ARCTIC FIRE

Published by Thomas & Mercer
P.O. Box 400818
Las Vegas, NV 89140

ISBN-13: 9781612183480
ISBN-10: 1612183484

ARCTIC FIRE

STEPHEN FREY

THOMAS & MERCER

PART 1

CHAPTER 1

TROY JENSEN was a daredevil. He always had been. It seemed as if nothing of this earth could stop him.

"You want me to go in there?" he asked in flawless Spanish. He was fluent in Russian and several Chinese dialects as well. He pointed tentatively at the fence, doing his best to convince the two older men he was scared. It was more fun that way. "Through that gate?"

The grizzled Mexicans exchanged crazy smiles.

"Sí," one of them answered, trying to hide his guilty, nearly toothless grin. He was worried the young American might see it and then see the light. He gestured excitedly at the gate to distract Troy. "Sí, sí. Vámonos."

"Take you with this thing," the other man offered in broken English, doing a better job of masking his own dentally challenged grin than his brother as he held out a rusty, bloodstained sword. This man still had most of his teeth, but they were crooked and yellow. "You will need it."

Troy took the sword just as a beautiful, dark-haired young woman trotted up and handed him a bouquet of flowers. "Gracias, señorita."

"You're welcome," she answered shyly. "Buena suerte."

"I don't need luck," Troy answered confidently, lifting the sweet-smelling bouquet to his face as he stared over it into the Spanish angel's dark eyes. "But I will need a kiss when this is done."

"Sí," she murmured. "I will give you." She glanced warily at the huge animal that was pacing around and snorting on the other side of the fence. "If you live."

"No," Troy said softly but firmly as he gave her that penetrating gaze they all seemed to love. "I want a kiss even if I die." He hesitated. "Maybe your touch would bring me back," he whispered. "Please, señorita."

He saw her imagining the fantasy. Then he saw her desire burning behind the fantasy. He loved being able to tempt her that way. He couldn't deny it.

Nature had blessed him with rugged good looks, a bravado women adored, and the ability to touch their hearts and souls quickly and deeply with his soft words and that haunting gaze. He used those blessings whenever he could.

The young woman tried to hide a guilty smile of her own from the two older men. "I will kiss you no matter what happens."

Troy nodded. "What is your name?"

"Selena."

He gave her another one of those gazes just for good measure. "I love it."

"You're incredible," she whispered as she turned to go.

He watched her walk away sexily, reliving their moment. He loved her caramel skin; those full lips; the erotic gleam flashing in those dark, exotic eyes; the way her long black hair shimmered in the sun; and that amazing passion she so naturally exuded. He'd been taken by all of it many times—for a night.

Regret rose in his expression when he thought about how Lisa had been the only one to ever really touch his heart, but how he hadn't delivered on his promise to marry her. How that bothered him…but not enough to make it right, because here he was wanting this woman.

But Jack was taking care of Lisa. He was making it right, at least for now. Troy pictured Jack knocking on Lisa's apartment door back in New York and holding the baby in that nervous way, and he almost smiled. Jack was the best brother anyone could have, even if he wasn't blood.

Troy's regret faded quickly as he strained to catch one more look at the Spanish angel before she disappeared into the crowd.

Then his gaze flashed to her father and uncle. They knew what he was thinking, and he knew how much they hated it…but to hell with them. They were trying to get him killed.

"Go on, gringo," her uncle muttered gruffly as he pulled the gate open just enough for Troy to pass through. The people hanging on the fence began shouting and screaming in anticipation as soon as he did. "Get in there."

Troy handed the bouquet to a little girl in a tattered dress who was standing by the gate. Then he patted her gently on her small head and stalked into the ring with just the rusty sword at his side.

Troy Jensen was only twenty-eight years old, but he'd already done more than most people would in a lifetime. He'd conquered the Seven Summits by climbing the tallest mountain on every continent, including Everest. He'd circumnavigated the globe in a sailboat, alone, twice. He'd slipped into remote areas of Russia and Mongolia to fly-fish for taimen—the world's largest and rarest trout—risking lengthy prison sentences by illegally crossing several remote borders. And now he was entering this makeshift ring in the slums of Nuevo Laredo to fight a frothing, wild-eyed bull in front of several hundred bloodthirsty spectators—all of whom, he figured, were betting on the bull.

Back home in Connecticut, people were whispering that he was obsessed with the edge, that maybe he even had a death wish.

So Troy knew it had come as no surprise to anyone when he'd called a week ago to tell his mother, Cheryl, that he wasn't coming to Greenwich next month for Thanksgiving because he'd joined the crew of an Alaskan crab boat. She was the *Arctic Fire*, and she was sailing out of Dutch Harbor for the season. The tiny port lay west of mainland Alaska on the Aleutian Islands, which stretched across the Bering Sea toward Asia like a lion's tail.

Dutch Harbor was little more than an isolated outpost. It was one of those glaring examples of why the global positioning system had been invented. Still, every autumn it served as the starting gate for the most prolific crab hunt in the world.

Troy was looking forward to hunting king crab on the Bering Sea. It was the deadliest job on earth, and it would be another box he could check on his daredevil list. But first he wanted that Spanish angel's kiss…and everything else that went with it.

He gestured to the massive midnight-black bull as it snorted furiously and tore at the bone-dry soil with its hoof. "Bring it on!" he shouted to the animal as the crowd roared. "Show me what you got!"

And it did. It rushed him as soon as he yelled to it, picking up speed fast for such a huge animal.

Troy dodged the long, sharp horns as the beast thundered by. But his expression turned steely as a cloud of dust swirled past an instant later. Plunging the rusty blade into the bull's neck with a kill thrust was going to be harder than he'd anticipated.

But that was fine, he told himself as he watched it wildly shake its head and turn to charge again. He didn't like easy; he never had. Nothing easy was really worth fighting for. His father, Bill, had taught him that a long time ago.

As the bull tore at the ground again, Troy noticed a man hanging on the fence of the small ring. The man was trying hard to blend into the crowd around him, but he couldn't. Everything about him looked authentic—except his teeth. They were too straight and too white. It was a tiny disparity hanging along that crowded fence, but Troy had been trained to pick up on tiny disparities.

He nodded subtly to the man, who nodded subtly back from behind his sunglasses.

Troy's eyes flickered back to the bull, which was starting its second charge. That man hanging on the fence could turn out to be so much more dangerous than this bull. The animal's agenda was obvious, and its actions were reasonably predictable. But the man on the fence could turn out to be a wolf hiding inside a suit of soft sheep's wool. He might say all the right things when they met later, but he might not mean any of them.

Troy was going outside the chain of command, which was strictly forbidden. But he was convinced that Red Fox One had gone insane, so he believed he had no choice. He believed he had to ignore his orders because the country had to come first no matter what. Those were his father's words too. And the orders from Red Fox One clearly did not put the country first. They were crazy orders from a madman who could not be obeyed.

One of the bull's horns nicked Troy's chest as the animal blew past again. It tore his shirt wide open and drew a long, thin swath of blood, much to the crowd's delight. He'd been thinking about those orders from Red Fox One. And he'd been trying to decide whether or not to trust the man who was hanging on the fence. Those distractions had nearly cost him his life.

"Come on, Toro," he muttered as he blocked out everything around him the way he'd been trained to do. So it became just the bull and him, and all other sights and sounds faded to nothing. "Come on, you bastard!"

* * *

"Tri-State Securities," Jack Jensen belted out angrily into the phone above the bedlam of the trading floor.

He was in a terrible mood. In the last ten minutes his bond portfolio had gone down over a hundred grand. He was short on a few big positions, and out of nowhere the Fed had flooded the financial system with cash. Bond prices were up across the board as interest rates plunged, and he'd been forced to bend over and grab his ankles while the situation unfolded on him out of nowhere. Now it was just a question of when to stand up and where to run.

"What do you want?" he demanded sullenly. Too late he recognized the caller's number.

"To remind you about this afternoon, son," came the gruff response.

Jack took a measured breath. He'd been hoping like hell Bill had forgotten about what was on tap for later. "Yeah, OK." But that had been a pipe dream. Bill Jensen never forgot about anything.

"Three o'clock at the house. That leaves us two hours to get to the airport and get prepped."

"I'll be there," Jack agreed grudgingly, worried that Bill might hear the dread creeping into his voice.

"Wheels up at five. That way we've got plenty of daylight left."

"Yeah, yeah," Jack mumbled, eyeing a pretty blonde woman on the equity desk who was shouting orders over the bulkhead at her trader.

He wanted to ask her out, but she was from a well-heeled Greenwich family and that could prove risky. She might find out that he hadn't actually been born with a silver spoon in his mouth. That the spoon had slipped past his gums a few months later. She might consider him an imposter at that point, and that would be a nightmare.

"Five o'clock, I guess."

"Don't make it sound like your execution, Jack." Bill chuckled. "There's nothing to worry about. It's a daylight tandem jump, for Christ's sake. You'll be hooked to the instructor. You'll be as safe as a baby kangaroo in its mother's pouch. All you've got to do is enjoy the ride down. The instructor does all the work."

Bill had definitely heard his fear. "Yeah, sure." And he was enjoying it.

"Next month you're doing a night solo with me."

"The hell I am."

Bill laughed. "Just get to the house by three."

"I'll be there already."

"You better post, son."

"OK. Look, I gotta take this call."

Jack hung up abruptly, then leaned back and rubbed his eyes. There was no other call coming in. He just didn't want to talk to the old man anymore. He hated to think about being hurled out of a perfectly good airplane fifteen thousand feet above the ground, even if the instructor was going to do all the work on the way down. Heights scared the hell out of him.

"Was that your dad?" Hunter Smith asked.

Hunter and Jack sat next to each other on the Tri-State trading floor. They'd prepped together, joined the same fraternity at Denison, and then become bond traders in New York City after graduation. They'd been best friends for a long time.

"Yeah, that was Bill," Jack muttered. "Why the hell did I pick up the damn phone?"

"It wouldn't have mattered if you hadn't. He still would have found you."

Jack managed a wry grin. "You're right, Hunt. He probably would have sent his marines over here if I hadn't answered. He's gonna make me jump out of the plane one way or the other today, even if it kills him."

"And the irony is *you'll* be the one who gets killed."

"Thanks for reminding me."

"Why do you think he wants to get you up in the sky so badly?" Hunter asked, grinning.

Jack winced as he checked one of the four computer screens staring back at him from the bulkhead. Now he was down over *two* hundred grand. It was wild how fast Wall Street could slam you. "He likes seeing me scared out of my mind." Thankfully, his portfolio was still up over four million bucks for the year. "It gets him off, especially when he knows he's the one who's scaring me."

"Maybe he's just trying to build a bridge between you two after all this time," Hunter suggested. "It makes sense."

"That's not it. He couldn't care less about building a bridge between us. He told me he's having the whole thing recorded."

"People always do that when they skydive. What's the big deal?"

"He's gonna grab that CD right after we land, pop it in the TV in his den as soon as he gets home, and laugh his ass off while he watches me scream bloody murder all the way down." Jack shook his head. "Then he'll show it to all his blue-blood buddies this weekend so they can see what a coward I am at fifteen thousand feet and get a good laugh too."

Hunter shook his head. "You're being too hard on him."

"Bullshit." Jack stared at the blinking screens in front of him. It was time to stop the bleeding. He wasn't risking any more of that four million bucks of profit he'd killed himself making all year for Tri-State. "I'm not being hard enough on him."

"Come on, Jack. It's not that he wants to see you scared."

"You know, you're right, Hunt." As he dialed a trader who could save his ass, it occurred to Jack that he was jumping from this bloodbath the same way he'd be jumping from the plane later on: panic-stricken. Hopefully he'd make out better then. "It's not that."

"Good man," Hunter said encouragingly. "Now you're getting somewhere."

"It's that he likes thinking Troy's a better man than me," Jack muttered softly enough that Hunter wouldn't hear. "He loves Troy and he hates me. It's that simple."

CHAPTER 2

TWENTY-FOOT WAVES and fifty-knot gusts roared across the open ocean as darkness closed in on the *Arctic Fire*. A bad storm on the Bering Sea could be a terrifying ordeal even for a veteran crab boat captain. For any normal greenhorn it was a nightmare that made him wish to God he hadn't been lured off dry land just by the prospect of making fast money.

But Troy wasn't any normal rookie. Fear wasn't an entry in his personal dictionary, and his only use for money was basic survival.

"How long we got?" Troy yelled over his shoulder. "How long till this storm goes nuclear on us, Speed Trap?"

"Five minutes!" Bobby Mitchell shouted back. "Ten, tops."

Mitchell was a strapping twenty-three-year-old with long blond hair any glam-metal rocker would have been proud of. His nickname was Speed Trap because over the last two years he'd chalked up five speeding violations—as well as a DUI and a resisting arrest over in Seward a month ago. Not surprisingly, he was driving on a suspended license. But then, so was half of Alaska.

"That's what they were saying on the radio right before I came out here."

"What are we supposed to get?" Troy shouted over the haunting wail of a powerful gust that was whipping through the mountain of huge crab traps stacked high beneath them. "How crazy at the top?"

"Thirty-foot waves and eighty-knot gusts," Speed Trap answered. "Maybe worse."

"No problem."

Surviving this storm wasn't going to be any worse than climbing Mount Everest in that blizzard two years ago, Troy figured, or fighting that crazy bull in Nuevo Laredo last month. The bull had charged him eleven times with those razor-sharp horns before he'd finally driven the rusty sword deep into its muscular black neck. After it collapsed on the dry dirt, he'd made certain its carcass was carved up and its meat given to the poorest people in the neighborhood.

Then he'd gotten that kiss from the Spanish angel. Then he'd met with that guy who'd been hanging on the fence. Then he'd gotten everything else from his angel. Then he'd kissed Selena's forehead as she was still sleeping and headed to Alaska.

"It'll be all right, Speed Trap!" Troy yelled reassuringly. "We'll be fine."

"Glad you think so," Speed Trap yelled back. "But you don't know the Bering Sea like I do."

The *Arctic Fire* had been on the hunt for king crab going on two weeks. This was the worst weather yet, and the storm couldn't have come at a worse time. With all of her traps back on deck and her surfaces coated with ice, the ship was top-heavy. Terribly vulnerable to rolling over in the rough seas and sending her crew plunging into the thirty-seven-degree water where they'd die of hypothermia in minutes without time to scramble into their orange survival suits—if they didn't drown first.

A frigid, salty spray whipped Troy's unshaven face as he crawled along the top of the carefully constructed mountain of steel-framed rectangular shapes. Several of the giant seven-hundred-pound traps on the bow's starboard side had torn loose. As the greenhorn, it was Troy's job to resecure the expensive gear so it didn't tumble over the side and sink to the bottom, lost forever. As the rookie on the boat, it was his job to do whatever the captain told him to do.

With her live tanks full of crab, the 118-foot vessel was grinding through the gale toward a processing plant in Akutan. If there weren't too many dead crabs in the tanks when they unloaded, this hunt would gross the ship a million dollars.

Half of that would go to Captain Sage Mitchell.

Another $250,000 would go to the captain's brother, Duke, who was the ship's first mate and chief mechanic.

And the last quarter of a million would be split equally among the remaining crew members: Troy and the other two deck-hands—Speed Trap and his older brother, Grant, both of whom were the first mate's sons. Bottom line: the three of them could each earn over eighty thousand bucks for two weeks of work.

The thought of the money made Troy grin even as the ship plunged toward the trough in front of the next wave. It had been risky to sail with these cowboys, but in the end it was going to be well worth it. When he'd gotten to Dutch Harbor three weeks ago, his checking account had seventy-three dollars in it. The balance was fourteen cents the day they'd sailed. And he didn't have credit cards. They weren't allowed.

He could have asked his parents for money, but he hadn't done that since graduating from Dartmouth six and a half years ago, and he wasn't about to start now. He had too much pride.

Besides, going to Bill might draw attention. His father was well known in certain circles—some obvious, some not.

"Move your ass, Troy!" Captain Sage bellowed from the bridge.

The bridge was eighty feet to the stern, and Captain Sage was warm and dry in there with Duke, protected from the driving sleet and slashing winds behind a thick pane of reinforced glass. But Sage could still shout orders to his crew through a series of rusty speakers that were positioned around the deck.

"Hurry up or we're gonna lose four or five of those traps!" he yelled. "If we do, we're gonna lose you too, you son of a bitch. I guarantee you that, Troy."

Troy glanced over his shoulder. Speed Trap was clinging to the crab trap mountain like he was part of it. He had a deer-in-the-headlights look in his eyes that was quickly morphing into one of sheer panic.

"Let's go, you mothafuckers!" Duke shouted, grabbing the microphone from his brother. "Now!"

"*Holy sheeeiiiiit!*" Speed Trap screamed like a terrified kid taking that first incredible plunge on a killer roller coaster as the *Arctic Fire* heeled dangerously to starboard and the trap in front of Troy almost went crashing into the sea. "I can't go any farther. I can't, man!"

"Move it, Troy!" Sage yelled, grabbing the mike back from Duke. "Damn you, Troy Jensen, get to those traps!"

"Help me!" Speed Trap pleaded as the ship began scaling the face of a twenty-five-footer. It was the biggest wave of the storm so far. "I can't hold on much longer. My fingers feel like they're gonna rip off."

"Just stay there!" Troy ordered. Speed Trap was worthless. He was petrified to the point of paralysis. "I'll be right back."

"Don't leave me!"

"Stay put! I *won't* leave you out here."

Troy hustled to the edge of the mountain, which rose thirty feet above the deck, and moved onto the trap that had barely stayed aboard moments ago. He hadn't bothered to hook into one of the bright yellow harnesses that would secure him to the ship by a long tether and keep him aboard in case what he was crawling on went over. He hated how the harness and the tether restricted his ability to move and react. He liked being mobile. He always had.

Speed Trap hadn't hooked up either, and Troy knew why. He was a veteran of these hunts and didn't want to look like he was more afraid of coming out here on the mountain than the green-horn. He was regretting that show of bravado now.

Troy took a deep breath and slid over the edge of the man-made cliff as the *Arctic Fire* hurtled to the top of the big wave, blew through the crest in a foam explosion, and then pitched forward and began barreling down its spine. Butterflies raced through his gut as he clutched the side of the trap he'd just been kneeling on and stepped the toes of his rubber boots on one that was two down from the top.

The mountain had been built with a slight stair-step fea-ture to it all the way up each side as the crew had stowed the traps back on board when the hunt was finished, instead of rebaiting them with cod and throwing them back into the deep to catch more crabs. They'd built it like this so they could get a toehold if necessary. Like Troy desperately needed one now.

He spotted the problem right away. Two stout ropes and a chain hung limply from the trap just behind and five below the one he was standing on. He could tell it was loose enough that if he didn't resecure it quickly, the *Arctic Fire* was going to lose more than just a few traps to the storm. She'd lose at least twenty to thirty because this particular trap was a key to the entire side of the mountain. And if the mountain crumbled, he and Speed Trap would be hurled overboard in a steel avalanche. They'd probably be crushed to death before they even hit the water.

With a smooth, pantherlike move, Troy reached the loosely tethered trap and moments later had it resecured. The critical trap would still move a little as the ship plowed through the rough seas, but it shouldn't go over and start that avalanche now.

A quick pull and a leap and Troy was back atop the mountain. He grinned when he spotted Speed Trap still hanging on for dear life right where he'd left the kid.

Troy hadn't gotten to know Speed Trap or the other three men aboard the ship that well since they'd sailed from Dutch Harbor, but they seemed like decent enough guys. They weren't very talkative, but there wasn't much time to talk. Just hour after hour of sinking traps to the bottom and hoisting them back to the surface after they'd snared more crabs.

It had been a hell of a grind as the traps kept breaking the surface teeming with the goods, and none of the crew had gotten more than a few hours of sleep a day. Even Troy had to admit that he was exhausted as their run across the Bering Sea was ending. But the money was going to be incredible.

He wouldn't be sticking around for the ship's second hunt of the season. Red Fox One had already communicated that in a coded message he'd sent to the *Fire* yesterday. After this run, Troy was headed to Eastern Europe.

As Troy got to where Speed Trap was crouched, his eyes flashed to the right, and for a moment he didn't believe what he saw. Something inside him wouldn't let his brain process the terrifying sight.

But it all turned hair-raisingly real when Captain Sage's panicked command blared through the speakers. It was the first time Troy had heard fear in Sage's voice.

"*Get off the traps, get off the traps!*" Sage yelled as he sounded the ship's foghorn. It was the ultimate warning. "*Now!*"

Through the sleet whipping across the ocean in the twilight, Troy saw the gigantic wave bearing down on them. If it hadn't been so terrifying, it would have been beautiful.

"We don't have time to get off the mountain," Speed Trap gasped as he gazed in shock and awe at the seventy-foot rogue roaring toward them. "We're gonna die, Troy."

CHAPTER 3

JACK WASN'T a daredevil like Troy, but he didn't back down from a challenge either. He just preferred having both feet planted firmly on the ground when he poked fate in the face, thanks to his acute fear of heights and his healthy respect for nature. Once he was more than fifteen feet up, he started getting nervous. Right now he was fifteen *thousand* feet up, and his heart felt like it was going to burst, it was pumping so hard.

"Come on, Jack!" Bill yelled as the jump supervisor slid the door open. The hum of the plane's twin props turned into a roar, and a cold wind whipped through the fuselage. "Let's go. This is it."

Jack had been dreading those words ever since they'd gotten into Bill's Mercedes a few hours ago and driven to the small airport outside Greenwich, Connecticut, to prep for the jump. "This is it." It had a terrifying ring to it.

Despite his fear of heights, Jack had forced himself to jump out of this same plane last month when Bill had shamed him into doing this same crazy stunt. But that jump had gone off during the daylight, and it had been a tandem jump. Back in October, Jack had been tightly secured to the instructor, who'd done all the work on the way down.

But this was a night jump, and Jack had to rip the cord himself. Technically, he needed more tandem jumps to qualify for a solo, especially a night solo. But the guy who ran the place was looking the other way.

Bill must have greased his palm, Jack figured. Money seemed to be Bill's answer to everything.

"Bill, I don't know if I want to—"

"Don't go there!" Bill shouted, anticipating what Jack was about to say. "Don't embarrass me." He moved quickly to where Jack was sitting and pulled him roughly to his feet off the wooden bench that ran along one wall of the fuselage. "Damn it, Jack. Don't make me throw you out of that goddamned door."

Bill and Cheryl had adopted Jack when he was only a few months old. He was thirty now, but in all that time he'd never told Bill about the terrible fear of heights he'd lived with ever since he could remember. It had been decades since the old man had served in the Marine Corps, but he'd never lost the semper-fi attitude. Phobias simply weren't acceptable in the Jensen family, especially with a blood son like Troy around who wasn't afraid of *anything*.

Jack had been hoping all day that by some miracle of God his fear of heights would evaporate or the crystal-clear weather would turn terrible—even though there wasn't a low-pressure system within five hundred miles. But neither prayer had been answered.

"Look, Bill, I don't have enough experience for this. Come on, you know that."

"You walk to the jump door, throw yourself out of the plane, count to five, and rip the cord. There's nothing to it. Any idiot could do it." Bill glared at Jack. "Any idiot with guts, anyway."

"This is insane."

Jack could feel his body seizing up like an overheating engine at the thought of taking even one step toward the door. He saw the jump supervisor roll his eyes over Bill's shoulder, but he didn't care. He wasn't going to be shamed into doing this. Not like he'd been shamed into doing that tandem jump last month when he'd almost had a heart attack during the first few seconds in the air. What if he couldn't find the cord? What if the chute didn't open? This was life and death, and he wasn't going to tempt the ultimate degree of fate just for Bill's entertainment.

"I'm not doing it," he said firmly.

"You will do it!"

"No I won't. Don't think just because—"

Bill grabbed him with both hands and wrestled him toward the door. He was more than twice Jack's age, but he was still a big, strong man, and he'd caught Jack completely off guard. They were only a few feet from plunging into the night before Jack even realized what was happening.

Just when it seemed they both would tumble into the darkness, Jack threw an arm around Bill's neck, stepped in front of him with one leg, and flipped him to the floor of the plane. Then he quickly retreated from the door. It was the first time he'd ever fought back, but it wasn't a conscious decision. The move had been purely instinctive, brought on by his terror of being hurled into the night sky fifteen thousand feet above Connecticut.

Bill struggled awkwardly to make it back to his feet in his jumpsuit. When he was up he shook his head and stared at Jack. "Why can't you be more like Troy?"

Then he turned, staggered to the open door, and plunged into the darkness.

* * *

The *Olympian* was three football fields long, and the four massive domes rising from her main deck were each twelve stories high. She was carrying more than 135,000 cubic meters of liquefied natural gas in those four holds, which for all intents and purposes made her a huge refrigerator, keeping what in nature desperately wanted to be a gas, a liquid.

In its liquid state, LNG took up less than 1/600 the volume it did as a gas. With an energy content of more than fifty-five Hiroshima bombs, the *Olympian* was one of the deadliest ships on the ocean. If one of those domes were suddenly pierced and the cargo detonated as all of that liquid instantaneously reverted to gas, the resulting fireball would destroy a city if the ship were close enough.

The leader smiled thinly as he stood on the *Olympian*'s bridge and peered past her domes into the darkness. That city was going to be Boston. In a few hours he and his crew would sail this massive cargo of LNG into the harbor—after presenting all necessary credentials to the waiting team of law enforcement officials, and then passing a rigorous onboard inspection. Then a Gulfstream 5 would come screaming from the sky and slam into hold 2 or 3. The horrible impact would instantly ignite that deadly fireball as the ship churned slowly along with a helpless flotilla of small-boat escorts. And millions of people would die.

Detonating an LNG tanker near a coastal city wasn't a particularly creative idea. Federal, state, and local authorities had been worried about the possibility for years, and they were extraordinarily careful each time one of the huge ships approached the United States. The key to executing this mission was having all of the correct authorizations—which they did, thanks to a series of bribes the leader had made to a well-placed individual in the United States.

Money was the American's Achilles' heel, he believed. You simply had to identify the weakest link in the chain and then offer him enough cash. The American wouldn't care that so many people had died, only that his bank account had grown much larger. Americans really were capitalist pigs. The one who'd sold him the authorizations certainly was.

It had been a long, exhausting voyage from Malaysia, and he had only a few hours to live. But in death he and his squad would become idolized immediately and revered forever. He couldn't wait to spot that plane streaking toward the *Olympian* and see the first instant of the explosion just before he was incinerated. He wanted to die. The other side was better. He'd been told that for a very long time, and he was ready to enjoy his harem of beautiful virgins.

"It will be the most beautiful thing I've ever seen," the leader murmured. "It will be a masterpiece of red and orange."

A moment later he lay dead on the floor of the bridge with his neck cleanly snapped.

The Navy SEAL who'd just carried out the execution lifted his wrist to his mouth. The rest of the crew had been killed a few moments ago by other members of his team. "All clear," he called loudly into his watch as he began to familiarize himself with the ship's control panel. "Let's get the bodies ready for the chopper."

CHAPTER 4

Troy grabbed Speed Trap by the neck of his orange poncho and half dragged, half pushed him across the traps as fast as he could. The air temperature was just twenty-seven degrees, and the spray whipping off the ocean combined with the sleet pouring down from above had made the top of the mountain treacherously slick. It was a situation made even more dangerous by the ship's steep angle of descent as it dived toward the bottom of the deep trough. Still, Troy and Speed Trap made it up the mountain to the forward masthead.

As the ship flattened out, Troy rushed Speed Trap into a harness. Then he grabbed another one and put it on himself as the ship began to climb.

The *Arctic Fire* wouldn't go up and over the mammoth wave that was bearing down on them. She was too long and heavy and the wave was too tall and narrow. She'd go through it, instead. She'd try, anyway.

At least the rogue was hurtling straight at them, Troy thought as he stared in awe at the huge wave. If it had been coming from either side, the ship wouldn't have a chance. The *Fire* would roll, and that would be that. It would take all of Captain Sage's skill, but the ship still had a chance with this wave coming straight at her bow.

As hell came hurtling down on them, Troy grabbed Speed Trap, took a deep breath of precious air, and shut his eyes tightly.

For several terrifying seconds he felt like a rag doll inside a tornado, and at the same time, as if he were encased in ice on the dark side of the moon. The ferocity of the wave and the bitter cold of the seawater cost him his grip on Speed Trap and forced a bloodcurdling scream from his lips. It was the first time Troy could ever remember thinking that the candle of his life was actually about to go out.

A second later the rogue blew past and Troy fell for what seemed like an eternity. When he finally crashed onto a trap, he opened his eyes, gasped several times, and took a quick inventory of his body. It didn't feel like anything was broken, but he was shivering so hard maybe he couldn't tell.

Then there was a throbbing in his left temple, and he pressed his hand to the spot. Blood covered his fingers when he checked them, but he was relieved by the sight of it because now he could feel the pain in his forehead—but no pain anywhere else. Given the awesome power of what had just slammed the ship, the wound was minor.

Maybe Red Fox One was right, Troy realized as he stared at the blood. Maybe he was untouchable. Maybe there was something otherworldly about it, as crazy as it sounded. He'd never believed in any of that, but what other explanation could there be? He always survived these life-or-death situations.

Troy glanced up from his fingers. The foredeck was a disaster area. More than half the ship's traps had been hurled overboard in the chaos. And many of those that remained aboard were now nothing but useless hunks of twisted steel.

As Troy staggered to his feet, a flash of adrenaline surged through his body and he caught his breath when the awful realization hit him. Speed Trap was gone.

"Where the hell is he, Troy?" Captain Sage bellowed through the speakers. "Did he go over?"

"Find my boy!" Duke cried, grabbing the microphone. "Please, Troy, find him."

Troy had already torn his harness off and was sprinting through the destruction. The ship was still pitching in the storm, but eerily, the waves had calmed and the winds had quieted now that the rogue was gone.

Then he spotted the tiniest tinge of yellow on the port side of the bow and raced for it. It wasn't much, but it was something.

As he reached the edge of the deck, Troy dropped to his knees atop a trap that was still in good shape. He peered over the side, and staring back up at him was the terror-stricken but very much alive face of the first mate's younger son.

Speed Trap was hanging from the ship literally by a thread, by what little remained of the shredded yellow tether that had connected the harness to the mast. At any moment it could break away from the trap it had somehow snagged onto and the kid would go plunging into the waves. Then the Bering Sea would finish the job and claim another victim.

Troy reached down, grabbed the harness with both hands, and carefully began pulling Speed Trap back aboard. He held his breath, afraid that the ragged strap would snap at any second.

But it didn't.

As soon as Speed Trap was back on deck, he jumped to his feet and hugged Troy tightly. "Thanks," he sobbed as tears of relief and joy streamed down his face. "You saved my life, for Christ's sake, *you saved my damn life*! I'll never be able to repay you. Thank you, thank you."

"You're welcome, pal," Troy muttered as Duke's sobs of relief blared through the speakers. "You're welcome."

* * *

Jack leaned against the Mercedes waiting for Bill to appear at the front door of the jump school. It was chilly out and the wind was blowing hard, much harder than it had been when they'd arrived a few hours ago.

He crossed his arms tightly over his chest. This wasn't going to be a pleasant ride back to the mansion. They'd actually had an OK conversation on the way over here—which was unusual because they didn't have many conversations to begin with and the ones they had were usually brief and unfriendly. But they weren't going to say anything to each other on the way home. He knew that.

Jack glanced up at the stars hanging in the cloudless night sky. He and Bill had been at it for so long maybe they just didn't know another way anymore. Maybe it had nothing to do with the fact that they weren't really related, that they were adoptive father and son. Maybe they wouldn't have liked each other even if they had been blood.

"Bullshit." Jack kicked a pebble across the nearly empty parking lot and then looked up. "Bill loves Troy." The only other vehicle in the lot was the owner's Explorer. "And it's all because Troy's his real son."

Jack pushed off the Mercedes when Bill came through the door. He could hear gravel crunching beneath the old man's boots as he walked across the lot. "Bill, I don't know what—"

"I don't want to talk about it right now," Bill snapped, aiming his key at the car. The lights flashed as the lock on the driver's side clicked open. "In fact, I don't *ever* want to talk about it."

Jack reached for the passenger door. "It's just that—"

"What do you think you're doing?" Bill demanded.

"What do you mean?" Jack lifted the handle, but the door didn't open. "I'm getting in."

"Not after that performance. Not after you embarrassed me up there on the plane like that."

"Excuse me?"

"Get another ride," Bill called gruffly as he climbed in and turned the car on. "Or walk."

Jack's mouth fell open as Bill slammed the car into gear and sped off, sending a hail of gravel flying across the parking lot behind him.

"What a prick," he muttered as he pulled his jacket around himself tightly and started to walk. "What a goddamned prick."

CHAPTER 5

SHANE MADDUX had been living in the darkest shadows of the global intelligence world for so long he'd almost forgotten how lonely and terrifying most people would find his existence. How it would probably send most nine-to-fivers head-on into a brick wall of hysteria to have to worry about assassins lurking around every corner and behind every door.

But he'd gotten over the mortal fears of the masses long ago because his love of country superseded his concern for self. Not many individuals could say that and honestly mean it, and he was quietly but intensely proud of how unselfishly dedicated he was to protecting the United States of America.

At any cost and any sacrifice.

That was his personal mantra, and he lived it every day.

Maddux glanced up in his naturally guarded way as Roger Carlson limped into the small, plainly decorated living room and eased onto the sofa on the other side of the dusty coffee table. It was the first time Maddux had *ever* felt uncomfortable about one of these meetings, and they'd been meeting like this for two decades. For twenty years Shane Maddux had run the Falcon division of Red Cell Seven for Roger Carlson.

"Hello, Shane." Carlson spoke up first as he usually did.

"Hello, Roger. It's good to see you."

Carlson was the only person in the world Maddux ever met with regularly, but that was fine. In fact, it was perfect. The deal he and Carlson had forged over the past two decades enabled Maddux to take what he wanted from the world with no strings attached and little risk of reprisal. It made him the ferocious apex predator he'd always dreamed of being as a kid when the bullies had kicked his ass around the playground like a soccer ball—and laughed at him while they were doing it. The apex predator he'd always dreamed of being as the priest had forced him into that dark, tiny closet and attacked him after he was too scared and paralyzed from his claustrophobia to even scream.

"It's good to see you too, Shane," Carlson said in his gravelly Georgia drawl. "Congratulations on nailing that situation headed for Boston Harbor. The *Olympian* is now in the capable hands of our Navy SEALs. Your Falcons came through again." Carlson's eyes lit up. "They're amazing."

"They are good," Maddux agreed, careful to show no emotion. Sometimes his Falcons were too good. Sometimes they needed to better understand the rules and their orders—one of them in particular. But he was taking care of that. "When did it happen?"

"Thirty minutes ago."

"Did we get the plane too?"

Carlson nodded. "It was a civilian G5. The guy ran for Europe, but one of our aviators from the *Reagan* intercepted him and shot him down in the North Atlantic. Played a little cat-and-mouse with him for practice and then took him out," Carlson explained.

"There's a recon team heading for the crash site now. Our pilot used a new laser technology to shoot the G5 down so there was no fireball. If there were helpful documents on that plane, the recon guys will find them."

"Good," Maddux said quietly. Once again he was careful to show no emotion. There might have been documents aboard the G5 that could pose a problem for him.

"It is good," Carlson agreed. "It's damn good, and President Dorn sends along his heartfelt congratulations. He's more impressed every day with how valuable you and your Falcons are. He's amazed at how you can find a needle in a haystack in the middle of a field at night when no one else can find the haystack. When some of our people can't even find the damn *field*, for Christ's sake." Carlson shook his head. "My God," he said quietly, "can you imagine if your guys hadn't gotten you the word on that ship? It would have been a nightmare for the president to handle an attack of that magnitude in his first year of office."

"It would have been *hell* for him," Maddux said fiercely, as Carlson rested his cane on the sofa.

There was no way to know for certain if the president had really sent along his heartfelt congratulations, if indeed the president was even aware of what could have happened in Boston Harbor. He'd never met any of the presidents. That was Carlson's area.

But that was all right. Maddux didn't care about accolades, and he didn't need much money—just enough to survive.

All he really needed was loyalty, because without loyalty the psychological infrastructure of trust disintegrated. When trust disintegrated, conditions turned to chaos and an every-man-for-himself situation developed—which never turned out well for anyone, including the country. And in Maddux's mind the country was as much of a living, breathing entity as any human being living within its borders.

That was why he'd taken the ultimate step against two of his Falcons. There simply had to be trust, there simply had to be loyalty, even if the orders coming from above seemed at odds with the best interests of the country. Even if those orders seemed insane.

Maddux's eyes narrowed. There had been a loyalty issue with two of his subordinates, and he had recently learned there was a loyalty issue with the president of the United States. And that was a problem for Red Cell Seven, a massive problem. A subordinate disobeying an order was one thing, but the president of the United States being disloyal was so much another. Maddux had felt comfortable addressing the first issue without seeking Carlson's approval. But he wasn't nearly as comfortable going after this second issue that way.

He would if he had to, though. He was committed to the path he'd already started down in the event Carlson didn't get on board quickly—as incredible as that was.

"It would have been more than hell for him," Maddux added. "It could have destroyed him. Then you both would have been sorry."

"I don't work at the pleasure of the president," Carlson responded evenly as his expression turned to stone. "I don't care who the president is. I'm indifferent about the man and his politics. You know that, Shane, and I don't appreciate the insinuation."

"Did you look into that situation we discussed the last time we met?" Maddux asked, boldly ignoring Carlson's rebuke.

"Of course I did."

"I can find out if you didn't."

Once in a while Maddux reminded Carlson that, despite the extreme secrecy involved, there were opportunities for checks and balances. And that he could take advantage of them if he chose to. He and Carlson trusted each other as much as two people in this situation could. But the remote possibility of distrust had to exist too.

It was an odd but essential paradox to their relationship. It was like God needing the devil for His warnings of fire and brimstone to be their most convincing. The possibility for personal disaster had to exist in any relationship for everyone involved to truly stay in line. Nothing in this life was pure, and anyone who believed in that fairy tale was stupid or naïve.

"I know you can, but that's not why I did," Carlson answered, "I looked into it because you asked me to and for that reason alone."

Maddux gazed at Carlson. The old man had formed Red Cell Seven forty years ago and run it ever since. He knew as much about what was happening in the world on a minute-by-minute basis as any person on the planet. He dealt constantly with every intel agency the United States operated, and his name was spoken with reverence at the Pentagon and the CIA. The few times it was actually spoken. Only a handful of senior officials knew who Carlson really was, and even fewer were aware of the immense power he wielded.

Carlson seemed like a calm, unassuming man who could blend into any background. But that was his cover and far from reality, Maddux knew. Despite his advancing age, Carlson could still act like a lion in its prime. He could still make a Brooklyn Mafia boss look like a petty thief and the chairman of the Joint Chiefs look like a private first class. And that was why Maddux was so worried about this meeting.

Maddux had gone outside the chain of command only a few times in his twenty-year career as the leader of the Falcon division, and he'd gotten away with it each time. But this target was different, very different. If Carlson ever found out about this work-around, there'd be hell to pay, and Maddux would probably pay that debt to the devil with his life. So he was praying to God

everything was going off without a hitch—even though he wasn't
at all religious.

"Which Falcon actually broke the Boston situation for us?"
Carlson asked. "Was it Troy Jensen?"

"Yes," Maddux answered, making certain his eyes remained
glued to Carlson's.

"He's been one of your top people for several years."

"He has," Maddux agreed brusquely. He wanted to get back to
the other thing. "Roger, we need to talk."

Carlson's expression turned serious. "What is it, son?"

Maddux loved that over the last two decades Carlson had
become his surrogate father. He'd hated his own father for a host
of brutal reasons—almost as much as he hated that priest—and he
hadn't shed a tear when the man had died of lung cancer a decade
ago. He couldn't have gone to the funeral even if he'd wanted to
because it would have been a perfect opportunity for his enemies
to identify him. But his relationship with Carlson had allowed
him to easily disengage from his father's painful struggle, and feel
no guilt at all for doing so. He and Carlson had their moments,
but he loved the old man.

Which made all of this so much harder.

"Everything all right?"

Maddux appreciated how Carlson had recognized instantly
that the subject change involved something crucial. "Is President
Dorn really on our side? Can we really trust him?"

Carlson eased back onto the couch and groaned. "This again,
Shane? I told you, I looked into the situation. This is turning into
an exhausting topic."

"Sorry, Roger, but I'm getting a lot of intel indicating that
President Dorn believes Red Cell Seven is more of a liability to
him and his administration than an asset. There's even some evidence that he wants to shut us down. And that's coming from
several sources." Exhausting was one of those code words Carlson

used when he felt disrespected. And disrespecting Roger Carlson was very risky. "Including my Falcons," Maddux added. He hadn't communicated that eye-opener to Carlson yet, and he knew it would have a dramatic impact.

"That's ridiculous," Carlson snapped. "I can't believe you'd say that. I can't believe you'd use your Falcons to manipulate me."

"*What?* Are you questioning my team's credibility? Are you questioning mine?"

"Sorry," Carlson said quickly, grimacing apologetically. "I shouldn't have said that."

Incredible, Maddux thought. He'd never seen the old man back off anything so quickly. There had to be at least a kernel of doubt in Carlson's mind too.

"Look, Shane, we've been over this several times. President Dorn's only been on the job for nine months. The Oval Office still has that new car smell for him. Wait until the one-year anniversary. Everything will be fine by then. I promise."

"But if the president's so damn appreciative of us figuring out what was heading for Boston, how could he have any doubts about how valuable we are to him and the country? I wouldn't be picking up any of these rumors."

"Have patience, son," Carlson advised paternally. "Give Dorn a little more time. He's young and, unfortunately for everyone, very inexperienced. He's new to how things work in Washington. He wasn't a senator or a congressman before he was elected commander in chief. He was a damn civil rights lawyer. He'll come around." Carlson chuckled softly. "You're putting too much faith in those guys of yours, Shane. Your Falcons aren't always right." His laugh grew louder. "There was that one time fourteen years ago when one of them was wrong."

In the twenty years they'd known each other, Carlson had rarely used humor to deflect anything. That wasn't his style. "Did you really tell the president what could have happened in Boston?" Maddux asked.

"Of course."

Maddux still had his doubts, but he knew he wouldn't get anything more out of Carlson. Despite how close they were, their relationship had its limits. It had to. "I hope so."

Carlson held up a hand. "I have something that'll take your mind off what you're hearing." The older man reached into his suit pocket and pulled out an envelope, then tossed it onto the coffee table in front of Maddux.

Maddux grabbed the envelope and tore into it like a wolf tearing into a fresh kill. When he'd finished reading what was typed on the single sheet of paper inside, he looked up gratefully. "Thank you."

"Enjoy it, Shane. You deserve it."

Maddux knew he should have left it at that, but he couldn't. He'd trained himself to keep his eye on the ultimate objective, but there were still times when he needed to make his peace too. "Be careful of President Dorn. I know you think there's no problem with him, but my information's coming from three sources, Roger. When it triangulates like that, there's an excellent chance it's accurate. In fact, I'd say the odds are almost a hundred percent at this point."

"Don't worry, Shane, everything's fine."

"Roger, I—"

"It's *fine*, Shane. Trust me."

Maddux slipped the envelope into his coat pocket and stood up. "I do trust you, Roger. You don't even have to say that." He started for the basement stairs and then hesitated. "I've never begged you for anything, but I'm begging you for this, Roger. Please look into it one more time." If Carlson did as Maddux asked, there would still be time to stop the train even though it had already left the station. If not, Maddux would move forward unilaterally. He loved the old man, but he loved the country more. "I'm telling you. President Dorn wants to destroy us."

CHAPTER 6

As QUICKLY as the storm had erupted, it had died. The sleet and snow were gone; seas had settled back to long, gentle swells of eight feet; gusts had calmed to less than thirty knots; and the *Arctic Fire* was cruising steadily toward a big payday in Akutan with only forty nautical miles left to go.

Troy stood at midship on the starboard side of the vessel, near the crane that pulled the traps back aboard. He shook his head. He still couldn't believe what had happened. He'd dodged *another* bullet.

The bridge was only thirty feet behind him, and he could see Sage and Duke up there through the reinforced glass yelling at each other, furious at losing so much expensive equipment to the sea. He couldn't hear them, but they were doing a lot of finger-pointing and waving, like they always did when things went wrong. Evidently they'd already put the fact that their nephew and son had cheated death by a yellow thread well into the rearview mirror.

Troy stared into the darkness shrouding the ocean, thinking again about how Speed Trap had come so close to death—but he hadn't. How they'd been standing right beside each other when the huge wave had smashed into the ship, but he'd come out of it so much better.

The same thing had happened before. He'd survived situations like that unscathed or barely bruised while others around him had been badly hurt, even killed. He hated to admit it because it was unnerving, but maybe Red Fox One was right. Maybe he was untouchable; maybe he was the ultimate survivor.

He leaned on the deck wall next to the crane and glanced toward the stern. Even though the sun had set, he could make out the shadowy shapes of the ever-present seagulls. And hear their sharp cries as they hung a few feet off the surface behind the ship, moving gracefully up and down with the waves. The same flock had been with them since they'd left Dutch Harbor, patiently waiting for any scrap of bait or piece of crab that might come their way.

It looked so peaceful to be a seagull, but it wasn't. It wasn't peaceful or easy to be any wild creature, Troy knew. Every day was a brutal struggle to survive, and there was no help for the sick or wounded. Only the strong made it, and that was nature's law. It was a cold reality, and it didn't necessarily work well for the individual. But ultimately it worked for the species, and that was the only thing that mattered to nature.

It was the same way for the United States. All that mattered was that she got stronger every day, even if brave men and women had to die. But the pain and agony those men and women endured was worth it if their sacrifices ensured the survival of the country and its place as the world's only superpower.

Troy touched his forehead. The gash he'd suffered in the chaos of the storm was only an inch long, but it was deep and he'd needed seven stitches to pull it together. He'd done the job himself with a sewing needle and black thread he'd found in an emergency kit on the *Fire*'s galley wall. He grinned as he thought about watching in the mirror as the needle plunged in and out of his skin. He was just glad his mother had no idea what had happened. She might have rented a boat in Dutch Harbor herself to come out here and get him if she had.

He knew his decision to sail on the Bering Sea had come as no surprise to his family, but that it was a bitter disappointment for her. She had hoped that after making it to the peak of Vinson Massif on a frigid Antarctic afternoon two months ago and completing the Seven Summits, he was finished tempting fate and had finally chased the daredevil demons from his soul.

She'd told him all of that very directly. She'd also told him that she wanted him to follow his father's footsteps into New York City's world of high finance. Bill Jensen was a Wall Street superstar, and she assumed her husband could get Troy any job he wanted at the huge bank he ran.

But Troy had made it clear to her then that a move to Manhattan still wasn't in the cards. That he still wasn't ready to trade in the razor's edge for a suit and tie, a cramped Upper East Side apartment, and a ride on a crowded six train down to Wall Street every morning. There were too many challenges left on his daredevil list, he'd told her over the phone from a distant corner of the world he wouldn't identify.

Maybe his mother was right, Troy thought to himself as he gazed into the darkness shrouding the Bering Sea. Maybe the razor's edge was finally getting too sharp.

"Troy?"

He whipped around, startled by the voice. He'd been a world away. "What?"

Sage and Duke stood beside each other in front of him. They were big-boned, broad-shouldered men who were each over six feet tall. Looming behind them was Speed Trap's older brother, Grant. Grant was a man-mountain who stood six-seven, weighed 270 pounds, and had even longer, starker blond hair than his kid brother. Speed Trap was nowhere in sight.

"We gotta talk, Troy," Captain Sage said.

It was strange to see the captain out here on deck. Since they'd left Dutch Harbor, Troy couldn't remember seeing Sage anywhere but on the bridge. "What about?"

Sage kicked at a crab leg lying on the deck, and Duke looked away.

Something in the back of Troy's mind clicked. He didn't like those looks in their eyes. "Hey, what the hell's—"

"You're going over," Sage interrupted in a steely voice. "You can jump, or we can throw you over. It's up to you."

Troy straightened up. His senses were instantly on full alert, and his pulse was racing. Sage and Duke were passing a death sentence. Their expressions were grim, but he could see that they were committed to carrying it out.

"So you don't have to pay me? Just so you can save eighty grand?"

"That was a lot of traps we lost," Duke mumbled in a hollow voice. "And eighty grand's a lot of money."

Troy's eyes flashed back and forth between the two men, searching for compassion from one of them. But he didn't find it. "This is how you thank me for saving Speed Trap's life?"

"It's a raw deal," Sage agreed.

"A raw deal?"

"Yup."

"That's all you can say?"

"Yup."

"Over eighty grand. That's what this comes down to?"

Captain Sage stared steadily into Troy's eyes for several moments. Then he shook his head slowly. "This ain't over eighty grand," he whispered. "You and I both know that."

How could Sage possibly know that? The question raced through Troy's mind as he brought his fists up.

Then it hit him. There'd been a sly wolf hiding inside that suit of sheep's clothing after all. The man hanging on the fence in Nuevo Laredo had rolled over on him. The man had said all the right things when they'd met, but he'd been lying the whole time.

Red Fox One was behind this execution.

CHAPTER 7

JACK SAT at the table in Bill and Cheryl's kitchen, thinking about what had happened in the plane as he gazed at his laptop and then at a tall glass of red wine standing beside it. He was going to spend the night here. His cramped apartment was another half hour away, and he didn't feel like driving after what had happened.

The fact that Bill had turned around and picked him up had been surprising. Shocking, really. They hadn't said a word to each other all the way home. But getting the ride had been a lot better than hiking all the way back to the mansion to get his car.

As he glanced out the wide bay window and into the darkness, he heard someone coming down the long hallway toward the kitchen.

"Hello, Jack."

"Hi, Cheryl." He stood up and gave her a kiss on the cheek as she passed him to get a glass of wine for herself. "What are you doing still up?" He eased back into his chair, relieved that it was Cheryl and not Bill.

She was tall, slim, blonde, and elegant. She was fifty-eight but looked ten years younger.

"I couldn't sleep." She ran her fingers through his dark hair lovingly as she sat down beside him with her wine. "So what happened? Why did I have to make Bill turn around and get you?"

Of course, Jack realized. They must have spoken after Bill roared away from the small airport, and she'd shamed him into going back. She was the only one in the world who could.

"I chickened out," he admitted. He wasn't proud of it, but he wasn't going to lie. "But damn it, I hate heights and I'm not qualified to solo, especially at night."

"Bill had you jumping out of that plane *by yourself*?" she asked incredulously. "At night?"

He didn't want to be that whining kid. He'd never accepted pity, and he never would. "It's done," he said quietly. "Let's just leave it at that."

She gazed at him for a few moments as she sipped her wine, and then she gestured at the laptop's screen. "Anything interesting?"

Jack pointed at the article he'd been reading on the *New York Times* website. "We blew away some mountain town in Afghanistan yesterday that was supposed to be a terrorist base." He'd seen a quick story about it yesterday afternoon on Yahoo!, but the *Times* article had more details. "We blasted the place to hell with cruise missiles, but it turns out all we did was kill a bunch of innocent civilians. No terrorists."

"You got a problem with that, Jack?"

Jack and Cheryl glanced up in surprise as Bill walked into the kitchen in his precise military stride. Neither of them had heard him coming down the long hallway.

"Yeah, I do," Jack answered, impressed as always by how quietly Bill could move despite his size. "A few of them, actually."

"Now, boys," Cheryl murmured uneasily.

"Like what?" Bill demanded as he sat down in the chair opposite Jack's.

"To start with, we killed a bunch of innocent civilians. And, according to the article, that included some kids."

"How do you know those people were *all* innocent?"

"The article said they were just townspeople. They probably didn't even know the United States existed."

"And you believe the article?"

"Sure."

"You'll never learn," Bill muttered.

"Want something to eat, dear?" Cheryl asked as she rose from the table and headed for the refrigerator. "A sandwich maybe?"

"That would be great, honey. Thanks." Bill reached across the table, pulled the laptop in front of him, and quickly scanned the story. "Consider the source, Jack," he said when he was finished. "It's the damn *New York Times*. It's the most liberal rag in the country. It's even worse than the *Washington Post*."

"Are you saying the *Times* manipulated this story? That they aren't telling the truth?"

"I'm saying they have an agenda. Senior people at that newspaper want us out of Afghanistan. Everyone knows that. If you want the straight dope, read the *Journal*."

"You're being ridiculous, Bill."

"And you're being naïve, Jack. But what else is new?"

"Wait a minute," Jack snapped. "Are you saying it's OK to kill a bunch of innocent kids as long as we kill a few terrorists at the same time?"

"Those animals don't care when they do it to us," Bill retorted, "as they've demonstrated time and time again."

"Aren't we supposed to be better than them?"

"It's a lowest common denominator situation, Jack. You have to fight these people on their level. Force is the only thing they understand. They're like dogs. You can't show compassion for them. The minute you do, they take it as a sign of weakness and they attack."

"Well, I was never very good at math, so I don't know much about all that lowest common denominator stuff. But I don't think you can justify killing kids for *any* reason."

"Why not? They grow up to be terrorists. Kill 'em while they're young, I say. Before they kill us."

Jack stared at Bill like he was crazy. "Are you serious?"

"Absolutely."

"Jesus Christ. I can't even begin to understand that way of thinking, especially when kids are involved."

"Let's talk about something else," Cheryl pleaded as she pulled cold cuts and a jar of mayonnaise from the fridge and headed for the counter beside the sink. "We're not going to solve the world's problems at our kitchen table tonight."

"I agree, Cheryl," Jack called over his shoulder. "There's no reason to—"

"Got any other problems with this?" Bill interrupted as he tapped the screen.

Jack tried to stop himself, but he couldn't. Sometimes Bill pissed him off too much. It had felt damn good to throw the old man to the floor of the plane up there in the sky, he couldn't deny that. It was pure macho bullshit, and it was incredibly stupid. But it still felt good.

"You're damn right I do."

"Like what?"

"Like it's not even our country we're shooting up," Jack said. "I mean, it's gotten to the point where we treat the rest of the world like our private gun range. We bomb anybody we feel like bombing whenever we feel like it. We don't even go to the United Nations anymore to get permission."

"Get real, Jack. We *are* the United Nations. Why do you think the damn building is in Manhattan?"

"We should still be going through the proper channels. We should be doing it the right way. We're the good guys."

Bill groaned loudly. "So we're supposed to stand by and play it straight while these maniacs who've been told that harems of virgins are waiting for them on the other side if they wipe us off the face of the earth train to do it? Is that what you're saying? Do you really think we're gonna get permission to bomb the hell out of someplace from a bunch of neutral pansies? Do you really think other countries that don't have a dog in the fight are going to vote like that in plain sight so these heathens who've taken a blood oath to kill anyone who does can see them do it?" he sneered. "Hell, we're the most powerful country in the world, the most powerful country to ever exist. And you're right. We are the good guys, we aren't the evil ones. We shouldn't have to ask for *anyone's* permission to do *anything.*"

Jack saw that vein on Bill's right temple pumping like mad, the way it always did when he started getting really worked up. "Maybe if we tried a little compassion and understanding first, we wouldn't have to worry so much about wiping each other out." Jack knew exactly how that sounded to Bill—like giant fingernails screeching down a giant chalkboard—but the chance to see that vein *really* go crazy was too tempting. "Know what I mean?"

"Christ," Bill hissed. "Let's get you some sutures for that poor heart of yours that's gushing liberal blood all over the cowardly left wing."

"A path of escalation never works," Jack fired back. "It can't. Revenge is our enemy. History shows us that."

"Well, isn't that profound? Why don't you tell that to all the kids who lost their moms and dads on 9-11?"

Cheryl grimaced as she fixed the sandwich. "Bill, I don't think Jack's saying that we should—"

"And my last problem," Jack cut in, "is that we're throwing six hundred billion dollars down the defense black hole every year while we go another *trillion* bucks in the red. At least, that's what the government tells us we're spending annually on guns and ammo. It's probably twice that when you take into account all of that black ops crap our intel people are up to just for fun. We could probably balance the damn budget if we blew up the Pentagon." He crossed his arms over his chest. "Tomorrow morning I'll probably read about how some super-secret US unit broke into an apartment somewhere in the Middle East and killed another suspected terrorist leader using some wild new personal cloaking device." Jack spread his arms wide. "And for what? So another prick with a death wish can take his place? It never ends this way, Bill. The war keeps going on forever. That's the point."

"The only way it ends is if we wipe them out. *That's* the point, you idiot."

"Bill!" Cheryl spoke up sharply. "Please."

"So we murder an entire population to kill a few bad apples," Jack said. "That's your solution to world peace?"

"It's the only solution we've got."

"How could we live with ourselves?"

"Happily. I know I could. And I'm not alone, Jack. You might be surprised how many people in this country agree with me and would be willing to use almost any means necessary to wipe out those people."

"OK, Adolph."

Bill glared at Jack. "You have no idea what it takes to run the greatest country in the world," he said in a grave voice, working hard to maintain his composure. "You have no idea how difficult it is to keep the United States safe and how many terrible decisions a few of our leaders have to make every day to do it." He shook his head as if he couldn't believe he actually had to say this. "You live in your beautiful little world in Greenwich, Connecticut,

Jack. Protected by men and women of honor who do things you don't want to know about half a world away so you can live in that beautiful little world. People who would laugh at your fear of heights because they do things that make jumping out of a plane at night look like walking a poodle through Central Park on a sunny afternoon." He inhaled deeply. "You accept their protection freely and completely even as you despise and denigrate them. It's pathetic, Jack."

Cheryl moaned. "Please don't do this, Bill."

"Those people you're talking about love what they do," Jack answered. "They love their high-tech weapons and their licenses to kill. They love to murder and mutilate just for murder and mutilation's sake. Most of them don't even care if they get paid as long as they get to kill or torture somebody once in a while. They're sadists."

"Those people," Bill hissed emotionally, "have more guts in their nose hairs than you have in your entire body. Maybe someday, if you and I are both really lucky, you'll understand that."

* * *

Troy nailed Sage in the face with a powerful right cross, sending the *Fire*'s captain crashing to the wet, slippery deck. A split second later he took out Duke with a swift, sharp uppercut to the chin.

But before he could spin back around to face Grant, the huge young man barreled into him from the side and sent him crashing to the deck too. Troy tried to get up, but Sage slammed him in the back of the head with a metal bucket. The impact didn't knock him out, but it rendered his arms and legs temporarily useless and he keeled over. He was aware of Grant and Sage picking him up and tossing him over the deck wall, but there was nothing he could do about it.

As he hit the water and the shock of the freezing temperature revived him, a terrible thought flashed through Troy's mind. Maybe this was how Charlie Banks had died too. Not on Mount Everest last year as Red Fox One had claimed.

PART 2

CHAPTER 8

TROY'S PHOTOGRAPH was prominently displayed on a large easel in the middle of the mansion's great room. In the picture he was standing on a dock in front of the *Arctic Fire* with his arms crossed defiantly over his chest as the ship lay at rest in Dutch Harbor.

A crewmate had snapped the photo minutes before they'd sailed, and Troy had e-mailed it out to Bill from the computer on the bridge as the ship reached open waters. That was three weeks ago to the day. The day Troy Jensen had finally taken on a challenge he couldn't conquer. The day his daredevil life had begun to catch up with him and the fuse leading to his death had ignited.

Jack felt that familiar pang of jealousy knife through him as he gazed at the picture of Troy that Cheryl had turned into a three-by-three-foot monument for the memorial service. Troy was still the headliner, still larger than life—even in death. He looked amazing standing there with his dirty-blond hair, chiseled cheeks, strong chin, perfect dimple, and sparkling steel-blue eyes that dazzled every woman who had the misfortune of glancing his one-night way.

"You bastard," Jack whispered. "How am I supposed to compete with you now?"

"That's a tough one, I'll grant you."

Jack's eyes raced from the photograph—to Hunter Smith. This was the first Jack had seen of Hunter today.

"I'd really started to think Troy was bulletproof," Hunter said as he gazed at the photograph. "Almost untouchable," he added in a reverent voice. "It's a good lesson for all of us."

"It's not a lesson. It's common sense. You can only give death the finger so many times before it nails you. He got what he was looking for. He got what he—"

"Don't say it," Hunter interrupted sharply.

"Say what?"

"You'll be sorry, Jack."

"Ah, you don't know what you're talking about. You're just trying to—"

"He got what he deserved. That's what you were going to say." Hunter shook his head as if he was relieved. "I'm just glad I said it first. See, that's why I'm good for you, Jack. I say the things you want to say but shouldn't."

Jack grinned faintly despite his irritation. "So that's why you're good for me, huh, Hunt? That's what I get out of us being friends?"

"Yeah and I'm still trying to figure out the symmetry. I'm still trying to figure out what I get out of being friends with you."

"Try this one," Jack suggested. "I introduced you to your wife and you're damn lucky I did. Amy's a hell of a catch."

Hunter squinted as if he were thinking hard about what he'd just heard. "Debatable."

"You've got no business being married to that woman, and we both know it."

"Well—"

"Don't even start with me on this."

A throw-in-the-towel shadow slid across Hunter's face like a cloud sliding in front of the sun. "OK, OK."

"Without me," Jack continued, "you wouldn't have had a chance with Amy."

Hunter put his hands up. "OK already, you're right."

"I was an idiot not to go for her myself." Jack searched the crowd quickly. "Maybe I should get her a drink and have a talk with her. Where is she anyway?"

"Stay away," Hunter warned. "I'll kill you if you go anywhere near her."

Jack's half grin grew into a broad smile. Hunter Smith was as gentle a man as had ever walked the earth. In the fifteen years they'd been friends, they'd never even come close to blows.

Jack couldn't say that about all of his old friends. He'd never been the one to throw the first punch, but he'd never been one to walk away from a fight either. He'd put two guys in the hospital with broken jaws after ducking punches, then firing back. Both of them had apologized later for what they'd said and for firing first, but Jack hadn't accepted. He didn't live by the second chance rule when it came to violence, especially when the violence had started after a comment about him being adopted.

"I'd never go behind your back, Hunt."

Jack had known Amy since grade school, and he'd gotten his chance to do that two years ago at a Jensen Labor Day party. She'd had too many cocktails during the course of the afternoon, and she'd tried to persuade him into one of the mansion's third-floor guest bedrooms. But he'd guided her straight back to Hunter as soon as he'd understood what was happening.

Amy had called him the next day to thank him for being a gentleman. Despite what had happened, Jack still figured she was a good girl and that Hunter was lucky to have her. She'd sworn it was the only time she'd ever come on to anyone since she'd been married to Hunter. And Jack believed her because he'd always known her to be a straight arrow, almost a prude.

"Never," he repeated emphatically.

Hunter looked down at the floor and nodded. "Yeah, I know you wouldn't," he acknowledged quietly. "I definitely know. Amy told me."

Jack had wondered if she had. Well, it had been two years and they were still together. It must have taken a lot for her to tell him, and Jack admired her for being so honest. He admired Hunter for sticking around too.

He glanced again at the picture of Troy standing in front of the *Arctic Fire*. Being with each other constantly was about the toughest thing two people could do, he figured. Which was why so many marriages failed, he believed, and why he'd always be a bachelor. He wasn't a loner, but he liked doing things his way. Compromise wasn't a priority for him. Not nearly enough of one to get married, anyway.

Women came on to him a lot even though he didn't consider himself that handsome. Pretty women too, and he found the attention curious. It had to be the money they thought he had. Or maybe they were trying to get to Troy through him. If that was the case, they wouldn't be coming on to him much anymore.

"Troy did get what he deserved," Jack said, still gazing at the photograph, "and I'm not afraid to say it."

Hunter checked around the crowded room, trying to see if anyone had heard that. "And I was so sure you'd be in a good mood today."

There was something about the picture that had really caught his attention. It was as if the picture were trying to talk to him, as if it were trying to send him a clue or a connection to something vitally important. But he couldn't figure out what that was, and it was driving him crazy.

"What's that supposed to mean, Hunt?" he asked, finally looking away, frustrated by his inability to decipher the message. He was almost sure he knew what Hunter had been driving at with the remark, and it was pretty brutal. But he wanted to hear the confession. "Well?"

"Nothing," Hunter said, guiding Jack away from the easel as two sad-eyed young women approached. "Come on, let's get a drink."

Jack thought about pushing it, but let it go. Hunter was one of the few people he hated to confront. With almost everyone else, it wasn't a problem.

It was early December, and Connecticut was enjoying an unseasonably warm and sunny stretch of weather. It was a good thing for the Jensen family too. So many people had come to pay their last respects to Troy that the mansion alone couldn't have accommodated the crowd. The place was huge, but not huge enough. Fortunately, the beautiful weather allowed Bill and Cheryl to use the sprawling stone porch at the back of the house too.

"Sahara scotch," Hunter ordered after they'd moved outside through a set of French doors and made it to the nearest bar. "Johnny Walker, half an ice cube, and an H_2O molecule." He held his hand up. "On second thought, hold that ice cube and the water molecule in the name of conservation."

Jack nodded to the bartender. "Same."

When they had their drinks, they slipped through the crowd to the stone wall framing three sides of the raised porch. From here they had a panoramic view of the Jensen barns and pastures, which stretched to an unbroken line of oak and pine trees a quarter mile away. From where they stood, they couldn't see another house. This was pricey real estate even in a pricey town. Wall Street had been good to Bill and Cheryl.

"Here's the thing," Jack said. "Troy took crazy risks all the time, and I don't care what anybody says about how modest he was and how he didn't care if people noticed. He cared, Hunt, he cared a lot. He was a show-off in his own way. Look at that damn front-page article he got himself in the *Wall Street Journal* about the Seven Summit thing. Jesus, what a stick-your-finger-down-your-throat-and-gag-yourself-until-you-puke crock of self-promotional crap that was."

"Your father got him that article," Hunter reminded Jack. "Troy had nothing to do with it. Your father's the one who's friends with that editor at the *Times*."

"You mean my *adoptive* father."

Hunter groaned. "You're thirty years old, Jack. When are you gonna get past this thing?"

"When Bill and Cheryl start calling me by whatever my real name is."

"What's wrong with Jack?"

Jack shrugged as he leaned down and rested his forearms on the wall. "Nothing. It's a great name. It's just not mine. It's the one they made up and hung around my neck when they brought me home to Connecticut in the limo from the secondhand baby supermarket in Brooklyn. It's the name they gave me so they could feel better about me. So they didn't have to call me Sonny or Vito or Carlo and think about who I really was every time they said it."

Hunter took a healthy gulp of scotch. "I love you like a brother, pal, but you are one stubborn son of a bitch, especially when the liquor starts talking." He made a sweeping gesture at all that lay in front of them. "Look at this place. It's amazing. And Bill's gotten us both jobs downtown, even the second one, even after we got canned at the first place. And if you ever did have money problems, you know Bill would take care of you. So if you don't mind me asking—no, no," Hunter interrupted himself, "even if you do mind, *especially* if you mind. What the hell are you bitter about? From what I've heard, if they hadn't adopted you, your ass would be riding the back of a garbage truck in the Bronx or sweeping the floors of some housing project in East New York."

Jack could feel the anger and frustration boiling inside him like it always did when he thought about this too much—especially, as Hunter pointed out, when the alcohol caught up with him. "They adopted me because they thought Cheryl couldn't have kids. When Troy came along out of nowhere two years later it was all over for me because he's blood and I'm not. Full stop. They would have given me back if they could have."

"That's bullshit, Jack, and you know it. They've always loved you. They've always treated you and Troy like equals."

"Now *that's* bullshit. At least as far as Bill goes."

Hunter shrugged. "Well, what do you expect? He sends you to Exeter, one of the best prep schools in the country. And the day after you get there you tell the headmaster your name isn't really Jack Jensen. You tell him it's really Sonny Carbone or something like that and that you're a made man in the mob. Then you tell him to fuck off in Italian in front of half the student body. Which would have been fine because he didn't understand Italian, but you flipped him the bird too."

"Yeah, well I'm not ashamed of whatever my real name is," Jack grumbled. "I don't appreciate Bill being ashamed."

"He isn't. He's just—"

"Look at me." Jack came up off the wall and rose to his full height of six two. "I look Italian. I look like my name ought to be Sonny Carbone. I've got jet-black hair and a Roman nose the size of New Jersey. I've even got a little olive to my skin, which means I'm a mutt even in Italy. I mean, could I ever pass for a blue blood? Would anybody ever believe my last name is really

Jensen? Of course not," he answered his own question quickly before Hunter could say anything. "Goddamn it, I've been trying to pass this joke of a twig of the family tree off for a long time, and I'm tired of it. I'm tired of the smirks and the eye rolls I get all the time when Bill introduces me to his society friends as his son. Everybody knows I'm really just an artificial limb."

"First of all," Hunter said, "your nose isn't the size of New Jersey." He grinned. "It's more like the size of Delaware, and what do you care? It's never affected your ability to get women. The way they throw themselves at you always amazes me. Troy too. He told me that last fall when he was home. I think he was really jealous of you for that."

"That's such a bunch of crap. He had absolutely nothing to ever be jealous of me for because—"

"*Second*," Hunter broke in loudly, "you're wrong about Troy. He didn't care about getting ink. I've never heard him talk himself up once, and this is coming from a guy whose brother is one of the biggest self-promoters of all time. Muhammad Ali was a modest man compared to my brother." Hunter paused when he saw that Jack was actually listening. "Third and most important, Troy did care about you. He cared a lot about you. I know that for a fact because we had a long talk about it that last time he was home. He told me how you always took care of him on the playground when you two were kids, and how much he learned from you over the years. How in a way you were still taking care of him. Which I didn't understand and he wouldn't be specific about, but I could tell he was being real serious. He said he missed you a lot too." Hunter paused again, giving Jack time to think about everything he'd just heard. "So I don't like hearing you say that Troy got what he deserved. You're a better man than that, Jack. A lot better. And Troy doesn't deserve to have that said about him, especially not by you. Look, he was a hell of a guy, and I know it wasn't easy having him as a brother because he was the real deal. Everybody idolized him, and that was tough for you. It would have been tough for anyone to deal with that. But he still ought to get better from you, especially now."

"I know," Jack admitted softly. "I guess sometimes how different I am from everyone else in the family catches up to me." He shook his head. "How different I am in every way. Even the way I think."

Hunter rolled his eyes and groaned. "You have another one of those political arguments with Bill?"

Jack nodded. "Yeah, I was over here one morning last week after we blasted that town in Afghanistan with cruise missiles, and Bill and I got into it."

"You call him Attila the Hun again?"

Hunter knew him so well. "Nah, this time I called him Adolph. I'm tired of calling him Attila."

"Did he tell you how you're nothing but a bleeding heart liberal, and how you have no idea what it takes to run this country? And how you have no respect for the men and women of honor who keep you safe at night?"

"Doesn't he always? And, for the record, I do have respect for those people, a lot of respect."

"I know you do. You just wanted to see how hard you could get that vein in his forehead pumping, right?"

Hunter knew him so *damn* well. "I just think the United States ought to act with more compassion. Being the bully never makes anyone respect you. It pisses people off and makes them do stupid things. It makes teenagers take guns to school. And it makes terrorists fly planes into buildings."

Hunter gazed out at the pastures. "Yeah, but I'm not sure compassion is the way either. Not with the freaks we're fighting now."

"Not you too, pal."

"You know which side I come down on, Jack. You always have. Maybe I'm not as far right as Bill, but every once in a while we have to back up our rhetoric with some serious action. That is, if the rhetoric's ever going to mean anything."

"Even if that action means we kill children?"

Hunter rolled his eyes. "Come on, Jack, that's not fair."

"OK, OK." Hunter was right. That wasn't fair. "Do you have a problem with us torturing people we believe might be terrorists?"

Hunter thought about it for a few moments. "No, I don't. I mean, as long as we're pretty positive they are."

"Jesus Christ, Hunt. You're just like Bill. Down deep you think we ought to wipe those people off the face of the earth."

"I do not, *damn it*. But I don't want to be on top of the new World Trade Tower one day and see a plane hit the building twenty stories below me." Hunter shut his eyes tightly. "I still think about those poor people who had to choose between being incinerated or jumping from a hundred stories up that morning. And I'm sorry, but I don't have a problem with some water-boarding if that keeps the skies over our country safe. Or whatever else they use to make those people talk."

"What if it's you someday?"

Hunter gave Jack a WTF look. "What are you talking about?"

"What if they arrest you and start asking you crazy questions about things you've said on the phone or they want to know about people you've met with? What if they tie you upside down on a plank and start dumping cold water down your nose? What then, Hunt?"

"That's ridiculous."

"Is it?"

"Of course it is. No one's going to arrest me for being a terrorist."

"How do you know? They didn't even give that guy in Yemen last year a chance to be tortured. He was an American citizen and they murdered him in his convoy."

Hunter stared at Jack for several moments, as though he couldn't believe what he'd just heard. "Are you talking about al-Awlaki? The dude who was a senior al-Qaeda guy?"

"Right," Jack agreed. "That guy."

"Come on, pal. Buy a ticket on the real world train and come to sanity town where it's always warm and sunny. We've got a nice couch waiting for you on the—"

"How do you know he was an al-Qaeda leader?"

Hunter winced as though he were in serious physical pain. "I know what you're going to say, Jack, but even the *New York* Fucking *Times* said he was. That wasn't a case of our government lying to us, not even close. That was a bad dude we killed."

"You never know, Hunter. I think we have to be very careful when we start executing our own citizens without a trial."

"And I think we have to protect our good citizens any way we can," Hunter replied loudly. "We have to trust our leaders to do the right thing."

"That's a big leap of faith in this day and age."

"In *any* day and age," Hunter agreed, "but we have to. That's why we elect them."

"I don't know." Jack finished what was left of his scotch and put the empty glass down on the wall. He closed his eyes as the realization that Troy was gone finally started sinking in. "Troy did deserve what he got, Hunt," he said quietly. "But I'm not glad he got it, I'm not glad he died." Why the hell had Troy gone on that damn crab boat? Why hadn't Bill steered him away from it? Bill had that power over Troy, the only one in the world who ever had. "At least, I don't think I am."

Hunter patted Jack's shoulder. "You better figure that out, my friend. And you better figure it out soon."

"Yeah," Jack agreed after a few moments. "I guess I better."

Hunter finished his scotch and put the glass down on the wall beside Jack's. "Have you ever wondered what Troy was really doing all this time?"

They were both facing away from the mansion, but when Jack heard what Hunter had said he turned to look at him. "What are you talking about?"

Hunter shrugged. "Doesn't it seem strange to you that Troy graduated from Dartmouth six and a half years ago, but he never settled down?"

"Not at all. Look, he was an endless-summer kid who never grew up. He loved how athletic he was and what he could do with all that talent. He loved being a rolling stone too. And he loved having all those different women." Jack snickered. "And he loved that Bill paid for everything."

"He was on the *Arctic Fire* to make money," Hunter pointed out. "And he worked in that mine in Argentina two years ago."

"He couldn't possibly have made enough money doing those things to support himself in the way he wanted to live. He was a Jensen, remember? A *real* Jensen. He needed money, and he needed lots of it."

"He wasn't like that and you know it. He wasn't materialistic."

Jack was getting annoyed. "So what are you saying, Hunt? Spin it out for me."

"I wonder if there was more going on with him than we realized. I've always wondered that."

"Like *what*?"

Hunter shrugged again. "I don't know. It's just something I've been thinking about ever since I heard he died."

Jack grabbed his glass off the wall. "Ah, you've always been a conspiracy guy. Accept the situation for what it is. A rich kid taking advantage of what he fell into just by being born."

"Maybe," Hunter said quietly, "but maybe not."

Jack waved at Hunter dismissively and shook his head. "I'm getting another drink."

As he stalked toward the bar, Hunter's words echoed in his head. Jack had been wondering the same thing for a while.

CHAPTER 9

"Good afternoon, Mr. President."

Carlson rose stiffly from the leather couch and extended his right hand beneath a practiced smile of indifference that came to his face automatically within the walls of the Oval Office after so many years. This was the eighth administration he'd served, and it no longer impressed him that he had direct access to the person the public and the press called the most powerful man in the world. Now he was more impressed by people who actually risked their lives every day in the shadows. People like Shane Maddux.

"I trust you've been well, sir."

"Of course, of course," President Dorn answered cheerfully. "I've got the best job in the world, I've got a wonderful family, and I've got my health. I have no excuse for feeling anything but absolutely outstanding. It would be a crime for me to complain about anything, Roger."

The president's greedy display of appreciation for his good fortune was a function of being in office less than a year, Carlson believed. The pressure of making decisions that affected billions of people every day—many of them negatively—hadn't gotten to him yet. As he'd told Maddux, Dorn's infatuation with the job would wear off around the first anniversary of taking that momentous oath on the Capitol steps on that blustery January day. At that point being president would turn into a grind, just like every desk job ultimately did.

Carlson always looked forward to that anniversary because dealing with a new president and his administration became infinitely easier. By that one-year mark the president no longer questioned the morality of what was going on in the shadows. By that time he fully appreciated knowing that there were people out there quietly killing the enemies because he'd come to realize how many people wanted to kill him and, bottom line, how vulnerable he was despite all of the Secret Service's efforts. In fact, after that first anniversary, the president usually started wanting more of what Carlson delivered—much more.

That was the progression with the liberals. The conservatives were in it up to their eyeballs right out of the gate, even before they took the oath—especially the neocons. They were the easy ones to deal with.

Unfortunately, President Dorn was as far left on the political spectrum as any commander in chief of the United States could be. He was a tree-hugger from Vermont who thought the ACLU was the most important group ever founded; that the death penalty was a barbaric ritual that only lunatics could support; and that the founding fathers had made a huge error in judgment when they'd decided that everyone had the right to bear arms. David Dorn made Bill Clinton look like Ronald Reagan, and Ronald Reagan look like Joseph Stalin.

"Well," Carlson said, "I'm sure we could get you off with a small fine and some community service if you did complain about something."

The president laughed heartily. "You're amazing, Roger."

Dorn was a tall, broad-shouldered man with a full head of dark hair who radiated charisma as impressively as the core of a nuclear power plant radiated energy, and couldn't have looked more presidential if he'd tried. In fact, Carlson thought of Dorn as the floor model. He just wished Dorn's political views weren't so severely left of left. He'd never cared about a president's political affiliation before, but he was starting to with this one. He hadn't fully dismissed Maddux's words of caution.

"You're in your seventies, right, Roger?"

"Seventy-three, Mr. President."

"But you look fifty-three."

That was crap, Carlson knew. His gray hair was thinning, he had deep creases at the corners of his mouth, crow's-feet at the corners of both eyes, and he'd started to get those brown spots on his arms and legs. And though he didn't really need the cane he used when he met with Maddux, he still hunched over when he walked because of a bad disk in his back that should have been operated on ten years ago—but there'd never been time. He looked like an older man because he *was* an older man.

Lately, he was feeling like one too. He was pragmatic, he always had been, and he knew his days of dealing with the constant pressure of running Red Cell Seven were numbered. It was almost time for him to be done with this crazy thing he'd been devoted to for over four decades. It was almost time to yield the awesome responsibility of this job to someone younger, and he knew exactly who that would be. There would be a quiet approval process, but it would be only a formality. He just needed to get President Dorn in line before he could turn over the reins to Shane Maddux and ride off into the sunset.

"And you act thirty-three," the president continued, gesturing for Carlson to sit back down. "I hear people half your age can't keep up with you."

Carlson turned his head slightly to the side, as though he was deflecting the remark. How the hell would the president know that people half his age couldn't keep up with him? How would the president know of anyone at all who was trying to keep up with him? He shouldn't.

Maddux's warning rattled around in Carlson's brain again, but he shook it off. The president's comment had to be just an innocent, off-the-cuff remark.

"How about we settle on me looking sixty-three and acting fifty-three?" Carlson suggested as he sank back onto the sofa. "That work for you?"

"All right, Roger, all right." The president chuckled as he sat behind his big desk. "So, how are you this fine, fine autumn morning?"

"Well, Mr. President, I woke up breathing."

The president raised one eyebrow. "As I recall, that's your favorite response to the question. It's what you say every time I ask you."

"You're right, it is." This was a first. The other seven men had never noticed that answer. At least, they'd never said anything about it. "I think it puts everything into perspective simply but elegantly, and I—"

"You woke up breathing all right," the president interrupted, his tone turning measurably less friendly. "You woke up without a limp too."

Carlson's eyes raced to the president's—and instantly he regretted his reaction. He hadn't been taken off guard like that in years, and his transparent response to the remark was infuriating. He'd confirmed the truth with his shocked look like some peach-fuzz-covered adolescent would have to his father about breaking a window with a baseball. The surprised expression had lasted only a second, but if he'd done that in the field, he'd be maggot-food right now.

"No cane when you went for your coffee at the Starbucks down the street from your house in Georgetown this morning," the president continued, "but you were using one the other day when you went out to that place you people have in Reston."

Here was more bad news. President Dorn knew about the web of safe houses they operated in Reston, a northern Virginia suburb of Washington. The houses looked like the typical neighborhood homes of normal upper-middle-class suburbanites, but they weren't typical at all. Dorn probably knew about the underground corridors that connected them too.

"Excuse me?" Carlson said hesitantly.

"You heard me," the president replied as he scanned a memo. "But I'll say it again. The other day you were limping. Today you aren't. The other day you had a cane. Today you don't."

There was no way for Carlson to deny any of this. Protesting would only make him look foolish. "So what?"

"Well, if you're deceiving people who've worked under you for decades and who idolize the ground you walk on, why wouldn't you deceive me someday? That's how I look at it."

Carlson made certain to stare back at the president with an unwavering gaze. "Is there a point to all of this?"

"There is, Roger," Dorn acknowledged, putting the memo down. "I want you to know that I have great respect for what you and your people do and the dangers you and they face every day. Your organization is a valuable weapon in what I'll call my twilight intelligence arsenal. It has been for many administrations, for many presidents before me. I get all that," he muttered as though he didn't get it at all, and didn't care that he didn't. He held up a hand when he saw that Carlson was about to speak, and his expression slowly became one of irreversible resolve. "But I'm not going to let anyone around me run free, even if they've had that room to run for a long time. It's too risky in this day and age, when every reporter out there is trying to break a career story every minute of the day and will stop at nothing to do it. So there will be limits to what you can do without my direct approval. Strict limits. I won't always be watching, but I could be. Make it easy on yourself and assume I am. That'll make it easier on *everyone*." He hesitated. "Another thing, Roger. You'll no longer have direct access to me. It's too damn risky to have you traipsing in here as some hush-hush special advisor no one knows. Too many people are asking questions.

"So I'm going to put a buffer between us," Dorn continued, "maybe even a couple of them. And that only makes sense because you'll be meeting with this person a lot more than you've been meeting with me, much more than I'd ever have time for. See, I want to know exactly what you're doing at all times because I'll be approving all of your major initiatives before you execute any of them in the field. No more running free in the shadows, Roger. No more freedom to handle things any way you choose. I know that isn't what you want to hear, but that's the way it's going to be. I am commander in chief of the United States of America and that's an order."

Carlson took a measured breath. He could have allowed that LNG tanker to sail into Boston Harbor and blow the city to hell— but he hadn't. In fact, he'd lied to Maddux because he hadn't told Dorn about the potential disaster that had been narrowly averted thanks to Maddux and his crew of Falcons, one of them in particular. About the plot Maddux had disrupted that would have killed so many people and thrown one of the nation's biggest and most important cities into total chaos.

Carlson exhaled the breath as deliberately as he'd taken it in. Maybe next time he'd let that tanker explode; maybe next time he wouldn't call the SEALs and avert the disaster. Maybe then the president would have more respect for his twilight intelligence arsenal.

He gritted his teeth at the awful thought. He could never do that. He could never let all those people die. He wouldn't be able to live with himself if he did. Those were the people he'd taken a blood oath so long ago to protect.

"Don't be upset with me, Roger," the president kept going. "It's all part of a process, all part of us figuring out how best to protect this country in difficult and changing times. Remember, at the end of the day we're all on the same team. We all wear the same jersey. Don't take it personally. You've made a great contribution to the country. You should be proud of most of what you've done."

Carlson wanted to puke. He wasn't proud of *most* of what he'd done. He was proud of *everything*. He had no regrets at all, and David Dorn needed to understand what an incredible insult he'd just tossed out there.

"Was there something else you wanted to see me about?" Carlson asked in a tone intended to make the president understand in no uncertain terms just how personally he'd taken everything. "Was there some other reason I was summoned to the mountain?" Carlson muted a satisfied smile when the president crossed his arms over his chest defensively. Dorn had gotten the damn message, and he'd gotten it good. "When I'm as busy protecting the country and *you* as I am."

The president blinked several times and cleared his throat twice. "There's been an inquiry about a young man named Troy Jensen. Do you know who he is?"

This time Carlson made sure his eyes shifted deliberately to the president's and that his expression displayed no emotion whatsoever even though that was a very interesting bit of information he'd just gotten. "No," he lied gruffly. He'd seen that intimidated shadow slide across the president's face moments ago. The sudden display of weakness and uncertainty that had appeared on the handsome face sitting behind the great desk was indescribably satisfying to Carlson. "No, I do not," he lied again, just as convincingly.

* * *

The young man—one of Maddux's Falcons—had stolen the leaky forty-foot fishing boat at ten o'clock last night and managed to sail it out of the small harbor fifty miles north of Shanghai by himself without attracting attention. Now he was a hundred nautical miles out in the Pacific Ocean, just a tiny dot on a vast dark canvas beneath a full moon. There were only two hours of darkness left before the sun would begin brightening the eastern horizon ahead of him. Fortunately, the skies were clear and the winds were calm. He doubted this bucket of rotting wood and rusty bolts could stand up to much in the way of weather. A squall line and a couple of ten-foot waves in a row and the thing would probably sink straight to the bottom.

He sure as hell didn't want to be out here long enough to find out, because that fisherman back in town was going to figure out very soon that his boat was gone. It wouldn't take much time for the local police to contact the Communist authorities in Beijing when the report of a stolen fishing boat came in. A few minutes after that, they'd scramble jets from several of China's coastal air bases, and a short time later one of those jets would send a missile screaming through the hull of this thing, and then it would definitely go straight to the bottom—in lots of little pieces.

The authorities in Beijing were onto the stolen fishing boat gig. They figured anytime that report came in now that the perpetrator was a Western spy getting the hell out of Dodge. Three times out of four they were right.

The handheld GPS device indicated that he'd reached the rendezvous location seven minutes ago. Since then, he'd been drifting along in neutral. The ocean was fairly well illuminated tonight thanks to the full moon and the stars, and he'd come out of the wheelhouse to the foredeck to get a better view.

As he checked his watch for the third time in the last two minutes, the conning tower of the attack submarine USS *Nevada* broke through the surface of the ocean inside a massive boil of bubbles less than a hundred feet from the fishing boat. This was the fourth time he'd been removed from country this way, but it still startled him when the massive sub rose from the surface just beside him like that.

Tremendous relief rolled through his system now that the cavalry had arrived. God, it was a wonderful feeling.

A few minutes later he was aboard the *Nevada* and the fishing boat was headed to the bottom of the ocean after two explosives experts from the sub had detonated enough charges in its engine room to put a gaping hole in the hull.

CHAPTER 10

JACK FOLLOWED Bill's longtime executive assistant into the spacious fortieth-floor office of the First Manhattan Bank headquarters and sat down in the wingback chair she pointed to.

"Your father should be back in a few."

She was Rita Hayes, and her voice still had the faint strains of a Brooklyn accent she'd been trying to erase for years—at Bill's suggestion. She was fifty-two and still very attractive and vivacious, but she'd never been married.

Which Jack had always found interesting. He'd caught her gazing at Bill in very affectionate ways before, though after thirty-three years together maybe that was understandable. Rita was good friends with Cheryl too. So there couldn't be anything going on behind Cheryl's back.

"Bill's downstairs on the equity trading floor with the head of syndications," she explained. "They're going over final pricing on a new issue that's hitting the street tomorrow."

Rita was basically part of the Jensen family. She and Cheryl often rode horses together out in Connecticut on weekends, and then she'd join Cheryl and Bill for dinner afterward. So she heard all the family dirt. Every last speck of it, Jack assumed.

Still, she was a professional and never let on to what she knew. She never gave Jack attitude when they saw each other or spoke on the phone, which he appreciated.

"Want anything to drink while you wait?" Rita called over her shoulder.

"No thanks."

When she reached the door, she stopped and turned around. "Was Bill expecting you? I didn't see you on his calendar."

Jack shook his head. "No, I just dropped in to say hi." He saw the surprise in her expression. He'd never come by on his own like this before. He'd always been summoned. "I wanted to surprise him."

"Oh, OK. Well, if he isn't back up here soon, I'll call and let him know you're waiting."

"Thanks."

When she was gone, Jack got up and moved cautiously to the office window. Wall Street was a long way down, and he could feel his heart starting to thump as he neared the glass. He stopped a foot from the window and leaned over to peer out. He'd always had nightmares about being way up in a skyscraper when an earthquake hit. He'd had one of those nightmares just the other night, after Troy's memorial service. And there was a serious fault not far north of here.

Wall Street was small and narrow, so most people were disappointed when they saw it for the first time, Jack knew. Despite its unimpressive appearance, the street was still one of the world's most competitive arenas. And Bill Jensen was one of its most successful players. He was a bona fide superstar because over the last three decades he'd made First Manhattan a fortune in fees taking companies public and presiding over what had become the top mergers and acquisitions department in New York City. Now he was CEO of the huge bank, which had offices in all fifty states and most countries around the world.

Jack backed away from the window and moved to a long credenza that was positioned against the opposite wall. Covering the credenza and the bookcases and attesting to Bill's incredible success was a gallery of tombstones. Lucite-encased announcements of the IPO transactions he'd led, which had originally been published in the *Wall Street Journal* when the deals had gone down. The many pictures of him shaking hands with politicians and sports stars, which rose from among the tombstones like tall buildings on the Manhattan skyline, only heightened the intimidation factor people experienced within these four walls, Jack knew.

Jack was thirty, but he still felt like a naïve kid when he came in here. That little brokerage shop he traded bonds for on the other side of the island was as about as important to the world of high finance as a pimple on the ass of an ant. First Manhattan was the lion that ate the anteater that ate the ant.

Jack picked up a photo of Bill standing next to the governor of New York and nodded. Bill always stood the same way in pictures. With his suit coat unbuttoned and his thumbs hooked inside his belt about a foot apart.

"Hello, Jack."

Jack looked up quickly at the sound of the deep voice. "Uh, hi, Bill."

Bill grimaced as he closed the office door and limped stoically toward the big leather chair behind the platform desk. He was a tall, silver-haired man who'd put on a few pounds after suffering a nasty knee injury playing squash several years ago—which was why he'd turned to skydiving to get his kicks. He couldn't cover a squash court anymore, but he could jump out of an airplane. He'd already reinjured the knee twice smashing into the ground on landing, but neither injury had stopped him from going back into the sky as soon as he could.

As Bill eased into the chair and it creaked beneath his weight, it struck Jack that he seemed worn out—physically and emotionally. He'd seen Bill tired, but not like this.

"Why have you always had such a hard time calling me Dad?" Bill asked somberly.

Jack put the photo back on the credenza and sat down in the wingback chair that was positioned directly in front of Bill's desk. It always reminded him of a witness stand whenever he came here. This time was no different.

"What do you mean?"

"You called me Bill just now. Why not Dad?"

"I don't know."

Because you try to throw me out of a plane in the middle of the night and then tell me you wish I was more like Troy when I fight you off.

That was what Jack wanted to say, but he didn't. He was looking for peace today. He'd thought a lot about what Hunter had said at the memorial service.

"I mean, I know I'm not your real father," Bill went on, "but I've taken care of you like your real dad would. So why don't I get that handle?"

"I guess because—"

"I don't feel any closer to you today than I did when you were a kid," Bill kept going. "Maybe not as close, and we weren't very close then. At least you called me Dad back then." He shook his head, still frustrated. "Jesus, we didn't talk at Troy's memorial service last weekend. I'm not even sure I saw you there. Were you?"

"Of course I was," Jack answered defensively. "You and Cheryl were so busy with everybody else. I didn't want to bother you."

"That's another thing. Can't you at least call *her* Mom? I guess it's OK if you want to call me Bill like I'm some old uncle you only see a few times a year at family functions. I guess I don't really care. But it would mean a lot to Cheryl if you'd start calling her Mom, especially now that Troy's gone."

Jack fidgeted with the cell phone he'd dug out of his jacket. He had no intention of actually trying to reach anyone, but he desperately needed something to do. "Well, I—"

"What do you want, Jack?"

Jack shrugged. "Can't I just stop in to say hi?"

"Sure, but I don't think that's what's really going on." A smug grin seeped its way into Bill's expression. "On your way to Brooklyn? Got something going on over there?"

Jack's eyes flashed to Bill's. "What?"

"Nothing."

Incredible. Bill must have had him followed at some point. That was the only way he could possibly know what was going on in Brooklyn. Christ, he was a control *freak*. How the hell could Cheryl have put up with him all these years?

"I mean it, Bill. If you're talking about—"

"I don't think you're stopping by just to say hello," Bill said loudly as his smug grin faded, "because of an e-mail I got a few minutes ago."

"I don't care about—"

"It's from Jamie Hildebrand."

Bill had called Jamie a few years ago when Jack and Hunter were fired from their previous jobs, and within an hour he had new positions for them. They weren't great jobs because Tri-State wasn't a great firm. But the salary covered Jack's living expenses, including rent on his one-bedroom apartment outside of Greenwich.

Of course, if Bill had really wanted to help, he would have gotten them jobs at his huge bank the way he was always offering to do for Troy. Good traders at First Manhattan made the big bucks, much more than traders at Tri-State, because they had so much more money to play with. But the old man had never done that.

Bill pulled out his cell phone, donned his reading glasses, and worked his way to the message. "It says here you walked into Jamie's office an hour ago and quit. Didn't give him a reason, didn't thank him for taking you and Hunter on when jobs in New York were scarce because the economy was in the tank. Just quit for no reason." He looked up over his glasses. "Mind telling me why?"

Despite that edge to Bill's voice, Jack felt a wave of positive energy surge through his body. It was time for them to connect, for them to get close, for him to lose his bitterness about being adopted. And he was convinced that what he was about to say would do it.

"I'm going to Alaska, Bill."

"Excuse me?"

That didn't sound good. "Uh, I'm going to Alaska, to Dutch Harbor."

"Why the hell would you do that?"

That definitely didn't sound good. "I want to find the captain of the *Arctic Fire* and see if he told the cops the truth about what happened to Troy. Or if there's more to the story."

"What do you mean, 'more to the story'?" Bill demanded. His expression was suddenly an angry mess. "Troy went overboard in a storm. He was out on top of the crab traps trying to tie one down when a rogue wave hit the ship. It happens up there on the Bering Sea, and it's as simple as that." Sadness rippled through

Bill's expression, mellowing the fire. "Troy never should have been on that damn ship in the first place. I should have told him not to take the job. It was my fault, not the captain's. End of story."

"Well, yeah, that's the official word we got. But don't you want to be sure?"

During the last few days Jack had researched the Alaskan crab boat business on the Internet and called an old friend from college who was living in Alaska to ask him about it. It turned out that most of the captains who sailed from Dutch Harbor were stand-up guys with good reputations. But a few weren't. Sage Mitchell, the captain of the *Arctic Fire*, was one of those men who weren't.

Something about that photograph of Troy standing in front of the ship was still bothering Jack too. Really bothering him. He felt like he was so close to making some kind of breakthrough, but he couldn't quite get there.

"There were four other men on the *Arctic Fire* that night," Jack kept going. "All of them survived the storm. It's always been the other way around when something like that happens around Troy. He makes it and the others don't. Or he saves the others." Jack shook his head. "It doesn't add up, Bill. Troy's a survivor. He's incredible when it comes to that. He was basically bulletproof, almost untouchable."

"How do you know there were four other men on the ship?"

"I've got a friend up there," Jack explained. "He's pretty connected, and he found out. It's not really that big a state when you get right down to it, not population-wise, anyway."

"Who is he? What's his name?"

That seemed like a strange question to ask right now. "What difference does it make? Look, I just think we ought to—"

"Stay away from Dutch Harbor," Bill warned as his expression turned steely again. "You hear me?"

"That's ridiculous," Jack shot back, rising out of his chair. This conversation wasn't turning out right at all. "You can't keep me away from there."

"I won't give you any money," Bill countered, coming out of his chair too. "You can't have much saved, which, I'm sure, is the real reason you're here. What are you going to do without it?"

"I'll figure it out." Though Jack wasn't sure what "it" was going to be. Bill was exactly right. He didn't have much saved. And it bothered him to hear how Bill knew that. "I'll figure it out," he repeated.

Bill glared across the desk. "Why are you really going to Alaska?"

"Because *you* haven't," Jack snapped. "Because you've been sitting on your ass for a week and you haven't done anything." It had taken every ounce of courage he had inside him to say that. "And I can't believe you haven't. I mean, you're so suspicious of everyone and everything, and you've bragged to me so many times about how being paranoid has been such a key to all your success in the business world. So why would you take some crab boat captain's word for what happened? Some guy you couldn't even pick out of a police lineup who claims Troy was the only one who went into the water that night. The other four guys on the ship are all family, they're all close. Troy was the only outsider. Something doesn't seem right about all that, Bill." Jack could feel perspiration seeping from every pore in his body, but he'd stood up to Bill Jensen in his office on Wall Street. It had been terrifying at first, but now it was an awesome moment he'd never forget. "You loved Troy so much."

"But I'm trying to figure out why you hate me."

"*What are you talking about?*"

"I've tried taking care of you, Jack. I've always tried making you feel like my own son even though—"

"See, that's the damn problem. You've always had to *try*. You never had to try with Troy."

"Well, I—"

"Admit it." Jack had a reputation for not taking crap from anyone. In fact, the only person he'd ever bowed down to consistently over the years was Bill. But now that was over, and it felt good. In that instant it had felt like he'd grown up all the way. "You know it's true."

"Leave Troy alone," Bill warned. "My God, what's wrong with you? What's all this really about?" As Bill's voice trailed off, a look of understanding slowly slid across his face. "Oh, I get it. You're trying to dig up dirt on him so you can throw mud on his grave. Still competing with him even though he's dead, are you?"

"No. I just want to—"

"Leave him alone!" Bill shouted. "Let him rest in peace!"

"Give me a break, Bill! Look, maybe if I go up there I can finally do some good for this family. Maybe then I'll feel like I'm part of it. Maybe then I won't think about how I'm adopted."

Bill gazed at Jack steadily for several seconds, and then his chin dropped slowly to his chest. "You really think that, don't you?" he mumbled. "That you're adopted, I mean."

"I think about it every day," Jack admitted, trying to figure out what the hell Bill was driving at. "I can't *stop* thinking about it."

He could have sworn he'd seen a mist in Bill's eyes as the old man's chin had gone down. He leaned slightly to the side and checked again. Sure enough, there were tears, and suddenly Jack felt a fear he'd never known. A fear that started as a slight uneasiness but quickly intensified.

Bill Jensen rarely talked about his emotions, and he *never* showed them—not sadness or fear, anyway. He hadn't broken down even as he'd given an incredibly emotional eulogy at Troy's memorial service. His voice hadn't cracked once even as people in the audience had sobbed.

It seemed surreal for Jack to see Bill like this. And for the first time he understood how much he'd depended on this man over the years for everything. How Bill had been everyone's rock for so long.

"What is it, Bill? What's wrong?"

Bill sank back into his chair. "You never figured it out," he whispered.

"Figured *what* out?"

Bill turned his head to the side and grimaced as if he were remembering something that caused him great pain. Like the image of a horrible accident that was burned so indelibly into his memory that even though the tragedy had happened years ago, it was still vivid in his mind.

"Come on. I—"

"You're Troy's half brother," Bill admitted almost inaudibly. "Cheryl's really your mother, but I'm not your—" He coughed several times as he fought to keep his composure. "Six months after we were married, Cheryl and I separated. We didn't get divorced, we just separated." His voice was shaking. "She went away for a few years because I was so damn focused on my career. And by the time I got around to begging her to come home, she was eight months pregnant with you by someone else. She stayed away until she had you, and then she came back. We kept everything very quiet," he explained, "and on the advice of a psychiatrist who was a friend of my father's, we told you and everyone else that you were adopted." He shook his head dejectedly. "It was stupid, but we were young and we didn't know any better. Once we told everyone, we couldn't take it back." He swallowed hard. "And I guess I was hurt, even though I had no right to be hurt because I was the one who wanted to be on my own again without any responsibilities. I was the one who sent Cheryl away, and I was such an idiot to do it. Anyway, the story about adopting you from someplace in Brooklyn was a bunch of crap. I...I just assumed you'd figured all that out for yourself somewhere along the line. Or that Cheryl had told you. I really thought she would have by now."

Jack stared over the desk as the old man went quiet. He couldn't believe what he'd just heard.

* * *

He stood behind the bedroom door, focused on his breathing, on regulating it as he'd learned to do long ago. The front door had just slammed shut, and the sound had sent an explosion of adrenaline bursting through his system.

He heard the footsteps on the stairs come closer; heard the man's humming grow louder; saw the figure flash past him through the crack between the wall and the door; and watched the man toss a jacket onto the bed and go into the bathroom, still humming happily.

Then he stepped from his hiding place and silently closed the bedroom door. The man wouldn't be humming much longer.

"*What the—*" The man whipped around as soon as he saw the reflection in the mirror over the sink. "Who the hell are you?"

"Death." It was what he always said at this moment, and simply uttering the word sent another mad rush of near-ecstasy-inducing adrenaline searing through his system. "Justice."

The man's eyes bugged out of their sockets as he stabbed in the air. "Get the hell out of my house right now, asshole, or I'll kill you!" he yelled. "I swear to Christ I'll tear you apart with my bare hands, you little shit."

For a split second Shane Maddux caught his image in the mirror behind the man and he had to smile. No wonder the man wasn't intimidated. The guy in the mirror *was* a little shit. Five-six and 140 pounds dripping wet, with a face only a father could love. Only his father hadn't loved him. And maybe that was ultimately why he'd grown so fond of the deal he'd forged with Roger Carlson. One of the reasons, anyway.

"Do you have any last words?" Maddux asked calmly.

The man rushed toward Maddux before he'd even finished, screaming wildly as he tore across the bathroom floor.

Maddux delivered a wicked chop-kick to the man's left knee-cap, then stepped smoothly aside as the man collapsed to the floor, writhing and screaming in pain.

Maddux's eyes narrowed as he stared down at the man struggling on the floor. The guy was a confirmed sex offender who four years ago had raped two young boys in the next town over. He'd admitted to everything during his initial interrogation with the detectives, but he'd gotten off when his case had finally come to trial because of a technicality and a young prosecutor's inexperience. In fact, he'd laughed about the prosecutor's mistakes in front of a crew of reporters on the courthouse steps a few minutes after the judge had been forced to let him go.

Maddux pulled a pistol from his pocket, pressed the barrel to the man's forehead above his terrified eyes, and fired.

The order Carlson had given him in that envelope had been executed—and justice had been served. The system didn't always work. Sometimes it needed help. Maddux was happy to provide that assistance.

He stared down at the dead man. Blood was pouring down the guy's face like a stream racing down the side of a steep mountain. Maddux had always wanted to do the same thing to that priest who'd assaulted him four times in less than two weeks when he was a kid. He'd always wanted to put a bullet through the bastard's head.

That priest was retired and living happily outside of Chicago. Maddux took a deep breath. Maybe it was finally time for a trip to the Midwest.

* * *

The moment he was past the doors of the First Manhattan building and out onto Wall Street, Jack lit a cigarette. After a week of warm weather, it had turned cold again in the Northeast. The temperature was down into the thirties, and the wind was whipping through the steep canyons formed by lower Manhattan's tall buildings and narrow streets. But Jack wasn't inhaling the smoke to warm himself up. He was doing it to calm himself down.

He wasn't Troy's adoptive brother after all. In fact, they were half blood brothers. He was a member of the Jensen family. At least, a lot more of one than he'd thought he was ten minutes ago.

It was so much to process, and his mind was still reeling. Who was his real father? Was he still alive? And why had Bill chosen that particular moment to drop the bomb? Was it simply that he was so weak because of Troy's death that he couldn't keep it to himself any longer?

Jack shook his head as he walked. Bill was a strategic and deliberate man. He usually had an obvious agenda for everything he did—and at least two more hidden ones. As far as Jack knew, Bill had never done anything out of weakness in his life.

He took a long drag off the cigarette as he headed up Wall Street toward the old Trinity Church. Well, to hell with Bill and this new information and to hell with trying to figure out why the old man had picked ten minutes ago to drop the bomb. The answers to all the questions would still be here when he got back from Alaska. They'd been waiting for thirty years. They could wait a little longer.

He was going to Alaska no matter what, he promised himself as he reached Broadway and stopped at the curb, waiting for the light to turn so he could cross. Something was calling him up there, something he couldn't ignore. And nothing was going to stop him from going.

Except money.

Bill was right. He didn't have much saved, and the trip was going to cost at least five grand, probably more. He'd been hoping Bill would offer to help, but that possibility had been flushed down the toilet right away. Bill wasn't going to give him a dime, even though he'd been proudly funding Troy's worldwide joyride for the last six and a half years.

When the traffic light at Wall and Broadway turned, Jack took one more drag from the cigarette, then flicked it away and stepped off the curb.

"*Hey, buddy!*" someone shouted from behind him. "*Hey, look out!*"

Jack's eyes flashed to the right. A white van was racing down Broadway straight at him.

CHAPTER 11

JACK TOOK several deep breaths, then knocked. It had been thirty minutes since the van had run the light on Broadway and almost killed him. But he still hadn't completely calmed down, he realized as the door opened in front of him. He still had that irony taste in his mouth from his lungs pumping so hard, and his fingers were still shaking.

"Hi, Jack," the young woman murmured from inside the apartment.

"Hi, Lisa."

Lisa Martinez was a twenty-year-old first-generation Puerto Rican-American who lived with her three older sisters on the third floor of this run-down project that was in one of Brooklyn's poorest neighborhoods. She stood slightly over five feet tall and weighed just over a hundred pounds. She had large, brown, almond-shaped eyes; lovely full lips; and caramel-colored skin. And her beautiful face was framed by long black hair.

"It's good to see you, Jack. Come in."

"Thanks," he said, following her into the apartment. "Are your sisters here?"

"No, I'm by myself. Except for the baby, of course."

"Of course."

She led him to a rickety dining room table, which stood in front of a grimy window. The window overlooked a row of basketball courts littered with trash and broken glass. They were used more for closing drug deals than anything else.

As they got to the table, Lisa gave him a warm hug and a kiss on the cheek, then pulled back and motioned for him to sit down. "Coffee?" she asked in her heavy Spanish accent. "It's really good. We just got it."

He liked her accent and the way she always waited a few moments to give him that hug and kiss every time he visited. It was as if she was nervous and had to find her courage to do it. "That's OK." He eased onto one of the four metal chairs ringing the small table. After just a few seconds of being with her he'd already started to relax. She had this soothing effect on him he didn't understand—but loved. "But thanks."

"Cherry Coke?"

He shook his head. "It's really OK, sweetheart." It was obvious that she wanted to please him, and he was thirsty. But he didn't like Cherry Coke, and it seemed like that was the only thing they ever had to drink here besides tap water. "I'm fine." He searched her dark eyes for clues to how she was really doing. She hid her emotions well for a young woman, though he wasn't sure she was trying to. It always seemed to him that it was a natural gift, that it wasn't anything she'd perfected. "Are you OK?"

She looked wonderful for having given birth only two months ago, maybe even better than she had when they'd first met over a year ago. She still had that pregnancy glow about her, but the extra weight was gone. In fact, she looked slightly thinner to him than she had before she'd conceived.

Lisa shrugged. "All right. You?" she asked as she eased onto the chair beside his.

"I'm fine."

He kept gazing at her. She was so nice and so beautiful, and he understood why Troy had been so attracted to her.

He let his chin fall slowly to his chest and took a deep breath. Troy…he couldn't bring himself to tell her.

"What's wrong?" she asked.

"Nothing, nothing at all."

"Are you sure? It looked like you were going to say something bad."

"I was just thinking about this guy I need to call," he lied.

"Oh."

He wanted to tell her about the terrible thing that had happened. But now that he was here and he was gazing into those soulful eyes and that vulnerable expression, he couldn't bring himself to do it. He couldn't make himself break her heart. He knew how much she loved Troy.

He reached into his suit coat and pulled out an envelope. It had five hundred dollars inside, and that was all he could spare right now. He figured he was going to need the rest of the money he was pretty sure he'd scraped together today to get to Alaska. In fact, he'd probably need more than that when it was all said and done. But he'd work that out later on the fly, while he was in the middle of everything.

"Here." He held the envelope out for her. "Take it."

Lisa caught her breath and put a hand to her chest when she saw the cash. "Ay dios mio!" she shrieked, springing out of her chair to give him a huge hug.

"Don't get too excited," he said when she finally pulled back. "It's just five hundred bucks. I'm sorry that's all I can give you right now."

"You're so good to me. Why?"

"I have to be," Jack answered simply. "That's just the way it is."

Lisa gazed at him for several moments, and then she turned and trotted into one of the bedrooms. A few moments later she was back, cradling her two-month-old son in her slender arms. He was wrapped snugly in a blanket and sleeping soundly, but Jack could see the tiny features of his handsome face as well as a shock of jet-black hair protruding from beneath his blue knit hospital cap. This little boy was her first child.

Lisa held the baby out and smiled. "Here, you hold him."

Just the thought of doing that sent Jack's heart rate into the stratosphere. He'd only held babies a few times in his life, and he'd been sweating profusely after only a few moments each time.

"Oh, no, I don't think so."

Lisa laughed as she pressed the little boy against Jack's chest. "Make sure you support his head."

"OK, OK." He took a deep breath as he gazed down at the tiny human being resting in his arms. "Well, hello there, little Jack," he said quietly. "It's nice to see you again."

CHAPTER 12

SPEED TRAP was eating dinner by himself at the crumb-strewn table in the galley of the *Arctic Fire*. Tonight it was two hot dogs and some baked beans that had been sitting in a big, uncovered pot on the stove since yesterday afternoon, undoubtedly attracting all kinds of attention from bacteria. Even in the frigid air on the Bering Sea, those nasty creatures survived. So he'd zapped his helping of beans and the two hot dogs in the microwave that was on the dishwasher beside the stove.

The ship would make Akutan in a few hours to unload a second excellent haul of kings—not quite as big as the first, but enough to make him another fifty grand. And he was using these last few minutes of downtime to put some much-needed energy into his system. He'd eaten nothing for thirty-six hours because they'd been hauling traps back on board almost nonstop, so right now any food at all looked good to him. Even things he wouldn't touch on land with someone else's ten-foot pole.

"Hey, little brother."

Speed Trap glanced up as he stuck the last bite of the first delicious mustard-covered hot dog into his mouth. "Hey, Grant," he said through the mouthful. His older brother was so tall he had to stoop constantly when he wasn't outside. "What's up? Other than your head on the ceiling."

"Funny, you little hemorrhoid."

"Shut up."

Grant took off his jacket and hung it over the back of the chair opposite Speed Trap's. On the back of the jacket was a large, multicolored image of the *Arctic Fire* cresting a wave and the name of the ship written in script beneath the image. Last Christmas, Captain Sage's wife had made the jackets for all four of the ship's regular crew members.

"I should take you up on deck and hang you over the side, you little shit."

"Try it," Speed Trap shot back. "See what happens."

Speed Trap had never gotten into a fight with Grant, and the truth was, he never wanted to. Grant was huge and mean. As far as Speed Trap knew, he'd never lost a fight. And when he got drunk, he looked for them. That was when Grant caused riots because people started stampeding out of his way.

"I'm serious."

"Shut up, little brother. You know I'd kick your ass."

After grabbing the biggest bowl he could find from the dishwasher, which hadn't been run in a week, Grant moved to the stove and ladled a healthy portion of beans into the dirty dish. After that, he grabbed some saltine crackers from the cupboard and sat down at the table in the chair opposite Speed Trap's without bothering to nuke his helping. He'd always had an iron stomach, and the fact that the beans had been around for a while didn't bother him at all. He didn't care that they were cold either, Speed Trap knew. Grant's priority when it came to eating was simply getting the food into his mouth and then his stomach as quickly as possible.

"Hey," Grant said as he shoved the first spoonful of beans past his teeth, "you just beat your DUI and your resisting charge over in Seward. How 'bout that?"

Speed Trap had been about to start in on the second hot dog, but when he heard Grant's headline the bun's forward progress came to an abrupt halt an inch from his mouth. "What?" He put the bun slowly back down on his plate and broke into a broad smile. "Really?" But his smile faded quickly. Grant was always teasing him or lying to him about something, and Speed Trap was worried that he was being stupid and gullible and just taking the bait one more time. He figured Grant was going to bust out laughing at him at any second. "Damn it, are you bullshitting me?"

"Nope. This is straight dope, dude. I was up on the bridge, and I overheard Uncle Sage talking to somebody on the phone about it. The shit's been taken care of. All your charges were dropped. You don't even have to go to court. They even gave you your license back. It's nuts."

Speed Trap gazed at Grant for a few moments, then finally decided he wasn't being set up for that sucker punch after all. "Why? I mean they had me dead to rights. When I went to first appearance the morning after I was arrested, the judge laughed at me. He told me with my record I'd get at least six months in the slammer, probably a year."

Grant shrugged. "I don't know what to tell you, pal." He gulped down several heaping spoonfuls of cold beans and then stuffed a couple of saltines in behind them. His eyes rolled back in their sockets, like a shark's did when its jaws closed down on prey. "Weird things like that always seem to happen on this ship," he said through his mouthful of food. "Know what I mean?"

"Yeah, like how about all those brand new traps that were waiting for us on the dock in Dutch after we put off that first load in Akutan? To replace the ones we lost in the storm, right? I figured we'd be in Dutch for at least a week waiting for new stuff." Speed Trap shook his head. "So what happens? One day in port and we're out of the harbor and back on the crab."

"Exactly," Grant agreed. "Nobody gets traps that fast. No fucking way." He stared at the microwave for a few seconds. "What about that guy we picked up in the raft west of St. Paul last year during the opilio season? That was insane."

"Yeah, that was insane."

"I mean, there's nothing at all on the radio about that guy. No heads-up from the Coast Guard boys, no chatter from any of the other boats. Then boom, there he is in the middle of the Bering Sea, waving us on from the raft and tapping his watch like he's late for a dinner party." Grant's eyes narrowed. "The weirdest thing about it all was that Sage didn't seem surprised. It was like he knew the raft was going to be there."

"Think he did?"

Grant hesitated. "I'll tell you this, little brother. We've never, and I mean *never*, dropped traps anywhere near that area of the Bering Sea before. Not during the king hunt or the opilio season. Even before you started crabbing with us we didn't."

"And the test line we sank out there wasn't very long," Speed Trap added, referring to the line of traps Sage dropped in places they were unfamiliar with to see if crabs were foraging on the bottom. "Uncle Sage doesn't drop many test lines to begin with, but when he does, they're longer than that. You know?"

"Yup."

"It was like he dropped that line to make us think he was into that spot, that he thought it could be a honey hole, but he really wasn't. It was more like that was our excuse to be in the area. I mean, when we pulled the traps back up there were crabs in them."

"But we didn't stick around. Yeah, I'm with you." Grant reached across the table, grabbed Speed Trap's hot dog, and took a huge bite—which was nearly half of it—before tossing what was left back on his younger brother's plate. "You know that guy stayed in Sage's room until we got back to Dutch too. He never came out once. Not that I saw, anyway. Sage doesn't let anybody use his room, not even Dad."

"And when we got to Dutch," Speed Trap said, pulling his plate far enough to one side that even Grant's long arms couldn't reach what was left of the hot dog, "he was off the boat and gone as soon as we got to the pier. He actually jumped off the boat before we even tied up." Speed Trap looked down at his plate dejectedly. "And we've thrown those greenhorns overboard," he mumbled. "That's the worst thing of all, Grant."

Grant chuckled dispassionately. "That's just because Sage and Dad want to save some money, little brother. That's just them being big old bastards." He finished the beans by picking up his plate and tilting it so they dribbled into his mouth. "You and I didn't see any of that money, did we?" he asked when the last bean was gone. "Technically, we should have split Troy's share, but we didn't. I got eighty-one grand. What did you get?"

"Same."

"I rest my case. Throwing those greenhorns over the side is just about the money. And we're not the only ship that does it."

Speed Trap remembered the terror he'd felt as he was hanging off the side of the *Arctic Fire* in that storm by what seemed like nothing more than one thin strand of the yellow safety harness. And that incredible sensation of overpowering relief that had rushed through his body when Troy had pulled him back on board. For a few incredible moments he'd actually loved Troy Jensen.

A little while later they'd thrown him overboard.

"Troy was a good guy. That's all I know."

"So he saved your life," Grant said callously as he stood up and the spindly chair he'd been sitting in fell over behind him with a loud crash. "Who cares?"

"What do you mean, *who cares*? I care. I care a lot. It sucked that Uncle Sage threw him over, and it sucked that Dad helped him do it. It sucked that you did too."

Grant pointed a long, menacing finger down at his younger brother. "You keep your damn mouth shut about it. Don't you say anything to Sage or Dad, or anybody else for that matter. You hear me?"

"I hear you."

"You better hear me, and you better not say anything. Or you'll be next. Got it? Well, *do you*?" Grant shouted when he didn't get an answer immediately.

"I got it!" Speed Trap shouted back. "Christ! Give me a break. I wouldn't be here if it wasn't for Troy Jensen. Don't you get that?"

CHAPTER 13

"Thanks for coming, Hunt. I appreciate it."

"No problem. I mean, it's not like you've got to try real hard to convince me to have a beer with you. So I'm guessing from your tone and the 'I appreciate it' that there's something else going on here."

"There is."

They were sitting at the bar of an Irish pub in lower Manhattan near Tri-State Securities. It was a place they'd gone more than a few times after a rough day on the trading floor.

"So, what's up?"

"What do you mean?" Jack had heard the suspicious tone in Hunter's voice.

"Where'd you go after you left the trading floor this afternoon? I thought you said you were running an errand, but you never came back. Then you called from your cell phone and asked me to meet you here." Hunter took several swallows of beer. "It was all kind of mysterious, and you aren't normally mysterious. You're more the in-your-face type, you know?"

"Uh-huh."

"So, *what's up*?"

Jack tore off the corner of the paper napkin beneath his beer glass as he thought about how much to tell Hunter. They were best friends, but this was a crazy thing he was doing. And the favor he was going to ask for would probably sound even crazier to Hunter than where Jack was going. He didn't want to have to explain both things tonight because the favor was going to take awhile. Plus, admitting that he was going to Alaska might lead to talking about that bombshell Bill had dropped today in his office.

Jack didn't want to go in that direction either. He was still digesting the news himself. He wasn't ready to share that with *anyone*.

He didn't want to tell Hunter about the trip mostly because he didn't have time—he had another meeting in a few minutes. But it was a little because of his close call with that white van on Broadway this afternoon too. Now that he thought about it, maybe it was more than a little about the van, maybe *a lot* about it.

"I resigned," he finally answered.

Hunter's eyes flashed up from his beer glass. "No shit?"

"After I left the trading floor this afternoon, I went into Jamie Hildebrand's office upstairs and quit."

"But why?" Hunter asked. "I mean, you never mentioned anything about it." He shrugged. "It isn't like you needed my OK before you did it. I just thought we were good friends."

"Best friends, Hunt. You know that."

Hunter leaned back in the stool and crossed his arms over his chest. "I've gotta say I'm a little surprised you didn't at least mention something to me."

"Yeah...I know." He could tell Hunter was hurt. "Sorry."

"Well, what are you doing?" Hunter asked when Jack didn't volunteer anything more. "Why'd you quit?"

Jack inhaled deeply. "I need to take some time off. I need to get away for a while."

"Because of what happened to Troy?"

"Is that so wrong?"

"Of course not," Hunter replied. "I'm sorry Troy died, but I think it's really good that you're taking it so...well, so deeply."

"I am." More than Hunter could know, Jack thought to himself.

"Where are you going?"

Jack glanced up. "Who said anything about going anywhere?"

"You did. A second ago you said you needed to get away." Hunter took several more gulps of beer. "It sounded like you meant you were getting away from the area. Or did you just mean you needed to get away from Tri-State?"

Jack needed to come up with something fast. Hunter would figure out pretty quickly that he wasn't around. The good thing was that Hunter never talked to Bill, so he wasn't worried about Hunt finding out that his real destination was Alaska.

"I'm going to Florida."

"*Florida?* Why?"

"It's almost winter. It's gonna get cold for good soon. I was thinking I'd head to the Keys and pick up a bartending job for the season. It shouldn't be hard to find something like that down there now."

"Bartending? Are you serious?"

"Sure. Why?"

Hunter shrugged. "I don't know. It's such a one-eighty. I know this thing with Troy hit you hard, but don't you think going to Florida to be a bartender is kind of drastic?"

Jack wanted to tell Hunter what the real deal was. And the words were on the tip of his tongue. "I just need some time," he murmured, glad he hadn't given in to the temptation to tell him about Alaska. He was probably being paranoid, but he felt better keeping Hunter in the dark about it. He'd tell him everything when it was all over. "That's all."

Hunter looked around the bar sadly. "Guess it'll be the last time we do this for a while."

"I guess."

"Why didn't we just talk on the train?" Hunter asked, checking his watch. "We could have taken a Metro North home together."

"I'm meeting someone else down here in a few minutes," Jack explained, checking his watch too.

"Who?"

"It doesn't matter."

"Oh, I get it. First you leave me by myself at Tri-State to go to Florida. Then you stonewall me when I ask an innocent little question. I guess we're not as close as we used to be. Is this guy your new best friend or something?"

"Give me a break, Hunt. He's just somebody I need to talk to about something."

The guy had been his and Hunter's boss at the firm where they'd worked before Tri-State. The guy had always said he felt bad for letting them go, and had always offered to help out. So Jack was going to put him on the spot tonight. He needed money badly now that Bill had made it clear he wasn't going to be an ATM if the use of funds involved Alaska and Troy. Bill had sent him a text a few minutes ago making that clear *again*—and warning him again to stay away from Alaska *again*.

"It's no big deal." He didn't want to tell Hunter what was going on because he didn't want Hunter getting curious and calling the guy.

Hunter held his hand up. "OK, OK. I guess I'm just cranky because my best buddy and his bad but loveable attitude are taking off. No more train rides in from Connecticut together, no more screwing around on the trading floor when things get slow, no more beers after work. I'm not gonna lie to you, pal. This sucks."

"It does suck," Jack agreed. He appreciated Hunter's candor. It made him feel good. "But I have to do this."

"I know. I guess," Hunter added as though he didn't really understand.

For a few moments Jack thought again about telling Hunter what Bill had told him this afternoon in the office—that he wasn't adopted. But again he decided against it. He had talk to Hunter about that other thing, and there wasn't much time to do that and get to his other meeting. "I need a favor."

"Name it and you got it. You know that."

Jack hesitated. He knew how this was going to sound, but he had to keep his promise. "I need you to look in on somebody while I'm gone because I might be away for a while."

"OK."

"And you can't tell anybody about it. OK?"

"Why not?"

"You just can't, *all right*?"

"*All right.*" Hunter paused for a few moments. "So who's this person?"

"She lives over in Brooklyn," Jack answered quietly. "Her name's Lisa Martinez, and she's got a little boy." He glanced around the bar and leaned forward slightly. "His name's Jack."

Hunter's eyes flashed to Jack's at light speed. "Aw, Christ, Jack. What the hell have you done?"

CHAPTER 14

JACK'S EYES moved from the late news on the TV screen to his front door when he thought he heard something outside the apartment. Then he heard what sounded like a knock, but he wasn't sure.

It was eleven twenty and he wasn't expecting anyone. He'd been lying on his living room couch listening to the anchorman's smooth voice, trying to forget what had happened today. And wondering how in the hell he was going to get to Dutch Harbor, because his seven o'clock meeting had turned out to be a dead end. The guy's wife had nixed the loan over the phone while they were sitting at another bar near the place he'd met Hunter. Now he had only fifteen hundred bucks left to his name after giving Lisa Martinez the five hundred.

He'd actually heard himself starting to snore as he'd drifted off listening to the news. But at the sound of the knock he was wide awake again and his heart was pumping hard.

He stared across the room through the flickering light coming from the TV screen. Maybe he was just being paranoid. Maybe he hadn't really heard anything outside. But after almost being killed by that van in front of Trinity Church today, he felt like he had a damn good reason to be paranoid. Thank God for whoever had yelled at him from the sidewalk. If not for that angel he'd be lying on a gurney in the morgue right now instead of on this sofa.

A voice in the back of his head had been telling him to get out of here for the last few hours…just like it had been whispering about that picture of Troy standing in front of the *Arctic Fire*. He'd called Hunter twice after they'd met for drinks to see if he could stay at his and Amy's place tonight, but Hunter hadn't called back yet. Which was strange because Hunter always called right back. Hunter's cell phone was basically part of his body.

This time the knock was loud and clear.

Jack glanced at his bedroom door as he rose up quickly into a sitting position. He was an avid bird hunter, and he had two shotguns in there. The over-and-under twelve-gauge was empty, but the side-by-side was loaded. He always kept that one loaded.

"Jack. *Jack*."

His shoulders sagged as he stood up and hurried to the door. He'd recognized the voice right away, but this was still a strange situation. During the three years he'd lived in this apartment, she hadn't come by once to see him. He was shocked that she actually knew where he lived.

"Hello, Cheryl," Jack said as he swung the door open. He cringed. Old habits died hard. "I, I mean…*Mom*." The word meant so much more now. "Come in. I'm sorry about the mess."

"Please don't apologize. It's fine."

"Can I get you something?" he asked as he closed the door behind her. It seemed surreal for her to be here. "Would you like something to drink?"

"No, thank you."

Jack watched her take in what little there was of the place. He saw her glance at the three pizza boxes stacked on the coffee table in front of the couch, the clothes draped over chairs and lying in piles on the floor, and the small desk in the corner, which looked like it had been hit by a tornado. "I wish I'd known you were coming," he said apologetically, flipping on the light and instantly regretting it. Now she could really see how bad the place looked. But she didn't seem to care. "I would have cleaned up."

"Don't worry about it, sweetheart. I keep telling you."

She'd always been so good to him. "I know, it's just that—"

"Bill told me about this afternoon," she interrupted. "He told me you came to his office, and he told me what he said." She took a few seconds to pull herself together. "I'm sorry we lied to you all these years. It sounds so worthless when I hear myself say it, but I really am sorry. I wouldn't blame you if you never forgave me."

A muffled sob escaped her lips as tears formed on her lower lids. The same way they'd come to Bill's eyes this afternoon. There was so much to talk about, but Jack had no idea how or where to start. "It's OK, really." He'd thought about calling her all afternoon, and he'd actually dialed her number twice. But then he'd quickly ended the call before the connection had been made.

"It's not OK," she murmured. "It's horrible."

It was horrible, but Jack didn't want to go there right now. This seemed like too harsh a way to begin what he assumed was going to be a long conversation. They should be easing into this, not barreling at it head-on.

"He told me that you're going to Alaska too," she said, "to Dutch Harbor."

That seemed like an odd topic to bring up now. When there were so many other more important things they needed to talk about. "Yeah…I am."

Cheryl moved so she was standing directly in front of him and their faces were close. "He told you to stay away from there, didn't he?"

Jack clenched his hands into tight fists. Maybe that was it. Maybe she'd come here to warn him too, and this visit was all part of a well-orchestrated bad cop, good cop routine. "I don't want to talk about Alaska," he said firmly.

She put her soft palms on his cheeks and stared up at him. "Don't let Bill talk you out of it," she whispered. "Don't let him scare you. Go to Alaska," she urged. "Do you hear me? Go."

Jack nodded hesitantly, not sure he really had heard her—at least, not right. He'd heard the words, but the message seemed full of static. "I heard you. I mean, I guess I—"

"But be careful, Jack. Be *very* careful."

"I will. Of course I will."

Her eyes widened, as if she'd just thought about something very frightening. "Don't ever tell Bill I was here tonight. All right?"

"All right."

"You *have* to remember that, Jack."

She suddenly seemed more terrified than he'd ever seen her before. "OK, OK, I'll remember."

She reached into her purse and handed him a thick envelope. Then she kissed him on the cheek and headed for the door.

But he caught her by the wrist and turned her gently back around. "Mom." Tears were streaming down her cheeks, and she wouldn't look up at him. "Mom?"

"What?" she answered, sobbing softly.

Jack swallowed hard. "Who's my real father?"

CHAPTER 15

HUNTER SAT in a comfortable chair, hands clasped together tightly in his lap, waiting patiently. He'd been sitting in the chair for hours, but they wouldn't tell him who he was waiting for or why they'd brought him here.

He'd been watching television the whole time, sitting with the two men who'd stopped him as he was heading down into the subway to go to Grand Central Station after meeting Jack. They'd flashed a couple of big, official-looking gold badges at him and then hustled him into a dark blue Town Car waiting at the curb. They hadn't forced him to get in, but he hadn't put up a fight either. He'd always heard it was best to do whatever you were told to do in those situations. To make sure you didn't piss anybody off and make things even worse for yourself later.

At first, Hunter was petrified that they were arresting him for a stock tip he'd gotten from an I-banker friend one night last month in a bar. The next morning he'd bought a ton of cheap call options on the target company's stock, knowing full well that a takeover announcement from a European conglomerate was imminent. The announcement had come two days later, and he'd instantly pocketed thirty grand. It was thirty grand he needed like hell because he was basically broke. It was also a clear-cut case of insider trading.

For the first hour of this ordeal he'd been panic-stricken, wondering how in the world he was going to survive in prison. Wondering if all those stories he'd heard about what happened in there to thin blond guys were really true.

Eventually he'd convinced himself that they weren't the kind of government people who cared about insider trading, so his initial wave of terror had ebbed.

Now his fears were growing again, though for a different reason. All they'd said the entire time he'd been here was that someone needed to talk to him. They wouldn't tell him who the person was or what branch of the government they were with. Worse, they wouldn't even confirm that they were actually with the government. And that was why he was getting nervous again. Maybe they weren't with the government.

He glanced at his watch. It was almost midnight. "Hey guys, I've gotta go," he said firmly, starting to stand up. "My wife will be—"

"Sit down," the guy in the chair closest to him ordered sharply just as there was a hard rap on the door. "Now!"

A few moments later the man who'd knocked on the door was sitting in a chair in front of Hunter and the other two men had disappeared into another room.

"Hello, Hunter."

The man wore an expensive suit, a sharp button-down shirt, and a Hermes tie. He looked more like a Wall Streeter than a government guy. He was small—short and narrow—but Hunter still sensed danger about him. He seemed to naturally emit it with his eyes.

"Sorry to keep you waiting so long," he said with a thin smile.

Hunter sensed that the smile and the friendly demeanor were forced. Maybe they were going to grill him on who'd given him the stock tip after all. Maybe they were after bigger fish and it was a plea-bargain situation. Well, he was going to get a lawyer before he said anything.

"That's OK." Hunter tapped his watch, trying to seem a little irritated. "But it's getting late."

"Cigarette?" the man asked, reaching into his suit coat and pulling out a pack.

"Nah."

"Well, look, I know you're wondering why you're here."

"To tell you the truth, that had crossed my—"

"Why did Jack Jensen quit his job at Tri-State this afternoon?" the man demanded. His friendly demeanor soured as he leaned forward.

"What?" Hunter asked, taken completely by surprise. "I, I have no idea," he stammered. "How the hell do I know why he—"

"Tell me!"

"All I know is that Jack quit. He didn't even tell me he was going to quit before he did. It was a shock."

"Bullshit, Hunter. You're his best friend. You know more than that."

"No, I don't." Hunter felt himself *really* starting to panic. There was something so terrifying about this man's eyes. "*I swear.*"

"Is he going somewhere?"

Hunter just hoped to God the man wasn't a mind reader and hadn't seen the word Florida flash through his brain. It probably didn't matter if he had, Hunter realized, because the word was probably tattooed on his forehead by now. "I...I don't know. *I'm serious.*"

The man glanced at something over Hunter's shoulder, but before Hunter could turn around, a clear plastic bag slid roughly down over his head, a rope cinched tightly around his neck, and his hands were clamped together behind his back. Through the bag shrouding his face, Hunter saw the man puffing on his cigarette, calmly watching.

Hunter struggled violently, but it was useless. There were too many of them and they were too strong. He couldn't move—or breathe. The bag was going halfway down his throat every time he tried to suck in air, and he could feel himself quickly losing consciousness.

As his eyes closed all he could think about was that conversation he'd had with Jack about being interrogated as a terrorist.

* * *

After grudgingly agreeing to pay twice the advertised rate up front in cash, along with a forty-dollar tip, the old man doing the graveyard shift behind the cheap motel's front desk hadn't required a credit card imprint or a name. However, the anonymity was providing Jack little peace of mind.

With one final heave, the heavy chest of drawers stood directly in front of the door to his room. Jack backed off slowly and sat down on the edge of the bed beside the envelope full of cash Cheryl had given him earlier. Maybe all of this was overkill and he didn't need to be so worried. Maybe that warning voice whispering to him from the back of his brain was wrong.

He shook his head as he reached for the loaded pistol lying on the mattress beside him. No way. Better safe than sorry, especially if being sorry meant being dead. Better to go the extra mile—an extra thousand miles if that was necessary—than get run over by a van.

Better safe than sorry. That was going to be his mantra until this thing was finished—one way or the other.

PART 3

CHAPTER 16

BALTIMORE, MARYLAND, was more than four thousand miles from Dutch Harbor, but that was where Jack had come to pick up the trail of truth about Troy.

A man named Ross Turner had pointed him there. Turner had been Jack's fraternity brother at Denison, and he was one of those few friends from way back Jack still had.

After graduation, Turner had gone to Alaska to hunt and fish for a year before going to Harvard Law School. Harvard had given Turner a deferral to get the Alaska bug out of his system. But one year had turned into eight, and any lingering thoughts of the law had been erased by images of the grizzly bears he'd shot and the king salmon he'd landed. Now Turner made his living hunting and fishing—as a guide.

Jack's second call to Turner in a week—a call Jack had made only minutes after almost being killed by the white van on Broadway—had prompted Turner to dig even deeper into Captain Sage Mitchell's sketchy reputation. During his years in Alaska, Turner had made contacts everywhere, including police barracks and Coast Guard stations up and down the seaboard. And it didn't take him long to uncover a fascinating piece of information that had somehow steered clear of the press.

The *Arctic Fire* had lost a greenhorn to the Bering Sea during last year's king crab hunt as well. His name was Charlie Banks, and he'd been thrown overboard by a rogue wave during a violent storm while he was up on the crab trap mountain trying to secure equipment that had torn loose in a gale. His body was never recovered, and Captain Sage had provided few details of the incident to the Coast Guard or the police. Banks's family and fiancée had flown to Dutch Harbor from the lower forty-eight to make sense of the tragedy, but Sage told them even less than he'd told the authorities.

Turner had learned from his source that Banks's family and fiancée had pushed hard for a more intense investigation, but there was nothing the state or local authorities could do. There was no body and no reason to suspect foul play, so they couldn't allocate what were always scarce law-enforcement resources in Alaska to the situation. And, after all, crabbing on the Bering Sea was the deadliest job in the world. Men and women who chose to sail those dangerous waters in November understood the risks. If they didn't, they were stupid. And in Alaska there was little sympathy for being stupid.

Charlie Banks's story was so chillingly similar to Troy's that as soon as Turner had called back this morning to relay the details, Jack had gone straight to Penn Station in Manhattan and bought himself an Amtrak ticket for Baltimore. Banks was originally from Baltimore.

More importantly, so was the girl Banks had intended to marry when he died.

* * *

Sidewalkers Cafe was just a hole-in-the wall joint on the Baltimore Harbor with twenty wobbly wooden tables and some corny fishing memorabilia hanging from the walls. But everyone around Jack in the Amtrak car had told him this was the place to go to get the best seafood in a city known for its seafood.

Jack leaned back in his chair to give the waitress room to put the plate down. It was piled high with two crab cakes, fried oysters, and a fried filet of flounder as well as heaping helpings of hush puppies and french fries. There was nothing healthy about it, but it looked and smelled delicious, and one bad meal wasn't going to kill him. He hadn't eaten since last night, and he was starving.

"Thanks." He smiled up at the waitress. He was glad the restaurant had gotten great reviews from people on the train, but he would have come here even if it hadn't. This place had been his ultimate destination all along. "Sure looks good."

"Can I get you anything else?" she asked.

The pretty young woman had long black hair, high cheekbones, glistening brown eyes, full lips, and a beautiful smile. All of that black hair was piled together haphazardly on top of her head in a wild bun; she didn't have makeup on, and she was wearing a loose University of Maryland white sweatshirt and baggy jeans. She wasn't dolled up, but she still looked great.

She was nice too, really nice. She'd seemed so genuine as she'd taken his order a few minutes ago. And during those brief moments Jack was convinced he'd seen a naïveté and an innocence hiding in her naturally trusting expression and those big brown eyes—which, of course, he was drawn to.

"More tartar sauce, please." He didn't want to wreck her night, and his first instinct was always to protect vulnerable women. But he had to stay focused on the fact that he was here to find out what had happened to Troy. "One dish won't get me through all this food."

"No problem." She gave him that easy smile. "Be right back."

Maybe he should let her finish her shift before he started firing questions at her, Jack figured as he watched her walk away. He hated the thought of making her dredge up such terrible memories.

"Here you go," she said as she got back to the table and put the dish of tartar sauce down beside his plate. "That should do you."

He gazed up at her, still going back and forth. "Thanks, Karen."

She'd been about to turn away, but the sound of her name made her freeze. She wasn't wearing a name tag, and she hadn't said her name to him when she'd first come to the table. Jack saw the emotion race through her expression.

"How do you know my name?" she asked in a hollow voice as she stared down at him intently.

It was like she'd seen a ghost, he realized. "I just want to ask you some questions." The anxiety in her eyes disappeared, and Jack saw a steely toughness rise up to replace it. "That's all I want, I promise. Please help me."

She gazed down at him for several seconds more.

Maybe there was a chance, he prayed. "Please."

But she turned and bolted for the door.

"Damn it!" He grabbed a crab cake off his plate and took a bite as he jumped up and sprinted after her. As he dodged his way through the tables, out of the corner of his eye he saw another waiter quickly put down his tray of food. "Why can't anything be easy?" he muttered to himself, tossing what was left of the crab cake down onto another patron's plate as he raced past the table.

He rushed through the entrance out onto the sidewalk just as Karen darted between two parked cars on the other side of the street. He took off after her, avoiding an older couple with a quick juke and an agile sidestep. As he did, he was aware that someone had burst out of the restaurant's front door behind him.

Karen was fast, and it took Jack several blocks to catch her.

"I just want to talk to you for a few minutes!" he yelled when he was finally only a few strides behind her. At thirty he was still in excellent shape. He'd been a good high school football and lacrosse player. Nowhere near as good as Troy, but good, and he still worked out. "Come on, stop!"

"I don't have anything to say!" she yelled back over her shoulder. "I already told you people that. Leave me alone or I'll call the cops."

"What people? I don't know who you're talking about." God she was fast. "My name's Jack Jensen. My brother Troy just died on the *Arctic Fire*." And she had stamina. She hadn't slowed down at all. "The captain said he was thrown overboard by a rogue wave, but I don't think—"

Karen pulled up so suddenly Jack could only avoid crashing into her by diving over the trunk of a car that was parked by the curb. As he scrambled to his feet, someone raced around the back of the sedan at him.

"No, Mick!" Karen yelled. "No!"

Jack heard Karen shriek frantically as he blocked the guy's punch with a forearm, then delivered a wicked body combination. Mick dropped to his knees and clutched his stomach as Jack coiled up to put the guy down for good with a right hook to the chin.

Before he could pummel whoever the guy was, Karen barreled into him from the side and knocked him away.

"What are you doing?" she shouted.

"What am *I* doing?" Jack demanded angrily between gasps for breath, impressed by her body block. She didn't look like she weighed much, but it had been powerful. Maybe she wasn't as vulnerable as he'd first thought. "That guy's the maniac." He pointed at Mick, who was still hunched over, clutching his stomach. "Who the hell is he?"

"A friend," Karen muttered, breathing hard too. "He was just protecting me."

"From what?" Jack asked, bending over and putting his hands on his knees.

"You."

"But I wasn't doing anything. I just wanted to ask you some questions. I told you that at the table."

"How was Mick supposed to know that? How was I? You chased me out of the restaurant like a nut job."

"Well, you ran out of the restaurant like a nut job."

"Well, you knew my name."

"OK, OK." Jack lifted off his knees and held his hands out apologetically. "You're right. I shouldn't have done it that way."

"What did you say your name was again?"

"Jack. Jack Jensen. A week and a half ago my brother went overboard off the *Arctic Fire*. The captain said it happened when a rogue wave hit the ship, but I didn't buy that. Then I heard about what happened to your fiancé and I had to talk to you. The captain of the *Fire* told the cops exactly the same story about Charlie Banks that he told them about my brother."

Karen knelt down next to Mick and patted his back. "How did you find me?" she asked Jack.

"I've got a friend up in Alaska who knows—"

The sound of screeching tires drowned him out. In the glow of the overhead lights he saw two men jump from a dark SUV across the street. Both of them had pistols.

"Come on!" he shouted, grabbing Karen's wrist and pulling her between the cars as the sounds of guns exploding and bullets pinging metal pierced the darkness.

"Wait!" she yelled, yanking her hand from Jack's. "Mick!"

But as Mick staggered to his feet between the cars, a bullet slammed through the back of his skull and tore out of his right eye, spraying blood and brain matter into the air. Karen screamed as Mick crumpled to the ground in front of her and the red and gray mess splattered her white sweatshirt.

Jack pushed Karen down on the sidewalk behind the car, then whipped the Glock 9 mm out of his belt. It was the same pistol he'd slept with last night at the motel, and now he was damn glad he'd listened to that paranoid voice inside his head.

He chambered the first round, rose up so he could barely see over the trunk, and blasted four shots at the men racing toward them. One of the men tumbled to the street on the other side of the car while the other peeled off to the right and dived behind a car that was several up from the one they were kneeling behind.

"Come on," Jack yelled, jabbing the barrel of the gun in the opposite direction of the way the second guy had just headed. "Let's go!"

"I can't leave Mick here."

Jack grimaced as he glanced down at her blood-spattered sweatshirt. "There's nothing you can do for him. Come on!"

"Wait!"

Jack watched in amazement as Karen reached to the small of her back and pulled out a revolver from a holster clipped to her jeans.

She dropped to the sidewalk, put the right side of her head onto the pavement so she could see below the bottom of the car, aimed, and fired twice. As Jack's gaze flashed in the direction the second guy had gone, he heard a scream and then a loud groan from the other side of the car—just as a dark silhouette appeared between the second and third cars up the street. He fired four shots at the silhouette, which quickly ducked down between the cars again.

As another SUV screeched to a halt behind the first one and two more men piled out, Jack and Karen helped each other up and raced away.

"There!" Jack pointed at the corner of a brick building in front of them, ecstatic that she was so fast and could keep up so easily. They cut quickly to the right and raced down the dark alley. "Let's get behind that thing and ambush them," he muttered, pointing at a Dumpster fifty feet ahead on the left. "They'll never see it coming."

"How many rounds do you have left?"

"I'm not sure. Not many."

"You have another clip on you?"

"No."

"No good, then," Karen gasped as she ran. "Not enough ammo, and besides, there might be more of them around. Better to get out of the alley altogether," she muttered as they sprinted past the Dumpster.

All of which made a lot of sense, Jack realized. "Were you in the military?" They'd almost made it to the end of the alley.

"No, I was a Baltimore city cop for two—"

Gunfire rang out behind them, and once again the air was filled with bullets.

A moment later Karen tumbled headfirst to the pavement and her pistol clattered down the alley in front of her.

✱ ✱ ✱

Amy Smith was tall and blonde with soft though not beautiful features. She was only thirty-two, but she dressed like a matron. It was as if she were advertising how much she wanted to be a mother.

But that hadn't happened yet.

Amy was the daughter of a Wall Street money manager who'd shot himself in the head six years ago just as the SEC was raiding his lower Manhattan offices. He'd defrauded his institutional clients of over five billion dollars, but no one had ever held her father's crimes against Amy. She'd never been involved with her father's firm, and she did a great deal of charity work for children.

She and Hunter were married several months after her father's suicide, and they lived in the guesthouse of an estate that was a few miles from the Jensen farm. They'd tried desperately to have children for the first several years of their marriage, but it hadn't happened. Now they were looking into adoption, hoping that would be the answer to their prayers.

Hunter sat on the couch and gazed at Amy, who was in a chair on the other side of the living room. He was wondering if they'd ever have a chance to follow up on their dream. He could see the tears running down her cheeks from beneath her blindfold, but there was nothing he could do. His wrists were tied securely behind his back, his ankles were taped together, and two men were pointing pistols at him.

The small man in the sharp suit and tie who'd interrogated him last night in the basement of the office building in lower Manhattan wasn't around tonight. Tonight it was a tall, big guy who was sitting on the coffee table in front of the couch.

"So," the big man began with a smirk, "perhaps we were wrong. Perhaps you don't know anything. I'm sorry for the inconvenience of the last twenty-four hours."

They'd forced the clear plastic bag down over Hunter's head four times since last night. He'd passed out each time, and as his eyes were fluttering shut the last three times he was certain he wasn't going to wake up. In fact, he was hoping he wouldn't.

"You're not sorry at all."

The man nodded. "No, I'm not."

"Let us go. Please."

"No," he said, "you can still be helpful to me."

Hunter saw him gesture to one of the other men in the room, who moved to where Amy was sitting and pulled her blindfold down roughly. She blinked several times and then glanced over at him, terrified.

"My number's programmed into your phone," the man explained, pointing down at Hunter's cell phone, which lay on the coffee table beside him. "It's stored into your memory as AAA. Anytime you speak to Jack Jensen, you call me immediately. He's tried to reach you several times since you two had drinks last night, so I suggest you check in with him as soon as you can. I want you to be in touch with him as much as possible, and I want you to find out all you can about where he is and what he's doing." The man hesitated. "But whatever you do, don't make him suspicious."

"You want me to spy on my best friend?"

"You catch on fast, Hunter."

Hunter glanced over at Amy. Her lower lip was trembling, and her tears were flowing in two steady streams. They were going to take Amy with them, and the man standing beside the coffee table was going to say that Amy would suffer the consequences if Hunter didn't help.

"I assume you know what's going to happen."

Hunter nodded. "Yeah," he whispered dejectedly, gazing at Amy. "I know."

"Good. By the way, don't try tracing my phone number. You do and your wife dies. And I will know if you or anyone else tries."

"OK."

The man leaned forward. "Hunter, are you absolutely certain you don't know where Jack Jensen is or where he's going?"

It didn't surprise Hunter when the clear plastic bag came sliding down over his face from behind and the rope tightened around his neck. But it seemed worse than the other four times because this time he could see Amy's horrified expression and hear her petrified screams as he tried pathetically to fight back. It was emasculating to have her watch him panic so badly, to struggle helplessly against his assailants and beg for mercy like a baby just before he passed out. He wanted to kill these men so badly.

It was the first time he'd ever had that horrible urge.

CHAPTER 17

FROM HIS hiding place in the dense grove of trees, Carlson watched Daniel Beckham pace back and forth in front of the small country store. It gave him immense pleasure to see the mounting frustration that was etching itself deeper and deeper into the young man's tight-lipped expression.

The store was set on the north side of a winding road that cut a narrow swath through the thick woods of central Virginia just east of the Blue Ridge Mountains' first wave. It was after nine o'clock, and the place had been deserted for hours. Except for the light coming from a bare bulb hanging above the front door, it was pitch dark out here. But the bulb was bright, and Carlson could see the aggravation burning in Beckham's eyes.

They'd been running him all over the state since two o'clock this afternoon, starting with his pick-up by Yellow Cab on Pennsylvania Avenue right in front of the White House. Thirty minutes later the cab had dropped him off at Dulles Airport, where a friendly agent of a privately owned northern Virginia security company had confronted him inside the terminal. That agent had quickly collected his two mobile phones before leading him into the handicap stall of a men's bathroom, where he'd stripped Beckham of a poorly hidden wire and a more creatively concealed transponder.

Then he'd escorted Beckham to the general aviation terminal and a waiting helicopter, which had flown southwest from the airport to a secluded farm. In the basement of the farmhouse they'd performed a fairly benign interrogation—for them—including a thorough strip search despite his violent protests. Then they'd put Beckham back on the chopper and flown him a short distance to a car, which was waiting at another farm. There were several more exchanges with other vehicles in secluded places around the state before they'd finally dropped him off ten minutes ago at this location, twenty miles west of Charlottesville.

Beckham was a senior aide to President Dorn's chief of staff, Rex Stein, and he wasn't accustomed to this kind of treatment, Carlson knew. That was obvious, and it was satisfying to see how easily they'd gotten into his grille.

When Beckham turned away with his head down, Carlson slipped out of his hiding place and moved to the end of the concrete slab that stretched from one side of the storefront to the other. He waited for Beckham to turn around and almost get to where he was standing before he spoke up.

"Hello, Danny."

"Jesus Christ!" Beckham barked, quickly backtracking several steps. "What the *hell*?"

"I'm Roger Carlson. It's good to meet you."

"Yeah, it's outstanding to meet you too, Roger," Beckham shot back sarcastically. "But next time I've got to go through a strip search to meet somebody, including a certain body cavity exam I know I'll never forget, I think I'll pass."

Carlson managed to mute his chuckle. Beckham had probably figured his first foray into the intelligence world was going to be more exciting than anything else he'd been doing for the last nine months in Washington—but not as exciting as this.

"You won't pass if your president tells you not to."

Beckham was probably wishing he could get back to the more comfortable surroundings of the West Wing as soon as possible. By the end of this battle he was going to wish he'd never come to Washington.

"You understand me, son?"

"Whatever," Beckham muttered.

Beckham was a tall, red-haired, rich kid whose family had amassed an enormous fortune trading commodities in the last hundred years and felt so guilty about it they'd moved to the left side of the political aisle two generations ago. That was how Beckham had ended up in Dorn's administration and not the GOP camp where he certainly looked like he ought to be with his tortoiseshell glasses and preppie wardrobe. He'd never had to really work for anything in his life, and that severely stacked the odds against him in this battle, Carlson knew.

Carlson also knew that the twenty-seven-year-old standing in front of him was only marking time in Washington to pad his résumé. He was planning to resign a year from now to found a private equity fund and make some serious dough his father and grandfather couldn't take credit for. Neither President Dorn nor Beckham's father knew about all that. But Carlson did, thanks to Maddux's team of Falcons.

"Let's go," Carlson ordered gruffly as a dark blue Town Car pulled up in front of the store. "Get in the back on the right side."

"Why did I have to go through all that crap anyway?" Beckham demanded when they were inside the car. It was moving through the woods, and the partition between the front and back seats was up. "Why the damn runaround?"

"Welcome to the intelligence world, Danny." Carlson had wanted to make certain no one was following Beckham, but he'd wanted to put Beckham through hell too. "Now, what do you want?"

"You know what I want, Roger. I'm your new contact at the White House. I report directly to the president on all matters related to what you and I discuss."

"You aren't reporting directly to the president," Carlson replied evenly. Now he was two steps away from the president—maybe more, maybe a whole staircase. At the least, Beckham and Rex Stein were in between his now-lost direct access. "You're going through the chief of staff on this. You're going through Rex Stein."

Dorn was a Washington rookie, but Stein was a DC veteran. The Democratic Party had chosen Stein to be Dorn's chief of staff, not Dorn. And Stein would have gotten an extensive download on Red Cell Seven during the administration's first national security briefing, which would have occurred at Langley within a few weeks of Dorn's election. Stein would never allow Beckham to report directly to the top of the chain on something as crucial as this. He was too savvy.

At least, that was what Carlson had believed a minute ago. But maybe this was even more serious than he'd imagined. Maybe Dorn was hiding this from Stein. That thought sent shivers through Carlson's body.

"Don't bullshit me, *Danny*."

"Think what you want, old man, I don't care. But here's the deal. From now on you and I will meet at least once a week but probably more like two or three times. And there won't be any more of this run-Daniel-all-over-hell's-creation crap when we do, or I can promise you Red Cell Seven will cease to exist immediately. Do you understand?" He paused. "Let me say that again so I'm sure you really hear it, Roger. RCS will cease to exist *immediately*. All I have to do is say the word to President Dorn and it's over. Even Rex Stein wouldn't be able to save your beloved cell at that point. I am the key to its existence and yours," Beckham added proudly. "What do you think of that, old man?"

Jesus. Dorn and Stein had even told Beckham the name of the cell. That violated all RCS protocol. "Watch your tone, Danny," Carlson warned.

Then it hit him like a freight train. Shane Maddux could be right after all. If Beckham really was reporting straight to Dorn on this, then everything Maddux claimed his Falcons had picked up in the shadows would make perfect sense.

"Red Cell Seven has been in business since the Nixon administration," Carlson began again. This time it was in a low, unsteady voice. He couldn't remember feeling this afraid in a long time. "And I've been—"

"Now that's something to be proud of," Beckham cut in rudely. "Jesus. If only we could erase that administration from the history books we'd be—"

"And it will continue to be in business for a long time," Carlson interrupted right back, forcing his voice to be strong. "A long time after you've hung up your Washington cleats for the private equity world a year from now. That's when you'll quit President Dorn's staff to start your firm in New York City."

"Red Cell Seven might continue to exist," Beckham retorted. "*Might*," he emphasized, "but not in its present state, I can assure you." He waved as if he didn't give a rat's ass about what Carlson had just said about him hanging up his cleats. "And big deal, Roger, so you found out about me making some money my father can't take credit for. Impressive, but not that impressive, because digging up information is one of the things you're in business to do. And if you use it against me, I'll deny it and say you're just being a prick and trying to make my life difficult, which Rex and the president will believe right away. Then I'll tell the president to blow up RCS immediately. Besides, my grandfather's one of Dorn's biggest financial backers. He won't want to piss my family off even if he does think I'm leaving." Beckham pointed at Carlson. "Here's the deal, Roger. By the end of this week I want a list of all your agents in the field as well as all overseas twilight contacts and your assets domestic and abroad. Like that maze of safe houses you run out in Reston. You need to understand that your fiefdom's about to become *my* fiefdom. And don't try to hide anything, Roger. We've got our own people in the field now, and they're watching yours. If we find out that you've held anything back on us, that you haven't been completely transparent, we could file criminal charges against you. Then everything would be out in the open. How do you like that, old man?"

Jesus Christ. This was worse than he could have imagined. Maddux had been *right* on target. So on target Carlson felt physically ill. President Dorn meant to shut down Red Cell Seven, and he meant to do it *immediately.* That was the reason he wanted a list of all those things Beckham had just reeled off. Dorn wasn't just trying to get a better handle on what RCS was doing. He had no intention of letting it continue to exist in *any* form. He was going to destroy it. That was the only way Carlson could interpret Beckham's request for all of that highly classified information.

Carlson shook his head in disbelief. Dorn had to understand what he was doing. He had to understand that this action would send shock waves down the corridors in Langley, at the Pentagon, and in the Capitol.

If Dorn didn't understand that, Stein certainly would. Stein would understand that there were many senior people within the CIA, the NSA, and the FBI who would be diametrically opposed to destroying the cell because over the past five years it had morphed into the glue that held the entire national defense structure together. It was the glue that had allowed domestic and foreign-based US intelligence assets to communicate seamlessly without turf wars breaking out all over the place like they had in the wake of 9/11. Those senior people in the respective agencies would view shuttering RCS as an action equal to Jack Kennedy's attempt to destroy the CIA in the early sixties. They'd view it as treason. For them, Red Cell Seven was indispensible, mostly because no one in RCS ever cared about getting credit for anything. RCS agents didn't care about credit because RCS wasn't even supposed to exist—and because they cared more about the country than themselves. Absolute demonstration of that loyalty was a requirement for initiation into the cell.

"By the way," Beckham said, "my name is Daniel, not Danny. Don't make that mistake again. You got it, Roger?"

"Yeah." Carlson had barely heard Beckham. "Sure."

"I'm your boss now, and one way or the other you will give me respect." Beckham's eyes danced. "This is about doing the right thing, Roger. This is about getting control of an intelligence cell that's been operating basically unchecked for forty years. It's about getting control of a cell that's become too powerful in the past five years, a cell that believes it's bulletproof and doesn't have to play by the rules. People must be held accountable from now on if the world is truly going to get along." Beckham sneered. "The hell with people; *you* need to be held accountable. You're the only one that matters. You're the Red Cell Seven dictator."

Beckham's image blurred in front of Carlson as he stared. He wasn't worried about criminal charges being filed against him or Dorn's people watching them. They were idle threats from naïve people who were already into the quicksand up to their necks, even though they didn't realize it yet. What terrified Carlson so completely was that he suddenly realized the country had an administration in power that believed it could protect the United States of America without Red Cell Seven. An administration that believed the country could survive without those agents who were willing to do all those terrible things in the shadows that no one wanted to talk about on the Sunday morning talk shows. An administration that seemed to think it could keep the United States safe playing by the rules, within some sort of ethically acceptable global framework.

Which was ludicrous, Carlson knew, *absolutely ludicrous.*

If Dorn was successful in destroying RCS, it could lead to a disaster for the United States on a scale of unimaginable proportions—abroad and at home. Terrorists would be *so much* freer to operate because the ability of law enforcement and the armed forces to short-circuit hijackings, bombings, and assassinations before they happened would be severely constrained. Advance information on terrorist activity would be cut to a minimum so that domestic assets would be operating basically in the dark— unable to anticipate, only react.

Carlson actually shuddered as the enormity of all that hit him right between the eyes.

"Do you understand me, Roger?" Beckham demanded harshly.

"I understand," Carlson replied softly. "I understand perfectly."

* * *

"Why are we going north, Uncle Sage?"

Speed Trap glanced at the compass on the bridge's control panel as the *Arctic Fire*'s bow cut a sharp wake through the day's relatively calm ocean. They'd finished unloading for a second time, and the king crab season was over. They'd reached their quota well before any other ship had, so they should have been headed west for a cod run or south to Seattle before coming back to Dutch for the opilio season, which would start in a week. But they were following a north-northeasterly heading.

"Why are we going this way?"

"Why are you such a question-head, kid?"

The less than friendly answer didn't surprise or anger Speed Trap. He was accustomed to Sage's demeanor after so long. "Just naturally curious, I guess."

"Don't be," Sage snapped. "It's irritating. You remember all those teachers in school who told you that the only bad question is the one you don't ask?"

"Yeah. So?"

"They were assholes. They didn't know what they were talking about."

The ship covered a few miles of rolling ocean before Speed Trap spoke up again. He'd thought about going below to get some sleep in the bunk room like Duke and Grant were doing. But he wanted to make sure Grant hadn't been bullshitting about the DUI and resisting arrest charges over in Seward. It still seemed too good to be true.

"Is there something you want to tell me, Uncle Sage?"

"What do you mean?"

"About my charges over in Seward."

"Jesus Christ," Sage hissed under his breath. "You and your brother are just like your father. Neither of you can keep your mouths shut. It's like I'm dealing with a couple of old ladies at a quilting convention."

Speed Trap rolled his eyes. "Well, is it true? Has everything been dropped?"

"When's your birthday?"

That seemed like an odd question. "Huh?"

"When's your damn birthday, Speed Trap?"

"Um, the day after tomorrow."

"OK, well, I was saving it for a surprise, but now Grant's ruined it. Yeah, everything's been dropped. You're free to get more tickets. But do me a favor this time, will you? Do it sober and don't start swinging at the cop when he pulls you over. Learn to say 'yes, sir' and 'no, sir' to those guys. OK?"

"Yes, sir."

"Good. Happy birthday early."

"Thanks. That's amazing."

"No problem. Don't mention it again, kid."

Speed Trap's ears perked up. "Why not?"

"Damn it, Speed Trap!"

"OK, OK. Sorry."

They went quiet again, and the only sound on the bridge was the constant hum of the two huge engines far below powering the *Arctic Fire* across the water.

Speed Trap glanced to port and out onto a desolate ocean. He was trying hard to follow Sage's order, but in the end it was impossible for him not to ask.

"I was just wondering how you got those charges—"

"*Goddamn it, kid!*" Sage roared. "What's your problem?"

It had been an incredible king crab season, the best ever, and Speed Trap didn't want to jeopardize getting paid the huge amount of money he was owed. But he couldn't control his curiosity.

"It's just that me and Grant were talking, and it seems like weird things happen on this ship. Like the time we picked up that guy in the raft last year in that place where we've never dropped traps before, and how he stayed in your room until we got to Dutch Harbor. Then there's this deal with us getting all that new equipment so fast after we—"

"Yeah, let's talk about equipment," Sage broke in. "Let's talk about rafts specifically."

Speed Trap swallowed hard. "What about them?"

"Why do we have a new one?"

"Huh?"

"There's a new raft in the equipment room downstairs. And an old one's missing. Why's that?"

Speed Trap shrugged. "Um, I don't know. I'm not in charge of that stuff. Grant is."

Sage lit up a Marlboro and inhaled two lungs full of the cancer stick. "Is there something you want to tell me, Speed Trap?"

Speed Trap tried to calm his pounding heart. As he was about to answer, he spotted something floating on the ocean several hundred yards ahead of the boat. "Hey, there's a raft out there—"

"I see it," Sage interrupted, taking another drag from the cigarette. "Time for you to get below."

"What? Why don't I help you—"

"Get below!" Sage shouted. "Right now, Speed Trap."

* * *

Carlson climbed out of the Town Car and trudged to the back of it. "Good night," he mumbled as he and Beckham came together at the trunk. The cold Washington night was making his bones ache. Suddenly he felt *ninety*-three, not seventy-three. "I'll be in touch."

"I want that list of agents and assets, old man, and I want it by Friday at noon."

Carlson covered his mouth to cough. "You'll get it."

"Well, I'm glad to see this spirit of cooperation from you, Roger. Frankly, I was worried that I wouldn't get it."

"I'm too old to fight," Carlson said as they shook hands. "And I do what my president tells me to do because this is the greatest country in the world and he's the leader of it. OK, *Daniel*?"

"OK," Beckham agreed, his tone softening. He hesitated for a few moments, then handed Carlson a thin envelope. "In that envelope is a piece of paper that details the president's specific information requests with respect to Red Cell Seven. Call me when you've answered everything. We'll exchange the info in person. No e-mails."

"Yeah, sure."

Carlson shoved the envelope into his pocket and climbed back into the Town Car. For all his education, Beckham was an idiot, at least when it came to the commonsense aspects of intelligence work. It was amazing that he even thought he had to mention not using e-mail to transmit that kind of sensitive information.

The ride back to Carlson's Georgetown house took just ten minutes, and Nancy, his wife of forty-six years, was sitting at the kitchen table doing a crossword puzzle when he came through the door. He smiled sadly as he sat down beside her and took her warm hand in his cold one. She was such a wonderful woman, still so beautiful to him even at sixty-nine. She'd always been so devoted, so loyal to the cause. They'd moved eleven times in those forty-six years, and she'd never complained once. She'd simply nodded and gotten to work every time he'd explained what had to happen.

She'd only asked him once what he did. That was forty-seven years ago, on their first date. He'd told her he was just a boring Washington bureaucrat, but he'd asked her never to ask him again. And she hadn't. She was old-fashioned that way.

Nancy put the crossword down on the kitchen table and took both of his hands in hers when she caught the look in his eyes. "What is it, Roger? Oh, God, what is it?"

After so many years together, they could read each other's moods and minds so easily. "I love you very much, sweetheart." He hadn't said that enough over the years, and he was going to make up for it with the time he had left. "I have bone marrow cancer," he explained softly. "I have six months to live."

CHAPTER 18

BEFORE JACK could get to where Karen had fallen in the alley, she'd already jumped back to her feet and hustled to where her pistol had come to a stop beside a smashed vodka bottle.

"You OK?" he whispered, ducking instinctively when a bullet deflected off the building beside them with a wicked echo. "*Karen?*"

"It's my left arm," she answered, grabbing her gun off the pavement and taking off with Jack. They were almost to the end of the alley. "But it's not bad," she said softly. "The bullet just grazed me. It stings like crazy, though."

At the end of the alley they dashed right and raced across the street. Overhead lights and restaurants had given way to darkness and warehouses. The big commercial buildings rising up all around them were surrounded by tall chain-link fences topped with corkscrewing razor wire. For a few moments there was no gunfire, and Jack thought about calling 9-1-1.

Then the bullets were back. A barrage exploded behind them, and the air was filled with flying steel again.

"This way," he said, bolting past her. "Come on."

They rushed down a narrow alley, between two chain-link fences that paralleled each other ten feet apart.

A few strides into the alley a huge Rottweiler exploded from the darkness and hurled itself against the fence directly to Karen's right. Its front paws and jaw were level with her head, and it barked furiously with its fangs bared.

She screamed and veered left. As she did, she ran into Jack and both of them tumbled to the ground. But they were back on their feet quickly—as more gunfire erupted behind them.

They took off again, darting right and left as the dog raced along the stair-stepped fence with them, barking madly as it kept up. As they reached the next street over, a pair of headlights flashed around a corner.

"Over there," Jack said, pointing across the street at a building that looked abandoned. Through the dim light he could see that most of the windows on the first and second floor were smashed out; the fence had been cut open in several places along the sidewalk, and a small door on one side of the building appeared to be hanging slightly ajar. "Come on!"

He sprinted to the closest slit in the fence, slicing his palm on the sharp, exposed end of a steel wire as he pulled the links back for Karen to crawl through. Then he caught his ear on another wire as he climbed through the hole after her. "Jesus," he hissed under his breath. He could feel blood trickling down his neck as he ran for the door to the building. "Friendly city you got here."

"Yeah, we don't take crap from anybody. *Now move!*"

Karen reached the door first, hurled it back, and they both piled through the opening one after the other as bullets smacked the wall around the door.

It was pitch dark inside, but Jack sensed that they were in a large room because of the echoes the door made when it slammed shut behind them. He reached out and grabbed Karen's wrist, pulling her along. As he pressed his back flat against the wall and slid along, it felt as if he were standing on a narrow ledge high up on the side of a building. He could feel those familiar butterflies starting to wake up in his gut, and he slowed down. Each step felt uncertain as he groped along the rough wall ahead of him with the hand holding the gun, and that fear of heights was suddenly screaming at him.

Then his eyes grew accustomed to the gloom, the butterflies calmed, and he started moving more quickly. He could make out shapes on the large floor in front of them in the soft light coming from windows on the far side of the building. They looked like stacks of wood or metal, and some were eight or nine feet high.

When they were several car lengths from the door, it burst open and both he and Karen turned and fired through the darkness. The door banged shut again, and Jack pulled Karen toward the closest pile. It was a stack of wood, and they dived behind it. When the door opened again they both pulled their triggers, but only Karen's gun fired. Jack's clip was empty, and he didn't have another one.

"Come on," he whispered as he made it to his feet and then helped her up. Through the dim light he'd seen what looked like stairs against the wall just behind them. "Let's go."

"Where?"

"Up those stairs."

"No, we should stay down here. Maybe we can find a way out. If we go up, we might get trapped."

"If we go up, it'll take them longer to find us. We can buy some time to call nine-one-one and get the cops here. By now they've probably got all the doors to this place covered anyway."

"Could you really tell the cops how to get here?" Karen whispered. "I couldn't and I live around here. The people at the door will get us way before—"

The door burst open a third time, and Jack pulled Karen hard toward the stairs. The voices over there were growing louder, and it sounded to him as if a lot of people were pouring into the building.

At the top of the stairway they hurried through a door. Then they turned and quickly climbed another set of steps to the third story. As they headed through the open doorway into the top level of the building, the hard floor turned to carpet and Jack realized that they were probably in what had been the administrative offices before the building had been abandoned.

They rushed down the corridor through the darkness and turned into the next-to-last office on the left, where he pulled his cell phone out and frantically dialed 9-1-1. As the phone began to ring in his ear, he thought he could hear the faint sounds of footsteps coming up the metal stairs. Maybe it wasn't going to take the people as long to find them as he'd hoped.

"Jack!"

His head snapped toward Karen's voice as the 9-1-1 operator came on the line.

"Let's go!" she urged.

Karen had raised a window at the back of the empty room and was waving him over. "What?" he asked, feeling those butterflies begin to rage in his stomach again. "What do you want?" But he knew exactly what she wanted. That was why the butterflies were back.

"This is nine-one-one," the operator called out in his ear. "What is your emergency?"

"Hurry, Jack."

He moved to the window as the operator continued to ask for information, following Karen's fingers with his gaze as she pointed down. The dark waters of Baltimore Harbor lay thirty feet below them. The side of the building went straight down into the water.

"We're jumping," she said.

The water looked freezing cold, and from where they were standing he couldn't spot any way out once they were in it. "Like hell we are."

She grabbed his arm. "They're gonna be here any second, and I don't want to die. We're way outgunned. This is our best chance."

"We don't know how deep that water is," he argued. "It might only be two feet right there. We'll die."

"We know we're gonna die if we stay here. We've gotta take the chance."

He hated to admit it, but he knew she was right. "You're gonna have to push me out."

"*What?* We don't have time for this crap, Jack."

"No, I'm serious. I think I can get on the ledge, but you're gonna have to push me off."

"Why?"

"No time to explain," he said as he started carefully climbing. "Just do it."

"Jack, you've got to jump yourself," she said, starting to climb out on the ledge too. "I don't want to push you."

"You have to." He could feel his body seizing up as he kept glancing down at the water. Another few seconds and he was going to dive back into the office so at least he had those walls around him again. "*Just do it!*"

CHAPTER 19

MADDUX SAT behind the wide mahogany desk in the farm-house's comfortable study. It was the same Virginia farmhouse they'd used earlier in the day to scare the hell out of Daniel Beckham.

A sardonic grin tugged at his thin lips as he remembered the horrified expression that had raced to Beckham's face when they'd told the bastard that the last step in the strip-search process was a thorough investigation of all body cavities. Beckham had screamed like a baby—before, during, and after.

Maddux's grin faded. Carlson had called ten minutes ago to deliver the sobering news that the rumors two of Maddux's Falcons had unearthed about the president were true. Dorn was going to destroy Red Cell Seven. Carlson had apologized pro-fusely for ever doubting the accuracy of the information—as well he should have, Maddux thought to himself resentfully—and then they'd started to plan.

Red Cell Seven would not be destroyed—at least, not without a fight. Dorn and his people had no idea what they were in for. It would be a war, and it would be carried out hand to hand in places Red Cell Seven knew well and would be comfortable with. In places Dorn's people would not be comfortable with—even the president's shadow operators.

During that telephone conversation, Maddux had considered coming clean with Carlson about what he'd done and how he'd acted without prior approval. He figured the old man might have understood the rationale now that he knew for certain President Dorn was a traitor.

But, ultimately, he'd decided against it. Telling Carlson still wasn't an option. He had to keep acting as if what had happened on the *Arctic Fire* was a terrible accident. He had to keep acting as if Troy Jensen had simply been lost in the line of duty. The same way he'd acted about Charlie Banks a year ago. He couldn't tell Carlson he'd specifically ordered Sage Mitchell to throw those young men overboard, because there was still a chance the old man might go ballistic—especially about Jensen.

Maddux glanced over the desk at Ryan O'Hara as he pushed aside thoughts of Troy Jensen and the coming battle with President Dorn.

O'Hara was a good-looking African-American kid with sharp facial features who'd graduated from Dartmouth eighteen months ago. Since then he'd been excelling in an intense training regimen at several military bases around the country as well as undergoing a battery of psychological tests in Arlington and San Diego. The demanding process was designed to make certain he was worthy of getting to this moment, that he was worthy of joining Maddux's elite crew of Falcons.

A week ago Carlson had decided to officially accept O'Hara into Red Cell Seven. Given his scores in every category, O'Hara was one of the strongest candidates to ever come along, and he was the first African American to make it in. There had been thirty-nine other AA candidates prior to O'Hara, but they'd all missed the cut.

Which wasn't surprising or in any way a result of prejudice. The attrition rate for all RCS recruits since the cell's inception was 98 percent—only two in a hundred candidates made the leap. And the 98 percent who didn't make it were sent to prized Special Forces assignments because they were still outstanding individuals who were completely dedicated to protecting the United States using whatever means were necessary. They just weren't outstanding enough to be members of Red Cell Seven.

"So, I've got a question," Maddux began. His elbows were resting on the polished arms of the chair, and his fingers were positioned cathedral-style in front of him. "And it's pretty obvious, at least, given that it's my first one." O'Hara had gotten a lot of hype from his instructors, and Maddux wanted to see the kid start living up to it right away. "Know what it is?"

"Of course," O'Hara answered confidently. "You're asking about my name. You want to know how in the hell a black guy from east LA gets a handle like Ryan O'Hara."

The young man had that smooth air of invincibility every member of Red Cell Seven needed. But his was even more impressive than most of the other young men in the Falcon division. His was on that same level with Troy Jensen.

Hopefully, he wasn't as inquisitive as Troy—or as completely polarized when it came to right and wrong. Troy could have been a valuable asset for a long time. But he couldn't see the shades of gray in between those two endpoints.

"My father changed our family name from Jefferson to O'Hara forty years ago when he moved to California from Alabama,"

O'Hara explained. "He told me he did it for me and my sisters, Meagan and Kristin, even though we weren't born yet. He said he wanted the top universities around the country to think his kids were Irish because you don't actually have to check the race box when you fill out college applications. It worked out pretty well too. I went to Dartmouth, Meagan went to Northwestern, and Kristin's a junior at Stanford. I hate to say it, but it helped in a lot of ways growing up. Not just getting into college."

O'Hara's father was a smart man. "You had to have the grades and the extracurriculars to get in too," Maddux pointed out. "Modesty's a good thing, but don't ever shortchange yourself. You're a good man, Ryan. Crazy brave. You wouldn't be here if you weren't." He hesitated. "But I admire your father's creativity."

"Thank you, sir."

Maddux glanced out the window into the darkness, thinking about how much he wanted to carry out justice on his own again. How badly he wanted to rid the world of another piece of trash like that child molester he'd just killed. How he didn't want to wait for another of Carlson's envelopes because it could be a long time coming.

So he was thinking about acquiring a target on his own without Carlson's OK—again.

He'd done that before. It had been several months ago, and the killing had gone off without a hitch. But there'd been another problem, and it had almost sent him tumbling into an abyss of trouble.

It wasn't that Carlson would consider the action going outside the chain of command the way he would the murders of Falcons Charlie Banks and Troy Jensen. Carlson would have no problem with scumbags being killed. What he'd have a problem with would be evidence of the scumbag killings showing up, because that could compromise RCS. That evidence had almost surfaced the last time, and he'd almost fallen into that abyss. If he hadn't killed Troy, it would have.

He glanced back at O'Hara. "Let me be official about it, Ryan. Welcome to Red Cell Seven." He paused. "So, how was the initiation?"

"Fine, sir. I was honored, of course."

"Do you have any questions?"

"Why the name Red Cell Seven?" O'Hara asked immediately. "What do cells one through six do?"

"Nothing," Maddux answered matter-of-factly. "They don't even exist. In fact, they never did. Red Cell Seven was created during the Nixon administration, when the Cold War was going strong. They called it Red Cell Seven to drive the Soviets crazy."

"What do you mean?"

"Back then, 'red' referred to the Soviet Union, which was by far our biggest enemy. So any intelligence cell we created with the word 'red' in it would logically be targeted at the Soviet Union. Our people knew they'd assume that, and, of course, we knew the Soviets would hear about Red Cell Seven sooner or later because it's impossible to keep anything completely secret in the intelligence world. Money talks, bullshit walks, and bribes are everywhere. Money and women can make a lot of men do almost anything."

"So," O'Hara said, "our people named it Red Cell Seven to make the Soviets think that cells one through six existed too. To get the Soviets to waste time and energy trying to find six other cells that were just figments of our imaginations. And theirs, right?"

"Exactly. And the more the Soviet higher-ups heard the cells didn't exist, the harder they tried to find them. I'll tell you what. They burned through a lot of money and resources in the process. See, the Russians are truly paranoid. I mean, all of us in this line of business are to some degree. But they're off the charts, and I guess I understand why. It's in their blood. Everyone's been spying on each other over there for so long, even neighbors on neighbors, that they can't help it. You know, I heard they were still looking for one through six even as the wall was crumbling and their world was falling apart."

O'Hara smiled. "Pretty smart, huh?"

"We have our moments," Maddux agreed.

O'Hara gestured around the tastefully decorated room. "Who owns this farm? Is it someone in Red Cell Seven?"

"He's not actually a member of RCS. We have a network of shadow support that's organized and run by the man who started the cell forty years ago."

Maddux was careful not to mention Carlson's name. The kid would have met Carlson at the initiation, but he would have met three other men too. None of them would have given away their positions within the cell to O'Hara because he was as green as they came. It would be several years before he'd learn the names of the Summit Level.

"The network is comprised of about twenty very wealthy individuals who have a general understanding of what we do and are dedicated to our goal of keeping the United States on top as the only superpower." Maddux held up one hand. "But none of them are ever briefed on our specific activities, which is for their own protection. We call them associates."

"So these associates make personal assets available to us?"

"That's right. Planes, boats, cars, and locations like this one."

"Money?"

"The best kind," Maddux declared. "The kind that can't be traced. Cash, and lots of it."

"But," O'Hara said, "I thought any deposit over ten grand had to be reported. What we need to run RCS must be way bigger than that. And I can't imagine somebody running around the country making lots of deposits that are less than ten grand. That would be a full-time job by itself. And the Fed would still get suspicious."

"The bank we use is huge," Maddux explained. "It has branches all over the world. But that doesn't really matter, because all our accounts are numbered. And, most importantly, we don't have to report any of our deposits no matter how big or small they are."

O'Hara nodded. "That works out pretty well."

"More than one black op cell has shut down because of a money trail. It can't ever happen in our case because there is no trail. Our bank makes sure of that."

O'Hara leaned forward in his chair. "So what will I be doing?"

"Pickups and deliveries to start with," Maddux replied. He saw the disappointment register in O'Hara's expression immediately. But it wasn't going to stay there. "Don't get me wrong, Ryan. These won't be normal, run-of-the-mill pickups and deliveries. You won't be driving a brown truck wearing a brown suit. You'll be taking top-secret orders and cash to agents in some of the most politically sensitive areas around the world. As well as bringing back vitally important information from those individuals about in-country activities. Don't believe this bullshit you see on the big screen. Don't believe that some guy at the CIA can talk to his top spy in Saudi Arabia by cell phone from the deck of his big, beautiful house in McLean, Virginia, while he's barbecuing. Not without the very real threat of that conversation being overheard by our enemies, anyway."

"You mean like Russell Crowe and Leonardo DiCaprio did in *Body of Lies*."

"Exactly." Maddux saw the gleam return to O'Hara's eyes. "I'm not saying they couldn't talk like that. Of course they could. What I'm saying is that you could never be sure that conversation is secure. I don't care what kind of cloaking or ciphering technology is used. As Americans, we tend to think our enemies aren't that sophisticated, that at the very least they aren't as sophisticated as we are. But that's just wrong. In some cases and with some technologies our enemies are more sophisticated than we are. Believe me when I tell you that the *only* way to safely communicate with an in-country agent is to deliver and pick up messages hand to hand. It's been that way since the beginning of civilization, and it'll always be that way." Maddux gestured at O'Hara. "That's where you and the rest of your Falcon brethren come in. You'll be going into countries that would execute you if they knew what you were really doing. At the very least they'd lock you away in a nasty prison for a long, long time while they tried to figure out what you were up to. So, whenever possible, you'll be going in with cover, with a story. To make it more difficult for them to figure out what you're really doing."

"What do you mean?"

"You'll be going in to climb a certain mountain or hunt a specific wild animal or explore a cave that's a major destination for only serious cave divers. And people will be set up there to guide you like they would be if you weren't on a mission. Like they would be if you were a normal person and you were going into that country just to climb a mountain or hunt or cave dive. Sometimes we even plant a story about it in a big newspaper in the US or Europe to *try* to draw attention to the trip to make it seem real. Being the athlete you are will help make the illusion seem even more real. Of course, there will always be people watching any American who comes into their country, so you'll still have to be very careful with every move you make."

"Of course."

"Then sometimes all of that won't be possible. You'll be slipping across borders by yourself, sometimes without the papers you need. We'll still give you a suggested story in case you run into trouble, but there won't be people waiting for you." The young man was definitely excited again. "You'll be on your own."

"Remember those three Americans who were taken prisoner by Iran a couple of years ago?" O'Hara asked. "I think it was two guys and a girl."

"You mean the three who were supposed to be hiking just across the border when they were arrested?"

"Yeah, and they told the Iranians they didn't realize they'd crossed the border when they were arrested."

Maddux shifted uncomfortably in his chair. "What about them?"

"Were they Red Cell Seven? I mean, that story sounds a lot like what we're talking about. In fact, it sounds *exactly* like what we're talking about."

Maddux shook his head. "If they'd been RCS, there wouldn't have been three of them. My Falcons go solo. The same way the bird hunts." He was ready to wrap things up. He wanted to get going because he'd decided to kill that target after all. "By the way, you can't have credit cards anymore. They aren't allowed. Everything's done in cash."

"I already gave my cards up before I got here."

"Good." Maddux hesitated. "Once you've been with us for a while, you'll start digging up information on your own. Here and abroad. Not just doing pickups and deliveries."

"Nice."

"We'll get more into that tomorrow."

"Yes, sir."

"And look, sometimes your assignment will simply be to take a job, a real job. I wanted to give you the heads-up on that now just to make sure you heard it early on and you weren't surprised when it happened. Sometimes we'll have you working off the books so you can earn money to survive without going on an official payroll. You're tougher to trace that way. It'll be good money and you'll earn it fast, but the work'll be hard and sometimes dangerous."

"What are we talking about?"

"You'll be on fishing and crabbing boats, on oil rigs, in mines. Those kinds of things."

"Got it." O'Hara motioned to Maddux. "If we work with a bank that has branches all over the world, why would I take cash to somebody?"

"We can't ever have our moles going into banks. That's too much of a risk. Hell, *you* won't ever go into a bank except to deposit paychecks from those legitimate jobs we just talked about. I'll be the one dropping you the money."

"Oh, OK. So, how many people are actually in Red Cell Seven?"

The kid was thirsting for information and that was good, but Maddux was only going to answer a few more questions. "About a hundred."

"How many Falcons?"

"Nineteen, including you."

"What are some of the other areas of RCS?"

"Divisions."

"What?"

"Divisions of RCS, not areas."

"Sorry, divisions. What other divisions are there?"

Maddux started ticking them off on his fingers. "Assassinations, out-of-country terrorism, counterterrorism, interrogations, and then there's intel communication and coordination."

"So I could be picking up or delivering information to or from other Red Cell Seven agents when I'm in those countries. They wouldn't necessarily be CIA people I was meeting."

"That's right." Maddux could see that the kid was still champing at the bit, but that was all he was going to get for now. "OK, well look, you're staying here tonight, Ryan. Get a good night's sleep, and we'll meet in the morning at oh six hundred," Maddux said, standing up. "Over breakfast we'll start getting into specifics of what those other RCS divisions I just mentioned do."

"Yes, sir," O'Hara said, standing up too.

"Again, welcome to Red Cell Seven, Ryan." Maddux came around the desk, and they shook hands. "We're glad to have you, kid. Very glad." He turned to go, but then hesitated. He wanted to get out of here, but he wanted to start getting a feel for the kid's thought process too. You could never start doing that quickly enough. "So you've shot questions at me tonight. Now I've got one for you."

O'Hara looked up expectantly. "Yes, sir?"

"What's the greatest terrorist threat to the United States right now?"

"What do you mean by 'greatest'?"

"What kind of attack has the most devastating effect on our country?"

"Death squads," O'Hara answered confidently. "No question. Three- to four-man kill teams who jump out of vans and shoot ten to twenty shoppers at big malls within a few seconds, then jump back into the vans and, *poof*, they're gone like they never existed. Maybe fifteen teams operating in this country, and they're constantly on the move and they never contact a mother base and the mother base never contacts them so you can't intercept communications. If they're well trained, they're almost impossible to stop, they're easy to set up, and they shut the country down economically once they really get going.

"Like those two snipers who killed people in the DC area and scared the hell out of everybody else awhile ago," he kept going. "Remember? They were amateurs, but people around DC were terrified just to fill up their cars with gas. It took the cops forever to find them and, candidly, it happened by accident. Setting up kill teams is basically the same concept, except this time the terrorists are using professionals. The best way to start it off would be simultaneous attacks on the biggest shopping day of the year. On Black Friday. What do you think, sir?"

"Keep that to yourself," Maddux ordered, wishing now he hadn't asked. The last thing the United States needed was for someone on the wrong side to hear that idea, because it was that damn good. "See you in the morning."

"Sir?"

"Yes, Ryan."

"I'm totally dedicated to Red Cell Seven. I'll do whatever you tell me to do, and I won't ask any questions."

Maddux stared intently into O'Hara's eyes for several moments. "That's what I want to hear," he said. They'd really drilled the message into this kid. "That's *exactly* what I want to hear."

"And, sir?"

"Yes."

O'Hara hesitated. "I...I know I'm the first black guy to make it into RCS. And, well, I know that means I have an even higher bar to hit."

Maddux shook his head. "I don't see black when I look at you, Ryan. All I see is courage. Do you understand me?"

O'Hara grinned. "Yes, sir."

"Good. Now get some rest. Tomorrow's going to be a long day."

"Yes, sir."

As Maddux watched O'Hara leave the room, he nodded to himself. This kid was going to be easy to control...which was a relief after all he'd gone through with Banks and Jensen.

CHAPTER 20

CAPTAIN SAGE grunted approvingly when he caught sight of a bright red raft through his binoculars. It was off the starboard bow at two o'clock about a quarter of a mile away, floating lazily up and down on the calmly rolling sea—exactly where it was supposed to be. He'd gotten the coded message from Maddux two hours ago that the drop had been made and the package was ready to be retrieved now that the sub had resubmerged and was a safe distance away. The kid the sub had picked up off the coast of China was almost home. The Falcon was almost back to its nest. Sage wasn't supposed to know they were called Falcons, but he'd overheard that last year after they'd picked up another one.

As he guided the *Arctic Fire* toward the raft, Sage's good mood faded. Speed Trap and Grant were asking too many questions. They weren't idiots. They'd figured out something was up.

He cursed under his breath. He was pretty sure Speed Trap had gotten a raft onto the ocean while they were throwing Troy Jensen overboard. That was why there was a brand new one in the equipment room. Speed Trap had tried to hide what he'd done, but the captain knew his boat too well. He knew his nephew pretty well too. The younger one wasn't cold like Grant. Speed Trap had a heart.

"Damn it!" Sage hissed, banging the control panel hard with his big fist. He couldn't blame Speed Trap. Troy Jensen had saved his life. He'd felt the ultimate loyalty, as he should have, like any good sailor should have. "I just hope to God Jensen never made it into the raft if the kid really put it out there," Sage growled to himself over the hum of the engines.

* * *

Maddux pulled himself up onto the sill of the first-floor window, then eased down onto the wooden floor inside. The small brick home was thirty miles from the farmhouse where he'd said goodnight to O'Hara an hour ago. It was well back in the woods at the end of a dirt driveway, completely secluded from prying eyes.

The place was owned by a young couple who had no children. They were both in their midtwenties, and they were both teachers at the local public high school.

But that was just the husband's cover. His more important job was to interface with and give aid to in-country Chinese spies.

Though Carlson hadn't yet received final confirmation that the CIA was a hundred percent positive of the man's complicity, Maddux didn't care. He'd seen the file, and he was sure of what this guy was up to—and it had to be stopped.

He closed the window quietly. The couple ought to be sleeping soundly. He'd watched the last light on the second floor go out thirty minutes ago from the tree line on the north side of the house. He was going to kill the man quickly, and then get out. He had no intention of harming the woman.

As he came around the corner of the living room and into the short hallway that led from the kitchen to the stairs, Maddux almost ran into the guy. For a split second they stared at each other in the dim light cast by the stove's bulb. Then the man tossed the milk and cookies he was holding at Maddux's face before barreling into him. He was a big man, and as he landed on top of Maddux on the floor and the wind rushed from Maddux's lungs, Maddux realized that he might have just made the biggest mistake of his life.

* * *

Speed Trap peered out from behind the deck door on the port side just beneath the bridge. He was well hidden here, and he could duck back down the stairs behind him and get to his bunk quickly if he needed to. He wasn't supposed to be up here, but Duke and Grant were still asleep so they couldn't rat on him, and he had to see what was going on.

His eyes narrowed as a young man climbed aboard. Sage was holding open the metal gate near the crane so the guy didn't have to climb over the deck wall. It was the same wall they'd thrown Troy Jensen over.

Speed Trap watched as his uncle and the guy shook hands. It was strange. The guy reminded him of Troy. He didn't look or talk like him, but the resemblance was still uncanny. He had a certain aura about him that was unmistakable. Just like Troy did.

Speed Trap pursed his lips as he remembered shoving the raft out onto the ocean that night from the back of the ship. He prayed that the Bering Sea fates had been kind to Troy. That somehow Troy had gotten to that raft and by some masterstroke of luck he was still alive.

Troy was too good a man to have died like that.

CHAPTER 21

"You OK?" Jack asked.

"I'm fine."

They were wet, cold, and exhausted after jumping from the warehouse into Baltimore Harbor, then swimming for their lives. They'd been in the water for at least ten minutes before finally finding a place to climb out, and at one point they'd almost been run down by a tugboat. The crew hadn't seen their frantic gestures as the big craft bore down on them. They'd barely avoided being crushed by the hull and sucked into the powerful whirlpool created by its two huge propellers.

Now Karen was sitting beside Jack on a side-street bench, holding her left arm gingerly.

"Do you need to go to the hospital?" he tried again, taking a slightly more specific tack. "Should we go to the emergency room?"

"I'm fine," she answered firmly. "But thanks."

He touched his ear and then checked his finger. The cut he'd suffered while crawling through that hole in the fence outside the warehouse had stopped bleeding. "You sure?"

"The bullet barely hit me, Jack. I'm fine."

"Yeah, I'm one of those people who says 'I'm fine' a lot too, Karen. So I know the code. It doesn't necessarily mean I'm fine. It means 'leave me alone.'" He paused. "Let me check it out, OK?"

She straightened up slowly and turned to look at him. "I told you," she said deliberately, "I'm fine. I meant it, Jack."

She was stubborn. "All right." But she was tough too.

He glanced at her arm again. The sweatshirt was ripped in the triceps area, and he thought he saw a dark stain around the torn material. But it was too dark where they were sitting to tell for sure, even as close as they were to each other. Maybe that was actually Mick's blood. He didn't want to say anything to remind her that her friend was dead.

"You're a tough girl, and I mean that as a compliment."

"Thanks." She leaned forward, put her elbows on her knees, and ran her hands through her still-dripping hair. "Why did I have to push you out of that window?" she asked. "Why didn't you jump? You have a fear of water or something?"

"Let's get out of here," he suggested. He didn't want to talk about his fear of heights now. "Let's get you someplace warm."

"I want to know what the deal is. Why did I have to push you out of that window?" she asked again.

"It's a fear of heights," he admitted.

"But we weren't up that high. Thirty feet, maybe a little more. I mean, come on, you're a big boy."

"Fifteen feet and I've got a problem, Karen. Not even that high sometimes."

"Really?"

"Really."

It seemed like she felt sorry for him, like that was a little bit of a pity smile. But that was OK right now. Anything that helped their connection get stronger faster was OK with him. And it wasn't like he was accepting her pity.

"More specifically, I have a fear of hitting something on the ground that makes my body splatter into a bloody, unrecognizable mass. That's what really gets to me."

"It all makes sense now," she murmured. "No wonder."

"I was just about to climb back into the office when you finally checked my boarding pass at the Jetway door and put me on the flight."

The second time he'd yelled at her to push him out, she'd done it with a solid shoulder to his hip as he knelt on the window ledge. Like the one she'd given him when she'd knocked him away from Mick as he was about to pummel the guy. Then she'd followed his scream into the water after somehow managing to pull the window back down so that the people who were chasing them wouldn't notice it was raised, figure out what had happened, and start scouring the harbor for them.

"How did you find me?" she asked.

Jack had been waiting for her to ask that question again. "An old friend of mine is a hunting and fishing guide in Alaska. He's been up there awhile, and he's got a lot of contacts inside law enforcement. I told him my brother was killed on the *Arctic Fire* and that I didn't believe the captain had come clean with his story about what had happened. He did some checking around and found out about your fiancé."

Jack didn't want to dwell on this because it had already been a terrible enough night for Karen. But she'd asked the question, and he wanted her to know he was disclosing everything and being as transparent as possible. He wanted her complete trust as quickly as he could get it because he sensed that, thanks to Ross Turner, he'd found someone who could be of great help with his search for what had really happened to Troy. He was positive now that he'd been right to stir up all those old memories, positive that Troy and Charlie Banks had suffered the same fate and that he was on the right track. He was sorry about causing Karen so much emotional pain, but he had to see this thing through.

"When I heard about what happened to your fiancé," he continued, "I was blown away. Like I said before, the captain of the *Arctic Fire* told the cops *exactly* the same story about what happened to my brother, Troy, as he'd told them about what happened to Charlie Banks." Jack shook his head. "Look, my brother was Superman when it came to the outdoors. I mean the real deal, you know, with the 'S' on his chest and the cape and all that. And he had beaucoup experience on the water. He made it around the world in a sailboat by himself twice, for Christ's sake. Plus he always had this crazy sixth sense in nasty situations about where to be and where not to be. People around him got hurt, even killed. The ones he couldn't save, anyway. But Troy never got hurt too badly. He got banged up and bruised, but he never took a hit that put him on the sidelines even for a day. He was one tough guy."

"Charlie was the same way," Karen said. "He was bulletproof. At least, until he sailed on the *Arctic Fire*."

Jack could see the memories starting to flood back to her.

"He was an incredible athlete," she continued, glancing past Jack into the distance, "and he knew everything there was to know about making it in the outdoors and on the ocean. Like you say Troy did. He never would have been the only one washed overboard if a big wave had hit the ship. He would have kept everyone else from going overboard." Tears filled her eyes. "I tried to make the cops up in Alaska understand that, but they thought I was just being emotional, I could tell. They wouldn't listen to me."

"One of them listened."

"Derek Palmer?"

"Yeah, that's him. He said you two stayed in touch for a few months after Charlie's death. He told me who you were, and he sent me a picture of you he'd saved on his phone from when you were up there. He gave me the name and address of where you worked too. That's how I found you." Jack hesitated. "I don't want you to be mad at him. He was just trying to help."

"I know," she said softly. "He was the one who called Charlie's parents to tell them he was dead. He was the first one to respond when the *Arctic Fire* got back to Dutch Harbor. He tried to push the investigation, but his superiors wouldn't let him."

"That's what he said."

Tears were streaming down Karen's face. "Sorry," she murmured, trying to wipe away the moisture. "I'm really sorry, I don't usually cry. It's just that I still miss Charlie all the time," she whispered. "I wanted to marry him. I wanted to have kids with him." She sobbed loudly as she dropped her face into her hands. "Sorry," she whispered again.

"Don't be." Jack slid down the bench so he was sitting right beside her. He couldn't imagine how awful she was feeling. "I think you're amazing," he said, slipping his arm around her shoulder. "I really do. You've already saved my butt a couple of times tonight. It's like you're not afraid of anything." He pulled her closer and gently guided her head to his shoulder. For several minutes they said nothing as she cried.

"So what do we do now?" she asked when the tears finally stopped.

"We go after these people."

She took a deep breath and wiped the moisture from her face one more time. "How?"

"We find out what really happened to Troy and Charlie. Then we go to the cops with what we have. At the end of the day I think we're gonna end up in Dutch Harbor."

She looked up at him. "You really mean it? You really want to do that?"

"Absolutely."

"You said 'we.' You want me to go with you?"

"Of course. Don't you want to go?"

"I do." She grimaced. "But I don't have much money, Jack."

"Don't worry." The envelope Cheryl had given him had ten thousand dollars in it. And there was a note along with the cash that said to call her before he needed more. "I've got you covered."

"You sure?"

"Yup." Jack slipped a finger beneath her chin and tilted her face up. "So, you in?"

She nodded. "Oh yeah."

"Good. I'm glad we got that settled."

She gazed back at him for several moments with a distant expression. Then her eyes narrowed. "Let me see your driver's license."

"Huh?"

"Your driver's license," she repeated. "Let me see it."

Jack dug into a pocket of his jeans, pulled out his wet wallet, and handed the license to her.

She scanned it carefully in the dim light. "OK," she said, handing it back to him. "I guess you really are Jack Jensen."

"I guess I am."

"That license better be real."

"Of course it is. What's the problem?"

"There's a place we should go on the way to Alaska," she explained after a few moments. "It's a cabin in northern Minnesota. It's Charlie's parents' summer place."

"Why there?"

Karen pursed her lips. "Can I trust you?"

"Of course you can. Haven't I already—"

"No, I mean *really* trust you."

"Yeah, damn it. I can't believe you'd even—"

"OK, *OK*, here's the deal. Before he died, Charlie told me he was part of some crazy government intelligence group called Red Cell Seven."

Jack's pulse jumped.

"He said it was a super-secret outfit buried in some black ops area of the defense department or the CIA or something."

"*What?* Are you—"

"Listen to me," she interrupted. "Let me finish."

So maybe Troy hadn't been joyriding around the world for the last six and a half years after all. Maybe he and Hunter had been right to wonder what Troy was really up to.

"Anyway," she continued, "Charlie told me that he and a bunch of other guys were responsible for digging up very secret information, and for delivering and bringing back classified information to and from American spies all over the world. Apparently they do crazy things in the countries where the spies are, like climb mountains and hunt wild animals, but they do those things just for cover. They're really in the country to make contact with our agents, and they do that when no one's looking. They're called Falcons, and they're one division of this Red Cell Seven group."

A chill raced up Jack's spine. Everything his brother had been doing since graduating from Dartmouth suddenly made so much sense. "Jesus Christ," he whispered. "Troy."

"Obviously, Charlie wasn't supposed to tell me that," Karen continued. "The reason he did was because he was convinced his superior had gone insane, that the guy had turned into a certified nut job. I think he was about to go to people in the government outside Red Cell Seven to tell them what was going on, but he never got the chance. I think Charlie's superior had him thrown off the *Arctic Fire* before he could tell anybody."

"Like Troy," Jack whispered.

Karen nodded. "Then a month ago I got this letter, and it told me about a box up in Minnesota I needed to get. Obviously Charlie wasn't the one who told me about it. He wasn't the one who sent the letter. He never said anything about a box in the cabin.

"The letter said there was a lot of valuable information in the box, and that I should get to it as soon as possible, read it, and give it to people who mattered, to people who could do something with the information in it." She grimaced. "But I haven't yet." She glanced around, searching the shadows near them. "The letter said one more thing."

Jack heard serious fear creeping into her voice. "What?"

"That guy I told you about. You know, Charlie's leader."

"The nut job? Yeah, what about him?"

"The letter said the guy was going to kill the president."

"Of the *United States*?" Jack asked in disbelief. "President Dorn?"

"Yes. It said that the guy was already taking steps to assassinate him."

"That's ridiculous. Why would someone in Red Cell Seven want to kill the president of the United States? They should be in business to *protect* the president."

"The letter didn't say."

"Well if that's true, then we know why Charlie thought the guy was insane. Why didn't you get the box?" he asked after a few moments. "Why didn't you at least show the letter to someone?"

"I didn't want to get involved. I'm not proud of it, but I had my reasons."

"Which were?"

"Some pretty scary people showed up at my door a few weeks before I got the letter and made it real clear I was being watched." She nodded across the harbor in the direction of the warehouse they'd jumped out of twenty minutes ago. "People like those men who chased us tonight." She shrugged. "And really, who was I going to show the letter to? People would have thought I was crazy if I'd handed them that thing. They probably would have thought I'd written it myself to get attention or something. Then I would have been arrested and thrown in jail for being a nut job. And I never would have been heard from again."

Jack shook his head. "I don't know." He glanced over at her. This was probably a dead-end question, but he figured he'd ask it anyway. "Did the person who wrote the letter identify himself?"

Karen nodded. "Yeah, and that's the other reason I didn't go to the authorities. I didn't want to get him in trouble."

"Well, who was it?"

She stared intently into Jack's eyes for several moments before answering.

"Troy Jensen."

CHAPTER 22

CARLSON NODDED solemnly to the other three men sitting around the table. They were about to make an incredibly important decision. And they were doing it in the unfinished basement of his Georgetown home over ham sandwiches and potato salad Nancy had fixed before going to bed to cry about his cancer. He felt bad for leaving her alone right after he told her, but this meeting had to happen immediately. The country still had to come first. They'd cry together later.

Ham sandwiches and potato salad in a Georgetown basement he'd never had time to finish, and it all seemed surreal to Carlson. It seemed too informal an atmosphere for them to consider an action so grave, an action that would change the course of history. He felt like they should be wearing tuxedos and toasting each other with fine wine in a private room of an elite club as they passed judgment on David Dorn.

"Before we get to the most important issue," Carlson began as the others ate, "I'll give you a few updates. First, one of our Falcons just left China and is now aboard the *Arctic Fire* headed for Dutch Harbor. I've already gotten preliminary information from him that the Chinese have, in fact, completed development of that tactical missile the DOD and the CIA are so concerned about. The information our Falcon brought back is excellent and should prove extremely helpful to our negotiators as they begin arms talks with the Chinese next week in Rotterdam. We'll have more details about the system when he gets to Washington tomorrow."

Carlson paused for a moment as he thought about Captain Sage Mitchell and the *Arctic Fire*. Captain Sage was a true patriot, a damn fine man. A significant amount of the country's recent success in terms of bringing back military and strategic secrets from and about China, Russia, and North Korea could be attributed, in part, to his ability to quietly pilot the *Fire* around the Bering Sea. They'd been smart to recruit Sage Mitchell a few years ago when he was almost broke.

It was too damn bad about Troy Jensen, and he hoped Sage wouldn't have any misgivings about helping Red Cell Seven in the future because he felt guilty about the kid getting washed overboard in the storm. Better than almost anyone else, Captain Sage understood why they called it the most dangerous job on earth. Accidents happened, especially on the Bering Sea. They were just one of those bad things in life that happened for no apparent reason. Like cancer.

"Second," Carlson continued, "in the past week our people executed two senior terrorist agents in the United States and three more abroad. From the chatter we're picking up out of Yemen and Syria, the agents in the US were even more vital to their organizations than we originally thought. And, we kept all of that out of the media."

Everyone was enjoying the food. He could tell how much because no one was asking questions. Nancy always had been a wonderful cook. Even her sandwiches tasted better than anyone else's. He smiled sadly. At least to him they did. He hadn't enjoyed her food as much as he should have over the years, but he was going to start now. He glanced down at his plate and the untouched sandwich lying there. Well, after this meeting, he would.

"Finally," he continued, "we've gotten word from our Falcons that it's likely another LNG tanker is being prepped in Malaysia by terrorists and will head toward another East Coast target soon. It'll be sometime after the first of the year, probably. This ship will be carrying almost two hundred thousand cubic meters of liquefied natural gas. We believe that Savannah, Georgia, is the target, but this time we'll board the ship farther out in the ocean, a few hundred miles, at least. We'll have a lot more firepower on the scene too, even some underwater. But, as I said, it's nothing we have to worry about right away. We've got a few weeks."

"Thanks, Roger," one of the other men said brusquely as he finished the last bite of his sandwich. "But what's going on with President Dorn? Let's get to why we're really here."

"Yeah, let's," one of the other men agreed. "Is the bastard really trying to screw with Red Cell Seven?"

"He's not just trying to screw with it," Carlson answered ominously. "He's trying to destroy us. He wants lists of all RCS personnel and where they're currently deployed. He wants all of our contacts abroad, the names of CIA and NSA in-country spies, and a list of physical assets here and abroad."

The room went deathly still as everyone stopped chewing and took a few moments to digest the information instead of the food.

"Then Dorn has to die."

Everyone's gazes flickered to the man at the opposite end of the table from Carlson who'd just spoken up in his deep voice.

"It's simply a question of when and where," he added.

Carlson glanced around the table. "Are we unanimous? Let me see hands."

Four hands rose immediately into the air. That fast, a death sentence had been passed. That fast, President Dorn had become a dead man walking. Because once Red Cell Seven identified a target, it didn't miss. It never had before.

"All right," Carlson said somberly, amazed as always by their efficiency. "We kill him."

"What about the vice president?" the man at the other end of the table asked.

"What about him?"

"Are we sure he'll be with us? We can't push this button twice in the same decade, Roger. There'd be hell to pay if we did. I mean, there will be this time too, of course." The man crossed his arms tightly over his chest as if a cold wind had just blown into the room. "But if we did it again…" His voice faded for a few seconds. "Well, that simply isn't an option."

"Agreed," Carlson said, glancing around the table. "I can assure all of you that Vice President Vogel will be very supportive of Red Cell Seven."

The room went quiet until the man at the end of the table spoke up again. "How long until David Dorn dies, Roger?"

Carlson stared down the table. Maddux was going to carry out the execution. "Two weeks," he answered in a grave voice. "Maybe less."

CHAPTER 23

"Mr. President, I should have looked at that list you gave Daniel Beckham this afternoon before you sent him to meet Roger Carlson."

Rex Stein was a short, wiry man with a full head of gray hair and intense hazel eyes set close together on his face. And he always wore bow ties. It was his trademark.

Stein was a consummate Washington insider who knew his way around the federal government as well as anyone. He knew how to get what he wanted without compromising in a town where few people got anything without giving away the farm.

Stein tapped a corner of the paper with his index finger so it popped loudly. "I just got this, and, well, with all due respect, Mr. President, giving Carlson this was a mistake." The party had chosen Stein for this position to keep Dorn out of trouble. He had permission from the nonelected leaders to be extremely direct with the commander in chief. "A *huge* mistake."

Dorn smiled stiffly at Stein from behind his desk in the Oval Office. "Thank you for your input, Rex, but you were busy this afternoon. You were working on the Europe trip we're taking next month, and I wanted to get this Red Cell Seven thing started right away." He chuckled. "Don't worry. Beckham isn't going to be reporting straight to me on this. He'll go through you just like everyone else does. Don't get your panties in a bunch."

Stein counted to five silently as he shifted in his chair. He knew Dorn didn't appreciate the directness. He could see the resentment for it building with each new day, and it was a function of Dorn becoming more and more comfortable in his position. But it was getting harder and harder for Stein to control his temper when Dorn decided to sling those sarcastic arrows across the desk.

"I'm not worried about that, Mr. President."

"Then what are you worried about?"

"Frankly, I'm worried that there could be repercussions for shutting down Red Cell Seven. We need to have more respect for how much support there is out there for RCS at the highest levels of—"

"I'm not shutting it down," the president interrupted. "I'm just getting control of it. That's all."

Stein glanced down at the piece of paper in his lap. "I have to tell you that a man like Roger Carlson will interpret this list as you shutting him down. I have a few more years of experience than you in terms of dealing with things like this and—"

"Rex," the president cut in sharply, "did you know that Carlson allows several of his direct reports to kill people? In fact, he condones it. He even sets it up in some cases."

Stein slowly raised an eyebrow. At his core he was a liberal, but he still had a healthy respect for Red Cell Seven and what the individuals in it did. Getting older had enabled him to start seeing both sides of the defense and intelligence coin. As had 9/11. He'd lost a brother when the North Tower had come crashing down.

"That's what they do, sir," he said deliberately. "That's their job. They kill the bad guys, and they do it in the shadows so you and I never need to know about it. So we have plausible deniability."

"I'm talking about civilians. He has them kill American civilians."

"Can you be more specific on that one for me, sir?" Stein asked calmly, aware that Dorn wasn't above telling a few white lies to make his point. He was like any other politician.

The president eased back into his big leather chair and made a contrite face to let Stein know that he hadn't told his chief of staff the whole story. "They carry out vigilante justice. They kill people who've dodged a bullet and gotten off serious crimes on a technicality."

Stein nodded. "Well, I can't really—"

"Don't tell me you agree with that."

"Justice can't be as blind as we'd like it to be. You know that."

"Whose side are you on?"

"The country's side, Mr. President."

Stein still wasn't convinced that Dorn had accurate information. And, even if the president did, Stein wasn't sure he cared. He'd had his doubts over the years, but now he was starting to think that what cells like RCS did in the shadows was necessary.

"How did you find out about this, Mr. President?"

"I've been president for ten months, Rex. I don't need you for everything anymore." Dorn had been looking at the painting of George Washington on the wall, but now he refocused on Stein. "A minute ago you mentioned repercussions for shutting RCS down. What did you mean?"

You don't want to know, Mr. President, was what Stein was thinking. But even as direct as he usually was with Dorn, he couldn't say that. He didn't want to mention the "assassination" word. "Are you really serious about *not* shutting down Red Cell Seven?"

"Absolutely. I respect what they do. They just need to be roped in some. Well, a lot," Dorn added.

Stein took a deep breath. He was going to try his best to do damage control on this, but it was going to be difficult. He knew that list on the paper in his lap had sent a very different message to Roger Carlson than what the president had just laid out. Unfortunately, there might be no stopping the intel reaction at this point.

* * *

Lisa Martinez carefully put the baby down in his crib, covered his tiny body with his hospital blanket, and headed for the living room. A few moments ago there'd been a loud knock on the apartment door. She was hoping it wasn't the super looking for last month's rent because she still didn't have it. The five hundred dollars Jack gave her had gone for formula, Pampers, and keeping the lights on.

When she pulled back the door, her eyes opened wide. Standing in front of her was a tall, older man with silver hair, wearing an expensive-looking suit.

"Can I help you?" she asked shyly. He looked so out of place here in the projects. Like Jack did when he came to visit her.

"My name's Bill Jensen," the older man said, moving into the apartment without being asked. "I'd like to talk to you for a few minutes."

* * *

President Dorn gazed into the autumn darkness outside the West Wing window. Rex Stein had left the office a few minutes ago, and Dorn was congratulating himself on what he considered an Oscar-winning performance.

Stein had left here thinking that his president really had no intention of shuttering Red Cell Seven, that it was all a big misunderstanding. He'd left thinking that his president was still inexperienced and didn't truly understand the grave message that the request for information would send.

Dorn chuckled. He'd played it perfectly. Now Stein was going to quietly run around Washington and Northern Virginia trying to convince the senior men in the shadows that it really was all a misunderstanding. Stein was going to tell those important individuals that the president was still wet behind the ears and had no idea how his message would be taken. That would give Dorn more time to get the information he needed to actually shut the thing down for good.

But there was no misunderstanding. Red Cell Seven was done as far as he was concerned. He couldn't have those bastards out there killing anyone they wanted to anytime they wanted to. It wasn't right. The world could never become the place it was supposed to be with men like Roger Carlson out there acting unilaterally. Even close allies would never truly trust the United States until the decks had been scrubbed clean of men like Carlson and his associates.

He picked up the phone. It was time to get a face-to-face report from Daniel Beckham without Stein around.

* * *

Hunter stared blankly into the darkness. The temperature had dipped into the thirties as the December night had fallen. But he barely noticed how cold it was as he stood beside his car in his shirtsleeves and smoked his first cigarette in twelve years.

They'd laughed as they'd led Amy away, and he'd heard her scream once after he'd lost sight of her. But there was nothing he could do to help her. They had him tied up and had let him go at gunpoint only after she was long gone.

He hadn't cried in a long time, but as he finished the cigarette and tossed it to the parking lot, sobs overtook him as his tears began to flow. They'd made it all very clear to him. Help them find Jack…or Amy would die.

CHAPTER 24

JACK GLANCED up as Karen came out of the bathroom. He wanted to take a shower, and he'd been watching a movie while he waited for her to finish.

"Hey there," he said as he stood up from the chair in front of the TV. "Feeling better?"

She had on the pair of jeans and the top he'd bought her at a Target on the way over to the hotel. He'd bought her a new coat too. It was chilly in Baltimore, but it was going to be a lot colder where they were going.

"So much better," she answered.

He'd offered to get her a separate room, but she wouldn't accept. There were two double beds in the room, and she'd told him that was fine, that she trusted him after everything they'd already been through tonight—and because the name Jack Jensen was printed on his license, which convinced her he was Troy's brother. It turned out she had only a few hundred bucks to her name, and she didn't want to be a burden.

He'd offered her the room twice, but she'd gotten that look in her eyes as he'd started to ask the second time, so he'd quit in midsentence. It was the same look she'd given him on the bench when he'd asked her if she wanted to go to the hospital. She looked so soft on the outside, especially now that she'd showered. But underneath she was turning out to be a firecracker.

"You look great." She did too. Her still-wet long black hair was down on her shoulders; she'd put on a little makeup she'd picked up at the store too, and she seemed to be in a much better mood. "I mean it." He liked that she'd put on that makeup. They'd already eaten and they had no plans to leave the room tonight, so it sent him a nice signal.

She smiled back at him. "Really think so?"

He checked her arm when he thought she wasn't looking, but he couldn't see anything. They'd bought some stuff at Target to dress the wound, and she'd covered it with bandages while she was in the bathroom. He thought about asking her how it was feeling, but he didn't. She seemed OK, and they were getting along too well. He didn't want another one of those looks flashing his way.

"Definitely."

"Thanks." She glanced uncertainly at their third-story window. "I hope we're OK here."

The hotel was in West Baltimore away from city center. It wasn't a great place, but it wasn't too bad. He'd wanted a place where he could bribe the guy behind the front desk so he didn't have to put down his credit card—the same way he hadn't last night up north—and that wouldn't have been possible at a nice place. With no credit card imprint on the room, he was confident no one would find them.

"We'll be fine." They were going to get a good night's sleep before heading west in the morning.

Karen sat down on the edge of the bed. "Do you want to see a picture of Charlie?" she asked.

"Sure."

He took the photo from her carefully after she took it out of her wallet. It was still wet.

Banks was an athletic-looking guy with a great smile, just like Troy. But that wasn't what caught Jack's eye. Instead, he focused on how Banks was holding his hands. His thumbs were hooked into his jeans with most of his fingers out of the belt and pointed straight down.

Jack counted the fingers in the picture again, for the third time. Four on the right hand and three on the left were pointed down at the ground. Only his thumbs and the last finger of his left hand weren't visible.

"My God," he whispered as it hit him, as four and three became seven. "Karen," he said loudly, "what did you say the name of that group was again? The one Charlie told you he was in?"

"Red Cell Seven."

"Red Cell Seven," Jack repeated. "*Holy shit.*"

"What is it?" she asked, staring at him intently.

In the picture, Charlie Banks was holding his hands exactly the same way Troy had been holding his hands in front of the *Arctic Fire*, as he stood defiantly in the photograph Cheryl had enlarged and put on the easel in the great room for the memorial service.

And the same way Bill was holding his hands in the photograph of him standing with the governor of New York that was on his office credenza. Thumbs hooked into his belt, seven fingers pointed at the ground—four on his right hand and three on his left, Jack remembered.

The realization hit him hard. This was no coincidence. It couldn't be. Charlie Banks and Troy Jensen were members of Red Cell Seven. Karen had made that clear as they were sitting on the bench.

But now he knew Bill was connected to it as well.

PART 4

CHAPTER 25

"Did you say you were a cop?"

Karen glanced over at Jack from the passenger seat of the rented Taurus as they sped west away from Baltimore. "Yeah," she answered deliberately. "So?"

He raised both eyebrows. "Wow." He was pretty sure she'd dropped that main-course cut of background data on him last night as they were sprinting down the alley trying not to get killed. "Isn't that interesting?"

"What's so interesting about it?" She held her hands out and signaled in with her fingers. "Come on, come on, let's have it."

He'd wanted to confirm it in the hotel room, but hadn't had a chance because she'd fallen asleep so quickly...which he liked. It meant she felt safe with him even though they'd just met.

"Oh, no," he said innocently. "I didn't mean to make it sound like that."

When he'd come out of the bathroom after taking his shower, she'd been curled up on her bed asleep hugging a pillow, and he'd pulled the covers over her shoulders gently. Her long black hair was still wet—the low-budget place didn't have hair dryers in the bathrooms—and he hadn't wanted her to catch cold.

"I just think it would be cool to—" He stopped himself. "I just think it's very cool. I really respect you for it."

"That's not what you were going to say."

He laughed loudly. "What are you talking about? Yeah, it is."

"Come on," she encouraged in a half-friendly, half-aggravated tone. "Say what you were really going to say, Jack. I bet I've heard it before. I've probably heard every crack about female cops ever invented. Don't be afraid."

"It's got nothing to do with being afraid."

"You don't have to worry about us getting off to a bad start."

That sounded good to Jack. "Well, I'm glad because—"

"Because we already have."

That didn't. "What? *Why?*"

Maybe it was the near-death experience they'd shared last night that had him interested in her so fast, he figured, trying to be analytical about it. Maybe being shot at together was an aphrodisiac, so then maybe what he was feeling was just infatuation.

But as he glanced over at her something told him that what he was feeling wasn't going to fade anytime soon. He was more taken by her every minute, but they hadn't been shot at in a while. Karen was definitely something special.

"What did I do?" he pushed.

She looked at him like it was obvious. "It's what you *didn't* do, Jack."

"What do you mean?"

"I had to push you out of that warehouse window last night. I mean, come on, who's really wearing the pants in this relationship?"

He didn't like his manhood being called out, but hearing that she thought they already had a relationship wasn't a bad thing. "I didn't even know we had a relation—"

"And let me tell you something," she interrupted as she pointed at him. "Yeah, yeah, I was a cop, but I love being a woman too. I love wearing cute dresses and heels and doing my nails and dancing like crazy at a cool club. Tell those guys on the trading floor that."

"Huh?"

"You know, all those animals you told me you work with in New York City."

"We're not animals," he said indignantly.

"Blah, blah. I've seen the movies about you Wall Street guys. And I've read the books. You're all blue bloods, but you're Neanderthals while you're on the trading floors."

"We're not all blue bloods either."

"Look, I'm not some stubborn bitch who gets off arresting men and gets offended by guys who treat her like a woman. I love it when a guy holds a door for me or stands up when I get to the table. I love being treated like a woman."

She reached out, grabbed the rearview mirror, turned it so she could see her face in it, and muttered angrily that despite brushing it out for fifteen minutes this morning, her hair still looked like a rat's nest because she'd slept on it wet.

He grinned as she muttered. Her hair looked sexy like that—not bad.

"That's how Charlie was," she continued. "That was one of the things that really impressed me about him on our first date. His manners were so awesome."

"I'll remember that." He would too.

"But what really impressed me was that it never stopped. He wasn't just doing it on our first date to get my attention. He cared about me enough to keep doing it." She hesitated. "I like being pampered, but I can handle myself in the tough situations too. I want you to know that, Jack."

"I think I've already seen you handle yourself in a tough—"

"So I'll keep wearing pants when it's the two of us if I have to," she cut in again as she turned the mirror back in the general direction it had been facing before.

"No problem." Jack adjusted the mirror so he could see out the rear window again.

"Charlie didn't have a problem with me being a cop."

"I don't either." He'd obviously hit a sensitive button on her personal remote.

In-charge women didn't bother Jack at all. He liked a woman who knew what she wanted and went out and got it…as long as she could be sexy and romantic too. OK, so his standards were ridiculously high.

That, along with not being much into compromise, was probably why he'd never gotten permanently hooked. But he wasn't like Troy either. He wasn't a one-night-stand guy. He enjoyed getting to know a woman and having a serious relationship. He just hadn't found a woman he wanted to spend the rest of his life with.

Jack looked over at Karen for the hundredth time since they'd gotten in the car. Not yet, anyway.

"Not going to argue about it?" she asked curiously. "Not going to get all macho on me and tell me you didn't really need me to push you out that window after all?"

"I definitely needed that push."

"Amazing," she said after a few moments, clearly impressed. "I've finally met a guy who admits to being scared of something."

"Hey, I hate heights. They scare the crap out of me. They always have, and there's nothing I can do about it." He gestured at her. "At least I had you push me out, right?"

"Yeah," she agreed softly, "you did." She reached over and touched his arm reassuringly. "Hey, I was just kidding about our start. I have liked it." She let her hand linger on his arm. "I mean, it's been kind of crazy," she said with an overwhelmed expression. "I've gotta give you a big 'A' for creativity and excitement. That's for sure. But I've got to go low in the safety category. The bullets were a bit much. A roller coaster would have been fine," she said with a grin.

"We're alive, aren't we?"

"So far," she murmured as her smile faded. "So, Jack, what were you going to say before about me being a cop?"

"I said what I had to say."

"You can't start something like that and not finish it."

"I sure can."

"Come on, I want to hear it. *I mean it.*"

"Don't boss me."

"I'm not. I would *never* do that." She laughed loudly, making it abundantly clear with her sarcastic tone that she knew very well she was bossing him. "Now tell me, *damn it.*"

"OK, boss."

"Now!"

He chuckled as he thought about whether or not to say it. He wanted to build that bridge to her quickly. He wanted her all-in as fast as he could get her there...so what the hell, he figured. "OK, OK. All I was going to say was that Baltimore seems like a good city to get arrested in now that I know you."

Karen rolled her eyes. "Why, because now you figure the force is all full of little hotties and it might be fun getting booked by a good-looking chick? What? Is that what you guys yak about on the trading floor in the afternoon when things get slow?"

She had this sizzle about her he couldn't resist. Those friendly eyes he'd spotted at the restaurant last night could flash red-hot quickly, but that was OK. She certainly wasn't as vulnerable as he'd first thought. But those tears she'd cried for Charlie last night had been genuine and heartfelt. That was obvious. She was tough, but it didn't seem like her skin was that thick.

"All I was going to say," Jack answered, "was that you seem like a really nice person, Karen. All the cops I've ever dealt with have been pricks, real hotheads."

Jack had been arrested both times he'd put those guys in the hospital with broken jaws. But the cops hadn't bothered to listen to how he'd been acting in self-defense either time. In fact, they'd told him to shut the hell up or they'd pile a resisting arrest onto the assault charge—which had been dropped quickly in both cases after witnesses had come forward and the facts had played out.

"But you aren't." He shrugged. "Maybe the police force you were on was better trained. That's all I meant, Karen."

"Oh." She hesitated. "Well, don't I feel like an idiot now?" she murmured apologetically. "Sorry, Jack. I guess I'm still a little sensitive about all those cracks I heard about being a woman cop."

He raised an eyebrow as he looked over at her again. "You think?"

* * *

Hunter sat at the kitchen table of their small country house gazing at a wedding picture of Amy in her long white dress. She looked more beautiful to him this morning than she ever had.

She didn't turn heads when she walked into a room, but she wasn't unattractive either. She was plain. That was the best way to describe her.

But that was fine with Hunter, because on the inside Amy was the most beautiful person he'd ever known. She'd do almost anything for anyone, and she cared so very deeply for any child who was in trouble in any way. And that was why he really cared about her. Because of her innate and uncompromising affection for human life and her desire to solve everyone's problems no matter who they were.

Hunter put the wedding picture down and picked up a photograph of Jack and himself together on a fishing trip out on Long Island Sound. They had their arms around each other's shoulders, and Jack was giving the camera one of those big, charismatic smiles he rarely gave anyone or anything. If he only understood how contagious that smile was and the confidence it engendered, he'd give it a lot more often, Hunter figured. But Jack still had so many issues, so many demons inside himself left to conquer. And most of them were born of still being so intimidated by Troy.

Hunter shook his head. Jack didn't need to be intimidated by anyone anymore—even Troy. He'd become his own very fine person over the last few years. Hunter had seen the progression from the front row and tried to help Jack see it too with as many psychological mirrors as he could find. But it hadn't worked. Maybe Jack never would see himself as that capable, confident person he'd become. Maybe that was the sad truth. And, perhaps, in an awful way, Troy's death had put a cover on that possibility forever. As Hunter had overheard Jack whisper to himself at the memorial service, how was he supposed to compete with his younger brother now?

They'd been friends for a long time, and now Hunter understood why Jack had acted so mysteriously at the bar the other night. He wasn't going to Florida for the winter to pick up some stupid bartending job. Based on what Hunter had been through in the last thirty-six hours, Jack was into something very dangerous. Though what that was, Hunter had no idea.

All Hunter knew for sure was that the little man who'd demanded information about Jack, used the clear plastic bag as his torture weapon of choice, and ultimately had Amy kidnapped was one serious motherfucker. Hunter had seen the evil in his eyes, and it had terrified him on a level he'd never even known he was capable of experiencing. The man was a predator and that was all. He knew no other way. Even more frightening, he obviously didn't *want* to know any other way.

Hunter placed the picture of Jack down beside the picture of Amy and took turns staring at their faces. He had to make a terrible choice between the two people who meant the most to him in the world. That little man had called early this morning and made him listen to Amy scream for help in the background, so he didn't have much time to decide. He had to make his choice very soon.

Jack had been his best friend for fifteen years, and he'd proven his loyalty time and time again.

Amy was his wife, and he loved her dearly.

He glanced at the cell phone lying on the table beside Jack's picture. There was one missed call registering on the tiny screen.

"My God," he whispered. "Somebody help me."

CHAPTER 26

MADDUX STOPPED O'Hara outside the heavy iron door with a strong grip to the shoulder. They were just about to enter the soundproof interrogation room, which was at one end of the narrow, stone-walled corridor of the farmhouse basement. It lay directly beneath the study in which Maddux had welcomed O'Hara into RCS.

"Put this on, Ryan," he ordered, handing the young man a crude hood. It was a faded white pillowcase with two small holes cut out of the poly-cotton blend near the closed end of the case. "And keep it on until I tell you to take it off."

"Are you serious, sir?" O'Hara asked, grinning self-consciously.

"I get the Klan irony," Maddux muttered as he slipped a hood on himself. "At least you don't have to wear the robe," he added in what was now a slightly muffled voice.

He was enjoying this moment, and he allowed himself a grin beneath the hood because now O'Hara couldn't see his reaction. Something inside Maddux had always enjoyed putting people on edge.

"Put these on too." Maddux pulled a pair of gloves from a pocket of his jacket and tossed them at the kid. "And make sure your shirtsleeves come down over the wrist end of the gloves at all times while we're in there."

"Why?"

"You said it yourself. You're black and you're the first one to make it in. Never give away anything about yourself you don't absolutely have to." Maddux nodded at the door. "Other than the man we're interrogating today, there's a guy from another RCS division in there as well. I don't want him seeing your hands and figuring out it's you if somehow he's heard through the grapevine about you making it in."

"Are you embarrassed by me?" O'Hara asked tersely. "Is that what this is about, sir?"

It was the first time Maddux had heard the kid's voice grab even a slightly irritated edge. And this one wasn't slight, it was pure resentment. "I don't want you identified *at all*," Maddux replied as deliberately as he could, controlling his rage at the kid's audacity in using that tone with his new superior, but at the same time showing the young man how irritated he was in no uncertain terms. "It has nothing to do with your skin color. I already told you, Ryan. I don't see color when I look at you. I see bravery." He hesitated. "The bottom line is I don't want any of my Falcons identified by anyone at any time. But everyone in RCS knows that we haven't had an African American make it into the Falcon division before you. If the RCS guy behind the door saw your hands, it wouldn't take him long to connect the dots. Understand?"

"Yes, sir," O'Hara mumbled. "Sorry."

"It's for your protection," Maddux continued. "That's all. I'd do the same thing for any other Falcon whether he was white, black, green, or purple. It's *always* best to fly under the radar whenever you can, even when you're flying over friendly territory. You've probably heard that a thousand times during your training, but it's true." He pointed a stubby finger at the kid. "Follow our training techniques at all times to the letter, son. I can't emphasize that enough. It *will* save your life one day."

"So, we stay that secretive even from other RCS divisions?" O'Hara asked.

"Absolutely," Maddux replied, watching the kid pull the hood down over his face. Maddux focused on the eye holes when the hood was in place, trying to see if anyone could tell the kid was black under there. But the holes were small enough to keep out any gaze, no matter how penetrating. "Pull those sleeves down," he ordered. "No skin showing."

"Why do I have to be worried about somebody from another Red Cell Seven division? Isn't he one of the good guys?"

"He is," Maddux agreed. "He's a counterterrorism guy and a damn fine one. But, in my opinion, he's got a big mouth." Maddux shrugged. "I mean, he doesn't say much because he is counterterror, but those guys shouldn't say *anything*."

"I don't under—"

"Not everyone's as smart as I am. Not everyone sees it all the way I do."

"Huh?"

"There's one more thing I have to make clear to you before we go in there," Maddux said quickly as he gestured at the door. "It's the most important to me."

"What is it, sir?" O'Hara asked expectantly.

"From now on you must be completely loyal to me no matter what happens. Do you understand that, Ryan? At this point it isn't about the rest of the Falcons, Red Cell Seven, the DOD, the CIA, or even the United States of America. It's just about your loyalty to me. Am I clear?"

O'Hara swallowed hard and gave Maddux a confused look. "Yes, sir, but if I could ask you just one more—"

"Let's go." Maddux hustled O'Hara toward the door. He didn't like the kid asking so many questions. He needed to put a stop to that ASAP.

Maybe it was a generational thing, Maddux figured. Maybe kids today simply couldn't keep from asking questions because there were so many ways to get information. As a result, they expected answers immediately all the time. Whatever the reason was, he didn't appreciate it. Young people were made to be seen and not heard, like his grandfather had always said.

He'd always liked his grandfather, but then the old man had up and died right in front of him of a heart attack when Maddux was only seven. And then he hadn't had any protection from his father's nightly beatings.

"We'll talk more after the session," Maddux promised as he pushed the door open.

"Yes, sir."

It was rare for Maddux to allow so new a Falcon into an inter-rogation like this, especially a session that would end up getting so brutal. But he had a good feeling about O'Hara, and he wanted to connect with the kid quickly. O'Hara was an expert marksman, one of the best to ever come along. The kid could literally put a bullet through the eye of an eagle in the sky from three hun-dred yards. Maddux wanted to practice with O'Hara over the next few days to try to improve his own marksmanship, which was excellent, though nothing compared to the kid's. Maddux wanted every extra bit of training he could get to make certain President Dorn died with the first shot.

Maddux's second reason for allowing O'Hara into this session was shock value. He wanted to see the kid's physical reaction to an actual torture session even if he couldn't actually see O'Hara's face. He'd still know what was going on behind the hood from the kid's body language and the debriefing meeting afterward. O'Hara had seen several gut-wrenching videos of sessions during his training, but never the live, in-your-face, blood-and-death performance.

He'd puked a few months ago while watching a particularly vicious session during which a subject had been slowly decapitated, but otherwise the kid had passed with flying colors. Most importantly, he'd never once questioned the need for brutal torture sessions as a tool to protect the United States. Not even if it involved American citizens.

Then there was that third reason Maddux wanted O'Hara in the interrogation session, which was the most important reason of all.

As they headed into the dimly lit room, Maddux motioned for O'Hara to move to the wall opposite the one the subject was hanging near. The guy's wrists were tied tightly above his head by a thick rope leading to a hook on the ceiling, and his feet barely touched the floor. He was moaning loudly while he tried to keep himself balanced on his toes as he strained toward the ceiling.

"Ready?" Maddux called in a low voice to the fourth man in the room, who wore a hood like the ones he and O'Hara were wearing.

His name was Nick Telford, and he ran the RCS counter-terrorism division for Roger Carlson. Maddux and Telford had come aboard RCS about the same time twenty years ago. As far as Maddux was concerned they had a healthy respect for each other, but that was it. Of course, that was the most intense relationship Maddux could have with anyone—except Carlson. He loved that old man—as much as his ultimate loyalty to the United States allowed him to love anyone.

"Have at it," Telford answered indifferently. "He's all yours."

The subject's name was John Savoy. He was fifty-two, but he looked older than that to Maddux, like he was in his early sixties. He had thinning brown hair, pasty skin, and an obvious paunch. He also had a wife and two kids in college, and he worked for the Department of Energy. He was a bureaucratic lifer, and he looked boring because he was boring, Maddux knew. His appearance and his career weren't covers at all. He was just an ordinary man trying to make a little extra money on the side by selling what he figured was a little harmless information.

He had no idea how big a shit-storm he'd stepped squarely into the middle of by selling that information—until now, anyway.

At Maddux's orders, Telford and several of his men had picked up Savoy in Arlington early this morning on his way into work, thrown him in the back of a white van, and whisked him down here to the farmhouse in central Virginia. As Maddux stared at Savoy, he could tell the guy was already on the verge of tears.

"Do you know why you're here, Mr. Savoy?" Maddux asked gruffly.

"No," Savoy whimpered. "I have no idea."

With no warning, Maddux delivered a sharp kick to Savoy's groin. Savoy screamed in agony and tried to double over against the pain. But he couldn't because his hands were tied so tightly above his head. All he could do was scream. Then scream even louder and more pitifully when Maddux delivered a second, even harder kick to the exact same body organs. Savoy lifted his knees to his gut, but he didn't have the strength to keep them there for long.

"We know who you are, you piece of shit!" Maddux shouted at Savoy, who was coughing so violently he was already starting to spit up blood. "We know what you're doing."

"I'm just a midlevel guy at DOE," Savoy gasped. "I'm a nobody in the Office of Fossil Fuels, for Christ's sake. I swear it."

"Like hell!" Maddux snarled. "You've given away some very sensitive information about LNG tankers heading toward American soil to the wrong person, haven't you, Mr. Savoy?"

"*What?* No, I don't even—"

Maddux delivered a blistering right cross to Savoy's jaw, which sent several of the older man's teeth flying from his mouth and into the room.

Savoy began sobbing hysterically through his pain when he saw Maddux pull a pistol from his jacket.

"Russian roulette," Maddux whispered as he moved close to Savoy and pressed the barrel to Savoy's head. "That's what we're about to play. Six chambers and one bullet, and I keep pulling the trigger until you tell me what I want to know or the gun goes off. Got it?"

Right away Savoy began screaming and shouting and doing everything he could to keep the gun away from his head.

Maddux chuckled as Savoy danced beneath the rope. He pressed the gun back to Savoy's head whenever he tired and went still for a moment. Finally, Savoy had nothing left in the tank and hung limply from the hook, exhausted and defenseless.

Maddux spun the gun's six-chamber ammunition cylinder so it sounded like a drumroll. As the clicking faded, he pushed the barrel to Savoy's head one more time.

"What the hell are you doing?" Telford demanded. "This guy doesn't know anything. He's a fucking bureaucrat, for God's sake. Let's get him out of here."

"This is my interrogation," Maddux snapped. "Not yours."

"Yeah, but—"

"Tell me what you know, Mr. Savoy, or I pull the trigger!" Maddux yelled as he pressed the gun hard to Savoy's head. "You gave information about those LNG tankers coming at this country to someone you shouldn't have on the outside, didn't you? Well, it turns out that someone on the outside was a person of interest to us." Maddux dropped the barrel of the gun from Savoy's head and forced it down the man's throat so he gagged violently. "*Don't deny it!*"

"*No, no, I didn't do anything like that!*" Savoy screamed past the gun barrel in a garbled voice as he gagged. "All I do is watch those ships after they leave port," he explained when Maddux pulled the gun from his mouth. "That's it as far as the LNG tankers go. I haven't given any information to anyone except my bosses at DOE. My information isn't even that important."

That wasn't all Savoy did, Maddux knew very well. He was selling himself short in a big way. Savoy also interfaced with Naval Operations in Norfolk, Virginia, to keep them up to date on where those ships were. So the military could track the tankers in case decisive defensive action was required.

Maddux knew this because *he* was the one who was paying Savoy *not* to tell the Navy that a huge LNG tanker called the *Pegasus* was heading directly for Virginia Beach and not toward Savannah, Georgia, where it was supposed to be heading. He was the one paying Savoy to tell the Navy that the *Pegasus* was still on course for Savannah. He knew all that because he was that person of interest, though Savoy couldn't tell, thanks to the hood.

Maddux smiled as he pressed the barrel to Savoy's head one more time. He'd told Carlson that the ship hadn't even left Malaysia yet. "Tell me, you bastard. *Tell me what I want to know!*" And, of course, Carlson had believed him.

"Please don't hurt me anymore," Savoy pleaded.

"*Tell me!*"

"All right, all right, I'll tell you what you want to—"

The bullet exploded from the pistol with a deafening blast and slammed through Savoy's brain. His body went limp instantly as blood and gray matter splattered the wall behind him.

"*What the hell?*" Telford shouted. "*He was about to break!*"

Maddux brought the revolver up in front of his face and stared at it for a few seconds. Then he glanced at O'Hara. "Did you not fix this gun like I told you to?" he demanded accusingly. This was the third and most important reason he'd wanted the kid in the room—so he had plausible deniability. "What the hell?"

Maddux pointed the gun at the ceiling, flipped the ammunition cylinder out to the left of the gun, and pushed the extractor rod. Five live rounds and an empty shell fell from the chambers and clattered across the tile floor. "Jesus Christ," he hissed. "This thing was fully loaded. What the hell's wrong with you, kid?"

"What do you mean?" O'Hara asked hesitantly. "I, I didn't... what are you—"

"Be loyal to me, damn it!" Maddux shouted. "Remember what we talked about outside. Why the hell didn't you fix this gun like I told you to? I told you to leave one bullet in it. That was it. *Just one fucking bullet!*"

O'Hara hesitated for several seconds, then looked down at the ground. "I'm sorry, sir," he finally mumbled, kicking at the cement floor.

"Christ," Telford hissed, yanking the hood off. He had a huge head with a square jaw and a shock of blond hair. "This was a fucking joke," he said as he stalked toward the door. He stopped before pushing it open and stared at Maddux. "Do you really not check your own guns before you come in here to do this, Shane?"

"I was too busy." The plausible deniability had worked. Telford was irritated, but not suspicious. "I didn't have time."

"What a moron." Telford banged the door open. "Fuck this. You guys can bury the body yourselves."

"You can take off your hood," Maddux said when Telford was gone. "You did great, Ryan."

"What exactly did I do?" O'Hara asked as he gazed at Savoy's body, which was still swinging back and forth beneath the hook.

"I didn't know anything about that gun. I didn't even know you had a gun on you."

Maddux pulled off his hood and tossed it into a corner of the room. "No, you didn't, Ryan. But you did the right thing."

John Savoy had been executed in the nick of time. Maddux had found out yesterday that the CIA was closing in on him. They'd determined that Savoy was giving some kind of vital information to someone outside the Department of Energy, though they hadn't identified who he was giving it to or exactly what the information related to. They'd intended to take Savoy to Langley for a tough round of questioning this afternoon that likely would have ended in his arrest, though not his death.

During the session, Savoy would have undoubtedly identified the man on the outside as Shane Maddux. He was too weak a man to keep his secrets for very long.

And that had left Maddux with only one alternative: murdering Savoy. He couldn't risk being identified as that person of interest and putting all of RCS—and himself—at risk.

Certain individuals at the CIA might understand and agree with Maddux's plan of causing a domestic disaster in order to scare the president and Congress into giving America's intelligence community greater powers. Those individuals might agree with the strategy, but they couldn't risk actually being involved in that scenario. It was far too risky for them personally, so they would have stopped the *Pegasus* from plowing into Virginia Beach.

Well, the CIA wasn't getting anything out of Savoy now. And, importantly, the man who would replace Savoy at the Department of Energy was an individual Maddux knew and trusted. A man who believed in everything Maddux and RCS were doing to protect the country. The fact that the *Pegasus* was heading for Virginia Beach instead of Savannah would remain a secret for a few more days. And that would be all the time Maddux needed. The crew would sail the ship right up onto the beach and then blow it up. The resulting fireball would probably kill half a million people in the Virginia Beach/Norfolk metropolitan area, wound another half a million, and scare the hell out of the rest of the country.

Liberal bastards like David Dorn who believed the United States needed to be a kinder, gentler nation would be ignored, laughed at, and scorned again—like they had been right after 9/11. Homeland security would once again become a top priority for the nation, and there would be no more discussions of doing away with critical groups like Red Cell Seven. Widespread wire-tapping, torture, and domestic spying would be available to those groups…again. The liberals would be sent packing and the neo-cons would rule the landscape…again.

Americans were becoming apathetic about security at home, Maddux believed. It had been more than a decade since 9/11, and people had forgotten how awful that attack had been. They needed to be reminded to keep the country strong. One way or another, Maddux was going to remind them. And keep remind-ing them.

A terrorist group in Syria would claim responsibility for the attack, and that was fine. Let the militant idiots shoot their guns off in the air on TV newscasts and grunt and cheer like the ani-mals they were. Let them think they'd won a glorious victory, and let their arrogance and their stupidity cause their demise. In the end, the attack by the *Pegasus* would only make the United States much stronger.

He grimaced. He didn't want to kill all those people in Virginia, but sometimes innocents had to be sacrificed. Sometimes indi-viduals had to die so the rest of the country could survive. This was one of those times.

"Sir?"

Maddux looked up. "Yes, Ryan?"

"I want you to know something."

"What?"

"I am loyal to you, sir," O'Hara said. "One hundred percent loyal." He motioned at Savoy's body, which was hanging almost still now. "I have no idea what just happened in here, but I won't ask any questions. I'll do whatever it takes to protect this country. I believe that you know what you're doing, and that you're doing the right thing."

For the first time in a long time, Maddux felt himself choking up. Ryan O'Hara was one of the finest Americans ever minted.

Fortunately for Maddux his cell phone rang, and he gestured for O'Hara to leave.

"Hello." He cleared his throat several times. "Hello," he said more firmly this time. No incoming number had appeared on the phone's tiny screen, but only a few people had this number, and they wouldn't call unless the issue was vitally important. "Who is this?"

"You all right?"

"I'm fine." It was Captain Sage Mitchell. Maddux recognized the voice immediately. "What do you want?"

"Do you know who this is?"

"Of course I know. *What do you want?*"

"We may have a problem."

Maddux checked the door to make certain O'Hara had closed it all the way. "What do you mean?" He could feel his chest tightening. He didn't like the tone he was picking up in Sage's voice.

"That excess ballast we tossed over the side a few days ago may not have gone to the bottom after all."

Maddux froze. "*What?*"

"One of my friends may have helped the ballast."

"*Christ! Why?*"

"The ballast had saved my friend's life right before that."

"You've got to be kidding me."

"No," Sage said dejectedly, "I'm not."

This could spell disaster in capital letters, Maddux realized. This could blow everything sky-high.

Because Troy Jensen had discovered that Maddux was planning to assassinate President Dorn. Because Troy had figured out that the *Olympian* was headed for Boston not to unload its cargo but to detonate it—and that Maddux was facilitating the ship's entry into Boston Harbor. And because Troy had discovered that Maddux executed American citizens who'd dodged justice on a technicality or were suspected of committing treason but hadn't been found guilty yet. Troy had dug up all of those skeletons and was about to go outside the chain of command to report what he'd found. Fortunately, they'd short-circuited Troy in Mexico.

Or maybe they hadn't.

If Troy was still alive, he and Carlson had a *huge* problem on their hands. The man in Mexico who'd met with Troy after the bullfight had taken copious mental notes. Troy hadn't been bluffing about what he knew.

"I'm having a conversation with the friend who might have helped the ballast when he gets back here later," Captain Sage explained.

Maddux was so angry he could barely contain himself. "You listen to me, and you listen to me good," he hissed. "As soon as you finish talking to him you call me and tell me what he said. Find out what you need to find out and use any methods you have to use to get answers. We *must* know what we're facing. Everything depends on it. You understand me?"

"I understand."

"I don't want to have to cut you off," Maddux warned tersely. "You wouldn't like the consequences."

"I'm sure," Sage agreed in a low voice. "At least I called to tell you what was happening."

As he should have, Maddux thought to himself. There wasn't anything heroic in making this call. "One more thing," Maddux said before Sage could disconnect.

"Yeah?"

"Any chance that ballast you threw over the side last year might have survived too?"

Captain Sage hesitated. "You mean—"

"Yeah, that's exactly who I mean."

No," Sage answered confidently. "I don't think so."

"Did that ballast ever wash up anywhere? Did anyone ever find it?"

Sage hesitated again. "Not that I know of."

Still, Maddux figured the chances that Charlie Banks had survived were minimal. They would have heard something by now. But you never knew. If this life had taught him anything it was that you could never count on something without absolute proof. Even then, you couldn't be a hundred percent sure.

Maddux took a deep breath. Suddenly he wasn't feeling very well. "Call me as soon as you know something," he ordered.

"I will," Sage promised.

"Out."

Maddux gazed at John Savoy's dead body as he ended the call. For some reason Savoy reminded him of the bully he'd killed when he was fourteen years old. He'd shot the kid with one of his father's pistols. Then he'd buried the body in the woods. Murdering the kid hadn't bothered him at all, not one bit.

In fact, he'd enjoyed watching the life ebb out of the kid as the son of a bitch had gasped for help from the ground with a bullet hole in his heart. He'd enjoyed watching the search for the kid's never-to-be-found body from the front-row seats too.

The only killing Maddux had ever regretted had occurred the other night, a few miles from here. He'd managed to turn the tables on the man who'd surprised him coming out of the kitchen in the brick house and break the man's neck, the man who was helping the Chinese. But not before his wife had come screaming down the stairs.

He'd been forced to kill her too, and he was sorry about that. But sometimes innocents had to die for the good of the whole. That had been one of those times.

As he gazed at Savoy's body, Maddux realized that he might need to go to Alaska—which meant that Ryan O'Hara would have to kill David Dorn.

CHAPTER 27

"I'M REALLY sorry," Karen murmured.

"Are you always going to think the worst of me?" Jack asked, trying to sound offended even though he wasn't at all. "Is that how ·it's going to be?" He gave her his best hurt-puppy-dog expression. "I try to give you a compliment about how nice you are and that's what I get?"

"I said I was sorry. OK?"

"OK, I guess." A sly grin slowly replaced Jack's sad expression. "Of course, the arrest would be even nicer if you were wearing a tight white blouse, a blue miniskirt, stiletto heels, and—"

"*I knew it*," she snapped, recovering from her momentary shock at his answer. "Sex is *all* you guys think about," she muttered with a disgusted groan.

"No, it's not." He'd spotted the flash of a grin tucked into the left corner of her mouth. She was trying to make him think she was angry, but she wasn't really. She knew he was kidding. "We have one or two thoughts a day that don't involve sex."

"At least you can admit it."

"I'm actually better than most guys. Some days I have three or four thoughts about other things."

"Whatever." She gave him a quick talk-to-the-hand wave along with a little neck jive. "Like I said, at least you can admit it."

"I'm sorry, but I couldn't resist. I'm just kidding."

She raised an eyebrow. "Are you?"

He hesitated. "Do you want me to be?"

"Not telling. You'll have to find out."

She was cool. She could take it as well as she gave it. He liked that.

As they made it to the top of a steep hill, the Blue Ridge Mountains appeared in the distance. "So, why'd you decide to be a cop?" he asked as he admired the view.

"I grew up in a house full of men," she answered as she gazed at the mountains too. "My mom died when I was little, and I'm the youngest of five. I have four older brothers."

Jack whistled. "Wow, four older brothers. And I'm sorry about your mom. But what does that have to do with—"

"My dad's a cop, and three of my older brothers went into law enforcement," she explained. "I wanted my dad's attention when I was growing up, but it was tough to get with all those boys running around doing crazy guy things he could relate to. Being a cop seemed like the best way to get that attention in the end. I mean, he didn't care that in high school I was a cheerleader or captain of the dance team. But that wasn't his fault," she added quickly. "Mom died real suddenly, and Dad wasn't ready to be a daughter's father when she did. He didn't know how to raise a girl or appreciate her. So I had to be the fifth son, I had to do something he didn't expect. You should have seen him when I graduated from the academy," she said, shaking her head nostalgically. "He couldn't believe it. It's the only time I ever saw him cry."

"That's nice," Jack said, thinking about how much he'd always craved Bill's attention as a kid. But it seemed like nothing he did ever topped Troy's achievements. And it wasn't Troy's fault. It wasn't like Troy was trying to excel. He was just that good at everything. "He must have been really proud of you."

The image of Bill crying in his office yesterday drifted through Jack's mind. That was the only time he'd ever seen Bill break down. At least Karen's father had been crying tears of joy.

"He was proud," she said quietly, "for a while, anyway."

"What happened?"

"I resigned a year ago."

Jack appreciated that Karen wasn't dodging his questions. This had to be a sore subject for her, but she wasn't shying away from it. It was another sign that she felt comfortable with him. "You mind telling me why?" he asked gently. He didn't want to push too hard.

She inhaled and exhaled deliberately.

As if she had to gather herself to answer this.

"It was a really rough time for me," she began. "I'd just gotten back from Alaska, from trying to find out about Charlie. I've never been so depressed in my life." She shook her head. "That's when it happened."

"What?"

She took another deep breath. "So I'm on patrol with my partner in the prowler the second night back, and we get a call about a robbery in progress at a store in East Baltimore. It's like four in the morning, and we're the third car to respond. By the time we get there, three other officers are already interrogating this guy. One of the first two cops to get there was shot and killed, and the unsub got away." Karen closed her eyes tightly for a few seconds. "The cop who was shot is facedown in a pool of blood in the alley behind the store, and the other three cops are going after this guy who they claim is the unsub's accomplice. I mean they're *really* going after him. They have him jacked up against a brick wall, and they're beating the hell out of him with their nightsticks." She shut her eyes again. "They're beating him in the arms and legs, you know? Nothing deadly, but I know it's still hurting like hell. I mean, he's screaming bloody murder."

Jack could tell by her expression that though it had been a year, the scene was still incredibly vivid for her.

"They start beating this guy in the chest and back when they can't get what they want out of him. He's begging them to stop, and they yell at him that all he has to do is tell them who the other guy is."

Jack winced as he imagined the attack. It must have been horrible to watch.

"The guy finally gets down on the ground, but they don't stop. In fact, it's the worst thing he could do because now they start hitting him in the head." Karen put a hand to her mouth. "I try to help him, I try to get to him, but my partner holds me back. I mean he literally holds my arms behind my back and won't let me go. He's a big guy and I can't break away. I can't do anything." She swallowed hard. "Then the guy goes still," she whispered. "One second he's screaming and yelling and begging for mercy, and the next second he isn't doing anything even as they keep beating him."

"Was he dead?" Jack asked in a low voice.

"Yeah, they'd literally bashed his skull in. I could see his brain."

"Jesus." Jack could taste the bile in his throat. "What happened after that?"

"They dump his body in the harbor," Karen answered. "Then they tell me and my partner if we ever say anything to anyone we'll be in trouble. They say they'll kill us, and they actually use the word *kill*. And let me tell you, we believed them," she said, nodding with her eyes wide open. "They were crazy. They were all guys who'd been around for a while, and they didn't operate by anyone's rules, especially when one of their own was killed. It was nuts. My partner and I even talked about how those guys had crazy reputations inside the department as we were going to the scene. But we never thought it would be that bad."

"Wow," Jack said quietly when she was finished. "I guess I was wrong. I guess the cops on your force aren't trained very well either."

"No, no." She spoke up firmly. "Most of the officers on the Baltimore force are good people. They're fair and honest and they're doing their best to protect law-abiding citizens. This was just a bad crew. My partner was a good guy, but he didn't want to screw with these guys either." She shrugged. "I couldn't blame him."

"So, you resigned?" Jack asked.

"Two hours later, and maybe I was wrong," she admitted, looking off through the passenger side window. "Maybe I should have fought those guys."

"Doesn't sound like it, Karen. Sounds like you would have ended up in the Baltimore Harbor along with the other guy. Your partner too."

She sighed. "I don't know."

"Did you tell your dad why you quit?"

"No, I made up some crap about burning out even though it had only been a year. I could see how disappointed he was and how he thought I was a quitter. But I couldn't tell him the real reason I ditched. He was old school all the way. Cops were never wrong as far as he was concerned, no matter what they did. And you *never* outed one of your own under any circumstances. It was an unwritten rule written in stone, and anyone who broke the rule had it coming. That was how he and his friends saw it, anyway. He told me that right before I graduated from the academy.

He would have told me I was dead wrong if I'd snitched on those guys."

"You wouldn't have been wrong," Jack said firmly. "Cops can't be allowed to do things like that. It's ridiculous. Today it's a killer's partner, but tomorrow it's somebody who happens to be in the wrong place at the wrong time. Maybe it's you or me. Citizens have to be protected, even if they end up being guilty. We have to let the system work. Everyone has rights for a reason. Even people who we think are guilty of terrible crimes have rights. I know some people think that's bullshit, but it's the only way." He paused. "And there's no excuse for torturing anyone, like those cops were doing to that guy. I'm sorry, but I can't accept allowing torture for any reason."

"I agree," she said somberly. "You couldn't be more right. And it sounds like you've said it before."

So she'd picked up on that. "Why?"

"It sounded like a sermon. One you've been preaching for a while."

"Well, I guess I—"

"Don't get me wrong. I appreciate it."

"Oh?" Something in her voice told him to press. "What do you mean?"

"Well, it turned out the guy those cops beat to death was innocent. He was a homeless guy, and it was exactly like you said. He was just in the wrong place at the wrong time. He had no idea who shot the cop. He was passed out when the gun went off."

"Oh, Christ."

"Awful, right?"

"But how do you know? I thought you said everything got swept under the carpet."

"A week after it happened, my partner was in the locker room after his shift and he overheard a couple of other cops talking about how this homeless guy they used to help out had disappeared. I guess they gave him food and stuff when they were on the beat because he was a nice guy and they felt sorry for him. And because he was helpful when it came to telling them what was happening on the streets. You know, he gave them inside stuff on who was dealing drugs, who was pimping girls, who was running the numbers. Stuff like that. Well, this guy had a big scar over his left eye in the shape of a hook." Karen bit her lower lip as she glanced down into her lap. "The guy they beat to death had a scar in the shape of a hook over his left eye. I'll never forget it as long as I live. I'll never forget looking at it as he begged them to stop beating him." She let out a long breath. "My partner and I had lunch a few weeks after I quit, and he told me what he'd heard in the locker room. I tried to convince him that we should do something, but he was still completely against it. He was still worried about what could happen to us if we did."

"And he was right," Jack agreed quietly, although he couldn't help feeling a tiny seed of doubt about what she *hadn't* done. The weak needed the strong, and sometimes the strong had to be crazy brave if the weak were going to get a fair shake. "He was right," Jack repeated, more firmly this time as he thought about it again. Maybe it wasn't fair for him to judge Karen that way. It would have been a terrifying situation, and there was no way for him to really understand it without experiencing it himself. Maybe she wouldn't be sitting here next to him in the car if she had tried to do something.

Karen looked over, and they stared at each other for several moments before his eyes finally flashed back to the road.

"Why did those guys show up out of nowhere last night and start shooting at us?" she asked. "They didn't even try to arrest us first. I mean, I don't know what they would have arrested us for, but my point is that they tried to kill us without even talking to us. Why?"

The same thing had been bothering Jack, but he didn't want to get into it with her. "If you aren't a cop anymore, Karen, why do you still carry a gun?"

"Don't ignore me, Jack. Answer *my* question first."

He'd been afraid of that. She didn't seem like the type who'd let something slide. "I was going to ask you the same thing, Karen. Why did those guys show up out of nowhere?"

"Come on, Jack!"

"Why's it my fault all of a sudden?" He glanced over and saw those dark eyes flashing angrily at him. "Maybe it was those cops coming after you. Maybe they heard you were talking to the higher-ups in the department."

"No way. I haven't gone anywhere near anyone in the Baltimore Police Department since I had that lunch with my ex-partner. That was almost a year ago."

"Well, you told me you were being watched. Maybe it was those guys who showed up at your door asking questions."

"No way. Look, you show up at the restaurant out of nowhere. You call me by my name even though I don't have a name tag on and I haven't told you what my name is. You chase me like a maniac—"

"I get it, Karen," he acknowledged stiffly, "but that doesn't mean I—"

"*And right after you catch up to me,*" she interrupted right back, "two guys jump out of a black Escalade and start shooting. Call me crazy, but I think there's a *direct* connection between you running me down and those guys showing up with their guns on fire."

As far as Jack knew, only three people in the world—Bill, Cheryl, and Karen—knew he was going to Alaska. What bothered him so much about Cheryl knowing was that she seemed so frightened of Bill finding out that she'd come to the apartment the other night to give him the cash. Jack had never seen her so scared.

And, apparently, Bill was involved with Red Cell Seven—as Troy and Charlie had been. Maybe for most people the way three men were standing in a few photographs wouldn't be proof positive of their co-involvement in a covert government intelligence operation. But it was enough for Jack.

As he gazed across the Maryland landscape, he thought about that white van barreling down Broadway through a red light. The near miss had happened only minutes after he'd left Bill's office, and Bill had been so completely against him going to Alaska. It seemed too coincidental.

And it still made no sense to him that Bill had accepted Troy's death so passively. The old man had clearly been devastated by what had happened, but he hadn't shown any interest at all in getting the details of Troy's death or questioning the captain's account of the accident. Some months the old man didn't accept his residential electric bill at face value, for Christ's sake.

Jack shook his head. He just hoped the answers to those questions were waiting for them in Alaska. Along with what had really happened to Troy.

"Talk to me, Jack," Karen said. "Why do you think those guys showed up when they did? And why were they so hell-bent on killing us?"

It was a clear, crisp morning, and everything in front of them was bathed in bright sunshine. They were only a few miles from the mountains now, and as Jack stared at the peaks he knew he had to tell her everything. What lay ahead could end up being even more dangerous than what had already happened, so he had to treat her like a true partner. After all, he was the one who'd asked her to come with him.

"My father's name is Bill Jensen," he told her. "He runs one of the biggest banks in this country."

"First Manhattan," she said. "It's huge. I know."

Jack nodded, impressed. "How?"

"Troy told Charlie and Charlie told me. Troy and Charlie told each other a lot. More than they were supposed to, I guess. He told Charlie a lot about your family. Not just that you were his brother."

"Oh."

"They were really good friends."

It was silly, but Jack was starting to feel a little jealous. "Troy never mentioned Charlie to me."

"I'm sure Troy never mentioned Charlie or Red Cell Seven to anyone outside RCS."

"Charlie mentioned it to you."

"I was Charlie's fiancée."

"Yeah, but—"

"Charlie and I told each other everything, and I mean *every-thing*." She reached over and put her hand on his arm. "He knew I'd never say a word to anyone. While he was alive," she added softly.

Jack winced. Charlie's death kept coming up. "Still, I think Troy would have—"

"Have you ever been engaged, Jack?"

"No."

"Then you can't understand."

Jack glanced over at her and nodded slowly. "I guess."

"It's just different."

He didn't want to push this. He was tired of making her sad. "OK." He could see she knew what he was thinking.

"According to Charlie," Karen said after a few moments, "Falcons aren't supposed to tell each other about their personal lives. But Troy told Charlie about your dad and how he ran First Manhattan. Troy never said as much because he seemed like a modest guy, but it was obvious to Charlie and me that your family's really well off." She paused and gave him a warning look. "I'm working class all the way, Jack, and I'm not trying to be rude, but I've never had much luck with rich people. I hate arrogance more than I hate anything else in life, and it seems to me like a lot of rich people are really arrogant."

"Am I arrogant?" he asked directly.

He'd never asked out that blonde on the trading floor because he hadn't wanted her finding out that he wasn't really a Jensen and then dumping him for it. Not that he thought she was that kind of person, he just hadn't wanted to take the chance. So he understood exactly where Karen was coming from.

Of course, now he knew he was a Jensen—halfway, at least. But he was still sensitive about that other half being an outsider.

"No," she said quietly. "But I haven't known you for very long."

"I'm not like that."

"We'll see, I guess."

"You just said Troy was a modest guy," Jack pointed out.

"I said he seemed to be. I didn't know him that well."

"Look, I didn't tell you about my father to impress you," Jack said. "I told you about him to warn you."

Her eyes raced to his. "Why?"

He could tell he'd gotten a hundred percent of her attention in that instant. "I think Bill's involved with Red Cell Seven too."

Her mouth fell slowly open. "Really?"

Jack nodded down at her purse. "Take a look at that picture of Charlie you showed me last night."

"Why?"

"Just do it, will you?"

She pulled it from her purse and held it up. "So?"

"Look at the way Charlie's holding his hands with his thumbs tucked into his belt."

"So?"

"Count the number of fingers he has pointing at the ground."
He could hear her whispering to herself as she counted. "Seven,
right?"

"Yeah," she agreed, nodding at him excitedly as she turned to
face him. "Seven. My God."

He could see the recognition in her eyes. She understood
exactly what he was saying, what seven fingers pointing at the
ground meant. "I've seen pictures of Troy standing exactly the
same way," Jack explained. "Like the one my mother used for his
memorial service." He hesitated for a moment as he replayed the
sound of himself saying "my mother." He'd said it so many times
over the years, but it meant so much more now. "He was standing
in front of the *Arctic Fire* right before she sailed a few weeks ago,
and in it he was standing just like Charlie's standing in this one."

"So you think that's how you can tell someone's a Falcon." She
glanced back down at Charlie's image. "But why would they risk
people finding out?"

"Secret groups always do things like that. I could show you
plenty of examples in history of hush-hush groups giving clues to
what's really going on. The cold, hard truth is that almost no one
in the world can really keep a secret."

Karen nodded. "Isn't that the damn truth?"

"Here's the really interesting thing," Jack continued. "While I
was in my father's office the other day down on Wall Street waiting
for him, I was looking at a couple of pictures on his credenza. In
one of them he was standing next to a guy and he had his thumbs
hooked into his belt the same way with seven fingers pointing
down." He didn't tell her that the guy beside Bill in the photo was
the governor of New York because he didn't want her jumping to
any conclusions about the governor.

Karen's eyes opened wide. "You think Bill Jensen is a Falcon?"
A puzzled expression clouded her face. "But Falcons are all young
and athletic because they go crazy places and do crazy things. At

least, that's what Charlie told me. And they try to be as anonymous as they can be." She shook her head. "Your dad's the chief executive of one of the biggest banks in this country. He's not a rock star or a star athlete, but he's still pretty well known. It would be hard for him to move around without being identified. Not to mention the fact that he's got to be in his sixties, right?"

"When I told him I was going to Alaska, he freaked out, and he never freaks out. He told me to stay away from there in no uncertain terms. He basically told me he'd do anything to keep me away from there. I've never seen him react like that before in my life. It was weird."

Karen's eyes opened even wider. "You think your father sent those men to kill us last night?" she asked incredulously. "Is that what you're saying?"

Karen didn't understand the dynamic. She couldn't; she'd never even met him. Bill was a fanatic when it came to the United States. He would literally do anything to protect it. Maybe even not pursue what had really happened to Troy because pursuing the truth about Troy might compromise some bigger picture he was unfailingly loyal to—as incredibly coldhearted as that sounded for a father.

And maybe Bill had always hated having someone living in his house who was someone else's son. Maybe Cheryl's out-of-wedlock kid had always been a terrible right-in-the-face reminder to Bill all these years that Cheryl had been intimate with another man. And having those guys shoot him last night would have been an excellent way to erase that awful reminder without Cheryl knowing who was behind the killing. It sounded so cold, but Bill could be a cold man.

"A week after he'd lost his younger son?" she asked.

"Yeah, I know how it sounds," Jack said dismissively, trying to act like what he'd implied was probably stupid, even though he didn't really think it was. He just didn't want to dwell on it right now. "I'm just trying to come up with some kind of explanation for what happened. Hey, you asked." He watched her slide the picture of Charlie back in her wallet. "So, why do you still carry a gun, Karen?"

"It's my old revolver from the force. I never handed it in, and they never asked for it back."

"But why do you still carry it on you? I mean, you're a waitress."

"Thanks for reminding me."

"Hey, that little bite of crab cake I got was awesome, and the place has a great reputation. But I'm sure you still get some complaints." He chuckled. "Do you really need to pull a gun when customers bitch?"

"Very funny."

"It certainly brings new meaning to the term 'dealing with customer complaints.'"

"Whatever. Look, like I told you, awhile ago I got a visit from a couple of guys who wouldn't tell me who they were or what they did. They asked me some really weird questions about Charlie."

"Like what?"

She hesitated. "Like if he'd tried to contact me recently."

"But he was…" Jack's voice trailed off. There it was again—Charlie's death.

"I told them he was dead, but they kept asking me. Finally, they left. A week later they showed up again at my door asking the same questions. But they were a lot more aggressive about it that time. After that, I started carrying my gun wherever I went."

"So then maybe that's why those guys showed up last—"

Karen sobbed out of nowhere, and it caught Jack by surprise. Tears were suddenly streaming down her cheeks.

"What's wrong?"

She tried to wipe the tears away, but they kept coming. "I was just thinking about Mick getting killed. He was just trying to help me."

The bullet had smashed into the back of Mick's head and out his eye. She'd been lucky not to have been hit by it herself, but she hadn't mentioned anything about him last night at the hotel or so far this morning.

"It's my fault he's dead," she whispered.

"It is *not* your fault," Jack said quickly and firmly. "Not at all."

"I feel so bad for him."

She was sobbing hard, and he reached over and took her hand. It was still early in their relationship, but he couldn't help himself. He couldn't stand seeing a woman cry like that. Especially one he was starting to care about so much. "I'm sorry. I really am."

"Thanks."

He started to pull his hand away, but she squeezed his fingers tightly and wouldn't let go.

CHAPTER 28

CARLSON HAD answered Stein's anxious telephone call at exactly seven o'clock this morning, as he was making sure to savor every delicious bite of the breakfast Nancy had made for him.

To reach him so directly, Carlson knew, Stein had used a cell number that had been subtly slipped to him at his first national security briefing—the one that had occurred in Langley, Virginia, a few weeks after Dorn's landslide victory.

On the call this morning, Stein had mentioned only that he wanted to place a bet on a horse named Big Blue. In response to the strange request, Carlson had given Stein odds of Big Blue winning, placing, and showing in the seventh race at Belmont Park that afternoon. Except they were the wrong odds, they weren't even close. A horse named Big Blue was actually running in that race, but the numbers Carlson had reeled off had a vastly different purpose than handicapping a horse race.

Immediately after giving Stein the numbers, Carlson had hung up. There was no need to say anything more, and Carlson wanted to finish his breakfast while it was warm. He hated cold food because he'd been forced to eat it that way so many times during his career thanks to inopportune phone calls like Stein's and being stuck in remote places where hot food wasn't even available.

While finishing the last few bites of the three-egg bacon and cheddar omelet, Carlson thought about how Stein was probably already staring intently at a laminated sheet of paper he'd also received at that same security briefing in Langley. By matching the numbers Carlson had given him on the call to specific columns and rows on the sheet of paper, Stein would be able to determine the location and time of the meeting. Carlson just prayed that Stein took his time with the calculations. He put his dishes in the sink for Nancy to wash. He didn't want to wait around. His time was too valuable—especially now that he'd seen the doctor again.

Fortunately, Stein had calculated everything correctly and arrived in Reston seven minutes ago, which was seven minutes early. Carlson was favorably impressed—so far. The only thing marring their first-ever face-to-face meeting was that Stein worked for David Dorn. Unfortunately, nothing could make up for that.

"Thanks for seeing me so quickly, Roger," Stein began politely after they'd shaken hands and were sitting down facing each other.

To Carlson's almost immeasurable satisfaction, Stein was acting low-key and deferential this afternoon, almost apologetic in his tone and manner.

"No problem, Rex," Carlson answered. They were meeting in the same room in which he'd given Maddux permission to kill that child molester. Stein had entered a house down the street and then followed one of Carlson's associates through a maze of underground passages to this house. "What's on your mind?" Carlson was confident he knew what was on Stein's mind. It was how the chief of staff presented his agenda that would be the interesting part of this meeting. "How can I help you?"

Stein adjusted his bow tie before answering. "First of all, Roger, let me tell you how impressed I am and, as a citizen of this country, how much I appreciate all you've done during your career to protect the United States. I'd heard rumors about it for a long time, of course. But I really had no idea what the amazing scope of your contribution to national security was until that first CIA meeting at Langley after the election."

It sounded so scripted, but that was all right with Carlson. Stein was starting off by kissing the ring—slurping on it, really— which meant that his assumption about Stein's agenda was exactly right. "So how can I help you?" Carlson asked a second time after nodding politely.

Stein grinned painfully, as if he wished he didn't have to answer the question. "My boss, the president of the United States, was," he hesitated for a moment as he searched for the most appropriate word, "shall we say, well, *emboldened* by his margin of victory in the national election a year ago."

The formality of Stein's delivery told Carlson that even though Stein was a consummate Washington insider, he'd never dealt with the guys in the longest, darkest shadows of the intelligence world. That gave Carlson a huge advantage in this meeting.

"Unfortunately," Stein continued, "and I say this delicately and with all due respect, President Dorn still feels the same way. Emboldened, I mean. He basically believed that his landslide victory gave him a mandate to do pretty much whatever he wanted. And he still does, Roger," Stein added after a short pause. "I've tried to steer him away from situations where he might have gotten ahead of himself and acted more like a bull in a china shop than a polished politician. I think I've been successful for the most part in doing that, and I think the Democratic Party appreciates that I have." Stein took a deep, obviously frustrated breath. "The problem comes when—" Stein interrupted himself. "*Problem* isn't a good word in this instance. What I really should have said was that—"

"For Christ's sake, Rex, leave the fucking bullshit back at the barn." Carlson could tell he'd shocked Stein with his outburst and instantly put him off his game. The guy looked like he'd just seen a ghost. Maybe he was supposed to be a ballbuster in the West Wing, but he was out of his element here. He wasn't just groping for words. He was groping for his way. "Say what you have to say. I don't have the time or the inclination to listen to all this crap. Be blunt, man."

Stein's expression turned into one of steely resolve. "Daniel Beckham met with you without my approval. I didn't see the asset list he presented you with before he presented it to you. A man in your position might get the wrong impression after seeing that list. The second I saw it, well, that was my reaction." Stein rolled his eyes. "I should say, when I *finally* saw it."

Carlson masked his grave disappointment. Without realizing it, Stein had just confirmed everything. President Dorn definitely intended to destroy Red Cell Seven. The simple fact that Beckham had been allowed to leave the White House without first showing *that* list to the president's chief of staff confirmed everything Shane Maddux and his Falcons had heard.

The president had no chance now. Carlson might have been able to stop the attack before…but not now. The assassination was a full-ahead go, and the president was a dead man. Now it was just a question of when and where the shooting would occur.

"Spin that all the way out for me, Rex," Carlson said calmly. "What are you saying?"

"You know exactly what I'm saying, Roger. I'm saying that President Dorn shouldn't have let Beckham show you that list. It was a goddamned huge mistake." Stein put his hands up and out as a clear indication of diplomacy and contrition. "And the president understands that. I promise you he does."

Bullshit, Carlson thought to himself. Bull *fucking* shit. "I'm glad to hear you say that, Rex, because, to be honest, I was concerned when I saw that list. *Very* concerned."

"You don't need to be anymore, Roger," Stein said quickly. He shook his head hard. "Sometimes the president acts too quickly. As I said before, for the most part I've been able to corral that impulse before it was too late." He exhaled heavily. "But not in this case." Stein glanced over at Carlson. "I'm sorry about all of that. But I'm glad we've been able to clear it all up before things got out of hand. Maybe the good in the bad is that you and I finally met face-to-face after hearing about each other for so many years."

Carlson didn't like Stein alluding to clearing things up before things got out of hand. It could mean that Stein understood exactly how dire the situation was for his boss. And if he could convince the president how dire the situation was, he might even be able to convince Dorn and the Secret Service to be more careful than usual for a while. So careful that Maddux might not be able to get his people in position for the all-important kill shot, which needed to happen sooner rather than later.

"Unfortunately," Stein kept going, "President Dorn still doesn't appreciate all that you do and how valuable you are. He says he does, but he doesn't. However, I guarantee you he will." He chuckled like what he was about to say was going to sound absolutely ludicrous. "He's got some pretty crazy notions about what you people do on the side, Roger. I mean, he must be reading some version of the left-wing handbook I've never read. It must be the Vermont version. They're pretty fanatical up there."

"What kind of crazy notions are you talking about, Rex?"

"He thinks you're running around the country carrying out vigilante justice. He thinks you're killing criminals who got off on technicalities. He thinks you're torturing American citizens to get information about the activities of others. He basically thinks you've become Big Brother or something. It's all a massive misunderstanding, Roger. I'm taking care of it, I promise."

Carlson laughed sincerely even though he wasn't being sincere at all. He'd learned a long time ago how important it was to do that. "We protect American citizens."

"Of course you do. And he knows that," Stein assured Carlson. "He just needs a little more time and some more of my coaching."

"Maybe you can do me a favor, Rex. I'd certainly appreciate it if you would."

Stein's eyes ran straight to Carlson's. "Of course. What do you need? Name it."

This had been bothering Carlson ever since the president had mentioned it at the end of their last meeting. "Your boss asked me about an individual when he and I last met at the White House. He said there had been an inquiry about him. The individual's name was Troy Jensen. Can you find out where that inquiry came from and let me know? I sure would appreciate it."

Stein nodded. "I'll get you a name as soon as I can, Roger."

* * *

The leader gazed out from the bridge over the five huge refrigerated holds of the massive LNG tanker *Pegasus*. Inside those five holds with the domed tops were two hundred thousand cubic meters of liquefied natural gas. The fireball this ship could instantaneously release would dwarf the explosive power of the *Olympian*, which had somehow failed to destroy Boston. They were still trying to figure out exactly what had happened there. No one at home had yet been able to contact the leader of that ship—or any of the other men who'd been on it.

He picked up his binoculars and scanned the afternoon sky. They were heading toward the Virginia Beach-Norfolk area of Virginia, not, as they were supposed to be, toward the Elba Island regasification facility that was just downriver from Savannah, Georgia. The clandestine change of direction was on the orders of the same man who'd secured the *Olympian* her documentation to sail into Boston Harbor. A man who seemed bent on assisting their group's goal of destroying an American city with a huge fireball from an LNG tanker.

The beauty of this attack plan was that the Norfolk-Virginia Beach metropolitan area had a population of almost two million people, the ship wouldn't be subject to any inspections, and he wouldn't need to present any documentation in order to reach a point near enough to shore to cause incredible damage to that population and its property. It wouldn't be quite as devastating to the United States as the obliteration of Boston, but the destruction it caused would still be made with an exclamation point. Especially because one of America's largest naval bases was in Norfolk.

The trouble with this attack plan was that US officials monitored the movement of all LNG tankers that had their bows aimed at American shores. There was a regasification facility farther up the Chesapeake Bay beyond Virginia Beach and Norfolk called Dominion Point Cove, so those officials wouldn't be surprised by an LNG tanker heading in that direction. Many did. The problem would come when they tried to figure out why the *Pegasus* was heading for Norfolk when it was supposed to be heading for Savannah.

United States military planes ran reconnaissance missions to monitor the progress of LNG ships headed for her shores. And, the leader realized ruefully, those planes would probably be on high alert after the US had intercepted the *Olympian*, which it somehow must have done. So if those planes sighted the *Pegasus* headed in the wrong direction, she would be boarded or blown up before she could get close enough to annihilate the Virginia Beach-Norfolk metro area.

But the man in the United States who they'd been working with claimed he had that covered. He claimed he was giving naval operations in Norfolk wrong information so the *Pegasus* could get close enough to complete her mission. So those planes wouldn't be looking for an LNG tanker heading for the mid-Atlantic and wouldn't have her coordinates. So they could literally drive the ship's bow right up onto the sandy beach, blow her up, and incinerate half a million people.

Maybe more.

CHAPTER 29

"THANKS FOR buying me this coat back in Baltimore." Karen pulled the heavy down jacket tightly around her slim body. "It's *freezing* out here."

"Yeah, it said eleven degrees in the car back at the gas station."

"And it's only December. How do people stand it here?"

Jack glanced over at Karen through his crystallizing exhalation. Her black hair was cascading down onto her shoulders in shimmering waves, she'd done her makeup just right, and she was wearing a cool pair of wraparound sunglasses. She looked more like a movie star who should have been walking down the streets of Vail, Colorado, with an entourage than an ex-cop stuck in the frozen northland with a crazy bond trader. But she wasn't complaining.

Despite being thrown together so intimately so quickly and coming from such different backgrounds, he and Karen were getting along great. They'd driven over a thousand miles since yesterday morning, but the time had gone quickly for both of them. She'd told him that very directly as they'd crossed into Illinois last night. And he'd agreed immediately. They'd laughed and joked, and in no time, it seemed, they were driving past downtown Minneapolis at midnight.

It had taken them another couple of hours to get up here to Bemidji, where they checked into a quiet, picturesque motel on the outskirts of town just after two a.m. Once again, Jack persuaded the man behind the desk not to take a credit card imprint. Once again, he and Karen stayed in the same room because she wanted to save him money. Once again, there were two beds in the room.

"Welcome to northern Minnesota," Jack said as he glanced around. "If you don't like cold and snow, you probably shouldn't stay long. And you definitely shouldn't live here."

The early morning sun was streaming down onto the snow-covered Upper Midwest through a cloudless blue sky. Despite the sunshine, it was brutally cold. Cold but eerily beautiful, and a place Troy probably would have loved, Jack figured.

"The guy behind the front desk at the motel was telling me that some years they grill out on Memorial Day in their coats and ski hats. On Labor Day too," he added.

"But I bet he said the summers are really nice."

Jack looked over at her in surprise. "He did say that, exactly that."

"All two weeks of them," she said grimly as she shivered.

She was exaggerating, he knew, but she probably wasn't that far off. "And I bet with all the lakes and ponds around here, the mosquitoes are terrible."

"The mosquito's the state bird, Jack. Didn't you know that?"

He chuckled softly. She was quick with those funny comments, and she had more jokes ready to go than most Wall Street traders—which was impressive. She was smart too—really smart, he was coming to find. They'd had a few intense discussions about certain highly charged areas of the world, and she'd actually changed his mind on a few things, which was also impressive. He couldn't remember the last time anyone had changed his mind about an important world issue.

* * *

"You sure you know where this box is?" he asked, nodding toward the Bankses' cabin.

The cabin was built in a small clearing not far from the shore of a large lake. The pine tree cover around the lake was dense, and anyone in the cabin would have had a difficult time seeing them even though they weren't far away. There were no cars in the small circular driveway in front of the cabin, and Jack didn't see any footprints in the three inches of snow covering the yard around the house. It didn't look like they were going to run into anyone when they went inside, but he was still worried.

"Troy's letter was very specific," she answered. "It's in the closet of the downstairs bedroom."

They'd left the rental car at a gas station out on the main road, then hiked to here along the quarter-mile driveway. They'd stayed inside the tree line the entire time to keep out of sight. It had taken a lot longer to get here than if they'd driven, but there was no way for a vehicle to get in or out other than the driveway. Jack didn't want to get trapped back here in case someone followed them in, and he wanted to approach the cabin as quietly as possible—in case it was being watched, or someone was inside.

"When did you get that letter from Troy?" he asked.

"Like a month ago, I think."

"Why would he put the box here?"

"He and Charlie hung out here. They had a pretty intense life, and this was a great place for them to get away to." She pointed through the trees at the glittering surface of the lake, which still hadn't frozen because it was too early in the season. "Charlie told me they fished a lot."

Jack didn't agree with everything Troy had been involved with, but he could still respect and appreciate most of what his brother had done to protect the nation. And he could certainly understand the need to get away from that intense life every once in a while. This would have been a great place to do it—despite the cold and the mosquitoes.

"He probably figured nobody from Red Cell Seven would ever think of looking here for anything now," she said. "Charlie's been gone a year. Why would anybody from RCS come here? I think it was a great place for Troy to hide something."

Jack glanced over at her. They hadn't talked about Charlie in a while, and he was glad to see no tears came to her eyes at another mention of his death. "All right, let's go. But keep your eyes peeled."

He had a bad feeling about this.

* * *

Speed Trap glanced up from his bowl of fish soup when he heard a pair of heavy footsteps trudging down the hallway outside the galley. They'd left Dutch Harbor two hours ago for a cod run on the Bering Sea to get bait for the opilio crab season, which was about to start. The engine hum coming from below was loud as the *Arctic Fire* churned up and down through seven-foot waves. He hadn't heard the footsteps coming toward him until they were close.

He knew something was wrong when he saw Sage's expression. "What's up?" he asked as his uncle sat down across the table.

Grant had stayed behind in the doorway—which was the only way out. "What's the matter?"

"What happened the night we threw Troy Jensen overboard?" Sage asked directly.

"What do you mean?" Speed Trap asked innocently.

Sage clenched and unclenched his jaw several times. "You know what I mean," he finally said, doing his best to keep his anger in check. "Did you throw a raft off the back of the ship to that guy?"

"No."

"He saved your life," Grant called out from the doorway. "You felt like you owed him. That's what you told me."

"Yeah, so?"

"Did you throw him a raft?" Sage demanded again. "Tell me the goddamned truth. It was dark. I wouldn't have seen it." He hesitated. "*Did you?*"

"No," Speed Trap shot back defiantly. He couldn't tell them the truth. If he did, they'd really take it out on him. If he kept denying it, they couldn't throw him overboard. Not with a clear conscience, anyway. "I didn't."

As Sage rose from the chair across the crumb-strewn table, he pulled a pistol from his coat pocket and pointed it at Speed Trap. "Get up," he ordered. "We're going out on deck."

"What the—"

"Grant," Sage called over his shoulder, "get your brother moving."

"Yes, sir."

* * *

Jack watched as Karen removed a stack of neatly folded towels from the bottom shelf of the cedar closet and placed them on the floor. Then she reached for the back of the shelf and picked up a black box the size of a thick hardcover book.

"Bingo," she whispered excitedly. "This must be it."

As Jack took a step toward her there was a loud banging on the front door. He froze as it quickly grew louder.

"Open up!" someone yelled. "Open up *now*!"

Jack hustled to the bedroom window and pulled the curtain back slightly. He couldn't see the front door from here, but he could see a police cruiser parked in the driveway. "We've gotta get out of here, Karen." They couldn't afford the time it would undoubtedly take to straighten this situation out with the cop. "Let's go!"

* * *

Carlson checked the number on his personal cell phone. It was Rex Stein calling. This wasn't the phone Stein was supposed to use in case of emergencies.

"Hello."

"Hi, it's me."

"I know who it is. What's going on?"

"I have that information you wanted."

Carlson nodded. Good for Stein. He'd followed up quickly on the request. "OK."

"Is it all right if I use names on this phone?"

Carlson nodded again. Good for Stein for asking that. He was showing respect for the man, Red Cell Seven, and the situation. Too bad it wasn't going to make a damn bit of difference as far as David Dorn's life went. He and Maddux were meeting later today to make final preparations for the assassination.

"It's all right to use names," Carlson said.

"OK, well, the person who called the president to ask about Troy Jensen was Troy's father, Bill."

Carlson was glad he hadn't been with Stein when he'd gotten this answer. He would have given away his surprise and disappointment with the shocked expression that had flashed across his face. The way he had with the same troubled expression the other day in the Oval Office.

"Are you sure?" Carlson asked calmly.

"Absolutely. One of the operators checked the incoming calls for me, and we traced the number to Bill Jensen. The call came in right before you and he met the other day."

"That doesn't necessarily mean—"

"And one of my direct reports confirmed that it was Bill Jensen who asked about Troy. President Dorn mentioned it to him."

Carlson wanted to ask another question, but Stein would quickly pick up on the obvious and might try to turn this situation to his advantage. That was politics and that was Washington, and while Stein was way out of his league in the intel world, he was a master at making hay in the marbled halls of downtown Washington.

"Did Mr. Jensen speak to the president?" Even in the silence coming from the other end of the phone, Carlson could hear Stein sensing an opportunity. "Do you know?"

"Yes, he did."

Carlson hated being in such a weak position. Thank God he rarely was. "Did you ask President Dorn about the specifics of their conversation?"

"I haven't had a chance to. I'll do that as soon as I can."

Bullshit. They'd probably spoken at length about the call. "That's all right," Carlson said quickly. "It doesn't matter."

"Troy is one of yours?" Stein wanted to know. "Is that right?"

"I hope you were being sincere during our visit yesterday," Carlson said, ignoring the question with another question and a stern warning tone.

"Uh, yes, I was. Of course I was."

"Good." That quickly he'd turned the tables back on Stein. "I'd hate to think otherwise." He paused for a moment. "Goodbye, Rex."

Carlson stared into space as he closed the cell phone and ended the call. He knew that Bill Jensen and President Dorn spoke at least once a month about the economy because, after all, Bill ran the biggest bank in the country and he was a great resource for the president to have on that subject. But Bill always alerted his old friend and RCS partner Roger Carlson that he was calling Dorn. He hadn't this time, though. This time Bill had violated their pact.

Carlson's eyes narrowed. Could Bill Jensen be putting his family in front of the country?

* * *

Jack slipped halfway through the back doorway—just as the officer moved around the corner of the cabin to the right.

"Go back," Jack whispered over his shoulder to Karen. He was pretty sure the guy hadn't seen him. "Now."

They retreated into the house, closed the door—the top half of which was a nine-pane window—and flattened themselves against either side of the kitchen wall beside the door.

"Open up in there," the officer called as he moved to the door. "I see your footprints in the snow coming across the yard. And I don't see any footprints coming back out. I know you're in there. Open up now. Give yourself up. My weapon is out and ready to fire."

Jack closed his eyes tightly. This was the last damn thing they needed right now.

* * *

"Jeeeeesus!" Speed Trap screamed as the *Arctic Fire* burst through the crest of a big wave. Salty spray went flying as the ship plunged toward the next trough. "Don't do this to me, Grant. Pleeeease!"

Grant was holding Speed Trap upside down by the ankles over the port side of the ship near where Troy had pulled him back aboard by that sliver of a yellow harness. The ship was plowing through the rough seas, and Speed Trap was absolutely terrified—almost as terrified as he'd been that day Troy had pulled him back aboard.

"Tell me the truth, Speed Trap," Captain Sage shouted down at him. "*Tell me the goddamned truth!*"

* * *

"Let him in," Karen whispered.

"Are you crazy?"

"Let him in," she repeated. "We'll talk to him."

"No way," Jack whispered back, his anger at her boiling over quickly. He was shocked that she'd do this, and suddenly the suspicious side of his brain was getting the better of him. "I'm not getting arrested. We don't have time for that. And you know that's what's going to happen if we—"

"*Open up!*" the cop yelled from outside.

"Do it," she ordered quietly. "Open the door or I will."

"Karen, you're going to ruin our chances of—"

"Do it!" she hissed. "Now."

Jack stared into her burning eyes. She wasn't backing down. That was clear. "All right, officer," he called loudly. "I'm opening it now." He stepped slowly in front of the door and pulled it back.

"Move into the kitchen slowly," the officer ordered as he aimed his revolver at Jack's chest. "Move it," he demanded, moving forward as Jack backpedaled. "Go on. But take your time."

As the officer moved past the door and into the kitchen, Karen darted out from the wall and slammed him on the back of the head with the revolver she'd whipped out of the back of her jeans. The officer tumbled limply to the tile floor as his gun crashed into the bottom of the stove.

"Jesus Christ!" Jack shouted, his suspicions gone that quickly. Now he was nothing but impressed. "What the hell?"

"Hey, we've gotta do what we've gotta do." She knelt down beside the officer to see if he was OK. "I hit him just right. No blood, just a lump. He's gonna wake up with a big headache, but other than that he'll be fine." She looked up at Jack. "He's gonna wake up tied to that chair too," she said, motioning at one of the big wooden chairs around the kitchen table.

Jack shook his head and grinned as he stared down at her. "I…I can't believe you just—"

"Go find some rope," she interrupted. "There's probably some in the garage. Hurry up!"

* * *

Maddux answered his cell phone before the second ring. "What?"

"It's me."

It was Captain Sage. "What do you have?"

"Well, we went at the friend of mine pretty hard, and he denied helping out the ballast."

"Are you sure he's telling the truth?" Something told Maddux that he needed to get to Alaska immediately. Captain Sage was a tough, tough man, but he might not have *really* put the screws to his nephew during an interrogation. "Absolutely sure?" He could already hear Sage struggling with his answer even though he hadn't said anything. Maddux's gut was telling him that Speed Trap had definitely floated Troy Jensen a raft from the back of the *Arctic Fire* that night on the Bering Sea. "I'm coming out there," Maddux said decisively, not even giving Sage a chance to answer. "If you're not in port now, get your ass back there within forty-eight hours."

* * *

"I owe you an apology," Jack said. They'd been driving in silence as they headed south from Bemidji. They were only a few miles from making it back to Interstate 94 and continuing their journey westward. He was hoping to reach Montana by late tonight. His target was Missoula.

"You thought I was going to ruin everything by trying to talk it out with that cop, didn't you?" Karen asked as a grin tugged on the corners of her mouth. "You thought I was going to tell him how I used to be a cop and all, right? You thought I was going to try and negotiate our way out of it."

"Maybe," Jack admitted as he eased off on the accelerator. He was doing ten miles over the posted limit. The last thing they needed right now was to get pulled over. "I sure as hell didn't think you were gonna nail him in the back of the head with your pistol."

She laughed. "Well, I guess you better watch out, huh? Maybe you better keep your eye on me." She opened her eyes wide and waved her fingers at him like she was putting a curse on him. "Woooo. Maybe I'm crazy."

He broke into a wide smile of his own as he watched her put her head back in the passenger seat and laugh even louder. He could feel himself falling for her. She loved life like no one he'd ever met. She wasn't scared of *anything*. And that laugh of hers was so contagious.

"I just hope that cop's all right," Karen said as her laughter faded. "I felt bad about that. The guy was just doing his job."

"He's fine. He was coming to as we left." Jack checked the rearview mirror. "I just hope he doesn't get out of there too fast, or we could be in real trouble."

Karen reached for the black box they'd taken from the cabin closet. It was on the floor by her feet. "How could we get in trouble?" she asked as she put it on her lap. "That cop has no idea what kind of car we're driving, and we'll be out of Minnesota and into North Dakota pretty soon. Then we're really fine."

"I guess," Jack agreed. "Hey, that was a pretty cool thing you did with the footprints."

As they'd moved across the yard toward the back door, Karen had followed in Jack's footsteps in the snow so it looked as if only one person had entered the house. He'd thought it was overkill at the time, and he'd needled her about it. But it had turned out to be a stroke of genius.

"That cop thought I was the only one in the house when I opened the door. If he'd seen two sets of prints coming across the lawn, he probably wouldn't have come inside and you wouldn't have had a chance to knock him out."

"Hey, I learned a few things on the force."

"A lot of things, actually."

She smiled appreciatively and then shook her head slowly. "You and Troy are so different, Jack."

He shifted in the driver's seat. He didn't like the sound of that. When a woman said something like that it usually didn't end on a good note. It usually ended up with him finding out that the woman wanted Troy—not him. "What do you mean?"

"You see things he didn't. Or maybe he saw them, but he wasn't willing to say anything." She hesitated, and then she shook her head again. "Nah, that's not it. He just didn't see them. His mind was on other things. I only met Troy a few times, but from what I picked up face-to-face and from what Charlie told me, he was only really into two things: being a daredevil and the Latin girls."

"There was more to him than that. A lot more."

"Yeah, but you know what I mean."

Jack smiled sadly. "I do."

"Troy saw the things he needed to see, things that would save his life while he was into his extreme situations." She nodded at Jack. "But you see a lot more than that. And you're willing to talk about what you see. That's the difference with you." She paused. "I love it."

Those last few words had sounded so good to him. "I'm older."

"Two years doesn't make any difference in terms of that. Not at the ages you guys are now, anyway." She looked down. "Sorry," she said softly. "The age he was."

Jack took a deep breath. It was time to tell her. "We were only half brothers, Karen."

Her eyes shot to his. "Really?"

Jack quickly told Karen the story of Cheryl leaving and being eight months pregnant with the child of another man when Bill asked her to come home. "I guess that's why we're so different."

"Wow."

"For a long time I thought I was adopted."

She stared at him for a few seconds. "You mean they didn't tell you what the real deal was?"

"No. Some psychiatrist told Bill and Cheryl to tell everyone I was adopted. I guess he figured it would be easier that way. Less explaining for Bill and all that." It seemed like it had always been what was best for Bill. "Times were different thirty years ago."

"Not that different."

Jack shrugged. "I don't know."

"Troy never mentioned that you were adopted. All he ever told Charlie was that you were his brother." She hesitated. "He said you were the best brother a guy could have."

God, he missed Troy. "I only found out a few days ago that Troy and I were half brothers."

"*What?* No way."

"Yup."

"How?"

"Bill told me in his office on Wall Street." Jack sped up as the turned onto the I-94 ramp. "It was after I told him I was going to Alaska to find out if we'd really gotten the truth about what happened to Troy."

"He waited all this time to tell you that you weren't adopted?" Karen asked in a hushed voice.

"Amazing, huh?"

"Disgraceful." She shrugged when Jack didn't say anything. "Well, it makes more sense now."

His heart sank as soon as she said that. He knew he shouldn't ask...but he had to. "What does? What makes sense?"

"You guys look so different."

Jack turned away so she wouldn't see his irritated expression. Women just couldn't resist Troy. It was so damn frustrating.

CHAPTER 30

BILL GLANCED across the kitchen table at Cheryl. For the last hour he'd been trying to find the right moment to talk to her. But he'd put it off every time he got the chance because he knew what was going to happen. Having "free and clear" money, as Cheryl had always called it, was a major hot button for her.

He couldn't stall any longer. Personal relationships had to run a distant second to the country's needs. The United States always had to come first. Lately he had to keep reminding himself of that. He never had before.

"Cheryl?"

"Yes, honey?"

"Why did you take ten thousand dollars out of your Citibank money market account a few days ago?"

Her gaze rose deliberately from the magazine she was reading. "*What?*"

He could see her eyes already burning. This was going to get nasty if he wasn't careful. Normally she avoided conflict like the plague, but not when it came to this. Having her own account gave her independence. At least, she thought it did.

"What did you do with the money, Cheryl?"

"How do you know I took money out of that account, Bill?"

"Because I—"

"That's supposed to be *my* account," she snapped as she slapped the magazine shut and slammed it down on the wooden tabletop. "*Only* my account."

He just prayed she hadn't given that cash to Jack. If she had, she'd probably signed his death warrant. There were people waiting for him out there who were extraordinarily talented killers, and Jack would be helpless against them. Almost anyone would.

"That's supposed to be my money to do whatever I want with," she reminded him icily. "You always said that once it went into that account you'd never ask me what I did with it."

"I never have."

"You just did."

"Things change," Bill answered solemnly. "There are exceptions to every rule." In all the years they'd known each other, he'd never seen her get this angry this fast. "You know that, Cheryl." He shuddered as he thought of what those killers would do to Jack. "I need to know what you did with that money."

"I can't believe you!" she shouted. "I can't believe you're doing this!"

"*Quiet!*" Bill hissed.

Rita Hayes, his executive assistant, was just down the hall. She'd taken a Metro North train out from the city yesterday afternoon to have dinner with them, and she'd stayed the night. This morning she and Cheryl had ridden horses while he'd worked in his first-floor office of the mansion. Now she was watching TV in the living room.

"I don't want Rita hearing us," he muttered under his breath, motioning toward the kitchen doorway. "Please."

"Do you have someone watching my account?" Cheryl demanded. "Are you so powerful you can have someone at another bank tell you when I make a withdrawal even though your name isn't on the account?"

"Yes," he replied.

"My God," she whispered. "You've been watching me all these years."

"Come on, Cheryl. You know what I do." He'd been watching that account all these years because he never completely trusted anyone—which was an awful curse. Until now she'd never done anything suspicious with all that money he gave her every month. "I run First Manhattan, for Christ's sake. It's the biggest bank in the country."

"I never thought you'd use your power against me."

It was time to drop another bombshell. The shock value might be just what he needed to get the answer he sought. "Do you know that Troy just had a son with a young woman who lives in Brooklyn?" He saw that the newsflash had taken Cheryl completely by surprise. "Her name is Lisa Martinez." She'd gotten no early warning about it from Troy. "The boy's only a couple of months old. His name is Jack."

Cheryl's expression turned from shock to confusion. "What? I thought you said—"

"Jack's been taking care of Lisa for Troy," Bill explained. "And since the baby was born he's been taking care of both of them. So she named the baby after Jack."

He watched emotion overwhelm his wife—for her lost son and her unseen grandchild. Then he felt heat come to his own eyes. He loved Cheryl so much. He didn't tell her that enough. In fact, he rarely did. He'd always regretted sending her away when they were young, when he'd been a foolish young man. And he'd always regretted not treating Jack like his own son when Cheryl had come back pregnant with him.

"So…we're grandparents," Cheryl murmured.

To a boy whose mother's last name was Martinez, Bill thought to himself in amazement. Never in his life would he have predicted that. But Lisa was a lovely young woman, and he was going to take excellent care of her—and Little Jack—now that Troy was gone. He was actually thinking of moving them here to the mansion.

"Yes, we are grandparents."

"I don't understand, Bill. Why wouldn't Troy have told us that he'd—"

"There's a lot you don't know about Troy." He'd explain all of that to her at some point, but there wasn't time for a discussion of that magnitude right now. "Right now we need to focus on the ten thousand dollars you took out of Citibank."

"Tell me what really happened to Troy," she whispered as the emotion building in her heart worked its way into her voice. "I know you know."

"Did you give that money to Jack?" he said, his voice steely. "Tell me, Cheryl."

She stared back at him for several moments. "What happened to Troy?"

"*Did you give that money to Jack?*" Bill roared suddenly, rising from his chair and coming around the table to where she was sitting. He'd had enough of this. If Rita heard, so be it. "Damn it, Cheryl, you've got to tell me!"

"Why should I tell you?" she shouted back, rising quickly too. "And why do you care if I gave money to Jack? Do you hate him that much?"

He didn't hate Jack. Down deep, he loved the boy. He'd just never been able to get over his bitterness at the fact that Jack was another man's child. It wasn't Jack's fault, but he'd never been able to climb that tall mountain of terrible regret. He hated to admit it, but every time he looked at Jack, he saw that other man. And Jack had paid the price.

God, he wished he could do things over.

"Have you spoken to Jack since that day you took the money out?" he asked, trying to push those regrets out of his mind for the moment. But he still couldn't. "You've got to tell me if you have." The only thing he could do now was try to help Jack. "You must tell me where he is."

"I'm not telling you anything."

Bill couldn't believe how hard she was fighting him. The few times they'd ever argued, she'd always crumbled when he'd started to yell. He'd never touched her in anger before, but he had to know what was going on. He grabbed her by both shoulders. "I've got to know right now—"

"What in God's name is going on?"

Bill's gaze shot to the hall doorway. Rita was standing there staring at him. He took his hands off Cheryl immediately, spread his arms, and tried to smile sincerely. "Rita, I was just—"

"Don't touch her again," Rita ordered sternly, stalking through the kitchen to Cheryl's side and taking her trembling hand. "I mean it, Bill. I'll call the police if you do. I don't care who you are, I'll call the cops."

"I'm fine," Cheryl whispered as she sobbed quietly. "I really am."

"No, you're not," Rita said calmly, shaking her head at Bill as she led Cheryl away. "Come with me."

Bill glared at them as they walked from the kitchen. Then he glanced out the bay window at the fields leading to the tree line in the distance. He couldn't believe what he was thinking. It was the first time he had in as long as he could remember.

Maybe the country couldn't always come first no matter what. Maybe there were actually times when family had to be the priority. Maybe this was one of those times.

He gazed at the far-off trees. He'd already lost one son. He couldn't lose another.

✳ ✳ ✳

"He's beautiful," Hunter murmured as he gazed down at the little boy Lisa was cradling in her arms. "This is Jack?"

She nodded happily. "Sí, this is Little Jack."

He glanced into Lisa's soft brown eyes. She was beautiful and sweet, and all she'd tried to do since he'd gotten here to Brooklyn was take care of him. She'd offered him food and drink over and over. She was a lot like Amy in that way. She just wanted to make people happy.

Hunter shut his eyes tightly. He still hadn't called Jack. But if he didn't soon, Amy would die. He was in hell, absolute hell. He was damned if he did, and damned if he didn't. He was paralyzed, and the only thing he could think of doing today to make himself feel better was coming here to see if Lisa and Little Jack were all right. It had worked a little.

"Are you OK?"

He opened his eyes at the sound of her voice and the warm touch of her hand on his arm. "Yeah, Lisa, I'm—" The knock on the door interrupted him.

"Will you see who that is?" she whispered. "If it's a man, please don't answer. It's probably my landlord, and I'm late on rent. My sisters and I won't have it until tomorrow or the next day."

"No worries."

Hunter moved to the door and peered through the tiny peephole. When he did, his body froze. There was a man standing outside, all right, but it wasn't the landlord. It was the little man who'd put him in hell. Hunter would never forget that face as long as he lived. He'd never forget how the man had watched calmly as the clear plastic bag did its work.

What in the hell was he doing here?

* * *

"Hello," Speed Trap answered hesitantly.

"Is this Bobby Mitchell?"

"Who wants to know?"

"My name's Ross Turner. I'm a hunting guide out of Wasilla. I got a buddy named Wilson Keats who told me he talked to you about a hunt you went on last year on Kodiak Island. He said you bagged a huge bear on that trip. A nine-footer."

"Yeah, that was in early October." Speed Trap knew a guy named Wilson Keats, so Turner's story sounded legit. "The thing was a monster."

"You're in Dutch, right? Wilson told me you're on one of those crab boats over there."

"Yeah, I'm on the *Arctic Fire*. So what?"

"Right. The *Arctic Fire*. Well, I'm gonna be over in Dutch real soon because I'm gonna try to hook on with a boat for the opilio season to make some quick cash. I was just hoping we could talk about your hunt. I'll buy you a beer while we do."

Just because Turner had mentioned Wilson Keats, Speed Trap wasn't buying the story at face value. He had too much experience with Grant telling him lies to go for the bait that quickly. "Or we could talk about it right now on the phone."

"We could," Turner agreed deliberately, "but I'd rather talk about it in person. That OK?"

The odds were good that Ross Turner didn't really want to talk about a bear hunt. He might at first, as a way in, but in the end he probably wanted to talk about something very different. Turner was probably a cop, and he probably wanted to talk about two people being lost off the *Arctic Fire* in two years—not what had happened on Kodiak Island last October. Uncle Sage might get away with throwing one greenhorn overboard…not two.

But maybe it would be OK to talk to somebody outside the circle about what had happened, Speed Trap figured. He'd been terrified while Grant was holding him over the side of the *Arctic Fire* by his ankles, and maybe he needed to make a big decision after all. Because he was pretty sure that the next time Grant held him over the side of the ship by the ankles, he was going to drop him into those freezing waters.

* * *

"Hi."

Bill looked up from behind the sprawling desk of his home office at the sound of the soft voice coming from the doorway. "Hi."

"Sorry about that scene in the kitchen," Rita apologized as she closed the office door and moved toward him. "You know I'd never call the cops on you, Bill."

There'd been that moment of weakness a few years ago, and he would forever pay the price if he ended this thing between them. Rita was careful to make that very clear every so often. "I know you wouldn't."

She went to sit on his lap, and she gave him a curious then irritated look when he didn't turn in the chair right away and swing his legs out so she could. "I gave Cheryl a sleeping pill. She won't be bothering us," Rita assured him as she turned the chair to the side herself and eased herself down onto his lap. "She's already out."

"Uh-huh."

"What's wrong?"

"Nothing."

"I did all that stuff in the kitchen for her benefit," Rita whispered, nuzzling his neck. "You know that."

"Of course." Why couldn't he have been stronger? He had been with everything else in his life. And he'd never even thought about cheating with any other woman, even when he'd sent Cheryl away when they were young. Why had he taken Rita to the hotel that day? Yes, yes, she'd been begging him to do it for months, but he should have been able to resist her. "And you were very convincing."

She leaned back and gave him her vixen smile. "I was, wasn't I?"

Rita was so damn passionate. Cheryl never had been that way during their lovemaking, not even when they were young. Cheryl had always been passive in bed, and he'd missed that passion in their relationship. But he still shouldn't have cheated. And now his weakness was putting him squarely in the crosshairs.

She kissed his neck. "Let's make love, Bill. Right here, right now."

"Jesus, Rita, I don't know if—"

"Don't do that, Bill," she warned sharply as the softness in her voice evaporated. "Don't deny me."

* * *

Hunter pressed his ear to the bedroom doorway. He'd hustled back here after he'd heard the man outside the apartment starting to jiggle the lock. It had occurred to him as he'd listened to the clicking and the rattling that the guy was probably capable of getting into anyplace he wanted to very quickly. He had that evilly competent look about him, even through the peephole, and it had scared Hunter to death—again. The same way it had the other night when the guy had his men force that plastic bag over his head the first time.

He'd been right to run back here. The guy had made it into the apartment only moments after he'd run into the bedroom and shut the door hurriedly.

The voices coming from the other side of the door were muffled, but Hunter could still hear the words. He felt terrible for leaving Lisa out there alone with the bastard, but what else was he supposed to do? If the guy found him here in the apartment, he'd probably kill him, which meant Lisa was in mortal danger as well because the guy wouldn't leave a witness to a murder. It would probably mean the end for Amy too, Hunter realized. So it was better for everyone for him to cower back here like a little kid.

"Where's Troy Jensen?" the man demanded loudly.

"I don't know," Lisa answered. "I haven't seen him in a long time."

"When was the last time you heard from him?"

"Awhile," she replied.

Hunter could hear her voice shaking with fear.

"When was it exactly?"

"I'm not sure."

"*When was it, damn it?*"

"*Ay dios mio.* Get your hands off me!"

"You don't tell me what I want to know, and I'll hurt your baby."

"No, please," she cried. "Please don't touch him! Please!"

Hunter reached for the doorknob. He felt so guilty standing here doing nothing. He'd told Jack he'd take care of the girl, and here he was hiding out like a complete coward.

But he pulled his hand back as soon as his fingertips touched metal. It was as though he'd been shocked by a powerful electric current. He'd never been in a fight in his life. What chance did he really have against the man out there? The guy was small, but Hunter sensed that he was still so very dangerous.

"Where's your damn cell phone?" the man asked harshly. "I want to see for myself if he's called you. Show me!"

"I don't have a cell phone."

"Yeah, sure," the guy muttered cynically. "Everyone has a cell phone. Even poor girls like you. Now where is it?"

"Ouch!" she screamed. "Stop it!"

"Give me your damn phone."

"Not my baby, not my baby!"

Hunter burst from the bedroom and raced straight at the little man. He couldn't take it anymore.

As Hunter was about to hurl himself into Maddux, the little man stepped aside and shattered Hunter's kneecap with a wicked chop kick.

"*Oh, Geeeoood!*" Hunter screamed in agony as he collapsed to the floor and shut his eyes tightly. "Oh my fucking God!"

When he grabbed his knee it felt as if the cap had spun around to the back of his leg. There was nothing but a depression where the kneecap should have been, and there was a huge lump at the back of his leg. He heard Lisa and the baby scream, but the pain in his leg was so intense he couldn't pry his eyes open.

Then there was a muffled bang and he thought he heard something fall to the floor beside him.

When he opened his eyes, he was staring directly into the pretty face of Lisa Martinez. It was only a few inches away.

"Lisa, are you—"

He cringed when dark red blood began pouring from her mouth and nose and pooling on the floor. Then he felt something pressing against the back of his head. It was the working end of a pistol with a silencer screwed to the end of the barrel.

Then Maddux fired a second shot from the pistol.

* * *

Rita pulled back from their kiss. "Do you love me, Bill?"

That was a question he didn't want to answer. Either way, it was trouble. "Rita, I—"

She pressed her fingers to his lips and smiled wryly. "Don't answer. I know you don't want to. I know you'll never leave Cheryl." She hesitated. "But you can love two women, Bill, I know you can. You're that kind of man. So I'll just assume you love me too."

The fact that Rita had even thought about him leaving Cheryl shook Bill to his core. It was all suddenly getting out of control. And he should have known that someday it would. "It's just not something we should—"

"Why did Jack come to visit you in your office on Wall Street the other day?" she interrupted.

"Um, he just…well…"

"Was it to talk about Troy?"

"Yeah," Bill muttered. "It was."

Rita kissed Bill on the forehead. "I'm so sorry about what happened. I wish he hadn't gone on that crab boat. He was such a good kid." She smiled sadly. "He was you."

"Thanks. That's nice."

He'd told Rita right away what had happened to Troy. For better or worse she was part of the family, and it would have been wrong not to say something to her immediately. It would have looked wrong too. It was a bizarre thing, but Rita and Cheryl were that close. If Cheryl ever found out what had been going on, she'd leave a husband and a best friend.

Bill shut his eyes. He'd been such a bad person. And Cheryl had always been so good to him.

"He was a great kid," Bill murmured.

"And that was why Jack came to your office? To talk about that?"

"Yes."

"That was the only reason?"

It seemed strange for her to push so hard. "Yes," he repeated. "Why?"

"It's just that I thought Jack told me he was going on a trip or something before you got to the office. I thought he said that, and I was just wondering where he was going."

Bill's eyes moved deliberately to Rita's as a cold chill crawled up his spine. Fortunately, he was able to hide its effects.

He couldn't believe what Rita had so blatantly asked.

* * *

"This is nine-one-one. What is your emergency?"

"There's been an accident in Building 2 of the Bayside Projects on Temple Avenue in Brooklyn," Maddux answered calmly. "Get somebody to apartment 312 as fast as possible. You've got two individuals down and a baby in distress." The two individuals who were down were dead, so there was nothing the EMTs could do for them.

"Who is this?" the 9-1-1 operator demanded.

But Maddux couldn't leave a baby alone in that apartment with his mother lying dead on the floor. He wasn't that cold. Close, but not quite. "Did you get the damn address?" he asked as he hustled toward the subway that would take him back to Manhattan, where he would catch an Amtrak to Washington.

"Yes, I got it. I already have a team responding. Now tell me who I'm talking—"

"Read it back to me," he ordered.

When the operator had read the address back correctly, Maddux ended the call with her immediately and dialed the man who was watching Amy Smith.

"What is it?" the man answered before the first ring had ended.

"She's expendable at this point," Maddux said matter-of-factly. "But make it humane. Got it? Don't drag it out. Don't even let her know it's coming."

"Yes, sir."

He tossed the cell phone he'd been using into a sewer. Then he pulled out one of the two other cell phones he was carrying. He cursed under his breath when he saw that there were no messages waiting for him on the screen.

They had to find out where Jack Jensen was going. If Troy really was alive, that was undoubtedly where Jack was headed. Jack would lead them right to Troy, Maddux was certain, and then they'd kill both of them. Then everything would be fine.

As Maddux slipped the phone back into his pocket, he thought about the *Pegasus* and the two hundred thousand cubic meters of LNG that were churning steadily toward Virginia Beach. And how so many people had no idea what was coming straight for them. Then he thought about how President Dorn had no idea what was coming straight for him either.

Just a few more days and everything would come together.

Maddux shook his head as he moved down into the subway. Troy Jensen was the only person who could crash the party at this point.

* * *

"I feel bad, Bill. I'm going in and check on Cheryl one more time. I'll be right back."

"OK."

Bill watched Rita trot back toward the mansion. As soon as she disappeared inside, he reached across the front of the Mercedes for her purse, which was sitting on the passenger seat.

He found her cell phone right away and scrolled through her saved numbers. There were no names attached to the numbers he quickly focused on, just unrelated letters as identifiers. But he recognized the digits anyway. One was Jack's cell phone and the other was the landline at Lisa's apartment. He knew because he'd dialed both numbers very recently.

Panic tore through Bill's system. He couldn't believe it. Rita Hayes was a spy. She'd gotten these numbers from his cell phone, which she always had access to for business reasons. It was the only explanation.

He'd known Jack was in danger. Now he knew Lisa was too.

CHAPTER 31

JACK FINISHED the last sentence, then placed the paper carefully down on the stack of pages he'd already read. The stack rose from inside the black box, which was sitting in front of him on the desk of the Missoula, Montana, motel room.

The story Troy had written on the pages was astonishing, almost unbelievable, really. It centered on a man named Shane Maddux…and another man named Roger Carlson…who seemed almost like mythic characters to Jack. Troy had basically told the story of Red Cell Seven.

After he'd placed the last page carefully back in the box, Jack lifted his hands in front of his face and stared at them. They were shaking like mad, and he couldn't make them stop.

Troy had been specific about dates and times and people other than Maddux and Carlson who were also involved with RCS. And he'd been specific about why he believed his direct superior was clinically insane by listing the reasons that provided absolute proof.

First, Maddux was going to assassinate President Dorn because he believed that Dorn intended to destroy Red Cell Seven.

Second, Maddux was going to create another horrific 9/11-type disaster by detonating an LNG tanker in Boston Harbor. He was going to blow the ship up to throw the country into chaos. So the United States intelligence infrastructure could gain broader spying and interrogation powers on citizens at home and abroad.

Last, Maddux was routinely carrying out vigilante justice. He was murdering people in cold blood who he and Carlson believed had wrongly escaped criminal justice. People who'd been released from prison or jail on technicalities, even people who'd been found innocent by juries but who Maddux and Carlson still believed were guilty. And they were killing anyone who the CIA believed might be spying on the United States. In some cases, people who the CIA didn't really have much tangible evidence against.

What *really* frightened Jack was that Troy had emphasized over and over in those pages how dedicated *and* incredibly capable Shane Maddux and Roger Carlson were. How almost nothing could stop them.

"So what do you think?"

Jack turned around as Karen sat down on the queen-size bed closest to the bathroom. She had only a towel wrapped around her slender body, and she looked sexy with her dark, wet hair hanging down on her slim shoulders. But he barely noticed how beautiful she looked. He was still so blown away by what he'd read.

"I think it's incredible."

Karen had read the material during the drive through North Dakota, but Jack had waited until he could concentrate completely on the pages. He'd gone through the single-spaced saga while Karen had taken a long, hot bath, and now he was glad he'd waited and that he'd asked her not to tell him anything about it. He would have been so distracted he might have run off the road and killed them both.

"I think we've basically got a time bomb on our hands."

"And *I* think it's as dangerous to us as it is to the entire intelligence network of the United States."

"Exactly," Jack agreed. He moved to the other queen-size bed and sat down on it so he was facing her. "If this got into the wrong hands, it would compromise the lives of so many individuals, and that could mean a lot of damn trouble for us. It's so specific about places and dates and people."

Karen nodded at the box. "Why would Troy write that?"

"He must have thought he was in trouble," Jack answered. "And he must have been really pissed off about it. That's the only explanation I can come up with. Troy was too much of a patriot. He was too damn dedicated to this country."

"He didn't send it to anyone," she pointed out. "He just wrote it. Maybe that was enough for him."

"Maybe." It seemed logical to assume that Troy hadn't sent the information to anyone. Why would he have taken the time to hide the box in the cabin and then send the letter to Karen?

"Do we call someone?" she asked.

Now Jack understood what Karen had gone through when she'd gotten Troy's letter. Who exactly were they supposed to call? If they gave all of this information to someone, they might never find out what had happened to Troy. Worse, they might become targets themselves. In fact, they almost certainly would, Jack realized. Even if they somehow got the information to the right people—whoever the "right" people were—it was logical to believe that the wrong people would ultimately find out what had happened. Presumably, those were people who knew how to kill very effectively and were comfortable taking that step to solve a problem or satisfy their desires for revenge—based on what Troy had written, anyway. And those weren't the kind of people Jack wanted to piss off, even if President Dorn's life was hanging in the balance. It sounded selfish, but after reading Troy's story, Jack had no desire to get into it with anyone from Red Cell Seven, no matter what was at stake.

"Do we at least call someone about Shane Maddux going for the president?" Karen asked.

Jack shrugged. "I don't know. I feel like we'd be looking over our shoulders for the rest of our lives if we did."

She nodded. "That's exactly what I thought after I read Troy's letter."

"Yeah, I get it now." He shook his head. "What's amazing is that Maddux and Carlson think what they're doing is right."

"Maybe some of it is," she said after a few moments.

Jack looked up. "What do you mean?"

"Well, I was just thinking. What if you and I were married and some animal raped and murdered me. Would you want him to go free because of some stupid technicality? You know, like the cops not reading him his Miranda rights or evidence being collected the wrong way? Which, I'm here to tell you as an-ex cop, happens all the time."

It was incredible that she'd just alluded to them being married, even if it was in a hypothetical situation. He'd actually thought about it during the drive today, and he'd been forced to admit to himself that he was totally into her. She was the woman he'd been waiting for. He knew that for certain. It seemed crazy for him to fall for her so fast, but maybe that was the crazy part about love. Maybe you knew right away because it was so right.

He glanced away from her and back toward the black box. He just wished she hadn't made that crack about Troy being so much better looking than him as they were getting on I-94 back in Minnesota this morning. It was stupid, but it was still haunting him.

"Of course, I wouldn't want that," he admitted.

"But if he did," Karen said, "wouldn't you want justice for me?"

"Sure I would. I'd do everything I could to get him another trial."

"What if that didn't work?"

He knew where she was going with this. "I don't know."

"Wouldn't you want to get justice for me any way you could?"

"You mean—"

"*Yeah*," she said emphatically. "Wouldn't you want Red Cell Seven's help?" She started ticking the facts off on her fingers. "You have irrefutable evidence, you have his confession to the cops, and you have him laughing to the press about it when he gets wrongly released. He's guilty, but he beat the rap and he's having fun with it." She hesitated. "Wouldn't you want Shane Maddux and Roger Carlson on your side?"

Jack took a deep breath. "But can that really ever be the right way to get justice, Karen? It's wrong to ignore the system, it's completely wrong. And you know it."

Karen rolled her eyes. "It's easy to say that when it hasn't really happened. But what if it did?"

"I understand."

Of course, he'd want to tear the guy apart with his bare hands. But agreeing with her that vigilante justice was acceptable, even in just a single case, would violate one of his most basic beliefs— which was that you had to let the system work and you had to abide by its decision even if you hated it. If not, society disintegrated and mob rule reigned.

"But I can't agree with you on having some secret government crew getting revenge for us. I just can't."

They stared at each other in silence for several moments.

"Let's go out for a while," she suggested, changing the subject. "There's a bar down the street I saw on the way in that looked pretty cool. Let's have a few beers and some laughs and try to forget about everything that's going on for a little while. What do you think?"

"Are you serious?" It was almost midnight and they still had a long way to go. "We should get some sleep. We've got another long drive ahead of us tomorrow."

"Please, Jack. Let's go out for a little while."

"Yeah, but—"

"Have I fallen asleep on you in the car?"

"No."

"And I won't. I'll stay right with you all day tomorrow. I'll do half the driving, and I won't sleep when I'm not driving. I promise. I know you're thinking I'll pass out, but I really won't. I'm good at that kind of stuff." She eased down onto the floor, crawled over to where he was sitting, and rested her arms on his thighs so that her face and those beautiful lips were very close to his. "I just want to have some fun. Come on. Please."

He gazed into those dark eyes of hers. He wasn't going to turn down that invitation even if he had to keep his eyelids pried open with toothpicks tomorrow.

* * *

From the bridge of the massive ship, the man gazed past the huge domes and into the darkness ahead. Then he looked up and cased the sky for any moving lights. But there were none.

The *Pegasus* was only two days from Virginia Beach, and he was getting nervous. He was prepared to die in the inferno they would create when they blew up the ship. But he couldn't take the thought of being stopped and boarded. He couldn't take the thought of living out the rest of his life in some awful prison somewhere, tortured every day.

He moaned in a low voice so the other man on the bridge wouldn't hear him. He wanted all those virgins he'd been promised on the other side. He only hoped that his contact in the United States was as crazy and bitter as he claimed to be.

CHAPTER 32

MADDUX AND Carlson were sitting in the same room of the central Virginia farmhouse in which Maddux had welcomed Ryan O'Hara into the Falcon division of Red Cell Seven. The only difference was that tonight Carlson was sitting behind the desk and Maddux was out in front where O'Hara had been.

They were the only people in the house. Carlson's driver was waiting outside in an idling Town Car, and Maddux had sent O'Hara to California yesterday to prep for his first assignment. It was the most important first assignment any Falcon ever had.

Carlson spoke up first. "Hello, Red Fox One."

It had been a long time since Carlson had called him that, but it didn't necessarily strike Maddux as strange. "Good evening, Roger." Maddux hadn't slept in three days. Despite that, he felt good. All in all, things were going well. There were challenges, but there were always challenges in this line of work. One way or the other, he'd overcome them. He always did. "I hope you're doing well."

"Doing fine."

"Do you have the information we talked about?"

President Dorn was going to Los Angeles and would be making two very public outdoor appearances while he was there. Carlson had acquired the details of the trip, including a dossier of the president's minute-by-minute schedule. Carlson had promised to bring that dossier with him tonight. Having those details would enable Ryan O'Hara to get in perfect position to take a clear shot at Dorn's head from no more than three hundred yards while the president was standing unprotected behind a waist-high dais. It would be a slam-dunk shot for a marksman of O'Hara's caliber, and Dorn's blood would end up splattered all over the California stage.

Maddux was disappointed he wouldn't be able to kill Dorn himself, but he had to get to Alaska quickly and there was no telling how long he'd be there.

He'd already informed O'Hara of who the target was, and O'Hara had claimed that he wouldn't be deterred from firing his rifle because he was aiming at the president of the United States. Several times during the briefing O'Hara had reaffirmed his absolute loyalty to Red Cell Seven—and, more importantly, to Maddux—and sworn that he understood the need to take such an extreme action during such an extreme time in the country's history. In fact, O'Hara seemed enthusiastic about using his skills so early in his career at RCS for such an important purpose.

But Maddux wasn't stupid or gullible. Another RCS agent who Maddux was close to and who hated President Dorn just as much would accompany O'Hara to Los Angeles to make certain the assassination went off as planned. That man would stand beside O'Hara to make certain the kid took the kill shot. To make certain O'Hara understood the grave consequences he would face should the president's blood end up not being splattered all over that California stage. He was the same man who'd gone to Mexico to talk to Troy after Troy had killed that bull in Nuevo Laredo.

"It's all right here." Carlson tapped his chest above his shirt pocket as he leaned over the desk. "Everything you need." He hesitated. "But before I give it to you, we need to talk about something."

"Oh?"

"We have a problem, Shane, a serious problem."

Maddux glanced up. He'd been checking one of his cell phones for another message from Rita Hayes, but nothing else had come in yet. She was doing her best to break Bill Jensen, but he was deflecting all her questions.

Maddux had been tempted to tell Rita to stop asking because Bill was no fool. He'd figure out what was going on sooner rather than later, and that could spell trouble. But now that Hunter Smith and Lisa Martinez were dead ends, Bill was their best shot at finding out quickly if Troy had survived his ordeal of being hurled from the *Arctic Fire*. And if Troy had survived, where he was. If Bill would just give them a clue about where Jack Jensen was headed, Maddux would feel so much better. Jack, Maddux was certain, would lead them straight to Troy.

Maddux had recruited Rita ten years ago to keep an eye on Bill, and until now she'd never let him down. He was confident she wouldn't this time either. Bill had too much to lose in all of this.

"What is it, Roger?" Maddux asked as he thought about how Bill owned the farmhouse he and Carlson were now meeting in. How Bill owned a lot of things Red Cell Seven used. They'd have to kill him if he figured out what Rita was doing or that RCS had killed his son, and replacing a man like Bill Jensen wouldn't be easy. But so be it. "What's the problem?"

"Remember I told you we shot down the G5 that was supposed to blow up the *Olympian* after she made it into Boston Harbor?"

"I remember," Maddux answered. "You said one of our pilots off the *Reagan* shot it down out in the Atlantic. He played with the G5 pilot a little bit while he was trying out some new high-tech stuff, but he took the guy out before he ever got close to Europe."

"I also told you that we had a recon crew heading for the crash site to see what they could find."

Maddux made certain to stare impassively at Carlson. "And?"

"And they found some documents."

Carlson's eyes were flashing in a way Maddux had never seen them flash before—which wasn't good. The old man was furious. "Oh yeah?" This was bad. "So?"

"Anything you want to tell me, Shane?"

Maddux leaned down to brush something off his shoe. "What are you talking about?" he asked innocently as he rose back up after a few moments.

"We've known each other too long to go through this stupid song and dance," Carlson hissed. "You know more about the *Olympian* than you've told me, don't you, Shane?"

"What the—"

"I can't believe it!"

"Can't believe what?"

"You were going to let that ship sail into Boston Harbor and blow it up. You got them the clearances they needed to get into the harbor, didn't you?"

"There were foreign terrorists aboard that ship. The CIA confirmed the identifications of several of the bodies from the *Olympian*. They were foreigners, and they were members of a terrorist group based in Syria that our people are very familiar with."

"You helped them," Carlson said accusingly. "You facilitated it. You got them their clearances," he repeated.

"I was the one who blew the whistle on what was happening, Roger. I was the one who told you the *Olympian* had to be stopped. This is ridiculous."

"It's not ridiculous at all," Carlson snapped. "You blew the whistle on that ship because you had to. Because someone else would have if you hadn't, and then you would have been identified as a traitor. I saw the documents they recovered from that G5. I knew the rat was you as soon as I saw the papers." He hesitated. "One of your Falcons figured out what you were doing, right? Is that what happened?"

"No."

"Was it Troy Jensen?"

"*No!*"

"You little bastard."

Maddux clenched his teeth together hard. "*What the hell did you just call me?*"

"How dare you go outside the chain of command, Shane? How dare you put me and Red Cell Seven in jeopardy like that? After all I've done for you."

"Look, I—"

"I know what you were thinking, Shane. You figured you'd blow up that LNG tanker, that some terrorist group would get credit for the disaster, and then we'd have another 9/11 on our hands. You figure the intel world gets *anything* it wants after that, and David Dorn has to bend over and take it up the ass when we want to tap people's phones and study people's credit card bills and torture anyone we want to torture whenever we want to." Carlson shook his head. "But you can't kill millions of innocent Americans, Shane. Those are the people we've sworn to protect. I mean, maybe a few could be sacrificed every once in a while. Maybe I could understand that. But if you'd been successful and the *Olympian* had blown up in the harbor, you would have destroyed one of the most important cities in our country. That's insane. *You're insane.*"

The old man needed to settle down. He wasn't thinking straight. Somehow President Dorn must have gotten to him, Maddux figured. That was the only explanation for all of the treason spewing from Carlson's mouth.

"Roger, you don't know what you're talking about." Deny, deny, deny. It was all Maddux could do right now. Carlson wasn't going to calm down, so he had to keep denying and hope the man would just let it go.

Carlson pointed at Maddux accusingly. "Was Charlie Banks really washed off the *Arctic Fire* by a wave a year ago? Or was he thrown off that ship by the crew?"

"That's not relevant right now, Roger."

"*Tell me, you midget,*" Carlson snarled.

Maddux could feel himself losing control. "Don't go there, Roger." He knew what Carlson was trying to do, and he couldn't let himself be driven out of control to the point of admitting everything. He was still hoping they could get past this.

"Did you have Charlie thrown overboard?" Carlson demanded. "Did you have Troy Jensen thrown overboard too?" The old man reached inside his suit jacket and pulled out his cell phone. "I think I better talk to Sage Mitchell myself."

Maddux stood up slowly from the chair. "Don't do that, Roger. Don't call Sage Mitchell."

"Are you threatening me?"

"I'm begging you not to make that call."

"You couldn't beg hard enough, Shane," Carlson retorted as he began to push buttons on the phone. "Nothing could keep me from making this call. I can't wait to hear Sage's answer."

"Roger."

Carlson glanced up angrily from behind the desk. "*What?*"

"I love you. I'm sorry about this."

Maddux raised his right hand, aimed the tiny dart gun at Carlson's neck, and fired. Carlson's eyes opened wide when the razor-sharp end of the dart hit his skin.

A moment later the old man rose unsteadily from the desk chair, staggered a few feet toward Maddux with his arms outstretched, and collapsed to the floor with a loud moan.

Maddux shook his head grimly as he gazed down. Carlson had actually been dead before he'd hit the floor. The shit really worked.

The dart inside the gun was filled with a concoction that perfectly simulated a heart attack. The bright orange liquid was basically an incredibly powerful shot of adrenaline that even a healthy young heart wouldn't have been able to handle. Carlson's heart had exploded in his chest almost instantaneously. The best thing about it: all remnants of the concoction would dissipate well before anyone could detect them during an autopsy.

Maddux knelt down, removed the dart from Carlson's neck, and began to perform CPR. The illusion had to seem real. Maddux's DNA needed to be in Carlson's throat, and Carlson's chest had to be bruised by his fists.

When he was done, he glanced at where Carlson had been sitting. The old man hadn't brought a cane tonight, and suddenly Maddux felt no guilt at all for what he'd done. Roger Carlson had been lying to him for twenty years.

Maddux reached into Carlson's jacket and pulled out an envelope. Inside it was the dossier for President Dorn's trip to Los Angeles. Now Dorn really was a dead man.

* * *

It was midnight and the bar was going crazy. The place was packed, the rock-and-roll band was in high gear, and alcohol was flowing freely. The clientele was a mix of locals and students because Missoula was home to the University of Montana, and right outside of town huge cattle ranches extended in all directions throughout Big Sky Country. So cowboys were dancing with coeds, and everyone was having a hot time.

Jack grinned as he watched Karen lean over the pool table to line up the last shot. She was wearing a sexy top, a snug pair of jeans, and cool suede cowboy boots. He'd bought her the outfit at a boutique in Bozeman, where they'd eaten dinner a few hours ago.

He took a long swallow of beer as he watched her stretch across the green felt to make the shot. His grin grew wider. He was glad she couldn't wait to wear her new clothes, because he couldn't wait to see her in them. And he hadn't been disappointed when she'd come out of the motel and he'd seen her in them the first time. She looked incredible.

He took another swallow from his mug. He was going to be exhausted when they pulled out of Missoula at dawn, but she'd been right to want them to go out. He'd had a great time for the past hour. She was awesome.

"Damn!"

The cowboys he and Karen had been playing for the last few minutes shouted their disappointment together as she dropped the eight ball in the table's far corner pocket.

It turned out he and Karen had something else in common. They were both excellent pool players. They'd held the table for the last forty minutes. No one had come close to beating them. And they'd won several hundred bucks.

Karen tossed her cue on the table, ran up to Jack, threw her arms around him, and gave him a huge hug. "I love this game!" she shouted over the music as she leaned back and gazed up at him.

He chuckled. "Me too."

"Know what else I love?"

"What?"

"That you're so damn handsome!"

He couldn't possibly have heard her right. "What?"

She smiled and shouted while she twirled around in front of him. "I think you're handsome, Jack. I love your dark hair and your eyes and how tall you are. I love everything about you."

"But you—"

"No, no, I said you and Troy looked different. I never said anything about who I thought was better looking." She stopped twirling and pointed at him. "I saw that face you made when I said it, even though you tried to turn away."

Jesus, she was amazing. It was as if she could read his mind.

She slipped her arms around his neck again and kissed him deeply. "Gotcha," she murmured when she pulled back. Then she kissed him again even deeper.

PART 5

CHAPTER 33

JACK COULDN'T believe his eyes when Ross Turner emerged from the seaplane at the dock on Puget Sound. For a few seconds he didn't think it was really his old friend. He figured the huge man squeezing through the narrow door and stepping down onto the plane's pontoon was actually a pilot Turner had hired to fly down from Alaska. The man didn't look anything like the tall, skinny, clean-cut kid Jack had known at Denison.

Jack didn't believe it was Turner until Turner stepped up onto the dock and introduced himself loudly to Karen, then gave Jack a bear hug that squeezed most of the air right out of his lungs. And the friendly slap on the back after the hug was so powerful Jack almost took an unplanned plunge into the sound's icy cold waters.

The last time Jack and Turner had seen each other was eight and a half years ago in New York. It had been a month after graduation, and they'd met for lunch in Manhattan at the Racquet Club, thanks to Bill, who was a member of the exclusive establishment. The next day Turner was leaving for Alaska. A year of hunting and fishing, and then he was coming back to the lower forty-eight to go to Harvard Law School. At that lunch Turner had still looked like the guy Jack had met in the Denison dormitory on the first day of college. He had still been a toweringly tall string bean with stooped shoulders.

But now Turner looked like the massive brown bears he hunted. He had a huge chest and broad shoulders, his brown hair fell well below his collar in the back, his dark red beard was full and curly, and his voice had gone lower. He even looked an inch or two taller to Jack.

After taking off from Puget Sound, they'd flown over open ocean with the Canadian and then Alaskan coasts off the right wing in the distance—until they'd reached Dutch Harbor. The town had less than four thousand full-time residents and existed solely to support the fishing fleet.

"So, tell me why you drove all the way across the country to Seattle instead of flew," Turner said as the three of them walked down a side street of Dutch Harbor through a raw, late-afternoon mist. Turner's seaplane was secured to a dock a few blocks behind them. "Why take all that extra time, Jack?"

"I was worried that if Karen and I flew commercial and I used a credit card to pay for the ticket—"

"Somebody would spot you," Turner interrupted. "Yeah?"

"Bingo."

There were only a few bars in Dutch, and, according to Turner, they were all dives. But at least the one they were headed for right now—the Fish Head Pub—was off the beaten track, Turner had claimed.

As much as anything around in Dutch Harbor could really be just off the beaten track, Jack had figured as they'd taxied to the dock a little while ago. As far as he was concerned, *everything* in this tiny town was *way* off the beaten track to begin with.

"So, it's that serious?" Turner asked.

"I almost got hit by a van on Broadway a few days ago, and I'm pretty sure the guy was aiming for me." Jack nodded at Karen. "And a few minutes after I met up with her in Baltimore, we got chased by two guys who jumped out of an SUV and started shooting at us without asking any questions."

"Holy shit," Turner muttered.

"That's what we thought." Jack hadn't mentioned anything to Turner about what was in the black box they'd retrieved from the cabin outside Bemidji. He figured it was better for Turner if he didn't know about all that. "So we drove."

"So this is more than just finding out if what happened to Troy is different from the official version you got?"

Jack took a breath and winced. The pungent odor of fish was everywhere in this town, and he still hadn't gotten used to it. "It didn't start like that, Ross, but that's how it's turned out. Look, I'll tell you the whole story right now if you really want to—"

"I don't want to hear the whole story," Turner said matter-of-factly as he stopped walking and motioned for Jack and Karen to do the same. "I don't care about any of the other stuff. In fact, the less I know the better. I just want to get this meeting with Bobby Mitchell over with. You're an old friend, Jack, and I want to help you with Troy if I can, if there's anything to find out." He glanced down at the ground and kicked at a pebble on the wet street. "Look, I got busted for cocaine possession a year ago," he mumbled, "and I can't get in any trouble while I'm on probation. I could lose my guide license if I did, and I can't have that. I'd have to leave Alaska, and I'd shoot myself before I did that. This is my home now."

Jack and Karen exchanged a subtle glance as Turner kept staring down at his shoes.

"Well, look," Jack said, "I don't want you to—"

"It's OK, Jack. I want to do this for you. Like I said, you're an old friend. And there was that time you pulled my ass out of the sling. The cops were going to arrest me for that DUI. I still can't believe you talked them out of it. That wouldn't have looked good on the law school apps."

Jack glanced over at Karen, who was smiling tenderly at him. He liked that smile. "How the hell did you get this meeting for us with Mitchell?" he asked, still thinking about how surprised he was that Karen had been able to cast her spell on him quickly and completely. He cared about her so much already, and he wondered if she had those same feelings for him. She'd acted like it at the bar in Missoula the other night, and then later in the room. But she'd seemed distant yesterday on the drive from Montana to Seattle. "I thought the captain of the *Arctic Fire* didn't let his crew talk to anybody."

"I didn't get this meeting for *us*," Turner answered. "It's just gonna be Bobby Mitchell and me in there. You guys are gonna wait outside, because if Mitchell sees you two with me, he'll probably run. I didn't tell him I'd be dragging an entourage. And, by the way, people in Alaska tend to be pretty skittish to begin with."

"OK," Jack agreed. "But how'd you get to him?"

"We have a mutual friend, and we all like to hunt browns." Turner glanced at the entrance to the Fish Head. It was just a few doors up the street. "And I think Bobby Mitchell wants to talk. It's just a gut feeling, but I think he's got a story to tell. It sure sounded like it when I spoke to him on the phone." Turner glanced around the area before going on. "I'm betting the captain of the *Arctic Fire* threw two people overboard," he continued. "Maybe he did it to save a greenhorn's share of the haul money. Or maybe he did it for another reason, now that I've heard about those people blasting away at you in Baltimore without even talking to you first.

Either way, maybe Bobby's getting amped about getting caught up in something bad. Maybe he figures it would be a good idea to tell somebody about it now so he doesn't go to jail for murder. So I can verify his story after the cops pick him up." Turner shrugged. "Or maybe he'll walk out of the bar as soon as I bring it up." He tapped Jack on the chest. "If he does, then you're stuck, because that's all I got for you. You understand?"

It would suck if Bobby Mitchell turned out to be a dead end, but Jack understood that Turner would have hit his limit as far as helping them at that point. "Yeah, I got it."

Turner started to move off, but then he turned around. "Are you both carrying weapons?" His gaze flickered back and forth between the two of them.

They nodded.

Jack spoke up. "That's another reason we drove to Seattle." He'd explained to Turner in the plane that Karen was an ex-cop. "We both wanted our guns."

"Good. Now I'm gonna give you some really good advice on surviving in Alaska. If you follow these three rules, you'll be good to go. First, don't be afraid to use those guns you've got. Don't die with them in your belt. Too many people make that mistake up here. They aren't for show. Second, always be ready for the weather to change, and not for the better. It can always snow harder here, and the winds can always blow stronger. Always assume it will get worse, not better." He hesitated. "And this is the most important rule of all. Never, and I mean *never*, ask a man what his last name is in Alaska. Let him tell you, let him volunteer it. If he doesn't, don't worry about it and walk away without looking back when you and he are done." Turner paused again. "An old man in a bar told me all that the first week I got here, and I'm glad he did. He was exactly right."

As Jack watched Turner head up the street toward the Fish Head Pub, he quickly committed the three rules to memory.

✳ ✳ ✳

"You shouldn't be out in the open like this." Stein was sitting behind the big desk of the hotel's top-floor suite, going through the president's detailed dossier for the next few days. "You'll be vulnerable on an outdoor stage like this," he observed, speaking up as he pointed at the line item on the dossier and then a picture of the venue on the opposite page of the thick green folder. "I think you should make this speech inside. We'll have much better crowd control if you're inside."

Dorn lay on his back on the comfortable king-size bed with his hands behind his head. He stared up at the ceiling fan that was rotating slowly above him. "I'll be fine."

"Yeah, well, I'm going to talk to the Secret Service again. I want their take on this venue one more time."

"I'll make it easy for you, Rex. They don't want me doing it there either. But it doesn't matter. I'm the commander in chief, and what I say goes."

"If the Secret Service says not to—"

"The people of California love me. They don't want to hurt me. They want to be close to me. Besides, I'm as popular as any president in the last hundred years. Look at the numbers."

"I've seen the numbers, Mr. President." Stein glanced through the window beside the desk, out over Los Angeles, so Dorn would be certain not to see his frustrated—and slightly disgusted— reaction. He still couldn't tell if the man was that arrogant or that naïve. "But it only takes one nut job."

"Go be useful, Rex," Dorn said.

The man from Vermont was so sickeningly full of himself. And it was getting worse every day. "What do you mean, sir?"

"Call Daniel Beckham and find out if he's gotten that list from Roger Carlson yet." Dorn sat up and swung his stocking feet to the floor. "The one that's supposed to detail all of those Red Cell Seven assets I'm interested in."

Stein gazed at the ocean in the distance. It was sparkling beneath the late afternoon sun. He'd tried to reach Roger Carlson twice today. Once on the regular number and once on that number he'd been given at that first national security briefing in Langley, Virginia. But he still hadn't heard back.

"Make that call, will you, Rex?"

"Yes, sir."

"Right now, Rex. Make it for me *right now*."

CHAPTER 34

TURNER POINTED at Speed Trap's chest. "Is that one of his canines?"

Speed Trap pulled a thin silver chain out from beneath his plain gray T-shirt and let the tusklike trophy tumble from his fingers. "It is."

"Damn." Turner's gaze intensified as he watched the sharp four-and-a-half-inch bear tooth swing back and forth across the kid's chest at the end of the chain. "I've never seen anything like it, and I've been tracking grizzlies up here for a while. That's impressive."

"How'd you know there was a tooth on the chain?"

"If I shot a bear like that, I'd do the same thing," Turner answered, tapping his own chest. "And I saw the outline of it beneath your shirt," he admitted. "How many rounds did it take to put that beast down?"

"One."

"Wow."

"I dropped him right where he was standing with my thirty-thirty, man. The bullet hit his head and his chin hit the ground. It was my best shot ever. The guide said it was a one-in-a-million pop because most times even a thirty-caliber bullet just gives them a headache and makes them mad. Their skulls are that tough."

"That's right," Turner agreed. "Well, like I said, it's damned impressive, pal."

"My guide thought so too."

"I wish I'd been your guide that day, Bobby."

For the last ten minutes Speed Trap had been telling Turner the story of shooting the massive, nine-foot Kodiak bear as they sat at the small, smoky bar of the Fish Head Pub. Turner was listening closely to the story of the hunt and seemed to be sincerely appreciating and enjoying every detail as they sat there drinking beers—which Turner was paying for.

It had been over a year, and Grant still hadn't bothered to listen to the whole story of what had happened on Kodiak Island that day. Grant always walked away whenever the topic came up, and Speed Trap knew exactly why—because his Kodiak bear was so much bigger than any bear Grant had ever shot. And Grant couldn't stand his little brother beating him at anything, especially hunting.

"Actually, Ross, people call me Speed Trap." He liked that handle so much more than Bobby. It made him sound important and daring. *Bobby* made him sound like a little boy.

Turner broke into a wide smile after taking several gulps of cold amber from his tall, twenty-two-ounce glass. "Got a few tickets under your belt, huh? So you like going fast?"

"I *love* it. I always wanted to win Daytona, you know? I always wanted to drive one of those cars for a living. Shoot, what I really wanted to do was fly fighter jets."

"Me too," Turner agreed. "But I was too tall. So what kind of rig you got?"

"An F-one fifty."

"Of course you do."

"But it isn't stock anymore, if you know what I mean. I made a few changes to the engine and the transmission and it goes now, man. I mean, it fucking *flies*."

"I bet." Turner took another long look at the tooth hanging from Speed Trap's neck. "Well, Speed Trap, people call me Griz."

It was Speed Trap's turn to smile broadly. "I can see why." He could feel the beer starting to kick in, and he chuckled loudly as he thought about Turner's nickname. "You look like a damn grizzly bear, and a Kodiak at that. Not some inland midget brown that eats nothing but bugs and berries."

"Yeah, well, I—"

"Did you really come to Dutch to talk about bears?" Speed Trap asked out of nowhere. "Or are you here to talk about something else?"

Turner stared intently at Speed Trap for a few moments. "What do you mean?"

"I called Wilson Keats right after you called me the other day."

"And?"

"And he said you'd been asking around about the *Fire* for the last week. He said you talked to some of your friends on the state force over in Anchorage about what happened to Troy Jensen. He said you talked to some of the Coast Guard guys about it too."

Turner nodded deliberately. "Yeah, I've been asking around. I'm not going to lie to you, Speed Trap."

"Are you a cop?"

"No."

"Well, what's the deal?"

Turner took a long guzzle of beer. "OK, here it is. I go back a ways with Troy's older brother, Jack. I'm doing him a favor on this."

Speed Trap finished what was left in his tall glass and put it down on the bar. Then he leaned back in his stool. He appreciated Turner being a no-bullshit guy.

"Want another one?" Turner asked, pointing at Speed Trap's empty glass.

Speed Trap wanted Turner to appreciate that he was a no-bullshit guy too. "You don't have to do that."

"Do what?"

"You don't have to bribe me with beers."

"I'm not," Turner answered firmly. "I'm just trying to find out for an old friend what happened to his younger brother."

Speed Trap thought about what was at stake here. This could end up being a mistake, he knew, but if Troy was still alive out there somewhere, he wanted Turner to find him. Troy had saved his life that night on the *Arctic Fire*, and he'd never forget the huge debt he owed the guy for as long as he lived. No matter what Sage and Grant did to him, he'd never forget.

* * *

Jack grabbed Karen's arm as they stood at the end of the alley down the narrow street from the Fish Head Pub. "Oh, Christ."

"*What? What's the matter?*"

Jack gestured at the two guys who'd just sauntered past them. One was a man-mountain with long blond hair, and the other was short and wiry. But the little one still looked to Jack like he could hold his own in a fight. In fact, he looked like he could hold his own in a fight with the devil. "Look at that jacket," he said, pointing at the guy with the long blond hair.

"*Arctic Fire,*" she whispered as she read the flowing white script that was embroidered on the black jacket beneath the colorful image of the ship bursting through the top of a wave. "What do we do?" she asked breathlessly. "We can't just leave Ross in there."

"We've gotta go get—"

"What's wrong?"

Jack and Karen whipped around. Turner was now towering over them. He'd exited the pub through the back door by the restrooms after taking a leak and walked up the alley behind them.

"Look at that." Jack stabbed excitedly in the air at the *Arctic Fire* jacket, which was about to disappear into the Fish Head Pub.

Turner glanced at the jacket and the man wearing it. Then he put one hand on Jack's shoulder, the other on Karen's, and leaned down so his mouth was close to their ears. "We've gotta get out of here, boys and girls. And we've gotta get out of here *now.*"

* * *

They were so close to the United States now the leader swore he could smell it. He swore he could smell the scents of trees and dirt and fresh water drifting eastward toward the ship on the wings of the prevailing winds. He was so close to guiding the *Pegasus* to its target, he realized anxiously. He was so close to changing world history forever.

He knelt down on the bridge and touched the dark, round scar on his forehead to the metal floor. Please, he prayed. Please let this happen.

* * *

"What did you tell that guy at the bar?" Maddux demanded angrily.

"What guy?" Speed Trap asked innocently. His wrists and ankles were tied tightly to a chair in the Arctic Fire's galley, and he was terrified. Over Maddux's shoulder he could see Sage and Grant watching from the doorway.

"Whoever it was that you met at the Fish Head," Maddux snarled. "I want answers, and I don't want to have to ask twice. I don't have time for this."

"I didn't meet anyone there. I swear to God."

"Liar!"

"No, no, I just went there to have a beer by myself. That's all!"

"That's not what the bartender said."

"Huh?" Of course the bartender would remember him talking to Turner, Speed Trap realized. Who was ever going to forget a guy like Ross Turner? "Oh, oh, *him*," Speed Trap said loudly, trying to make it seem like he'd just remembered Turner. "He was just some guy in the bar. He was there when I got there. I'd never seen him before in my life and—Oh, *God!*" Speed Trap gasped.

Maddux had nailed him with a crushing right fist to the stomach that felt like a bowling ball had hit him squarely in the gut going a hundred miles an hour. Maddux was small but he packed a hell of a punch, and for what seemed like an eternity Speed Trap couldn't breathe. Finally, the air began seeping back into his lungs as Maddux grabbed his long blond hair and roughly pulled his head back.

"It hurts, it hurts," was all he could gasp as he stared up helplessly into Maddux's cold eyes. "It hurts so bad."

"But you can keep it from hurting again if you tell me everything you told that guy."

"We just talked about a bear hunt I went on last year when I shot this trophy bear on Kodiak." Speed Trap tasted blood as he spoke. "That's all. I swear it was."

"Did you float a raft out the back of this ship to Troy Jensen the night he went over the side?"

Speed Trap shook his head hard. "No, no," he answered, try-ing to watch Maddux as the man walked behind him. But he couldn't turn his head far enough to see what was happening. "I'd never do that. I'd never—"

Speed Trap's lies were interrupted when a clear plastic bag came down over his head roughly and wrapped tightly around his neck. Within seconds he could feel himself starting to suffocate as the plastic went down his throat deeper and deeper with every breath. But there was nothing he could do about it. All he could do was watch Sage and Grant watch him pass out. All he could do was pray they'd help him.

* * *

"Mr. President," Stein began as soon as he moved past the Secret Service agents who were posted inside the suite doorway of the Los Angeles hotel, "you've got to listen to me."

"What is it?" Dorn snapped as he straightened his tie in the mirror. "What do you want now, Rex?"

"I spoke to the agent in charge, and she's very concerned about this speech tomorrow. You've got to reconsider. It's not too late to move the thing inside."

"This is California, not Texas. People are born here with a big liberal 'L' stamped on their foreheads. You know, 'medicinal' pot, hippies, Hollywood, and all of that. No one's coming after me out here, I assure you."

Stein could hear the rage creeping into Dorn's voice for the first time since he'd taken on the job as chief of staff. But he didn't care. His number one responsibility was to do what was best for the country, and therefore what was best for the president. If Dorn wanted to get angry, so be it.

"Sir, I've got to—"

"No more," Dorn hissed, ordering the Secret Service detail outside the suite and into the hallway with a curt wave. "That's it," he continued when the door was shut and they were alone. "You raise this issue again, Rex, and I'll fire you on the spot, so help me God. You're really becoming a major pain in my ass." Dorn hesitated. "Maybe I'll fire you anyway. The powers that be who hired you for me a year ago can't control me anymore. I'm too popular. It's my show now, and there's nothing they can do about it."

Stein stared at the president, wondering what he was supposed to do. Dorn was right. He could do anything he wanted now and none of the party heavyweights could do a damn thing about it at this point.

"Yes, sir," he said quietly.

"Did you call Beckham?" Dorn demanded. "Did you find out if Carlson sent the information over to him?"

"No, not yet."

"Well I suggest you do, *damn it*. When I give you an order like that I expect you to carry it out immediately. One more screwup like that and I will fire you, Rex. And I'll make sure you never work in Washington again." Dorn's eyes narrowed. "I never liked you, but at least I respected you." He shook his head. "But I don't even respect you anymore. Now get the hell out of here."

* * *

"You OK?"

"I'm fine."

Jack and Karen were standing on the dock where Turner's seaplane was lashed, waiting for the big man to come out of the general store that overlooked the pier. He was inside, using cash Jack had given him to pay for the spot the plane had been using.

Karen hadn't looked up when he'd asked her that question, Jack realized. She usually looked him straight in the eye whenever she answered him about anything…but not this time.

"I'm glad Troy's alive," she said softly.

"*Could be* alive," Jack reminded her. "The only thing Ross said was that Bobby Mitchell admitted to floating a raft to Troy out the back of the *Arctic Fire* the night the other guys threw him overboard." Jack was trying to be low key about all this, but he had to admit he was damn excited. Just the possibility that Troy might still be alive had sent his spirits on a rocket ride. "But Mitchell couldn't tell if Troy made it into the raft. It was too dark."

"I guess we'll find out. But I've got a really good feeling about it, Jack. I think you're going to see Troy again."

"We both know the chances are still so small," Jack cautioned. "Mitchell said they were still forty miles northwest of Akutan when they threw him over. Even if Troy made it into the raft, the thing could have flipped over or sunk or just headed out to sea."

Karen shook her head. "It didn't sound like Ross thought that was the case while we were walking over here. He seemed to think with the winds and the tides that were going on that night the raft would have gone to shore somewhere east of here. He said he'd checked into all of that, and he was pretty sure the raft wouldn't have been taken out to sea. Right?"

She was still looking down at the ground. "What is it?" Jack moved in front of her. "You seem…well, you seem kind of sad."

"It's nothing."

He ran his fingers through her hair. They'd made love the other night in Missoula when they'd gotten back from the bar. It had been awesome, and afterward he'd held her in his arms until they'd gotten up a few hours later to drive to Seattle. It had seemed like the most natural thing in the world to hold her like that too. They'd fit together all night like two puzzle pieces, which was a new experience for him. Every other time he'd held a woman all night, he'd gotten up in the morning with a stiff neck and an arm that was fast asleep.

He hated to think it, but it was almost as if she now regretted what she'd done. And that was going to hurt so badly if it was true. He'd already started missing her when she was gone for just a few minutes. He was hooked on her, and he didn't like thinking that she wasn't hooked on him. Especially after she'd told him she was the other night. She didn't seem like the kind of woman who'd change her feelings like that so quickly. But, when it really came down to it, he didn't know her that well.

"It's something, Karen."

"I was just wondering what I'd do if somehow Charlie's still alive too." She touched Jack's arm. "I guess I'd have a problem on my hands. I guess we both would."

He couldn't even bring himself to think about that possibility. "Well, I guess—"

"Come on," Turner called loudly as he emerged from the store's entrance. "Let's get out of here. Let's go find Troy."

Jack watched Karen hop down onto the pontoon and climb into the plane. He shook his head. How could he possibly hope that Charlie Banks was dead? How could he be that terrible a person?

* * *

"You're not shooting my son!" Duke yelled at Maddux as he barged his way past Sage and Grant into the *Arctic Fire*'s galley.

Maddux swung the barrel of the pistol quickly away from Speed Trap's forehead and straight at Duke. It stopped Duke in his tracks five feet from his son, who was still tied tightly to the chair and beginning to sob.

"It's a matter of national security," Maddux answered matter-of-factly. Speed Trap had just finished telling him everything. "Your son must die."

The kid had admitted floating the raft to Troy that night on the Bering Sea, and to telling a man named Ross Turner the same thing a few minutes ago at the Fish Head Pub. He'd also informed Maddux that Turner was working with Jack Jensen and that they were heading out in a seaplane right now to look for Troy. If those two found Troy first, everything Maddux had worked so hard to execute might be stopped a foot short of the goal line, and Roger Carlson would have died in vain. Maddux simply could not accept that outcome.

"I have no choice, Duke."

"Please don't kill me," Speed Trap begged, starting to cry hard. "I don't want to die."

"*You're not killing him!*" Duke shouted. "Don't worry, son," he called past Maddux.

"I have to," Maddux said evenly. "And if you try stopping me, you'll all be killed by the men waiting for me on the dock." He nodded to the dock side of the ship. "Speed Trap too, so what's the point? You might get me, but they'll definitely get you. And it won't be pleasant. They'll make you pay." He glanced quickly at each of them in turn. "You know me, you know what I do, and you know I'm telling you the truth. Don't fuck with me. You'll live to regret it…and then you'll die."

Duke shook his head as he glared at Maddux. "I don't care. You can do whatever you want to me, but you're not killing my son."

"Get back, brother," Sage urged. "We knew what we were getting into with these people. We didn't have a choice. We owed the bank so much money from that other boat that sunk." He shook his head sadly. "Speed Trap shouldn't have gotten involved in this, Duke. He shouldn't have thrown that raft out the back of the ship. It's terrible, but it's his own damn fault."

"Troy saved his life," Duke shot back angrily, taking a step at Maddux. "What did you expect my boy to do?"

"Get back," Maddux ordered. "*Now.*"

Maddux was worried he was going to have to shoot Duke too—which could cause a major problem because Sage might not be able to handle seeing his brother go down. A nephew was one thing, but a brother might be different. And Maddux had to get out of here. Jack Jensen and Ross Turner were widening their lead on him with every second. He could feel them getting ahead, and he could feel himself starting to panic—and he never panicked.

"Let him go!" Duke shouted, taking a step toward Maddux, then two steps back when Maddux brought the gun up quickly with his finger on the trigger. "*Please.*"

"Stay back!" Sage yelled.

"*Don't kill me!*" Speed Trap screamed. "I'm sorry, I'm sorry. I shouldn't have done it. But I'll never tell anyone."

"See," Duke yelled, "he'll never say anything! He'll never say a word!"

Maddux swung the gun at Speed Trap and then back at Duke, who came at him again and then retreated again.

"Don't kill me, don't kill me. Please, God, don't kill me!"

"I can't have this," Maddux muttered to himself. "I can't have this right—"

The explosion shocked everyone as the chair Speed Trap was tied to tumbled backward with a loud crash. The gunshot had sounded *incredibly* loud inside the galley. Even Maddux had thrown himself to the floor out of instinct when the bullet blasted from the gun.

Maddux scrambled to where Speed Trap lay. He was still secured to the chair, which had crashed to the floor, and Maddux tried to find a pulse in the young man's wrist and then in his neck. But there was none in either place. The single, well-aimed bullet had blown Speed Trap's heart to bits, and he was dead.

Maddux glanced up at Grant, who was still aiming the smoking gun at his younger brother. "Good job, son," he muttered to Grant approvingly as he stood up and moved to where Sage was standing with his hands to his face. "Get this ship out on the Bering Sea right now, Sage. And I mean *right* now." Maddux glanced down at Duke, who'd crawled over to Speed Trap and was sobbing pitifully as he rested his head on his dead son's bloody chest. "I might need you out there."

Maddux patted Grant on the shoulder as he went by. "Good job," he repeated. "The United States thanks you."

When Maddux emerged onto the deck of the *Arctic Fire*, he glanced up just as a seaplane roared overhead. He knew who was in that plane.

It occurred to him as he signaled to the three men who were waiting for him on the dock that the man who'd just flown overhead was risking everything to save his brother. And that the man below had just killed his brother in cold blood.

CHAPTER 35

"RED, RED, *red*," Karen shouted excitedly as she pointed down at the ground through the late afternoon sunshine. She was sitting on the right side of the plane, directly behind Jack, who was in the front seat opposite Turner. "Red at two o'clock!"

"I see it, I see it," Turner confirmed as he banked the seaplane a few degrees right so they were heading due east toward what Karen had spotted. The mass of material lay on the ground at the end of a brittle-looking wooden pier. The pier extended into the wide inlet behind the barrier island and the Bering Sea. "That's what Bobby Mitchell told me to look for. He said red was the color of the rafts on the *Arctic Fire*. He said his Uncle Sage always had orange survival suits, yellow harnesses, and red rafts."

"I don't know if it's a raft." Jack stared down at the crumpled mass lying on the sand by the end of the dock. "But it sure is bright red."

Everything seemed to be falling together, but he had to be ready for a dead end too. If he didn't and Troy wasn't in that lonely house a hundred yards inland from the pier, he'd be devastated. He'd always had the habit of preparing himself for disappointment, not anticipating success, because he never wanted to feel vulnerable. And he still couldn't let go. He'd finally thought he could in that Montana bar the other night, when he and Karen seemed to be doing so well. But now she was being so distant. At least he knew why, though that didn't help much.

"Great spot, Karen," he called over his shoulder above the hum of the two propellers.

"Thanks."

Other than her excited call about what was lying at the end of the pier a few moments ago, that was the first word she'd spoken in the plane.

After taking off from Dutch, Turner had pointed the nose of the seaplane east-northeast and then hugged the top of the Aleutian archipelago. They'd flown past Akutan and Mt. Gilbert, and then Turner had brought them down to three hundred feet as they reached the west end of Unimak Island. Since then they'd been skimming along the north side of the island looking for anything that might lead them to Troy.

Using the *Arctic's Fire*'s approximate location as a starting point—which Speed Trap had given Turner at the bar in the Fish Head Pub—he'd done some rough calculations using winds and tides from that night. The calculations indicated that the best chance of spotting anything was on the north side of the island chain between the east end of Unimak Island and Nelson Lagoon on the Alaska Peninsula.

If this turned out to be a dead end, it would be too dark to spot anything else once they were up in the air again, Jack realized. They'd have to cover the rest of the search area tomorrow, if the weather cooperated—which it wasn't supposed to.

Turner landed the plane on the calm waters of the inlet in front of the little two-story house, which was in desperate need of repair, Jack saw as he jumped from one of the plane's pontoons down into the shallow water Turner had taxied to. His heart was starting to pound hard. Mostly because he was close enough now to the mass of red material Karen had spotted to see that it was indeed a deflated raft—but also because he'd never done anything like this in his life and he was loving it.

Now he understood why Troy was constantly challenging nature. It was crazy to be out here in the wilds of a remote place like this. Maybe it wasn't as dangerous as climbing Mount Everest or as remote or exotic a destination as Nepal, but it was still exciting as hell. And it was a lot better than sitting at Tri-State Securities trading bonds. If there was one thing he'd figured out from all of this, he knew he never wanted to work another desk job again.

"Everybody got guns?" Turner asked as he came around the front of the plane and slogged out of the shallow water. He was holding an over-and-under shotgun.

And, Jack saw, Turner had a .44-caliber Magnum in his wide belt. The thick, black handle protruded ominously. "Yeah, I've got my nine millimeter," Jack answered with an impressed grin. Ross Turner was one damned intimidating presence. And Jack was damned glad he was here with them.

Turner pointed at Karen. "You?"

She gestured at the small of her back. "I've got my thirty-eight."

"OK, let's go."

Jack pointed at the small, weather-beaten house as they walked toward it. "Why do people live like this, Ross?"

"What do you mean?"

"There isn't a town anywhere near here. Hell, there probably isn't another *house* that near here. Who lives like this?"

Tucker shook his head grimly. "People who *really* don't want you to ask them what their last name is."

As they closed in on the house, the front door burst open and an older woman dressed in jeans and a sweatshirt rushed out onto the porch brandishing a shotgun. She looked pretty weather-beaten herself, Jack noticed, but she certainly wasn't lacking in the guts department.

"What do you want?" she demanded angrily, aiming the weapon at Turner before he could raise his gun.

"Easy, ma'am," Jack called out loudly, stopping quickly and holding both hands out with his palms facing the porch. "We sure don't want any trouble."

"What *do* you want?" she asked again.

"I'm looking for my brother, Troy."

"Never heard of him and never seen him," the woman answered. "Now get the hell out of here."

"What about that raft?" Jack asked, motioning over his shoulder toward the pier. He didn't want to let this go. It had felt like Troy was so close. "We think it's the kind he would have been in."

"That's just an old raft from my husband's fishing boat."

"What boat? I didn't see any—"

"He's out on the ocean right now," the older woman interrupted, stepping forward and swinging the shotgun in Jack's direction. "So I'm alone, and I got a real itchy trigger finger when I'm alone."

It felt to Jack as if his heart actually dropped out of his chest just then. He'd been so ready to see Troy, so certain that they were seconds from reuniting. And he realized that no amount of prepping himself for disappointment would have been enough to ease the sadness he was suddenly experiencing. Apparently, they were going to have to head back to Dutch Harbor and try looking farther east tomorrow.

But he'd come so far.

"Ma'am, I don't mean to—"

"I told you," the woman said, bringing the gun up and aiming it directly at Jack's chest, "I don't know who he is."

"I believe that's our cue to leave," Turner said quietly, backing off two steps very slowly. "Let's go, Jack."

"OK, OK," he murmured softly. "Well, I'm sorry we bothered—"

"Hello, brother."

Jack's gaze flashed to the left as a slim figure stepped out from behind the worn, gray shingles on that side of the house. "*Troy!*"

"Jackson!" It was the nickname Troy had used for Jack since their playground days.

They hustled toward each other and hugged hard, slapping each other on the back and shoulders over and over.

"Sorry for that cat-and-mouse crap," Troy apologized, "but I had to make sure who it was."

"No problem. God, you're thin," Jack said, still experiencing the overwhelming wave of emotion that had hit him as soon as Troy had stepped out from behind the house. He brushed tears from his eyes and cheeks as he finally pulled back from their embrace. "I knew you weren't dead. *I knew it,* goddamn it!"

"What are you doing here?" Troy asked as he wiped away tears of his own.

"Saving your ass."

"Yeah, yeah, but *why*? *Why* are you here?"

"We heard you were washed off the *Arctic Fire* by a rogue wave." Jack shook his head. "I knew that wasn't true when I found out that the other four guys aboard the *Fire* were OK. I was convinced you would have been the last to go off that ship, not the first. So I came here to find out what really happened." He pointed at Turner. "This is an old friend of mine from Denison. His name's Ross Turner."

"Hey, Ross." Troy waved at Turner. Then he smiled and nodded at Karen. "Hey, Karen."

"Hello, Troy." Her eyes were watery too. "I'm so glad you're OK."

"You're not the only one," Troy agreed with a roll of his eyes. "Beeeelieve me."

Everyone laughed loudly, even the woman on the porch.

"I remember your name," Troy said, pointing at Turner. "I remember my brother talking about you."

"Ross lives here in Alaska," Jack explained. "He's been a big help getting me this far, let me tell you."

"Thanks, Ross," Troy called out. "I can't tell you how much I appreciate it."

"No worries, pal," Turner called back. "Your brother's a good man. I wanted to help him any way I could."

Jack put a hand on Troy's bony shoulder and smiled. "By the way, Troy, we really are brothers. Half brothers, anyway."

Troy's eyes opened wide. "*What?*"

Jack quickly explained what Bill had told him in his office on Wall Street. And then they hugged again…even harder this time.

"I can't believe it," Troy muttered, shaking his head. "This is *awesome*."

"We got that box from the Bankses' cabin in Minnesota," Jack said. He gestured toward Karen. "She got your letter and told me about it. We stopped at the cabin on the way out here."

"Any problems?"

"Not really."

"What does that mean?"

"I'll explain later." Jack would tell him about the cop when they had more time.

"Did you read what I put in there?" Troy asked.

"Every word. It's incredible."

"Yeah, well, that guy Shane Maddux is crazy. I mean, *really* crazy. What about President Dorn?" he asked worriedly.

"He's OK," Jack answered, "as far as we know, anyway. There wasn't anything on the news when we left Dutch. We haven't heard about any kind of assassination attempt."

"What about an LNG tanker blowing up in Boston Harbor?"

"No."

Troy's shoulders sagged. "Thank God."

"Yeah, really."

"Well, did you call someone after you read the stuff?"

"Who was I supposed to call, brother? And not get arrested or thrown into an insane asylum. *And* not get Shane Maddux and Roger Carlson very, very pissed off at Karen and me."

"I didn't think about that," Troy admitted.

"Candidly," Jack continued, "I wasn't sure you really wanted her to contact anybody. I couldn't figure out why you'd write it all down and then put it in a box. I couldn't figure out why you wouldn't report Maddux yourself."

"I put all that in there in case I was killed. I had a feeling something was up, and I wanted Maddux to go down if he murdered me. I was going to take out Maddux before he could shoot President Dorn, but I never got the chance. He took me out first."

"He thought he did," Jack said defiantly. He was remembering what Hunter had said at the memorial service. "But you're one of those untouchables, brother. I swear you are."

"Maybe." Troy gestured at the house. "There's no landline here, and cell phones don't work this far out. But we need to talk to people fast. I'm sure Maddux is still planning to kill Dorn. It's just a matter of time, I'm telling you. He hates the guy."

"We can be back in Dutch Harbor in less than an hour. You can make your calls from there. Let's grab your stuff and go."

Troy chuckled as he pulled the pockets out of his jeans and then spread his arms wide. "You're looking at everything I own." He nodded toward the front porch. "Before we go there's someone you need to meet." Troy grabbed Jack's arm. "But hurry. We've got to make those calls soon."

As they were climbing the porch steps toward where the older woman was standing, Jack had to catch Troy. He was weak, and it was strange for Jack to see him so fragile. He'd always exuded so much strength and energy.

"This is Betty," Troy said, smiling affectionately at the older woman, who was still holding her shotgun when they made it to the porch. "Betty, this is my older brother, Jack."

Jack stepped forward and hugged the woman gently. He loved the way it had sounded when Troy had said the word "brother." It was accurate now. "Thanks for taking care of him, Betty."

"She sure did take care of me," Troy agreed. "She was basically my nurse. I would have died without this woman. I didn't even wake up for a few days after I got here."

"Actually, it was almost a week before you woke up," Betty corrected him in her gravelly voice, balancing the gun on her forearm as she pulled a pack of Camels from her coat pocket and lit one. "I was worried he was gonna catch pneumonia," she explained, stuffing the cigarettes back into her pocket, "but he fought it off. There were a couple of bad nights, but he's a strong kid."

Troy smiled. "I think it was your fish chowder that saved me, Betty." He glanced at Jack. "I couldn't even pick up a spoon for a day or two after I woke up. She had to feed me."

"How'd that feel?"

"Pretty pathetic." He put a hand on Betty's shoulder. "But thank God she was here."

Jack pointed at the ocean beyond the wide inlet and the barrier island, then at the raft. "So Troy washed up on the beach over there?"

The woman exhaled a thick cloud of cigarette smoke as she shook her head. "My husband found Troy when he was out

fishing. He was about five miles offshore when he spotted the raft
and pulled him in."

"And your husband's out fishing again?" Jack asked.

"Yeah, he's gone a lot."

Jack gazed at the deflated raft. He'd noticed how Troy hadn't
mentioned Betty's last name when he'd introduced her.

"Thanks, Betty," Troy whispered into the older woman's ear
as he hugged her. "We've gotta get going, but I'll be back to see
you soon."

"You better."

He kissed her on the cheek, and then he and Jack moved carefully back down the stairs after Jack had given her another hug as
well.

"You all right, brother?" Jack asked.

"I could use five thousand calories a day for two weeks, and
a month of R and R," Troy admitted, moving as fast as he could
in his weakened condition. "But we don't have time for that. Do
we, Jackson?"

"No, we don't."

"How did you and Karen hook up?" Troy asked as they
headed for the seaplane with Turner and Karen lagging behind a
little to give them privacy.

Jack explained how Turner had pointed him toward
Baltimore—and Karen.

As Jack finished explaining, Troy broke into a huge grin. "You
like her, don't you, Jackson?" he asked quietly.

"What?"

"I can tell what's going on with you two," Troy said good-
naturedly. "It's obvious."

"What's obvious?" Jack demanded defensively. "What are you
talking about?"

"You're into her, and don't even try denying it. I saw the way
you've been looking at her."

"I haven't looked at her once in the last five minutes."

"No, it's been twenty times in the last two."

"That's ridiculous."

"She's into you too, brother."

Jack's eyes raced to Troy's. "You really think so?"

"I knew it!" Troy pumped his fist several times quickly. "I knew you liked her."

"I more than like her," Jack admitted as he leaned toward Troy. "But how did you know?"

"I'm your brother."

Jack glanced over. "Yeah, right." He thought again about how it sounded so good to hear that—and to realize it was true after all the years of thinking he was adopted.

Troy patted Jack on the shoulder. "Well, good for you. I'm really glad you found each other. Charlie would be glad too. And I mean that."

Jack wondered if Karen had heard him. Troy had said it pretty loudly. "Thanks." He wanted to look back at her, but he didn't.

"So how are Lisa and Little Jack?" Troy asked.

As he was about to answer, Jack heard a thumping in the distance that sounded like the heartbeat of a giant. Seconds later, two small black helicopters appeared on the horizon out of the dusk. They were skimming thirty feet above the water's surface.

"Jesus Christ!" Troy stopped short and stared intently for a second at the two choppers that were bearing down on them. "Everybody back to the house!" he shouted. "Now! *Go, go!*"

"What the hell?" Jack yelled as they all turned and sprinted the way they'd just come. "What's going on?"

"Those are the new MHs!" Troy shouted, already breathing hard. "Those are Special Forces' Little Birds, and they are very dangerous machines. I'd recognize them anywhere, even from that distance. And I'm sure Shane Maddux has something to do with them. That's his style. Believe me, they aren't coming to save us."

Jack held Troy's arm as they loped along, trying to support him. "Shouldn't we try to get to the plane and get out of here?" He was worried Troy was going to fall as they ran.

"Negative," Troy replied decisively. "Even if we somehow got airborne, they'd shoot Turner's plane out of the sky like it was a hot air balloon floating through a summer evening. It'd be a turkey shoot."

"Jesus."

"We'd never make it into the air, anyway. Those things will be here in a few seconds. They're damn fast."

"Why didn't we hear them before now?"

"They've got six blades up and four on the back. The more blades a chopper has, the quieter it is. They're built for stealth... and killing."

They were still twenty yards from the house when the lead chopper roared overhead and laid down two lines of withering fire ten feet apart. The bullets barely missed Jack, Troy, and Turner as they blew by in exploding parallel paths. But Karen shrieked loudly and tumbled to the ground just as the second helicopter— trailing directly behind the first one—held up and hovered above them.

Jack turned around to help her, but Troy grabbed him by the shirt collar and tried to keep dragging him along toward the steps leading up to the porch. "No, brother!" he yelled as Jack struggled against him. "It's too dangerous out here. These are *serious* motherfuckers. We need to be inside and behind cover to have any chance."

"I've got to get to her," Jack shouted above the roar of the engine above them and the hurricane-force winds whipping down all around them. "I can't leave her out here."

A rope dropped from the right side of the hovering chopper as the other one roared back around from the far side of the house only a few feet off the ground. Two figures dressed in black dropped quickly down the rope, one after the other, as the first chopper settled to the ground two hundred feet away from the house. It landed directly behind the spot where the two men had just hit the ground. The rope blew wildly around beneath the still-hovering helicopter without the weight of the men on it.

As Jack whipped his Glock 9 mm from his belt and ripped free from Troy's grasp, there were two loud blasts from his right. He raced for Karen, who was trying desperately to get to her feet, when one of the two men who'd just dropped down the rope hurtled backward. He'd been hit in the chest by a blast from Turner's shotgun.

Jack squeezed the trigger of his Glock four times in rapid succession, and he dropped the other guy who'd slid down the rope from the hovering chopper. But not before the man raked Turner's huge body with machine-gun fire.

Turner hurtled backward as the chopper above Jack descended suddenly until it was only a few feet above him, sending him sprawling to the ground. When he looked up through blowing dirt and sand, he saw another man jump from the helicopter, grab Karen, heave her into the chopper, and then haul himself back up into it.

"No, no!" he shouted as the helicopter lifted up and raced away. He fired every round left in his clip at the helicopter as it disappeared into the fading light above the Bering Sea, but that quickly Karen was gone. "Damn it!"

Four more men raced through the twilight at Jack and Troy from the second helicopter. Jack dashed to Turner's body and ripped the .44-caliber Magnum from his belt. "Brother!" he shouted as hurled the gun at Troy.

Troy caught the .44 neatly out of midair and in the same motion dropped to the ground and began firing as Jack grabbed Turner's shotgun and fired at the men too.

At the same moment, two shotgun blasts exploded from an upstairs window of the house, and one of the men racing at them went down. Then Troy put another one of them to the ground just as Jack saw another figure toss something at the window.

The top floor of the house exploded a second later.

And then a brilliant flash exploded directly in front of Jack. His nose filled instantly with the foulest stench he'd ever smelled, and then everything went black.

CHAPTER 36

As JACK came to consciousness, he heard someone shouting but he couldn't really understand the words—or see anything. The anesthetic released in the explosion outside had been terribly powerful. His head was pounding like it never had. Like on top of having the worst hangover ever, his brain was being split in two by an ax with each word being yelled. Then the words began to make sense, but he still couldn't make out the images around him. Everything was still a blur.

As his vision finally began to clear and the pounding subsided a little, Jack realized that he was tied tightly to a chair, and that Troy was secured to another chair a few feet away. A small man dressed all in black stood directly in front of Troy. Jack recognized him right away. He was the man who'd been walking beside the tall guy with the long blond hair wearing the *Arctic Fire* jacket in Dutch Harbor.

"*What information did you give away, Troy?*" the little man yelled. "*And who did you give it to?*"

"Screw you."

"Address me properly. I am your leader. I am Red Fox One."

"Fuck you, Maddux. You aren't my leader anymore."

So this was Shane Maddux, Jack realized as he glanced away from Maddux and toward the only other person in the room. This man was standing by the doorway of the cramped living room holding a small machine gun with both hands. He was dressed all in black too. But, unlike Maddux, his face was obscured by a ski mask.

"You just signed your brother's death warrant," Maddux said gravely. "You shouldn't have said my name, Troy."

"You're gonna kill us both whether he knows your name or not. Don't act like you aren't."

"But I might have been humane about it."

"Don't give me that shit. You love it. You can't wait to torture both of us."

"I need to know what information you've given away and who you've given it to," Maddux demanded again as the tone of his voice turned urgent. "And I need to know *now!*" he roared. "Do yourself and your brother a favor. Tell me quickly and I'll have some sympathy for you."

"No."

Maddux motioned at Jack. "Do you really want to see what I'm capable of doing to him?"

"Fuck you, Shane," Troy snapped. "You just threw a grenade at a sixty-year-old woman and blew her to bits. Do you think I really have any doubt about what you're capable of doing to my brother?"

"She killed one of my men. She had it coming."

"Too bad she didn't kill you too."

Maddux moved several steps over so that he was standing in front of Jack. "This won't go well for you, and you have your brother to thank."

"Fuck you, Maddux," Jack said defiantly, making certain the little man understood that he knew his name. "Do you really feel OK about killing that poor woman upstairs?"

"She's inconsequential to my life or to the well-being of the United States." He raised both eyebrows and shrugged. "She had to die for the good of the whole. It's as simple as that." He shook his head. "She was probably a criminal, anyway. So we're better off without her."

"You're sick. I feel bad for you."

"Don't feel too bad, because I'm going to—"

Maddux's words were drowned out by the blast of a large-caliber bullet. The man clutching the machine gun stumbled back against the wall, spraying the ceiling with bullets as his finger constricted on the trigger.

As the machine-gun fire stopped, an older man stepped through the front door into the living room, aimed a revolver at the masked man, and calmly fired a head shot. Blood exploded from the man's head, and he keeled over limply as the older man swung his gun smoothly at Maddux.

"You bastard," the old man whispered. "That woman you killed upstairs was my wife."

* * *

Jack trained the .44-caliber Magnum on Maddux, who was now tied to the same chair Jack had been tied to only minutes before. Troy had lashed Maddux to the chair and then told Jack to watch him carefully before going somewhere with the old man. "Where's Karen?" he asked.

Maddux laughed loudly. "You'll never get anything from me I don't want you to get."

"Where the hell is she?" Jack demanded again.

"You're wasting your time," Maddux retorted arrogantly.

"He's right," Troy said as he moved through the front doorway and into the living room. He was followed by the old man, who gazed at Maddux sullenly while he stood over the body of the man he'd shot a few minutes ago. "You're wasting your time, Jack."

"So what do we do?"

Troy lifted the crude wooden box he was carrying and gestured at Maddux. "Get him to tell us everything we want to know."

"You just said it was a waste of time trying to get him to talk."

"No. I said what *you* were doing was a waste of time. But I know how to get to him."

"We're not torturing him," Jack said firmly, stepping between Troy and Maddux. "We're not torturing anyone."

"We're doing what we need to do, Jack. Get out of my way."

"No."

"Are you out of your mind?" the old man asked incredulously. "This guy killed my wife. There really isn't anything left of her upstairs. I saw a few fingers and a leg, but nothing else I recognized as human. That's all I have left of her, and you have sympathy for him?"

"I have no sympathy for him at all," Jack assured the older man compassionately. "But we can't sink to his level. We have to do the right thing here."

Troy stepped toward Maddux, but Jack intercepted him. They were standing face-to-face in the middle of the room.

"I'm not letting you do this," Jack said evenly. "I don't know what you think you're gonna do to him, but I can't let you do it. We have to let the system work, Troy."

"There is no system for a man like Shane Maddux. Who would we turn him over to? He has immunity from everything, Jack. He really is bulletproof, at least from the United States government. If they prosecute him, every other agent who has his kind of immunity quits because they can't trust what they've been told, and then the country's fucked. Believe me when I tell you that we'd have chaos on our hands if that happened. There are plenty of very brave men and women out there protecting us who need that immunity. Our enemies would take immediate advantage of it if we took it away from them." Troy shook his head. "Shane Maddux will never be prosecuted for anything, Jack. He'll go free a day after we turn him over to the authorities, if not sooner. Then you and I are fucked." He pointed at Maddux. "Because that man would never stop looking for us until he found us and killed us."

"Don't worry about it, Jack," Maddux called defiantly from the chair. "Let him torture me." He laughed loudly. "He won't get anything out of me."

"You can't imagine what that guy was going to do to you," Troy said, nodding over Jack's shoulder at Maddux. "And he wouldn't have given a damn about how much pain he was causing you. In fact, he would have enjoyed watching you suffer."

"I don't care." Jack couldn't give in to this. It went against everything he believed in.

"Just like I don't care about what's happening to Karen right now," Maddux said. He laughed harshly. "They've probably got her bent over something and they're all taking turns on her. I just wish I could too. But I'll get my chance at some point. Troy's right. I have immunity from *everything*."

"Get out of my way," Troy ordered.

"I bet they're doing her real good right now!" Maddux shouted at Jack. "And there's nothing she can do about it. She's just got to take all of them any way they want to take her and deal with it."

Jack shut his eyes tightly, trying to block out what Maddux was yelling.

"And then they'll kill her real slow when they're done with her," Maddux continued. "So maybe I won't get my chance with Karen after all. But that's OK. I'll just do it to some other bitch I feel like doing it to. Yeah, I'll do it to—"

"Shut up, Maddux!" Jack shouted. "*Shut your fucking mouth!*"

"What's wrong with you, Jack?" the old man demanded. "How can you protect this prick? Did you hear what he just said?"

"He can handle doing nothing because he's a goddamned faggot!" Maddux roared. "That's what's wrong with Jack Jensen."

Jack clenched his teeth, calling on all of his self-control. "Let's just get him out of here and turn him over to someone."

"Didn't you hear what I said? There's no one to turn him over to." Troy shook his head. "Jackson, what's wrong with you?"

"I can't let you do it, Troy."

"But I can," the old man said firmly, placing the barrel of his pistol against Jack's head. "Give up your weapon," he demanded calmly, "or I shoot. I swear to God I shoot. I can't watch this any longer. Five, four—"

"Give me the gun, Jack!" Troy shouted. "Don't let him shoot you. He just lost his wife. He's not thinking straight. He's gonna kill you, for Christ's sake."

"Three, two—"

"Jack! *Drop the fucking gun.*"

"One—"

Jack's gun banged loudly on the floor after he dropped it.

"You did the right thing," Troy muttered breathlessly. "Now get out of my way."

Jack turned around and watched Troy approach Maddux. He could barely feel the steel barrel of the pistol the old man was still holding to his head. He could barely feel anything at this point. He was completely numb, physically and emotionally.

"What do you think you're gonna do with that?" Maddux asked smugly, staring at the wooden box in Troy's hands.

Troy smiled thinly. "I found your diary, and shame on you for keeping one. You always told us Falcons never to write anything down. But you broke your own rule, and now you're going to pay." Troy held the box up so Maddux could get an even better look at it. "I just made this thing, and I know it doesn't look very good. But it'll work just fine." He placed the box on the seat of the empty chair beside the one Maddux was lashed to and pulled a dark plastic trash bag from his back pocket. "Now," Troy said calmly, "tell me what I want to know."

"Fuck you, asshole. You'll never get anything out of me and you know it."

They were defiant words, but Jack had seen a chink in Maddux's armor. He'd seen that slight wince as Maddux looked at the box sitting on the chair beside his.

"Where's Karen?" Troy asked as he opened the bag. "Tell me now or I put you in that tiny, tiny space you can't stand. The same tiny space that priest put you in when you weren't a good little boy. When you wouldn't do all those terrible things he wanted you to do in that room beneath the altar."

Maddux licked his lips over and over and shook his head hard. "No. Fuck you."

Jack saw how fast Maddux was starting to breathe. Troy was getting to him.

"Where and when is President Dorn going to be shot?" Troy demanded. "Is there another LNG tanker coming at the United States? Where's Karen? Tell me everything, Shane, or your head goes in the box. That hole in the bottom of it is for your neck. See, I put the bag over your head, then the box over the bag, and suddenly you're in that closet that priest made you go in."

"No, no!" Maddux shouted as he began to strain frantically against the ropes holding him to the chair.

"Claustrophobia," Troy hissed. "That's what's waiting for you inside the bag and the box. You can't take the tiny, dark spaces. I know it because I read it on those pages. You did all those terrible things for the priest because you couldn't handle the darkness in the closet, and you hated the way you thought the walls were coming in on you. Like he told you they were. You couldn't handle the thought of him making you go back in there." Troy moved toward Maddux with the bag wide open. "And you still can't." He hesitated a few inches away as Maddux strained desperately against the ropes and moved his head wildly from side to side. "*Now where's Karen?*"

"Fuck you! Fuck you!"

Jack grimaced as he watched Troy roughly pull the bag down over Maddux's head. Then Troy picked up the box off the chair, closed it on Maddux's head using the hinges, and hooked it shut.

For several seconds Maddux managed to remain calm. Then he began to shout and scream from beneath the bag and the box, and suddenly he and the chair went tumbling over. As he hit the floor, his screams grew louder.

Instinctively, Jack took a step forward to help.

"Don't move," the old man ordered, grabbing Jack's arm and pulling him back. "Stay right where you are, son."

After listening to thirty seconds of screaming and shouting, Troy removed the wooden box from Maddux's head and then pulled the bag off. "Now talk," he ordered firmly. "Tell me everything."

Maddux couldn't spill his guts fast enough. In a matter of seconds he'd told them everything.

First, he told them where Karen had been taken. Then he gave them details of President Dorn's imminent assassination. Then he told them that the *Pegasus* was heading for Virginia Beach, not Savannah, and that the huge ship had almost reached its target.

When Maddux was finished answering Troy's questions, Jack stepped forward as the old man let the gun barrel drop. His eyes narrowed as he stared at the bastard who was still sprawled on the floor tied to the chair. "I've got one more question."

After Maddux had answered it, Jack glanced at Troy. "What now?"

"We find the *Arctic Fire*. Fast!"

"How?"

"We take that chopper outside."

"Can you fly it?" Jack asked incredulously.

"I sure can, Jackson." Troy smiled. "I can fly almost anything."

* * *

The leader of the small band of desperate men sailing the huge ship westward gazed ahead through the darkness. The *Pegasus* was only hours from reaching the Atlantic Coast of the United States of America. They were going to make it after all. He could feel it.

* * *

Stein stared through the darkness at the ceiling fan, which was rotating slowly above him as he lay on his hotel room bed down the hall from the president's suite. He had a terrible feeling about this, like no feeling he'd ever had before. He hated David Dorn now, but the man was still the president of the United States.

He ran both hands through his gray hair and swallowed hard. What would he do at that critical moment if it actually occurred? He honestly didn't know.

Emotionally, that was tearing him apart.

CHAPTER 37

"THERE SHE is," Troy called out as he pointed through the helicopter's windshield toward the lights in the distance. "That's got to be her. She's supposed to be the only ship in the area."

One call to the Coast Guard station on Kodiak, a quick call back moments later from the CG, and they had the *Fire*'s position. Captain Sage had only gotten about thirty miles outside of Dutch Harbor, and the chopper was coming up behind the ship quickly.

"You ready, Jack?"

There were no doors on the chopper, just open spaces where the doors *definitely* should have been as far as Jack was concerned. As he peered cautiously down over the side of the helicopter at the dark ocean they were skimming across, he held on to his seat with a death grip. They were only thirty feet above the water's relatively calm surface, but thirty feet was thirty feet. It was twice

fifteen, and the chopper was bouncing around in rough turbu-
lence, which made everything even more gut-wrenching.

"Yeah," Jack answered in a hollow, unconvincing voice, more
to himself than Troy. But he had to go over the side if he was
going to save Karen. "I'm ready."

After Troy had removed the box and the bag from Maddux's
head, and Maddux had answered all of Troy's questions, he'd told
them that Charlie Banks had to be dead. That there was almost
no chance he could have survived the way Troy had. It had been
a year. Someone would have heard something by now. And Speed
Trap hadn't floated a raft to Charlie.

The Coast Guard was heading for the *Fire* too, by air *and* sea.
But Jack and Troy weren't waiting for them. Every second was
precious, and they had to get to the ship and get on it as soon as
possible—if they were going to save Karen.

"You really think we should have left Maddux with that old
man at the house?" Jack was trying to think of anything but how
he had to go over the side to get down to the *Arctic Fire*. "You
know he's gonna kill Maddux."

"If he does, then I don't have to."

Jack shook his head. "You're really going back to that house
after this to kill him?"

Troy nodded regretfully. "I told you. We don't have any choice.
If we turned Maddux over to someone, he'd be free almost right
away, and sooner or later he'd come after us. We'd live the rest of
our lives looking over our shoulders. And we probably wouldn't
see him until it was too late, no matter how hard we looked. If
Maddux doesn't want to be seen, he won't be. He has the infrastructure available to him to remain invisible as long as he wants.
That's what people don't understand. You could never stay hidden
like that, Jack, but Maddux can. He has fanatics around the world
who'll help him do almost anything."

"Why didn't you just kill Maddux before we took off?" Jack hated to admit it, but what Troy had just laid out scared the living hell out of him. He'd already been nervous because they were racing over the ocean with no door between him and the water, but now that speech had him *really* thinking. "Why make it so you have to go back?"

"I don't want to kill anyone in cold blood, even that bastard. I...I..." Troy faltered.

"What?" Jack asked loudly. "What is it?"

"I hope the old man does kill him." Troy grimaced. "That's a terrible thing to say, but I do."

Jack had been wondering about this since he'd found out that Troy was in Red Cell Seven, and now seemed like an appropriate time to ask the question. "You ever killed anyone, brother?"

"We'll talk about that someday, Jackson. I'll tell you everything. But not now." Troy pointed at the ship. They were almost to it. "This is gonna have to be fast!" he shouted over the roar of the rotor and the engine. "There's only one of you, and surprise is the only advantage you've got. You can't hesitate at all when we get close. You're gonna have to be on the rope and ready."

"Jesus," Jack muttered. His heart was already pounding so hard his vision was blurring with each beat.

"I wish I could do it for you!" Troy yelled. "But somebody's gotta fly this thing." He reached over and patted Jack's leg. "Maddux said they didn't leave any Special Forces guys behind on the *Fire* after they dropped Karen off." He grimaced. "But if you think you see one of those guys, get over the side of the ship right away and throw yourself in the water. They've got too much training on you. The Coast Guard will pull you out of the water when they get here." He hesitated. "Unless, of course, the sharks get you first or the SF guys shoot down the CG chopper."

"Jesus," Jack muttered again. He wasn't finding this outdoor stuff at all exciting or invigorating anymore. All of a sudden trading bonds at Tri-State was looking pretty good again.

When they were a hundred yards off the *Arctic Fire*'s stern, Troy patted Jack's leg again. "Time to go over! Come on, pal."

Jack glanced down at the water again and instantly felt his body seizing up the same way it had on the plane that night over Connecticut after the jump door was open. The thought of even tossing the rope over the side of the chopper was paralyzing him.

"Come on, brother! You've got to do it." Troy grabbed Jack's chin and pulled it left so they were staring into each other's eyes momentarily as the helicopter barreled ahead. "*Show me something, Jackson!*"

Jack gazed back into his brother's piercing stare. Troy was right. He cared about Karen too much to let this stupid phobia control him. He'd asked her to come along with him on this crazy ride, and it was his responsibility to get her out of what he'd gotten her into. And he needed to show Troy that the little brother wasn't the only one in the family with guts.

He tossed the rope over and watched it drop sickeningly fast down toward the water. That was where he had to go.

* * *

Maddux stole through the back of the house and into the night. There were no ties that could bind him permanently. Troy Jensen was as good as any man alive at securing a prisoner, but it didn't matter. Harry Houdini was a rank amateur compared to Shane Maddux when it came to escape.

He'd thought about killing the old man, but then decided against it. He had nothing against the guy, and, in a small way, he felt bad for killing his wife. The woman had fired on him and killed one of his men during the battle, but she'd been protecting her home. If she hadn't been shooting at him, he wouldn't have tossed the grenade at her. It had been a kill-or-be-killed situation in battle, and that was all.

Maddux took a deep breath. He had a long trek ahead of him, but that was all right. He was back in the shadows where he felt completely comfortable, and he loved it. There were enemies to kill.

* * *

When Jack dropped to the deck of the *Arctic Fire*, Grant was on him before he could even draw his pistol. In seconds, Grant had him pinned to the deck wall near the crane and was lifting him over the side as Troy circled above in the helicopter, unable to help.

But just as Grant was about to toss him into the frigid water, Jack got his right arm free, whipped Turner's .44 Magnum from his belt, and slammed the big man in the head with it. Grant crumpled to the wet deck just as Duke emerged from a doorway beneath the bridge.

"Don't move!" Jack shouted, leveling the huge pistol at the man as he sucked in air. "I'll shoot you where you stand if you do." He'd had enough. He had to help Karen if she was still alive, and he didn't care what he had to do to find to her. If he had to shoot this man, so be it.

"Please don't shoot," Duke begged, throwing his hands in the air.

"Where's the girl?" Jack shouted.

"I'll take you to her," Duke called.

Moments later Jack and Karen were in each other's arms. She'd been hit in the thigh during the initial helicopter attack on Unimak Island, but the wound wasn't life threatening and Duke had bandaged her up after Maddux's people had dropped her off on the *Arctic Fire*.

"Thank God you got here," she murmured. "I was beginning to think you wouldn't."

Jack smiled down at her as he shook his head in disbelief. "My brother's a pretty amazing guy."

She smiled back at him. "So are you, Jack."

* * *

Ten miles, the leader realized as he stared sadly through the night-vision binoculars. Two fighter jets were streaking toward the *Pegasus* through the darkness. Just ten short miles and they would have plowed into the sands of Virginia Beach. That was how close he'd come to changing world history.

He saw a flame erupt from the wing of the fighter to the left, and he knew that the remainder of his life could now be measured in seconds. They could have boarded the ship, but the United States military had decided to send a message to any other would-be terrorists. And that message was clear: they weren't afraid to blow an LNG tanker to hell.

The explosion was felt as far away as Washington, DC.

* * *

"I can't get through to him," Jack muttered as he looked over at Troy. They were standing on the bridge of the *Arctic Fire* and Jack was using the ship's phone. "He must be asleep. It's late on the East Coast."

"Try him again."

"You sure Dad's on our side?"

Jack had explained to Troy about the white van on Broadway, how the thing had almost run him down right after he'd left Bill's office that day. How it seemed like too much of a coincidence. But Troy had dismissed any notion that his father would be behind anything like that. He'd explained that Bill was a Red Cell Seven associate, but that he wasn't so fanatical that he'd try to kill his own stepson.

"You sure he's going to want to stop this assassination?"

"Dad would do anything to stop the president of the United States from being assassinated," Troy answered firmly. "He may not agree with Dorn's politics, or even like the guy, but he'd never want him dead." Troy hesitated. "I don't want you to take this the wrong way, OK, Jack?"

"OK."

"You don't know Dad like I do."

Jack couldn't argue with that. "Tell me who else to call," he urged. "We can't wait any longer."

"I don't trust anyone else," Troy replied. "Who knows how deep the conspiracy goes?"

"Well, we know if we don't call someone, President Dorn's going to be shot." Jack gazed at Troy intently. "What the hell are we supposed to do? You got through to Naval Ops in Norfolk and told them about the *Pegasus*. They listened to you."

"That's black and white," Troy explained. "Norfolk Naval Ops has to put planes in the air as soon as they get a call like that from someone like me. They can't ignore it. It's standard procedure. And if there's an LNG tanker out in the Atlantic where it isn't supposed to be, they board it or blow it up. It's as simple as that." He shook his head. "But if we call the wrong person about President Dorn being assassinated, the message might not get through to people who can do something about it. And by calling without knowing exactly what's going on, without knowing exactly who we're talking to, we could give people inside the conspiracy a heads-up that we know about it. And, again, we'll have people after us we don't want to have after us. They might not be as deadly as Maddux, but it still won't be a situation we want to deal with."

Jack stared at Troy for a few moments longer. Then he grabbed the bridge phone and dialed Bill's number again.

* * *

Stein's cell phone began to vibrate just as President Dorn began his speech. The street in front of the stage was mobbed, and people were hanging out of windows and off trees just to get a glimpse of David Dorn. It was just seven o'clock in the morning, but the people of Los Angeles had turned out en masse to see their president.

Stein pulled his phone out of his suit pocket and read the first few words of the urgent text message from Bill Jensen. Just as Dorn's deep voice began reverberating through the huge speakers on both sides of the wide stage.

Stein didn't bother finishing the message. He threw the phone down, jumped out of his seat on the left side of the stage, and sprinted for the president.

* * *

Ryan O'Hara took a deep breath as he stared through the telescopic sight that was mounted atop his favorite rifle—an Accuracy International L96 he'd owned for a while. He never missed with this weapon.

He exhaled half the breath he'd just taken as he caressed the trigger gently with his finger. President Dorn had just started his speech.

It wouldn't go on for much longer. O'Hara had a perfect shot at the president's chest from here, from just under two hundred yards away. The leader of the free world was about to die. This was one of the easiest shots he could have.

As O'Hara squeezed the trigger, he was aware of someone running toward the president in his peripheral vision.

* * *

Stein didn't hear the explosion of the bullet being fired, but he felt it rip through his chest just as he reached the dais and threw himself in front of Dorn. As he lay sprawled on the stage floor, he began to taste blood and a terrible sadness overwhelmed him. He wasn't sad about his own death. He was sad that David Dorn was lying beside him. The bullet must have passed through him and into the president—or the shooter had fired again. Either way, Dorn had been hit too.

As his eyes shut for the last time, a small smile still tugged at his lips. He hated Dorn, but he'd still tried to save the president's life. He was a true patriot. They would write good things about him in the history books.

CHAPTER 38

JACK AND Karen sat side by side on a wooden bench outside the Anchorage hospital. It had turned very cold this afternoon, but they were wrapped up in warm down jackets. And they were enjoying the crystal-clear night sky that was full of glittering stars.

"You sure you're all right?" Jack asked. It had been more than twenty-four hours since he'd rescued her, and they'd snuck out of the hospital a few minutes ago, after visiting hours were over. "I don't want you to overdo it, OK?"

"My leg's a little sore. But I'm fine."

"Yeah, you're fine. Remember, I get that one."

"OK, it's a lot sore." She slipped her arm into his and rested her head on his shoulder as they sat on the bench. "But I don't want to go back inside yet. I don't want you to leave. I'm not over being taken away from you like I was yesterday. I didn't think I was ever going to see you again."

Jack turned his head and gazed straight into her eyes as she picked her head up off his shoulder. She was one tough person... and one incredibly beautiful woman. "Look, I don't know if this is the right time to tell you, but—"

"I know," she interrupted him. "Troy told me. Charlie's definitely dead. Shane Maddux made that very clear."

Jack nodded. "Yeah, I'm sorry about that," he said gently.

She reached out and touched Jack's face. "I'll always love Charlie," she murmured.

"I know you will."

"But I'm looking forward to us. I feel like I know you pretty well already, but I can't wait to get to know you better."

"Really?"

"Oh yeah. I think you're incredible, Jack. I can't wait to spend lots of time with you."

He gazed into her eyes for several moments more. Then he leaned forward to kiss her. But just as their lips were about to touch, she pulled back quickly. He frowned at her good-naturedly. "Hey, what the—"

"Look at that," she said excitedly, pointing up at the vivid greens and yellows that were dancing across the sky above them magnificently in dazzling waves. "It's the northern lights. It's arctic fire."

CHAPTER 39

JACK, TROY, and Bill stood in a hallway in Walter Reed Hospital in Washington, DC, waiting exactly where they'd been told to wait. They'd been standing here for nearly thirty minutes and they were getting impatient. They would have walked out by now if they'd been iced like this by *anyone* else.

"I've got to ask you a question," Jack said as he glanced at a nurse who was hurrying past. He'd wanted to ask this for a while, and now finally seemed like the time.

Bill glanced up, obviously aggravated by the delay. He'd been jingling the change in his pocket loudly for the last few minutes as he'd stared down the corridor. "What's on your mind, son?"

"Son." It was starting to sound right to Jack. He and Bill still had a long way to go, but they'd spent a lot of quality time together over the last few weeks, and things were finally getting better between them. A lot better. Though Jack still wasn't calling

Bill "Dad" yet. He wasn't quite there, even though Bill had mentioned it several times this week.

"Why did you tell me I wasn't really adopted that day in your
office? Why'd you pick then to drop the bomb?"

Bill thought about his answer for a few moments. "You may
find this difficult to believe, but I don't know for sure."

That was difficult to believe. But then maybe Bill wasn't as
hard a man as Jack had always assumed. Maybe the emotional
waters ran deep beneath that tough CEO exterior, but maybe
they were there nonetheless. How could he really know if Bill was
always so calculating, if he always had hidden agendas and ulte-
rior motives? After thirty years, he and the old man were just now
starting to understand each other.

"Subconsciously," Bill continued, "maybe I actually wanted
you to go to Alaska. I know I warned you not to, but maybe I
really did. Maybe I figured knowing you were blood might help
you at some critical moment, that it might give you that extra
boost just when you really needed it. I do believe the mind works
on many levels at the same time, most of which we're not even
aware of." He shrugged. "I don't know for sure." He patted Jack
on the shoulder. "All I do know for sure is that if you hadn't gone
to Alaska, Maddux would have tracked Troy down to that house
and killed him. He would have overpowered that poor woman in
a heartbeat if you and Ross Turner hadn't been there." He paused.
"And I'd only have one son now."

"That's right," Troy said heartily. In the last few weeks he'd
gained back all the weight he'd lost, and he was his typical, ener-
getic self. "I owe you my life, Jackson."

"Thanks, brother." Jack glanced back at Bill. "Why didn't you
call Roger Carlson to find out what happened?"

"Carlson didn't know," Troy answered for Bill. "Maddux was
already way off the reservation by going after Charlie and me
like he did. He was doing more and more things like that outside

the chain, without telling Carlson what was really going on. The assassination and the LNG tankers were the shining examples."

"And Roger wouldn't have told me about Troy even if he had known," Bill added. "God rest his soul. It's just too bad he had that heart attack."

Jack glanced down the corridor both ways before saying anything. "Why wouldn't he have told you? I mean, you're an RCS associate, for crying out loud."

Bill shook his head. "It didn't matter. Those were Roger's rules. The country always came first. No exceptions. I wasn't actually a member of Red Cell Seven. Therefore, I still couldn't know something so crucial even though it involved my son."

Jack couldn't accept that. He was black-and-white about a lot of things, and this was one of them. Family would always come first for him. Karen believed that with everything she had, and she'd convinced him to think that way too.

"Have they found Rita yet?" Troy asked.

"No. And I doubt they ever will."

"Think she's dead, Dad?"

"Damn good chance, I'd say," Bill said grimly. "Wouldn't you?"

"Yeah, Maddux always covers his tracks."

Bill gestured at Troy and then Jack. "Which is why both of you must be very careful at all times. Never let your guards down. He's out there somewhere, and he'll be coming at some point."

Jack's eyes flashed around. He was searching the shadows constantly these days.

"So she was Maddux's plant, huh?" Troy asked.

"She was," Bill replied, "and I still can't believe it. More than thirty years with me, and she turns out to be a spy. It's almost more than I can—"

"Gentlemen."

The three of them glanced in the direction of the voice. Stewart Baxter was calling to them from down the hallway. Baxter was President Dorn's new chief of staff. He was a big man with an ego to match.

He waved to them and snapped his fingers twice. "This way, please. Hurry up."

A few moments later Jack, Troy, and Bill were standing at President Dorn's bedside after shaking hands with him carefully.

Jack stared at the president as he lay on the bed with tubes running in and out of him everywhere. The bullet had torn through his right lung after killing Rex Stein. It had been three weeks since the assassination attempt, and the president was still pale and drawn, but he would survive. If not for Stein deflecting the bullet slightly, the doctors and the forensics experts had determined President Dorn would have died on that stage in Los Angeles too. He looked terrible, but he seemed in good spirits.

"Thanks for coming," he said feebly.

"No problem," Bill answered for the three of them.

"Let's keep this short, sir," Baxter encouraged.

"Take a walk, Stewart."

"Sir?"

"Leave us," Dorn ordered in as strong a voice as he could muster. "I want to be alone with these men."

"But—"

"Now."

"Yes, sir."

When Baxter was gone, Dorn smiled at the three Jensens and chuckled softly. "Well, well. Two liberals and a neocon. Exactly what I'm looking for. This way it'll be two to two at crunch time."

"Excuse me?"

"I'll get to all that in a minute, Jack," the president said. "But first I want to thank you guys for saving my life. I understand each of you had a part in it. Second," he continued before they could say anything, "I want to tell you that I've had a lot of time to think, and I've come to a couple of very important conclusions."

"Which are?"

"I don't want death knocking on my door again anytime soon, Bill. Not for another thirty or forty years, anyway. I love my family too much. I love life too much. So I'm going to be much more careful about my personal security going forward."

Bill nodded approvingly. "Good. I may not agree with your politics, but you need to stay alive. You are the president of the United States, and you are my president, sir. I don't want you dying on my country or me."

Dorn reached out and touched Bill's arm. "Thank you. That means a lot to me, a lot more than it did a month ago."

"What's the other conclusion you came to?" Jack asked.

"I've decided this country needs men and women in the shadows after all," the president answered gravely. "Lots of them, maybe even more than we have now. I've decided that I was a fool for wanting to destroy Red Cell Seven. Staring death down has a way of making you see how wrong you were on a lot of things. I know it has for me." He shook his head. "You know, that first LNG tanker almost made it into Boston Harbor, and the second one came within *ten miles* of Virginia Beach. I know both of those crews had help from Shane Maddux. But I also know that neither of the ships would have been stopped if Red Cell Seven hadn't come through." He nodded appreciatively to Troy and Jack. "More importantly, since I've been able to sit up a little during the last week and start working again some, I've had a chance to dig into what Roger Carlson did over the last four decades. I've read through a lot of files, and I've spoken to a few very senior people at the CIA and the DOD who know the truth. What I found out is incredible. If the American public had any idea how many times RCS has saved this country, they'd be amazed."

"And terrified," Troy added.

"Right." President Dorn smiled wanly. "So let's make sure we don't tell them. I can't have a panic on my hands."

"Yes, sir."

"It is incredible what Roger accomplished," Bill said. "I'm glad you're finally seeing it that way, Mr. President."

"I didn't appreciate it before." Dorn paused. "But I do now." He shook his head as if he couldn't believe what he was about to say. "Maybe in a strange way I even understand why Shane Maddux was trying to kill me."

"In a *very* strange way," Bill said quickly, shaking his head hard. "Killing the president of the United States can never be—"

"I know, Bill," Dorn agreed with a wry grin. "Believe me, I'm not crazy. I'm not advocating my own assassination. The point is, Maddux was doing what he thought was right and necessary to protect this country. As misguided as he was, he was willing to do anything to make this as strong a nation as possible." The president paused as he took several labored breaths. "Ultimately, he was a bad apple, clinically insane probably, but I can't punish all of the outstanding people in Red Cell Seven just because of him. RCS must continue to exist. In fact, it needs to get stronger." He glanced up at them. "That's where you guys come in."

"How?" Jack asked.

"I want all of you working for me." Dorn gestured at Bill first. "I want you taking over Red Cell Seven immediately. I want you taking over for Roger Carlson."

Bill put his hands up. "Mr. President, I can't just—"

"I know, I know. You feel a loyalty to your shareholders at First Manhattan. You feel like you can't just quit your job like that when you're the CEO of a huge Wall Street firm. You think that might crater the stock."

"Well, I—"

"I know, I know," Dorn broke in again exactly the same way. "You're too modest to say it, but that's what you're thinking."

"Anytime any CEO resigns suddenly there are questions."

Dorn raised both eyebrows. "But I thought you put America in front of everything, Bill, even your family. I thought even as just an RCS associate you were committed to that loyalty."

Jack glanced at Bill. He could see his stepfather struggling for an answer. Just like that Dorn had boxed him in, and it was an unusual sight. Jack had never seen Bill like this, and it was actually a little satisfying. Dorn was good, even in his weakened state.

"Let's do it this way," the president suggested when he saw Bill was about to speak up. "Keep your CEO title for now. In the next few weeks you'll announce an orderly transition, which will take enough time to placate the stock markets. But you'll take over Red Cell Seven immediately. You can do two things at once. You are right now."

"But I'm not sure I'm the right person," Bill argued gently.

"You're *exactly* the right person," Dorn countered. "You're an ex-marine. You already know a great deal about Red Cell Seven. You already command a great deal of respect in multiple circles in New York and Washington. And, most importantly, I trust you completely." He laughed hard for a few seconds, but it was too painful and he ended up groaning and shaking his head. "I'm entrusting my life to a Republican. I never thought I'd do that." He gestured at Bill. "And you might actually be an even more effective economic advisor if you aren't the CEO of First Manhattan. You can be even more candid with me."

"How about these two?" Bill asked, gesturing at Jack and Troy. "You said you wanted all of us working for you."

The president's eyes moved deliberately to Troy and then Jack. "I've thought a lot about this, and I want you two men to be my personal ghosts in the shadows. You'll be deep, deep undercover. The only people in the world who'll know what you're doing will be your father and me. I'll call you my Gray Men. Troy will no longer be a Falcon." Dorn smiled mischievously. "And Jack, you need a job anyway, so it works perfectly for you."

Jack laughed. "I do need a job. But I'm not sure about being a Gray Man. This is right up Troy's alley, but it sounds a little crazy for me. I'm not trained for that."

"From what I understand, you did pretty well in Alaska."

"Still."

"I'll convince you," Dorn assured Jack as his gaze turned intense despite his weakened condition. "The icing on the cake for me is that you're a liberal, Jack. Though, like me, maybe not as much of one as you were a week ago," he said, smiling grimly. He gestured at Bill and Troy. "So you can keep an eye on these two for me. You can make sure they don't go too far to the right when I'm not looking." He smiled a little. "You three won't have to worry about the bad guys killing you. You'll probably kill each other first."

They all chuckled for a few moments.

"My biggest regret," Dorn said as their laughter faded, "is that I didn't appreciate how good a man Rex Stein was. I treated him like shit, but he still saved my life."

"He was a patriot," Bill said.

"He was a patriot," the president agreed. "And I didn't understand how important that really is until I was lying on that stage with blood pouring out of me. It's all about trust at this level. Nothing is more important," he said in a hushed voice. "And that's why I want the three of you to work for me. I trust all of you completely."

CHAPTER 40

"I FAILED."

Maddux nodded to O'Hara. "You did fail, Ryan. But don't feel bad about it. We got what we wanted. Red Cell Seven survived. President Dorn no longer wants to shut it down. I got that from a very good source this morning. It's definitely true."

"Good." O'Hara stared down at the ground. "Still, I wish I'd finished the job. I take pride in hitting what I aim at."

"You did hit him."

"I was aiming for his heart, not his lung."

Maddux nodded appreciatively. "Well, the primary goal was achieved. And it took a superhuman, suicidal effort by Rex Stein to save Dorn."

"It was a superhuman effort," Randy Hobbs agreed. "I was shocked the guy could move that fast. I couldn't believe it when he tore across the stage like that."

Hobbs was short and wiry, like Maddux, with thinning brown hair cut very short. He and Maddux had been close friends for a long time, and Hobbs was the man who'd accompanied O'Hara to Los Angeles while Maddux was in Alaska hunting Troy.

"You just got a little unlucky." Hobbs chuckled snidely. "Look at it this way, kid. You got a two for one, and that must be some kind of presidential assassination record. It took Oswald three shots to get Kennedy and Connally in Dallas. Unfortunately for us, you killed the *other* guy."

Maddux sneered. "Like it was just three shots in Dallas."

"Like it was just Oswald," Hobbs added quickly.

The three men broke into loud laughter as they stood beneath a secluded grove of oak trees in the Missouri state park. Back here in these woods at this time of night they were miles from anyone. They could enjoy a good laugh without worrying about anyone hearing them.

"What are you going to do now, sir?" O'Hara asked Maddux when their laughter finally faded.

"The same thing I've been doing, Ryan. I'm going to make sure the elected officials of this country never forget what happened on September 11, 2001. I'm going to make sure those officials keep giving the leaders of the United States intelligence infrastructure everything they need to protect the citizens of this country. I'm going to make sure the doves don't build a nest under the eaves of Capitol and start making us vulnerable again with all their bleeding-heart liberal bullshit. I'm going to make sure no one even considers shutting down Red Cell Seven ever again."

"By engineering what look like foreign terrorist attacks against the United States?" Ryan asked evenly. "By scaring those elected officials on Capitol Hill out of their damn minds with more rogue LNG tankers sailing into American harbors?"

"By doing whatever it takes." Maddux's eyes roamed to O'Hara's by way of Hobbs's. "You got a problem with that, kid?"

O'Hara stared back at Maddux for several moments. "No, sir," he said, shaking his head as he reached for his pocket. "No problem."

Before O'Hara's fingertips got to his pocket, Hobbs had whipped a pistol from his belt and leveled the barrel at O'Hara's head. "Easy, kid."

"It's information for Shane," O'Hara said calmly.

"Take it out slowly, Ryan," Maddux ordered.

O'Hara withdrew a folded piece of paper and handed it to Maddux as Hobbs slid the pistol back into his belt.

Maddux pulled out a small flashlight and scanned the piece of paper after he'd unfolded it. "Very nice, Ryan," he said appreciatively.

"What is it?" Hobbs asked.

"A list of suspected Chinese spies who are living and operating in this country," Maddux answered. "I'm staying in the assassination business as well," he said, slipping the paper into his pocket. "And, based on this list, it looks like I'll be busy, Randy."

"I got it from a contact of mine at the Office of Naval Intelligence," O'Hara explained. "There's more to come. Apparently, the Iranian list is pretty long too. I should have that one for you next week."

Maddux nodded at O'Hara and then gestured at Hobbs. "I told you he was good, didn't I?"

"I figured that out in Los Angeles two minutes after I met him," Hobbs agreed. "Actually, it was less than that."

"Then why'd you pull the gun on me a few seconds ago?" O'Hara demanded.

"Training, boy," Hobbs replied with a gleam in his eyes.

O'Hara pushed his chin out defiantly. "Well, watch it, pal. And there's no need to call me 'boy.' I know I'm black."

"Easy, Ryan," Maddux urged. "There's no need for *that*."

"He's just young," Hobbs said condescendingly as he glanced off into the darkness. "Ryan's a good boy, but he's still got a lot to learn. We'll teach him, though. We'll—" Hobbs stopped short as he turned back toward the other two men. O'Hara was now holding a pistol to *his* head. "What the hell?"

"You know I was the shooter in LA," O'Hara explained. "I can't have that, *boy.*"

Hobbs's gaze flashed to Maddux. "Shane?" he mumbled in a gravelly whisper, suddenly panic-stricken.

"Sorry, pal. There's nothing I can do."

"*My God,* Shane, I—"

Hobbs collapsed to the ground as soon as O'Hara pulled the trigger. Spasms racked his body for several seconds as he moaned pitifully, and then he lay still.

"He was a good man," Maddux said as he stared down at the dead body. "But he was expendable, and he was past his prime." Maddux smiled thinly. "I liked the way you got pissed at him there at the end, Ryan. Good acting. It put him at ease. It made him think he was better than you."

"It's what you told me to do, sir. And he reacted just like you said he would. He looked away, and it gave me plenty of time to pull my gun."

"Well, I've won a lot of money off him at poker, so I had an advantage. He always looked away from the bet when he had a good hand." Maddux laughed softly. "You know, I almost believed you myself when you asked me what I was going to be doing now. If you crash and burn out of RCS, Hollywood could be an option."

"Thank you, sir, but I don't plan on crashing and burning out of Red Cell Seven."

"Excellent answer." Maddux pointed down at Hobbs's body, then into the darkness. "Throw him in the river at the bottom of the hill, will you, Ryan? Weigh him down with a few rocks so his body doesn't show up for a while. I know you're not religious, but say a prayer as he disappears, OK?"

"Yes, sir."

"And keep me as up to date as you can with what's going on in Red Cell Seven, all right? Without making anyone suspicious, of course."

"I will," O'Hara promised. "In fact, there's some kind of announcement coming in the next few days. I spoke to another Falcon and he thinks we're about to find out who's going to replace Roger Carlson."

Maddux nodded. "Good. Let me know as soon as you find out."

"So, where you headed?" O'Hara asked as Maddux took a step into the darkness.

"I'll tell you this time," Maddux answered after a few moments of uncomfortable silence. "But don't ever ask me that question again."

"Yes, sir," O'Hara agreed solemnly. He understood his mistake. He wouldn't make it again.

"I'm going to Chicago, Ryan. I've got some unfinished business there. Then I'm going to kill a few spies. After that, who knows?" Maddux raised one eyebrow. "Maybe I'll go shopping."

"Sir?"

Maddux patted O'Hara's shoulder. "Call me when you have that list of Iranians."

"Yes, sir."

O'Hara watched as Maddux disappeared into the darkness, and then he chuckled as he bent down to pick up Hobbs's body. That was one scary son of a bitch, he thought to himself. Maybe someday he'd be half as good.

CHAPTER 41

"I KILLED a man outside that house in Alaska."

"He was about to kill you, Jack."

"Still."

"Would you rather be the one in the ground right now?"

Jack shook his head. "No, I would not."

"Then you did the right thing by killing him first."

Jack and Troy were sitting on the huge back porch of Bill and Cheryl's mansion looking out over the horse pastures as they drank hot coffee. It was a chilly, though not bitter cold, December afternoon. Not nearly as cold as that day in Minnesota, Jack remembered.

"It's still strange to think about taking a man's life, about him never taking another breath."

"Do you think about it a lot?" Troy asked.

"It's the first thing I wake up to every morning."

Troy nodded. "That's how it was for me the first time too," he admitted. "But I got past it."

Jack glanced up at the dark clouds scuttling low across the sky. Christmas was a week away. "How?"

"I killed again," he said quietly as he took a sip of coffee. "The second time was easier. It didn't bother me nearly as much."

"Jesus," Jack whispered. How could it not bother him as much? Could it really get easier? And if it did, was that a good thing?

"Hello, boys," Bill called loudly as he came through the French doors and sat down with them. "How's everything?"

"Good," Troy said. "How about you?"

"I'm making my announcement tomorrow about stepping down from First Manhattan. I'll stay on for six months, but my COO will be taking over the day-to-day responsibilities immediately. He really already has. You all right, Jack?" Bill asked.

Jack had been thinking about probably having to kill again if he was a Gray Man. It must have been obvious that something was bothering him from his expression. "Yeah, I'm fine."

"Mom says dinner should be ready in about an hour. When's Karen getting here?"

Jack leaned forward in his chair and gazed at the tree line in the distance. "She just sent me a text. She should be here in a few minutes."

"Good. I like her a lot. I hope it works out for you two."

Jack stared carefully at that spot in the trees a moment longer, and then he looked over at Bill. "Thanks, Dad. That's really—"

The thirty-caliber bullet struck him squarely in the chest, and he tumbled backward over the chair.

There'd been someone hiding in that tree line after all, Jack realized as he gazed up at the sky. His chest hurt so much.

EPILOGUE

REGGIE WAYNE had retired from the Washington, DC, Metro Police Department last month after twenty-three years on the force. During his time on the streets of the nation's capital he'd seen it all—murders, rapes, robberies, riots, fires.

He'd even been on duty that clear, crisp September morning when the jet had slammed into the western side of the Pentagon, right across the Potomac River from Washington. As word of the awful explosion had spread, Reggie had watched congressmen and women race from the Capitol. And later he'd spoken to other cops on the force who'd seen the president run from the White House into a waiting limousine headed directly for a waiting Air Force One. Along with New York, it was the most pressure-packed city in the country for all levels of law enforcement.

During those twenty-three years, Reggie had experienced a thousand times more panic attacks and adrenaline rushes than

STEPHEN FREY

most people would in a lifetime. He'd even been shot once. And been told by the attending surgeon, as they were wheeling him into the operating room, that his chances of surviving the chest wound he'd suffered while breaking up a bank robbery were fifty-fifty at best.

So this security-guard gig at Tysons Corner was nice. The money wasn't as good, but it was a hell of a lot safer here in northern Virginia where the well-to-do lived, shopped, and ate out at Morton's, The Palm, and the Capital Grill. After his years on the force in DC, he felt like he'd dodged the ultimate bullet by getting out alive. He was proud of himself for that too. He hadn't waited too long. And the pension he'd draw from the city in another couple of years would more than make up for the difference in pay.

Tysons Corner was located just outside the Capital Beltway fifteen miles west of the White House. And there were two massive shopping malls less than a mile away from each other. The first—Tysons One—was an upscale mall for the relatively wealthy, and the second—Tysons Two—was a super upscale mall for the super wealthy. A week before Christmas both of them were jam-packed with customers.

And shoplifters.

"Reggie, Reggie," the voice blared through his walkie-talkie. "Pick up."

He grabbed the device from his belt and pushed the red button. "Yeah?"

"We got a lifter at the L.L. Bean. He's on the first floor. The store manager's waiting for you at the mall entrance to point the guy out."

"Got it. On my way."

He shoved the walkie-talkie back into his belt and hustled through the crowded large corridor toward Bloomingdale's, which was at the north end of the mall. He enjoyed these calls. It broke up the monotony of the day and kind of took him back to his days on the street. It wasn't like there was anything he could really do to a shoplifter. He smiled thinly—except scare the hell out of him. And he intended on doing just that.

But his smile faded as he neared the store. After twenty-three years on the Metro force, he recognized evil immediately. He'd developed that sixth sense about it, and the four grizzled-looking men walking toward him in long dark trench coats were definitely evil. *Pure* evil.

"*Oh, shit*," he muttered to himself when he saw the working end of a sawed-off shotgun poke out from beneath one of the trench coats.

This was the mother of all mall nightmares, Reggie realized. These men intended to create hell on earth.

He wasn't armed and he was outmanned, but his training took over. The men were fifty feet away, but he was still going to try to take them down. He might, *just might*, be able to surprise them, get one of the guns, and shoot the other three before anyone was killed.

Reggie inhaled deeply and then took off toward them. Forty feet, thirty, twenty. None of the men were even looking at him. He was going to make it. He was going to get one of their guns and save this mall.

But with only a few strides to go, one of the men lifted his shotgun smoothly from beneath his coat and hit Reggie with a deafening blast to the stomach. Reggie doubled over and tumbled to the corridor's tile floor, screaming.

Then all four men turned their weapons on the crowd.

As Reggie clutched his bloody wound, he saw a young woman holding a baby crumple to the floor and then an older man shot directly in the face.

Tysons One was in chaos. The dead and dying lay everywhere as the fortunate fled in panic.

Reggie watched the mob run until his eyes slowly closed for the last time.

* * *

Within seconds of shooting Reggie, the four men had killed and wounded another seventeen people. At that point they raced back outside to a waiting van and took off.

They quickly changed vehicles in a remote area of the huge, crowded parking lot and then switched vehicles again two miles away in the parking lot of a strip mall. Before the first wave of police could respond, the assailants had disappeared.

An hour later they were back in their apartments in central Virginia watching television. Watching the results of what they and others around the country had just done.

The same scenario had played out in ten other major malls around the country at the same time, and Americans were suddenly barricading themselves inside their homes, terrified. Seventy-three people were dead and over two hundred had been wounded.

Two days later it happened again. This time the casualty list numbered over four hundred.

The United States was under siege...

ABOUT THE AUTHOR

STEPHEN FREY is a former investment banker and private equity specialist. He is bestselling author of sixteen novels, including *The Takeover*, *The Chairman*, and *Hell's Gate*. An avid fly-fisherman and fan of college lacrosse, Frey lives in Chestertown, Maryland.